'And where dost tha' think tha's bin?'

Mary gasped in fright at the angry voice.

'I've been helping out,' she faltered. 'Eliza had her baby this evening—'

'I'm the one who employs you,' interrupted John Crowther, 'and I'd thank thee not to come in at this late hour like a common trollop.'

The injustice of this remark hit Mary and she flushed. 'I couldn't leave Eliza. There *was* no one else...' she said, passing him as he sat slouched at the table.

He reached out and caught her hand. 'No, don't go,' he muttered. 'I didn't mean to be angry.'

She hesitated, trying to think of a way of disengaging herself.

'Such a lovely face,' he continued. He reached up to stroke her hair, and his perspiring face and bloodshot eyes loomed close. She drew back, knocking an enamel basin to the floor. The sound brought him to his senses and he sat up.

Mary edged towards the door. 'If you'll excuse me, Mr Crowther, I'm very tired, and I need to be up early in t' morning.' With that, she made her way up the stairs and into her room, turning the key securely in the lo

Dee Yates was born in Somerset, raised in Surrey, and moved to Yorkshire forty-two years ago. She graduated from Leeds University Medical School and worked as a family planning doctor and part-time general practitioner, in-between bringing up three daughters. For eleven years she has lived in a railway cottage alongside the busy East Coast main line. She is already a published poet, and the romance of the early railway and a study of the village census returns for the late eighteen-hundreds have led her to imagine what the cottagers' lives were like, and were the inspiration for this, her first novel. Dee is currently working on her next novel, *Silver Apples of the Moon*.

THE RAILWAYMAN'S DAUGHTER

Dee Yates

M&B™ and M&B™ with the Rose Device are trademarks of the publisher.

First published in Great Britain 2007 by Harlequin Mills & Boon Limited, Eton House, 18-24 Paradise Road, Richmond, Surrey TW9 1SR

THE RAILWAYMAN'S DAUGHTER © Dee Yates 2007

ISBN-13: 978 0 263 85696 5
ISBN-10: 0 263 85696 8

41-0407

Printed and bound in Spain by Litografía Rosés S.A., Barcelona

I would like to thank all my railway
and non-railway friends for imparting their knowledge
and for helping me to write this book.

Foremost among these is the late Harold Thompson,
my elderly neighbour and for many years a railway
signalman, who shared his memories and his
photographs of the age of steam.

To Rachel, Wendy and Liz…
my inspiration and my joy.

PROLOGUE

FROM the vantage point of the bridge the view suggested a gigantic Snakes and Ladders board. The flat landscape, which the dark hedgerows had divided into squares as far as the eye could see, held the ageing river in its final reach to the sea. The river pursued a sinuous and unhurried course, carrying the excesses from the towns and cities upstream, so its once clear water was tinged orange and bubbles of foam congregated in hollows in the banks. From time to time the wind caught the froth and sent it scudding over the fields, where it became trapped in the tall fronds of purple willow herb along an embankment.

The embankment supported the gleaming tracks of a newly-opened stretch of railway, built to connect the important rail centres of Doncaster and York. It had taken years to overcome the monopoly that the 'Railway King', George Hudson, held over the region and another six before the forty-mile ladder of line was opened on 2nd January, 1871. With the line came stations, seven in all, and with the railway came the men to maintain and run it.

The small village of Templesforth was chosen as the site of one of these stations. Lives ruled until now by the land and the seasons and the fickleness of weather and water, were changed for ever. Farmers grumbled at the disruption to their fields but soon welcomed the ease with which their beasts could be transported to market and animal feed and fertiliser reach them with the minimum of inconvenience. Women grumbled about the noise and the dirt but welcomed the opportunity to visit the nearby town or venture even further afield.

Alongside the station a row of railway cottages was built to accommodate the influx of workers. Opportunities arose for the young men of the village to join the railwaymen and pursue a future different from that of their fathers and grandfathers and as far back as they could all remember.

In 1875 Tom and Susan Swales and their five daughters took up residence in the end cottage of the row. Although small, it was a palace compared with their previous home near the east coast line four miles away. The front of the dwelling looked out over the busy yard, flanked on its left by Station House, the dual purpose of which, as living accommodation for the Stationmaster and his family and as the pivotal building of the railway station, meant that, of necessity, it nestled against the line itself and bore the brunt of all the noise, dirt and general inconvenience of the railway. When iron bedsteads in the cottages trembled and ornaments danced, the same vibrations in Station House would cause kitchen utensils to clang together in tuneless percussion and bring ornaments crashing to the floor. Engine smoke, that left sooty smuts on Susan's washing, worked its way into every nook and cranny around the windows of 'the House', leaving a daily deposit of dust and grime. But still, the house was large and slightly elevated in position, as befitted its superior rank. The cottages stood fifty yards or so back from the line but, even so, every vibration, hiss, grumble, screech and blast of steam or soot was experienced by their occupants.

The eldest daughter of the family, Mary, thirteen years old when they arrived in Templesforth, went into service in the big house of a neighbouring village. For four years she was happily employed as general maid but new members of the family moved in, bringing their own servants, and Mary's help was no longer needed. What was she to do? She returned to her parents' cottage but, with her sisters growing rapidly, there was no room for her to stay indefinitely. Her recent friendship with an elderly villager was giving her an increasing interest in the cultivation and use of herbs but the small amount of knowledge she had so far acquired would not enable her to support herself. It only strengthened her desire to stay in the countryside she knew and loved, rather than leave for work in the city. The two things she needed most—a place to work and a roof over her head—seemed impossible to find. And then, by chance, she learned that the Stationmaster was looking for help.

CHAPTER ONE

'WELL, my dear, you've excelled yourself today,' Jonah Maynard Crowther said sarcastically, scowling at the stodgy syrup sponge his wife had placed in front of him. 'I don't think I've ever tasted a dinner so burned. And if you think I'm going to eat this mess, you can think again.'

He pushed the plate from him with such force that it skimmed across the table and landed upside down on the carpet, where the custard splattered in all directions like the petals of a sunflower around its seed head. Annie jumped up from her chair with a gasp and turned towards the kitchen to fetch a bucket of water and a cloth.

'Sit down, woman. You can see to that afterwards. It seems that after eighteen months of being married to me you know no more than when you were with your parents. God knows what they taught you. Not a lot by the look o' things. It's a thousand pities they didn't let on to me what a useless article you were, instead of cheating me out of a proper wife. I'd certainly have thought twice about taking you on. It seems you can't do anything right.' Annie lowered herself timidly into the chair, her fright at this sudden outburst showing in the heightened pallor of her face. She bit her bottom lip and stared at the tablecloth.

'Any road, I've found someone to help you, seeing as your brain is addled. She's starting next week.'

'Who is it, John?'

'What's the matter? Are you worried that if I bring another woman in, she'll show you up? She will, more than likely. It'd be hard to find someone lazier than you are. Nay, it's Tom Swales' eldest daughter, him from t' cottages. She was housemaid in the big house at Bankside but apparently her services weren't wanted any more. So she's back living with her family at the moment but there's no room for all of them there. Her father seemed more than pleased when I suggested she come and work for us. For some reason he weren't too keen about her living in but he knew it made good sense, them being so short of space.'

'Have you seen her? How old is she?'

'Oh, you don't need to worry. She's old enough to do any of the work that you're so useless at doing. And, yes, I've seen her.' His gaze shifted from Annie to the window. 'She's just turned eighteen, pretty as a picture. In fact, I'd place money on it, she could teach you a thing or two about more than cooking my meals. Yes, she'll do fine for us.' A smile flitted across his face. He got up, scowled again at the congealed pudding on the carpet. 'Get this mess cleaned up. I'll have my cup of tea in the parlour. Perhaps you can make a decent job of that.'

Slamming the door behind him, he climbed the stairs to the parlour and crossed over to the window. The object of his conversation was at that moment gathering in washing from the line. He stood looking at her as she reached to unfasten the clothes and stooped to place them in the basket before stretching again, her shapely waist outlined against the brick wall of the cottage behind her. He grunted in appreciation and watched her walk to the door with the basket on her hip and disappear inside. Then he turned away and sank into the easy chair, which moulded itself around his substantial frame. Resting his legs on a small stool drawn up in front of the chair, he closed his eyes, the smile again hovering around his mouth. Yes, she would do very nicely.

His dreams were interrupted by the entry of his wife. She set the tray on the small table by his side, poured a cup of tea and scuttled from the room. He yawned widely, opened his eyes and sat forward. Thoughtfully he stirred two spoonfuls of sugar into the tea, eased himself from the chair and strolled over to the window. The garden was empty. He stood drinking noisily, looking at the sleepy row of cottages. Then he placed the cup on the windowsill, checked the time on his pocket watch before slipping it back into his waistcoat pocket and made his way heavily downstairs.

His wife stood waiting in the dining room. Turning his back to her, she heaved the heavy jacket up his arms and he shrugged his shoulders into it. Then he settled his hat squarely on his head and caught hold of her by the arms as he bent to bring his mouth close to her ear.

'I shall be in early tonight,' he said under his breath, 'and I don't want any of your excuses about being too tired. I'm your husband and you'd do well to remember it.' He kissed her hard on the mouth and pushed her suddenly away from him so she lost her footing and fell against the sideboard. The Stationmaster stood looking at her where she cowered, rubbing her arm, then turned on his heel and marched quickly from the house to await the arrival of the goods train from Doncaster.

CHAPTER TWO

'IT'S grand,' exclaimed Mary, stepping from the back yard into the scullery and seeing a copper boiler in the corner and a stone sink under the window and rows of shelves, upon which stood every size of saucepan and every kind of cleaning equipment that a maid could wish for. The fact that the copper was tarnished, the pans not altogether clean and the array of equipment piled haphazardly on the shelves, she could easily remedy, she thought. Tiptoeing reverently across the stone flags, she entered a large kitchen complete with cooking range and long wooden table. She spun round in excitement to face Annie. 'You've no idea what it's like at Mam's,' she said. 'We've just the one room downstairs for everything—cooking, eating, living. There's a set pot for washing t' clothes but it's in the outhouse and middlin' cold in winter. We've a range, like, in t' room but it's smaller than thissen and much harder work, like as not.'

She followed Annie through into the dining room and, from this, up a flight of stairs to the floor above. On one side of the landing a door led into a comfortable parlour.

'This is where John has his rest after dinner, before he goes back to the station. He doesn't like to be disturbed,' Annie warned.

'Why do you call him John?' asked Mary. 'I thought his name was Jonah.'

'It is—' Annie laughed '—but he says that the Jonah you read about in the Good Book is always complaining and he's not going to be called after someone like that. So I have to call him John.' She looked at Mary and smiled. Mary smiled back. From what she had seen of the Stationmaster, she wondered whether his character might be more than a little like the name he despised. But she would not expect Annie to say that, even if it was what she was thinking.

Across the landing another door led into a long corridor that spanned the entrance hall. From this, doors led to three bedrooms. The first was to be Mary's. She gazed around in awe. It was plainly furnished with dressing table, wardrobe and washstand and a single bed that jutted out into the room. In one wall there was a small fireplace. Curtains billowed out in the cool breeze from an open window and she crossed the room and looked out on to the row of cottages, the end one of which was occupied by her family.

'Mrs Crowther, it's wonderful. I've never had a room of my own. At home I have to share a bed with my three younger sisters and even in t' big house I were sharing a room wi' another servant girl.'

'Please don't call me Mrs Crowther. You must call me Annie. I want us to be friends. Come along and see the rest of the upstairs.'

The second room was the nursery. From its window they were able to see Annie's baby asleep in his perambulator in the garden. At the end of the corridor Annie held the door open and cast a diffident glance at the bed. 'This is where John and I sleep.' It was a large room with windows at the front, giving a view of the railway, and at the back, so that they could see over the yard and the cottages beyond.

'I should be able to manage these without any trouble,' Mary said, closing the door and looking out of the corridor window on to the platform beneath. She was interrupted by the noise of a heavy goods train that clanked slowly through the station. The walls vibrated and a drift of dust insinuated itself around the windows and settled on the sills. The two women looked at each other and laughed.

'Don't talk too soon.' Annie wrinkled her nose. 'The dust is back within a few minutes of you removing it. Your work will never be done here! And another thing…be careful where you put vases of flowers. They're likely to finish up on the floor whenever a train goes by.'

The Stationmaster walked along the platform and glanced up at the window where the two women stood. Mary stepped back quickly, out of the line of his gaze.

'Come along,' said Annie. 'John said I must introduce you to him. We mustn't keep him waiting.' They sped down the stairs and back through the rooms. 'What you have to remember is that we live in just a small part of the building. Most of the ground floor belongs to the railway.' Through the entrance hall, past the ticket office and on to the platform Mary hurried after Annie. They reached the general office, just as the Stationmaster emerged resplendent in his dark blue uniform.

'John, this is Mary Swales. She says she can start work as soon as we want her. Isn't that good?'

'It is indeed. I'm pleased to make your acquaintance. I've been looking forward to seeing you. You can start work straight away, as far as I'm concerned. I hope you'll be happy with us and knock some sense into this wife of mine.'

'She doesn't seem lacking in sense to me,' Mary retorted, fixing her gaze on her new employer. A look of surprise tinged with amusement washed over the Stationmaster's face.

'Aye, well, you don't know her as well as I do. Any road, come with me and I'll show you what's what.'

Mary followed in his wake as he strutted from room to room, pointing out the waiting rooms and the general office, from which led the porter's office and the parcels offices. It was obvious that he was proud of the orderliness of his station, and Mary, while conscious that she did not need to know about the station buildings, was nevertheless interested.

'That's about it,' he concluded, as they stood once more in the entrance hall. 'You best get on. I want my dinner on time, don't forget, and I want to enjoy it. So, if you've a mind to start today, Mary, I've certainly no objection.' And he looked her up and down in a way that made her blush.

'Come on, Mary,' his wife broke in. 'I'll show you round the kitchen, then you can get on with the dinner while I give little Johnny his meal.'

Mary gave the Stationmaster a quick nod and followed Annie through the entrance hall. As they turned towards the entrance to the house she glanced back. John Crowther still stood there and his eyes were fastened on the two women. She turned away and lifted her head high. She wasn't going to be intimidated by the likes of him. It was Annie she was there for. In any case, she would have very little to do with Annie's husband. How he made her feel was of no consequence at all.

Within an hour saucepans were boiling excitedly on the range and water hissed and spat as it hit the hotplates beneath. It was warm in the kitchen and Mary had to keep brushing back from her face a curl of dark brown hair that had come loose from its fastening. She turned red-faced as Annie entered the kitchen, her baby son astride her hip.

'I'm sorry.' Annie struggled with the weight of her baby as she sat down with him, well away from the complaining kitchen range. 'John always insists on a good meal at noon. He says it sets him up for the rest of the day.'

'My father's never in at this time of day.' Mary fastened the strand of hair in place. 'He takes sandwiches with him to work—lovely in the summer but not so good now. There, Annie. Johnny's dinner is ready.'

'I hope he takes it today. He struggled so much yesterday I had to give up. The book says to give this Mellin's food, once they start to teethe…' She offered him the food but the baby began to struggle and gag as soon as he felt the cold metal of the spoon against his tongue. With Mary's encouragement Annie persisted and gradually Johnny settled and began to look forward to the next mouthful.

'Look, he's opening 'is mouth like a baby bird.' Mary smiled. 'He'll soon get the hang of it. Afore you know it, he'll be sat at t' table with 'is dad.'

It was one o'clock precisely when John Crowther stepped into the house. In the dining room he removed his heavy jacket, hung it over the back of his chair and sat down at the head of the table. He took up his soup spoon and looked round as Mary entered, a few seconds later, with a tureen of steaming oxtail soup. She ladled a generous helping and placed it in front of him, sensing the stale smell of sweat that mingled with the aroma of the soup. He grunted, ripped apart his bread and began to eat. Mary returned to the kitchen to strain the vegetables and check that the gravy was neither too thick nor too thin. Annie had taken the baby to the nursery for his afternoon nap and, when Mary next entered the dining room, Annie was in her place at the table and toying with a crust of bread. Her bowl of soup stood almost untouched.

'...And another thing,' her husband was saying, 'I don't want you turning up late for meals. There's the babby to think about now. What kind of example is that to 'im?' He glared at Annie, who said nothing but sat staring into the bowl of unfinished soup.

Mary took the plate, glancing sympathetically at John Crowther's wife. Didn't he realise that it was the baby she was thinking about—and her husband? She had hurried to settle their son for his afternoon nap precisely so John could have an hour of peace before returning to his work. Mary stacked the bowls noisily, placed the dinner plates firmly in front of them and served the meat and potatoes with quick precision. The Stationmaster's attitude to his wife was irritating her already and she had only been in the house a few hours. She vented her frustration on the pile of dirty pots stacked in the sink. It was only when she heard the front door slam that she relaxed and began to enjoy her new surroundings.

'I wish I could prepare meals like that.' Annie came into the kitchen as Mary closed the larder door and began stacking the plates in the cupboard. 'I can't even boil an egg. Take a look at these.' She crossed to a shelf and lifted down four heavy volumes, which she placed with a thud on the table. 'John sent for them. He said they would teach me how to cook and a lot else besides.' She turned the pages and read aloud. '"*We feel inclined to tell you how many ways there are of boiling an egg badly.*"' She looked at Mary and smiled. 'I don't need to be told. I already know. And if I didn't, John would tell me. He's already complained about my overcooked beef and heavy sponge cakes. And the bread I attempted a few weeks ago had to be fed to the chickens.' The two women laughed.

'I'm lucky, I suppose,' Mary said, leafing through the pages of the book. 'Mam taught me early on how to cook, her time being so taken up, like, with our Alice. Though there were times when I would far rather have been off over t' fields playing. Mindst you, I couldn't cook the like of these dishes—bullock's heart à la mode,' she read, stumbling over the unfamiliar words.

'I love ground rice pudding, though, and that's easy to bake in t' range. Did your mam not teach you how, when you were little?'

'My parents didn't teach me anything useful, so I never learned how. They were elderly when I was born. I suppose they loved me but they didn't seem to know what to do with me. I was left on my own a lot. I read books. Father had plenty of those in his library. He was in the church, you see. And Mother, well, she was always delicate. As early as I remember, she'd spend her day lying on the couch, like as not with a cold handkerchief on her forehead and a bottle of smelling salts nearby. We had a maid who lived in and did all the cooking and mending and cleaning. She had been looking after my parents for so many years when I was born that I seemed to be in the way when I tried to help. Mother was always too ill to show me how things should be done. As soon as I was old enough, I looked after her as well as I was able. Father used to be out most of the day. He was very strict and, apart from church, I wasn't allowed out, except with Hilda—she was the maid—or with him, which wasn't very often. So you see, I don't know much at all.'

'These books have a lot of helpful information.' Mary leafed through the pages of the volumes. 'Look—care of the sick, how to make baby clothes, looking after chickens, even.'

'Well, I hope that's something you enjoy doing,' Annie said, getting up from her seat, 'because it's a job I can't wait to pass on to you. Let me show you the chickens. I need to collect the eggs in any case. If I leave the hens sitting on them any longer, they'll be hard-boiled by the time we fetch them in.'

Mary followed Annie down the garden between the raspberry canes on one side and the rows of blackcurrant bushes on the other, to where a dozen or so chickens pecked in the hollowed-out bare earth. On the far side of the run stood a handsome cockerel. He turned a mean eye on the two women as they approached and began to strut slowly through his drowsy harem.

'He's the reason I don't like coming down here.' Annie pointed in the cockerel's direction. 'I hadn't been here a week when he attacked me. It was freezing weather, trying to snow, and I'd been gathering the eggs. I could hardly hold them, my fingers were that cold. Anyway, he decided he didn't like me being there and started to come after me. I was in such a hurry to get out that my legs went from under me and I finished up sitting in the mud. My dress smelled evil!' She wrinkled her nose. 'The worst of it was, the eggs all broke and John was angry because there wouldn't be any for his breakfast. He didn't seem to care about whether I was hurt or not, even though I was expecting our Johnny… That was the first time I saw John lose his temper.'

As evening drew on Mary strolled with Annie down to the henhouse to lock up the birds for the night. Framed by the over-arching heaven they stood in silence together, soothed by the gentle clucking murmur of the chickens. The sky, pink at first, turned a deepening blue and became patterned by stars. In the hedgerows birds, brave in their spring finery, sang a lullaby and a blackbird's warning call startled the two women. An owl made silent progress from the barn and a perfect V of geese whirred above their heads. As the sky darkened candles were lit in the cottages and shadows moved, huge and wavering within the windows. Mary looked across at her parents' cottage, feeling herself suddenly outside its warm cocoon of safety. Then she looked at Annie and smiled. She liked this woman and her young son. The house behind them, black now apart from the muted light from the open scullery door, stood as a challenge. She would clean and polish till it shone. She would help Annie to adapt to the role of wife and mother and teach her the things that she herself had been fortunate enough to be taught in childhood. About her employer she was less certain. But she would surely go about her business without their paths having to cross more than once or twice a day. She gave a contented sigh and turned to follow Annie up the dew-wet grass towards the house.

CHAPTER THREE

MARY carried her sister into the brightness of the early
September afternoon. At fifteen years of age Alice had
grown long and gangling and Mary was glad to lay her
down on the warm grass in front of the cottage. It was
a patch planted specially by Tom for this purpose, the
rest of the garden being given over to feeding the family. Their mother had insisted on a row of sweet peas,
these being her favourite flower, so Tom had constructed
a little haven of peace—the bed of grass for their Alice,
backed by a low wooden trellis which separated the
garden from the path connecting the five cottages. Up
the trellis twined a profusion of sweet peas, pink and
purple and palest yellow and so sharp smelling that it
made Mary want to weep.

''Appen we'll have a few minutes in t' sunshine before the girls get in from school.' Mary smiled, turning
to her mother, who had rounded the corner of their cottage. 'I asked Annie if she minded me calling in to say
hello to my sisters on my way back from t' shops. I
daren't stop long, though. I must get back over as soon

as I've seen them. Mr Crowther'll be none too pleased if his tea isn't waiting for him when he comes in at half past four.'

Susan sat down heavily in the grass and closed her eyes. She looked older than her forty-nine years, her dark hair scraped into a loose bun at her neck and liberally streaked with grey, her face lined and lacking the healthy glow of so many of the country folk around her. In contrast, her eldest daughter's lithe body, clear tanned skin and dark brown curls radiated life. They sat listening to the drone of the bees in the flowers and enjoying the few snatched minutes of quiet. As if to deny them even this interlude of calm, a low-pitched rumble began in the distance, accompanied by a shrill whistle. The rumbling grew steadily louder until, with a deafening roar, it materialised into a gleaming green locomotive with a haul of rhythmically grumbling wooden coaches. The train swept through the station in front of them, enveloping the platform, the cottage gardens and Susan's washing in a huge cloud of sooty smoke.

'The three forty-five from Doncaster,' said Susan, without opening her eyes.

As the sound of the train retreated into the distance a loud wail could be heard coming from the baby carriage that stood in the shade of a lilac tree at the side of the cottage.

'That train wakes Johnny from his afternoon nap better than any alarm clock.' Mary laughed and jumped up to fetch the crying baby and sit him on the grass by her sister.

'How's Annie doing now with t' babby?' asked

Susan, running her fingers through the little boy's unruly brown hair. 'He certainly looks well since you moved into Station House. It seems like ages you've been living there. We see so little of you now.'

'I know. I'm sorry, Mam. But I can't just drop everything and come over here whenever I feel like it. After all, I *am* paid to be a live-in servant. You'd see even less of me, like as not, if I wasn't working so close by. It doesn't seem possible I've been there six months already. Johnny were only a couple of months old when I got the job. Don't you think he's coming on grand? Annie can cope much better now than she did at first. I think it all got too much for her, moving to a strange place and having the babby straight away when she were still new to the village and didn't know anyone. And Mr Crowther's so busy, an' all.'

'Hmph,' was her mother's reply. 'From what I've heard, he could care for his family a lot better, busy or not.' She looked sharply at Mary, who hesitated, torn between loyalty to her employer and friendliness to her mother. Should she voice the uneasiness she had begun to feel whenever the Stationmaster was around the house? It was not just his overbearing manner with his young wife, which kindled Mary's anger and forced her to bite her tongue for fear of saying something that would make things worse. There was more than this. It was a feeling that she herself was constantly under observation when the Stationmaster was at home. It could not be that he was unhappy with her work, which she knew from Annie to be satisfactory. So was it she herself that her employer found peculiar or perhaps distasteful? She couldn't put her finger on it. She knew only that, whenever he entered the room, she became self-conscious under his furtive scrutiny and, if he approached, or worse, brushed against her in passing, her flesh began to crawl uncontrollably.

She turned to her mother, determined to seek her advice. But Susan had closed her eyes and tipped her head back to feel the sun's warmth on her skin. Mary stared at her and sighed. No, she couldn't burden her mother with another worry. She had more than enough already, in the shape of the crippled daughter lying on the grass between them.

'How's Alice been this week?' she asked instead. 'She's very quiet at the moment. Are you waiting for your sisters, Alice? They'll be here soon enough and then there'll be no peace and that's a fact.'

Alice responded with a tuneless shriek and an agitation of her arms and then lay quietly, enjoying the feel of the sun on her face. At least that was what Mary assumed, though she had no way of knowing for sure. She believed that her sister understood a lot of what was said to her, even though she was incapable of making the appropriate response. Little wonder that she was prone to outbursts of frustration.

'She's been in one of her rages more often than not this week,' complained Susan. 'I think she's missing you, Mary. I wish you didn't have to live away.'

'Me too,' sighed Mary, 'but that was what Mr Crowther required when I were taken on. And Annie has needed me there all the time, while she hasn't been well enough to cope with t' babby. And, in any case, there really isn't room for me here, is there?'

It was true. The tiny railway cottage was full to over-flowing with Mary's sisters. When Susan and Tom had moved into the cottage there had seemed room enough, but with the three younger girls growing fast and Alice more of a handful than they would ever be, there was not an inch to spare. They were lucky, though. Tom had applied for the job of ganger and been appointed as a result of his reputation for good work at his last post. He was to be in charge of the platelayers, whose responsibility it was to maintain a not insubstantial stretch of the new line. They had hardly believed their good fortune when they had been given first refusal of the brand-new cottage, one of the row that had been built to accommodate the workers on the newly opened stretch of railway.

There were five cottages in all. Tom and Susan and their family had the first in the row, which had the advantage of an extra triangle of garden, in the corner of which was sunk the well. Every inch of the garden was used to provide vegetables for Tom's growing daughters. The cottages were linked by a path, which ran directly in front of them and separated each from its garden, which, in turn, was the only thing that came between them and the dusty, bustling station yard.

A shunting line diverted smaller goods trains into the yard, so they could be divested of their cargoes of seed potatoes and fertiliser for distribution to surrounding farms. In return lambs and calves made their complaining way on to the trucks to travel the short distance to Selby market. Four large coal cells ran parallel to the platform and occupied a substantial stretch of the yard.

These formed the limit, beyond which the children of the cottages were not allowed to go. Tom and George, his neighbour, had built a platform at the side of the coal store and from here the children could wave to drivers and firemen, passengers and livestock, as the trains slowed or stopped at the station. The presence of the yard meant that, like it or not, there was never a dull moment in front of the cottages.

The back yards were quieter, though hardly more appealing, for the malodorous privy was situated in one corner and a heap of coal in the other. Each cottage had its own washhouse, a wooden makeshift building, situated either behind the cottage or joined with that of a neighbour. But the view beyond these necessary though unattractive particulars of cottage life was of the fields, stretching into the distance and broken only by Manor Farm and its outbuildings. When the men of the cottages wanted some peace on their return from work, they preferred to saunter down the path to where it gave out well beyond the buildings and gaze in admiration at the hairy backs of five pigs, each in its own sty, making comparison between the size and proportions of their own beast and those of their neighbours.

Mingling with the drone of the bees and the hustle and noise of the yard, there came the sound of children's voices. It was the girls arriving home from school. Alice heard them too and shrieked in excitement.

'Mam, our Mam,' Lucy shouted, as soon as she saw Susan in the garden. 'We got a lift. Nathaniel let us ride in t' cart.'

'And I sat agin' him and helped him with t' horse,'

added Sarah-Louise, emphasising her privileged job as oldest of the three.

'Me too, me too,' joined in Laura. Her curls had entangled straw from the floor of the cart and, being indistinguishable in colour from her own hair, this gave her an even more unkempt appearance than was usual at the end of a long day at school. For it was a long day, especially for Laura who had just turned five. There was talk of a new school in the next village but, until that became a reality, they were forced to walk two and a half miles at the start of the day and again at its close. It was fortunate that the older children of the row were able to walk with the younger, for their mother, tied as she was with Alice, would never have been able to make the journey once, let alone twice a day. As it was they had to take their dinner to school. Susan sent them off with a potato apiece to bake in the embers of the school stove or, if she had dripping, she would spread it thickly between two slices of bread for each daughter. No wonder they were hungry when they reached home.

'Where's Nathaniel now?' asked Mary, who had blushed deeply at the mention of his name and was now looking expectantly towards the road.

'Oh, he had to go on to Landing Corner to meet a boat that's sailing up the river with some goods for t' farm,' said Sarah-Louise in an offhand manner, 'but he said he'd see you as planned the day after tomorrow,' she added mischievously, as she saw Mary's crestfallen look.

The two younger girls sat down with the baby and began to amuse him with songs they had learned at school. Susan rose from the grass with difficulty.

'Keep an eye on our Alice for a minute while I get you all a drop o' milk,' she said, turning to Sarah-Louise. 'Mary, you come with me.'

'Aw, Mam, I want to go and tell Mr Morritt what I've been doing at school today,' complained Sarah-Louise. 'Can't I go, Mam?'

'You'll do as I've asked you,' replied Susan sharply. 'You can go and see him later.' Sarah-Louise slumped down in the grass next to her two younger sisters, who were still playing with the baby, and their mother made her way into the cottage, followed by Mary. She stood a moment to let her eyes adjust to the darkness.

'She's too fond of disappearing off when there's work to be done, that one, especially when I've asked her to keep an eye on Alice,' Susan complained to her oldest daughter. 'Given half a chance she'd spend more time with George in the box than she does at home.' She indicated towards the signal-box, where George Morritt's large profile could be seen as he leant his weight to the levers in preparation for the up train from York. 'It's easy for him,' she concluded. 'Just his wife and the one lad to take care of.' She slammed down three cups on to the table, lifted a jug from the shelf and poured each daughter a drink of milk. Mary opened her mouth to object at the unfair comment but Susan gave her no opportunity.

'Any road, Mary, what's this about you meeting that Nathaniel? Does your dad know about this?'

'It's nothing, Mam. You know how Sarah-Lou likes to tease. Nathaniel's only being friendly. It's nothing more than that.' Her mind told her that it probably was no more than that but her heart hoped otherwise.

'Well, you be careful, lass. There's a lot of men as are up to no good. And we don't know much about…'

She stopped at the sight of Lucy's worried face peering around the door.

'Mummy, Mary. Alice is poorly again. Come quickly.'

Stopping only to pick up a spoon wrapped in a strip of cotton cloth and used for such emergencies, Mary ran after her mother and Lucy into the garden. Alice was rigid, her eyeballs rotated upwards, the skin of her face turning puce. Mary forced the spoon between Alice's clenched teeth, turned her with difficulty on to her side and held her there as the stiffness gave way to rhythmic convulsions. Her skin turned darker still and bubbles of saliva drooled from the corner of her mouth.

The fits had been frequent when Alice was little. As she grew they had lessened to once or twice a week but their ferocity had increased and those around her were frightened when she had one. Susan had taught her daughters not to be alarmed and, even as she and Mary steadied Alice, the younger ones gathered round, stroking her hair and talking quietly to her.

The jerking grew less, stopped. Alice lay, still as death, while her body recovered from the buffeting. Her lungs drew in a huge gulp of air and the blueness retreated from her face, which flushed pink before taking on an unhealthy pallor.

Alice's transition into womanhood was bringing with it a big increase in the number of these fits. It was plain to see they were wearing her down. Her parents were reluctant to leave her unattended, fearing that the worst might happen if she were left alone. Mary grieved that she was no longer able to take her part in caring for the sister to whom she had always been close.

A shadow fell across the little group gathered round the unconscious girl.

'Na' then. Is it our Alice poorly again?' Tom took a large and not very clean handkerchief from his trousers pocket and gently wiped the trail of saliva from his daughter's mouth.

'Can I do owt to help?' It was George Morritt, returning home at the end of the early shift. He stood aghast at the sight of Alice. 'Here, let me hold open t' door.'

Tom picked up his daughter and carried her into the house. He sat down carefully with her and cradled her head against his chest, stroking her hair softly as his daughters had done. Mary saw the glint of a tear in her father's eye, a tear that he quickly blinked away. She busied herself with taking the neglected drinks for her sisters and returned to the room with the baby astride her hip. It wasn't fair, she thought, not for the first time, that her parents should be so tied to Alice and her every need. For her eldest sister was utterly dependent on her parents. Her limbs, even in the relaxing summer warmth, refused to unbend, elbows tight, fingers deformed, legs scissored and incapable of bearing her weight. Every now and then there was an involuntary arching of her neck.

Susan had some time ago told Mary of the circumstances of Alice's birth. Mary knew that she herself wasn't Susan's firstborn. Far from it. Susan had become pregnant twice and lost both babies before successfully giving birth to Mary. Then she had lost another. When she had become pregnant a fifth time, Tom had unexpectedly put his foot down and said she must go and stay with his parents.

'I didn't have the energy to refuse,' she explained to her eldest daughter, 'but I doubted whether Tom's folks would be able to look after me. They were ailing themselves by then. Needed to be looked after themselves, like. But we moved, thee and me, into the cottage at Beckley two months before the baby was due. Your father walked the three miles from Thorpe each evening. Winter was drawing on. It was dark when he finished work and dark again when he left the cottage in the early hours to get back to work on time. It wasn't easy for any of us.'

Mary listened, picturing the scene on the disastrous night of her sister's birth. The snow had come early. And so did the baby. One bitter night, four weeks before her due date, her mother began in labour. In the flat landscape that held the ageing rivers in their final reach to the sea, there were no barriers to the snow. It fell for hours and was blown in huge, arcing drifts against trees and barns and cottage doors. The waves blocked the narrow road to where the midwife lay asleep and oblivious in her cottage. By the time Tom had battled through the snow to wake her and the two of them had made even slower progress back, Susan had been many hours in labour. When the little girl was born at last, this had been the result.

'I can see it all now, just as clearly as when it happened so long ago. We feared she wouldn't last the night but somehow she did. Then we feared she wouldn't last the week. A poor, helpless little scrap, she were. Couldn't feed, nor nowt. She stayed wi' us, though, 'gainst all the odds. But she's never got no better, all these years.'

There were other children after Alice—quite a long time after, for Alice took every ounce of her mother's energy. She had given birth to three more daughters. She never knew whether the lost babies would have been boys. Five daughters then, for Tom and Susan. Susan told Mary that her father didn't mind a family of girls but she was disappointed all the same for his sake that she hadn't given him a son.

'You'll have a drop of tea with us?' Susan asked George, setting the kettle on the range. 'Your Eliza and little Alfie aren't back from t' farm yet.'

Mary could sense her mother's eagerness to foster this friendship between Tom and his neighbour, her worry that her husband would feel himself over-whelmed in this house of women. Tom was gently rock-ing Alice back and forth, attempting to soothe her into a more restful sleep than the one that had ended her fit. The house was peaceful again. The younger children finished their milk and, kissing Mary goodbye, set off to their platform beside the coal store to watch the ar-rival of the next train and attempt to attract the attention of friendly passengers by their frantic waving. Mary walked towards the door, the baby still astride her hip, and paused to have a word with George.

'How's Eliza?' she asked. 'Mrs Riley was asking after her only the other day. She's not long to go now, has she?'

'Nay, lass. 'Appen a week or two. She's very tired now…she's middlin' old to be having babbies, tha' knows. It were hard wi' 'er last time. We're just hoping this un'll be easier.'

'Is there none of your folk who can come and help?'

'No, more's the pity. Wi' us being older, our parents are dead and gone, God rest their souls. It's hard for 'Liza. If only she had a sister who could gi' us a hand. Think I'll tek a walk along t' road to meet her and t' little lad.' George got up and followed Mary to the door. ''Appen Alfie will be wanting to tell me about riding on t' tractor or some such thing. I just hope he's not been in wi' t' pigs. He's that fond of 'em. We've all on to keep him clean at the best of times.' He nodded to Susan. 'Thanks for the tea, missus. I hope the little lass'll be all right.'

Mary felt sorry for the Morritts. She would have liked to help but her responsibility now was to the Stationmaster and his family. She knew from her friend, Martha Riley, that things were not going well in Eliza Morritt's pregnancy, but what could she do? She would not have known how to help, even if there were the time. Since starting work for John Crowther and his family she had not once seen Eliza.

'I must be off too,' Mary said. 'Johnny needs feeding and I've the tea to get for Mr Crowther and Annie. Are you sure you can manage?'

'Aye, love, you get off,' said her father. 'Alice will be back to normal when she wakes up.'

Susan turned from the open door, where she had been watching George's substantial frame receding into the distance.

'Remember, Mam, I'm only living on the other side of the path. Come across if you need owt.'

Her mother walked with Mary to the perambulator and stood looking out over the garden towards the yard as Mary strapped Johnny in and turned the baby carriage towards Station House. The early summer vegetables had taken on a crinkled, careworn look. Plump sprouts were developing on their stalks and a few cabbages still dotted the hard earth, but the feathery rows of carrot tops stood in disarray and mint, sage and lovage had flowered and run to seed. Trees and bushes alongside the embankment were exhausted, dusty leaves edged with brown, life force draining back to the core, anticipating winter. A glaring yellow sun sank to the horizon and painted the outline of a great grey billow of cloud. A chill wind blew from the east.

Susan shivered. 'It'll soon be winter again,' she said bitterly. 'I hate it, shut in with nowt to see and hear but the station yard. You be sure to come again soon, now. It's been grand to see you.'

She was right, thought Mary. The station yard was the limit of her mother's horizon. The shackles of her life would intensify with the cold dark days ahead. Glancing at her, Mary thought how she looked as exhausted as the rows of crinkled vegetables lit up by the setting sun. She hugged her warmly and set off across the track, sad at her mother's predicament and her own inability to help.

CHAPTER FOUR

TOM and his men clambered up the steep embankment and on to the bridge, where they stood a while to catch their breath and admire the view. The ganger had decided that, the river being so low, the bridge should be inspected before the weather began to deteriorate. The platelayers did this regularly. Tom remembered well the disastrous floods of fifteen years earlier, when the river had struggled unsuccessfully to cope with the melting snow and burst its banks just upstream. Water had covered the fields as far as his parents' cottage more than two miles away. There had been no railway then to add to the dangers that the floodwater brought with it.

For there was no denying that the railway had brought danger in its tow. The men lived with it, respected it and were on constant lookout for it. As ganger, Tom's first job each day was to walk his section of line, checking for any loosening of the pegs which held rails to sleepers, examining the sleepers for signs of rot, looking for subsidence in the ground that held them firm. Putting right these deficiencies was their most important task. If the line was in good working order, the men would then be set to scything and trimming and fence-mending along their stretch of line. Used as their lives were to the background of the trains, they must not for one moment forget the hundreds of tons of steel which could bear down on them at any time.

The three workmen were proud of the part they played in the running of this iron master. You could hear it in their voices at the end of the day when they sat enjoying the last of the evening sun and a welcome tankard of beer. They stood now, relishing the prospect of a stroll through the village to the Wheatsheaf Inn.

Along the road to their left a young woman was walking. Her lilac-coloured skirt was pinned back to keep it from becoming soiled with the dirt of the road and the sleeves of her tight-fitting jacket were pushed up above her elbows, revealing bronzed arms. She was hatless and her dark hair, caught loosely behind, curled to her waist. Her muddy boots bore her along in a lively, self-confident way, despite the heavy pail of milk she was carrying.

From the opposite direction Tom saw a wagon approaching. As it drew near the woman it slowed and stopped and the carthorse, taking advantage of the break in the journey, bent her head to the sweet grass along the roadside. Its driver, a tall young man with a mass of curly fair hair, turned and spoke to the woman and she rested her pail of milk on the ground and laughed in reply.

'Well, now,' exclaimed Wilf, the most senior of the platelayers, turning to Tom. 'Looks like your lass has an admirer.'

'Lucky divvil,' said Robert under his breath. He was the youngest of Tom's gang and made no secret of the fact that he entertained ideas of courting Mary himself.

'And, more to t' point, so does many of me mates,' he had ventured one evening after his second glass of beer, causing Tom to look across at him in alarm.

'It's Nathaniel from t' end farm, if I'm not mistaken,' added Wilf.

'Aye,' nodded Tom. ''E's been giving our Lucy and Laura lifts 'ome from school recently. 'Appen he wants to make an impression. Don't reckon 'is old man will be o'er impressed, though. He'll be wanting grander things for 'is son and heir.'

A distant whistle alerted them to an oncoming freight train and the three men stood well clear of the rail as the huge engine and its haul of wagons grumbled past, coupling links clanking, a line of sooty smoke trailing in its wake. As the smoke dispersed, Tom looked down again at the road but his daughter was nowhere to be seen and Nathaniel and his cart had passed the chapel, rounded the bend in the road and were pulling up at the Wheatsheaf. Tom licked his parched lips. Carefully taking out his pocket-watch, the sole memento he possessed of his father, he saw that it was only fifteen minutes off their normal finishing time. It was too late to start another job. They would make their way back to the stores with their tools, then he would stroll along to the inn for a pint with Wilf and Robert.

The Wheatsheaf stood at Landing Corner. Here, a huge loop in the river brought it within a few feet of the road. In times past boats would come upstream to this point, the tidal limit, and load and unload their cargo. But the river often ran shallow and navigation was difficult, so when the Knottingley-Goole canal had opened more than fifty years earlier it took much of the river traffic on its easier and more direct route to the Humber. The network of railways that now wove in all directions through the countryside had also taken trade away from the river, so it was with some curiosity that Tom and his gang approached the corner, for the tall mast of a sloop could be seen beyond the sloping roof of the inn. Its sails had been furled and the rigging slapped lazily against the mast. A gaggle of excited men stood around, beers in hand, admiring the gleaming polished woodwork of her deck. Nathaniel and the owner of the sloop were deep in conversation. Money changed hands and the owner went below and proceeded to drag one sack after another of rich fertiliser from the hold. A group of willing volunteers loaded them on to the cart. The transaction completed, Nathaniel turned to the sailor.

'You'll have a pint with me before you sail?' The two men sat down at a convenient table. The other helpers also sat down expectantly and when Geoffrey Marriner, the landlord, appeared, Nathaniel ordered drinks all round. Geoffrey, like the men who were now sitting on the benches in the evening sun, welcomed the infrequent visits of the boats, for the flurry of activity always brought him extra trade. He disappeared into the dark interior of the inn and emerged several minutes later with a tray of tawny-coloured, thirst-quenching beers, which he set down on the table in front of Nathaniel.

'While I think on't,' said Nathaniel, as Geoffrey was

turning to go, 'I'd like to bring Princess for shoeing later this week. I've worked her hard in the last few months and she's well due.' Princess had just been relieved of the burden of her cart by one of the village lads and, tethered to a nearby tree, was contentedly munching the remains of a bale of hay.

'Aye, lad. Tha' can bring 'er Friday. I've nowt else that day.' Geoffrey made no secret of how much he relished his job as a blacksmith. It gave him satisfaction to get a horse with hooves overgrown and shoes worn or, worse, twisted off by an unsuspected rabbit hole, to file and hammer and shape, surrounded by the white glow of the metal, the hiss of steam and the acrid burning smell of hoof and to send the horse on its way, walking straight and tall and comfortable. But it was hard work. At the end of a hot afternoon he wanted nothing more than to sit and rest his aching back and drink a pint of his own thirst-quenching ale. Instead he would have to open the inn just in time for the men, thirsty from their own labours. Without Jane's help he would not be able to manage. But, just as he loved the horses, she enjoyed running the inn. He had to acknowledge that it was her dedication which made it the place to which the men of the village were drawn when they wanted to relax.

Tom waited until Geoffrey had served Nathaniel's helpers and then ordered ale for himself and his colleagues. He was fond of Robert, a young fresh-faced boy, eighteen years old, though looking much younger, and instructed him carefully in the intricacies and dangers of their job. Wilf, an incomer like himself, had worked on the railways more years than he cared to re-

member. He was a regular at the Wheatsheaf, well
known for being the first to arrive and the last to leave.
He sat now, waiting for his beer, his face deeply scored,
his nose bulbous and purple, a drip constantly forming
at its end, despite the warmness of the weather. He was
a man of little conversation, morose and brooding. It
was rumoured that he had only married his wife, who
was ten years his senior, because no one else would have
him—and that it was a step he had regretted ever since
because she made his life hell. Tom couldn't help smiling at the story of Wilf being escorted home by his wife
a few weeks ago because he had overstayed his welcome at the village inn.

Few words were spoken as the men savoured their
drinks. It had been an exhausting day and the ale
coursed through their aching limbs and relieved them
temporarily of the cares that hung around them.

'I mustn't stop overlong,' said Tom. 'Our Alice won't
settle without her night-time kiss. And 'appen the little
ones will be waiting to tell me what they've been up to
at school.' He rose to leave and, glancing up, Tom saw
Nathaniel looking at him. The lad nodded to him and
took a sip of his drink. If there had been nothing to take
him away from the inn, Tom would have lingered, hoping to have a word with the boy. Hardly a boy. He was
the elder of Henry Varley's lads, well into his twenties,
Tom guessed. And it was obvious that he shouldered
considerable responsibility within the family. He nodded back with a brief smile and turned to go, leaving
Wilf to settle back with another beer and another, until
several pints later he would be escorted home by Robert

or some other kindly acquaintance. Unless, of course, his wife should appear to do the job for them.

Robert sat, absent-mindedly sipping his beer. Tom could guess the thoughts that he was entertaining. He had seen the flicker of attraction that had passed across his face when he'd caught sight of Mary on the road below. He could not help but feel that Mary's path would be straighter if she was attracted to Robert rather than, as he suspected, to Nathaniel. But he was not one to interfere in affairs of the heart. He and Susan had been right for each other and, despite their difficulties, he had wanted no one else. If Nathaniel was interested in Mary and Mary felt the same way, then so be it.

CHAPTER FIVE

'SHH, don't make a sound,' Sarah-Louise whispered to Mary, who had entered the signal-box breathless from the steep climb. 'Come over here quietly and see the pheasant babbies.'

Mary tiptoed over to where her sister and George stood at the far window, watching a family of pheasant chicks follow their mother down the embankment, the five or six little mottled-brown bodies running hither and thither through the tufted grass, tumbling head over heels in an effort to keep up.

'There's a family of swallows up in the eaves of Station House,' Sarah-Louise went on. 'George says they've had three lots of babbies this year and they're rushing to get the little uns flying and away before the cold weather starts. He says you never saw parents so devoted to their babbies.'

Mary looked at George, who smiled back.

'Aye, I know all about the swallow family. I've had t' windows to clean that many times in the last couple of months!' They looked up to the eaves of Station

House, below which a fan of white droppings littered the bricks. A swallow looped into its nest with a mouthful of food and a moment later flew off again in an effort to keep up with the passing of the season. From such a distance they couldn't see the babies, but the sisters had seen the birds build their muddy homes in the eaves of their cottage too and watched the row of little black heads craning to be fed every time the parent arrived, and heard their frantic quarrelling to be first in the queue.

'You certainly get a bird's eye view from up here,' Mary went on, her gaze taking in the row of cottages, the Station House and the road beyond, where she had so recently been chatting with Nathaniel.

'I saw you on t' road with Nathaniel,' Sarah-Louise said, echoing her thoughts. 'You can't have any secrets from us in t' signal-box.'

'Best shift to be on is the morning one, of course,' George said, turning to the girls. 'You can see all sorts then. The other day there were a flock of goldfinches in yon thistles. Reet pretty they were, dancing around, twittering and calling to each other. I've seen foxes too on t' banking. If you're lucky, you can get a glimpse of the mother with her cubs.... Any road, you haven't come here to listen to me. How can I help you, Mary, love?'

'I've come to tell Sarah-Lou that I've got the evening off, so I thought we might have a chat.'

Sarah-Louise hurriedly gathered up her school bag, which she had dropped at the back of the signal-box. 'I've been helping George to polish the levers. Don't they look beautiful?'

The two sisters surveyed the tidy room, its floor

swept free of mud, its windows sparkling and the mul-
ticoloured row of levers with their brasses polished till
they shone. A truncheon was propped against the far
corner of the box, for George was also the village po-
liceman and was fond of telling callers that he *'had to
keep folks on t' right lines, just like t' trains'.*

'Thank you for the almonds,' she said to George.
'George bought me and Alfie some almonds from Dick
the tinker when he came through t' village the other day.'

'Be sure and share them with your sisters now,' he
called in reply but she was halfway to the ground, her
boots clattering on the iron steps. At the bottom she
turned and looked up to where he stood.

'I'll come again soon,' she shouted, as if she were
doing him a favour.

'Where's tha' been?' questioned her mother abruptly
as Sarah-Louise entered the cottage. 'I need thee to go
along to t' farm for some eggs. Always disappearing off
when she's wanted for owt,' she added, turning to Mary,
who had followed her sister in. 'It's good to see thee
again, Mary, love.'

Mary put an arm around her crestfallen sister and
hugged her close. 'Thee and me'll walk along to t' farm
together,' she said. 'We'll have the chance of a chat on
the way.'

'Tha'll stay a while here as well?' her mother interrupted anxiously.

'Of course I will. I want to see all of you, Father too.
When will he be home? Where is he, any road?'

'He often calls in at t' Wheatsheaf if he and 'is men
finish in time. 'Appen he's there just now.'

'In that case let's go along to t' farm now, Sarah-Lou. We can pick up the eggs and we might meet Father coming back.'

'I'll have some tea ready for you,' Susan said to her daughters as they left the cottage.

'Thanks, Mam, but I can't stay long. I'll be in trouble wi' Mr Crowther if I'm not back before nightfall.'

'I don't see why you've got to rush back to that old man in t' Station House,' Sarah-Louise said. Her face had brightened as soon as they were away from the vicinity of the cottage and she linked arms with her sister as they set off towards the dusty road.

'Sarah-Lou, tha' mustn't talk like that about my employer.' Mary laughed, glancing up at Station House and unable to suppress a feeling of relief at her sister's irreverent words. 'Remember he pays my wages. And, any road, I work for Mrs Crowther mostly—and she's not old.'

'No, she's nice. Why did she have to marry someone like him? I don't like him. He gives me the creeps!' Mary looked at her sister, whose astute observation accorded with her own feelings about her master.

'Well, she must have loved him, else she wouldn't have married him.' Mary breathed in the fresh autumn air and sighed. 'Let's not talk about them. Let's enjoy this time together while we can. Tell me about school. How are you getting on?'

'Miss Thompson says I'm best in t' class at writing,' Sarah-Louise replied proudly. 'Last week she made us write a letter. I 'ad to pretend I were writing to someone who lives in Leeds. I 'ad to tell 'em all about 'ow we go on in t' countryside. I telled 'em about t' pheasant chicks in t' banking and t' swallow babbies getting ready to fly to Africa. I said about us watching the huge engines with their carriages of posh folk from t' cities, looking out from t' carriage windows when they stop at t' station.'

'But they're the people you're writing to. They'll not be o'er pleased if tha' calls them "posh".' Mary smiled.

'When I'm a grown lady, I shall go and visit Leeds and, if I like it there, I shall stay,' announced Sarah-Louise, 'and you shall come and visit me.'

'I've heard that it's dirty and dark and busy, that people live o'er close to each other so that there's no room to breathe and t' children run barefoot in t' streets and there's no pheasants or rabbits or foxes and all the wild things tha's so fond of. Nathaniel says that houses spread row on row for miles and it would be easy to get lost and never be found again. He says that York is a beautiful city, much nicer than Leeds, wi' all walls running round it, hundreds of years old, and a huge church in t' middle with steeples reaching up to t' sky and middlin' of shops and big houses where all t' posh people live. But I wouldn't like owt to take me away from t' countryside. I love it here in t' village. Here is where I want to stay and work and bring up my family.' She had not mentioned her meetings with Nathaniel so openly before and her mention of his name and of her expectation of a family caused her to blush self-consciously.

'I like Nathaniel,' said her sister. 'He's funny and he makes me laugh. I hope that he's falling in love with you, Mary. I think he might be, cos he's always asking questions about you.'

'What kind of questions?' asked Mary, striving to affect as offhand a manner as possible.

'Oh, just questions. Any road, Miss Thompson says there's only one way to better us selves and that's by learning our letters and being able to read and write,' went on Sarah-Louise. ''Appen Mother and Father'd be able to live easier if they had learning.'

'Thou mustn't say a thing like that, Sarah-Louise. There were no proper schools when Mother and Father were growing up. Father learned his letters at Sunday school but Mother never had the chance. She's determined we all get learning, though. She puts aside three pence for each of you every week, tha' knows. It must be hard for her to save that much. And, in any case, it wouldn't be learning that would make life easier for them; it would be not having to toil so much with our Alice.'

Mary knew that her sister and her parents didn't always see eye to eye. She knew how hard it was for Sarah-Louise when all their parents' attention was focused on the sister who could not help herself. They continued along the road in silence.

'I wonder where Mrs Riley learned her letters,' continued Sarah-Louise at last. 'She must be able to read so as she knows how to mix her potions.'

They were passing a small, ramshackle redbrick cottage, which stood sideways on to the road. A high brick wall enclosed its garden, the contents of which therefore remained a mystery to the casual passer-by. Both house and wall were almost completely covered in ivy, which was sending fingers stealthily up on to the roof, seemingly in an effort to hide the secretive cottage completely. The building, its occupant and the surrounding garden were viewed with apprehension and fear by the children of the village and with apprehension and respect by the grown-ups. It was the home of Mrs Riley. She was always given the married title although no one had ever known or seen a Mr Riley.

'All t' children in t' village says as how she's a witch,' went on Sarah-Louise. 'We have a skipping rhyme for her. Does tha' want to hear it?' Without waiting for a reply, she began to chant,

> 'Old Mother Riley, a witch is she,
> She'll ask you in for a cup of tea,
> With frogs and mice and beetles too,
> She'll make a brew for me and you,
> Old Mother Riley.'

'Sarah-Lou!' Mary laughed '—she's not a witch at all. She's a kind old lady. She's full of wisdom.'

'Doesn't she frighten you when you go to visit her? Don't you worry that she might put a spell on you and you'll be a prisoner behind the brick wall for ever and ever?'

'Of course not, silly. It's just that she keeps herself to herself like and folk haven't got to know her. And now she's badly wi' 'er legs and can't get out, I doubt if they ever will. We're lucky, I suppose. We came wi' t' railway and folks have accepted us along wi' trains. Any road, Mrs Riley is a quiet lady. She's happy wi' 'er own company. Though, I dare say, if one or two cared to pay her a visit, she wouldn't turn them away.' She paused for a second. 'You might go sometimes, Sarah-Lou. I can't, now that I'm working for Mr and Mrs Crowther. I've only called maybe once or twice since I've been in service…and then I couldn't stay long.'

The enclosing brick wall and the covering ivy made it impossible to see whether the old lady was at home. She would most likely be in the garden, pottering among the flowerbeds or sitting among the herbs, where she could enjoy the mixture of sweet and pungent fragrances drawn from them by the cooling air of evening. It was true; her age and frailty did confine her for the most part to the house and garden. She struggled even to venture to the nearby shops.

It was when Mary's job in the big house in Bankside had come to an end that she had struck up a friendship with the old lady. They had met one day when Mary had been shopping for her mother and Mrs Riley had been posting a letter to 'an old friend', as she'd confided to the girl. They had walked slowly back along the road together and Martha, as she insisted on being called, had invited Mary to see her garden.

Mary had been amazed at the variety of herbs and flowers contained in such a small area and fascinated with the scents they produced and the insects they attracted. The friendship, like the old lady's garden, had blossomed and soon Mary had begun to learn about the herbs that were growing in the little garden and in the wider hedgerows and fields beyond. With Martha's guidance, she had begun to gather plants and herbs according to the season. She was, as Martha had put it, the old lady's hands and feet.

She had started to harvest in spring when the comfrey bushes dotted the hedgerows, sturdy and green, lighting up the road with their pink and blue and purple bells. It was the first herb of the season around those parts and the first that Mary had learned about. She had known little of its use, other than that it was considered to be a miracle plant, and even less about the preparation to render it miraculous.

When summer had warmed the fields she'd picked angelica, meadowsweet, tansy and sorrel. As autumn had approached she'd harvested rosehips and pulled golden hops, with their rough, bristly coils, from the trees bordering the farm that belonged to Nathaniel's father. Under Mrs Riley's instruction she had slowly learned the uses and preparation of this hedgerow bounty.

In addition there was the garden, where rosemary and tarragon, chamomile, feverfew and mint grew with dozens of other herbs in tight-knit confusion. Mary's mind had reeled, at times, with the information it was being given but she loved to feel, as she always had done, that she was at one with the turning of the seasons, that she could learn the secrets of the soil, how to grow and harvest and use the herbs for the benefit of their neighbours.

The men and women of the village sought Mrs Riley's advice for those illnesses—and there were not many—that they could not deal with themselves. Her knowledge had been handed down from those who came before, who were skilled in the use of plants and herbs to treat ailments and improve health. It was compounded with the wisdom of experience that Mrs Riley had accumulated over her long life. The old lady's skills were vital when the doctor lived so far away and the villagers could not, in any case, afford his advice.

And then it had all come to an end, or nearly so, as Mary had known it would. How often she had dreamed, as she was abroad in the fields and hedgerows, of making this her life's work, as Martha had done. She had no idea how Martha had been able to live in this way, for she never accepted payment for the salves and potions that she mixed. She assumed that the old lady must have some private means at her disposal for how else could she have lived so long unsupported? Mary had no doubt that, much as she wished it, she could not follow in her mentor's footsteps. What was more, she had been in service before and knew how long were the hours that she would be expected to work and how little time off she would be given. Although Martha Riley lived only a stone's throw from the Station House, there was little opportunity to visit now. Mary bitterly regretted the passing of that time, the more so when she compared its freedom with the disquiet stirred in her by her present job.

'I don't know what tha' sees in all those boring old leaves,' Sarah-Louise said to her sister, jolting her from her reverie. 'They don't run or jump. They don't move at all. And they don't even say anything!'

Mary had tried before and failed to explain the fascination she felt. She was not surprised that, with the impatience of a ten-year-old, Sarah-Louise preferred the excitement of animals, which hopped, ran, flew and fed their young. She could understand how her sister loved the busy farmyard at milking time, the weaning of the piglets, fastened like oversized pink leeches to their mother's belly, the bustle and excitement of harvest time when the two huge horses, attached to the reaping machine, worked from sun-up to sun-down and everyone scanned the skies and prayed for the weather to hold. She remembered the summer storms of last year, which had arrived only a week or two before harvesting was likely to commence. The crop had been flattened and lay soaked and mouldering while the dykes filled and the river ran dangerously high. Men who had been taken on as casual labour had been laid off and returned to their homes nearby or far away, disappointed and complaining, with empty pockets. But they all knew that they were at the mercy of the weather and that the weather was under the control of a higher power than themselves. And this year their prayers had been answered.

Last year Nathaniel had been only a name, a farmer's son, battling, as were they all, with the elements. This year he meant so much more. Or was she being presumptuous? After all, he was the eldest son of a tenant farmer, she a mere general servant, daughter of a railwayman. And, although she was very proud of what her father did on the railway, she doubted whether his status matched that of the farmers, generations of whom had worked long and hard to tame the land in this temperamental corner of Yorkshire.

Manor Farm, the first they passed on their walk, was untenanted. Edwin Simpson at Bailiff Farm, towards which the two sisters were making their way, was tending the land belonging to both farms and a hard job it was. Granted he hadn't faced the unpleasantness that Henry Varley, Nathaniel's father, seemed to get from his men at Temple Farm, the other side of the railway line, but the combined land which he was working covered so many acres that there was not a minute left in the day.

'Yon house looks reet sad wi'out anyone there to care for it,' said Sarah-Louise. It was true; it did look neglected. Its windows stared like unseeing eyes. The magnificent roses in the front garden, the pride and joy of the previous owners, had run riot in the absence of the usual strict discipline inflicted on them. The gate swung on its hinges.

Bailiff Farmhouse was as busy as its neighbour was desolate. From the side door Bessie Simpson's plump figure emerged, surrounded by several small restless children, like bees round a honey pot. Bessie was fond of the two girls. In the short time they had lived in the village they had often lent a hand with the little ones. She did not know how she would have managed without their help when Edwin was so busy.

The younger children took hold of Mary and Sarah-Louise and escorted them to the hen house, where they all set to, searching in the straw for the golden-brown eggs. It was warm in the enclosed space and one or two hens were still sitting. Sarah-Louise showed the little ones how to put their hands gently beneath the soft feathers to retrieve the eggs. The hens glared fiercely and tried to peck at the less than clean skin of their chubby arms. Mary felt herself lulled by the warm close atmosphere of the hen house and found it difficult to comprehend the sudden commotion that accompanied the appearance of Bessie. It was her two younger sisters.

'Mrs Morritt's been took poorly,' gasped Lucy, 'and Mrs Riley's ailing herself so she's asked can you see to her. Mam said we'd find you here.'

Mary straightened up and looked at them in dismay.

'I hope she's not starting with t' babby. I don't know owt about bringing babbies into t' world.' And, leaving Sarah-Louise and her sisters to follow on behind, she ran with a racing heart back along the road to the cottages.

CHAPTER SIX

ALFIE was not to be comforted. 'I want my mummy. Why won't Mummy get up? I want Mummy to get up,' he intoned miserably. His words greeted Mary at the door and followed her as she hurried through the room to the foot of the stairs. From above came the sound of voices, which she recognised as those of her mother and Eliza Morritt.

'Come on, Alfie.' Mary took his hand. 'Show me where your mam's bedroom is.' With difficulty they climbed the narrow stairs together, Alfie reluctant to relinquish the hand that was giving him his first bit of comfort that day.

The small room seemed crowded. On the bed, which took up most of the space in the room, lay Eliza. Susan Swales was sitting on the edge of the bed, holding her hand and talking to her. Alfie let go of Mary's hand and ran to his mother's side, trying to climb on to the bed with her. At that moment Eliza was overcome with a painful contraction and turned her face away to hide her distress.

'Thank goodness you're here,' said Susan, looking at her daughter, relief written over her face. 'She were took bad wi' her pains a few hours since. She were planning to wait while George kem in from work, but our Lucy found Alfie here crying in t' garden and fetched me. If you ask me, I don't think things are right at all.' She gestured towards the middle of the bed, deformed by Eliza's swollen belly. ''Appen Mrs Riley's not well enough to come?'

'No, she can't get out at all now,' replied Mary, lifting Alfie, kicking and complaining, off the bed and noticing, with alarm, a dark red stain that was spreading outwards from under Eliza's body.

Sarah-Louise called from the foot of the stairs. 'Can I do owt to help?'

'Oh, Sarah-Lou, I'm glad you're back. Come on, Alfie. Let's go and find Sarah-Lou. She'll give you some tea. I'll be back up in a minute, Mrs Morritt.' Taking Alfie's hand again, they made their way clumsily down the stairs, followed closely by Susan. In the neglected living room Susan turned to her daughter.

'I must get back to Alice. I've left her too long already. Will you be all right?'

Mary thought for a moment and turned to her younger sisters, who were clustered at the doorway.

'Lucy and Laura, you run down the road to the inn and tell Mr Morritt that he's wanted at home. Tell him not to bother finishing his ale but to hurry back straight away. Sarah-Lou, can you take Alfie and look after him?' She glanced over at Station House. 'And call on Mrs Crowther for me. Make sure you talk to her, mind, and not her husband. Explain that I might be delayed. Tell her why. I'm sure she'll be all right about it. Aye, Mam, I'll manage. You get back to our Alice. I'll go back up to Alfie's mam now.'

As Mary swiftly but reluctantly climbed the stairs, she told herself that there was no point in panicking. That wouldn't help anyone, least of all Mrs Morritt. After all, she thought, whatever she could do was better than no help at all. And Mrs Riley was only just along the road and she could run to her for advice.

'Mrs Morritt…Eliza,' she added, surmising that in this most intimate of circumstances Christian name terms would be more apt, even if such familiarity did not come easily to her. 'Eliza, how often are you getting your pains?' The older woman turned to Mary, relief written on her pale, tired face that here was someone who could help.

'At first they were coming reet often,' she said, 'but now there's not so many. But they're o'er painful when they do come.' As if in confirmation, another agonising contraction forced her to clutch Mary's arm until Mary could feel her skin throbbing in its grip. The red stain grew.

'Has there been anything else apart from t' pains?' Mary asked, not wanting to alarm Eliza by drawing attention to the bleeding, which she felt sure was not normal.

'Well, the waters broke this afternoon, 'appen a couple of hours since,' Eliza replied.

'Waters'? What does she mean by 'waters'? thought Mary frantically. If only she had been able to spend more time with Mrs Riley, she would not feel so ill prepared.

'What about during the time you were expecting— any problems then?'

'Not really. I've been o'er tired, but then, as my George keeps telling me, I'm middlin' old to be 'aving babbies! Oh, and these last few weeks I've been losing some blood. Not a lot, tha' knows. Nothing to worry about.' The tears filling her eyes suggested she was much more concerned than she cared to admit.

So, thought Mary, *at the very least she needs something for t' pain and I need to know what's the cause of the bleeding.* But she couldn't leave her unattended. She would have to wait until George arrived. She went downstairs to heat water—that much she knew was necessary. The range had been neglected and she gingerly encouraged the few remaining red embers into life before adding more coal. The hotplates had thankfully retained most of their heat and she lifted saucepans from the shelf and filled them. Thank goodness George had been to the well before setting off for work that morning. She had been worried she would have to do that job too. She hurried up the stairs as Eliza cried out in pain, the sound fuelling Mary's anxiety. She felt helpless.

When the pain had settled, Eliza told Mary where to find linen and retrieve Alfie's baby clothes. They would prepare the crib later. Next Mary decorously withdrew the sheet that covered Eliza and put a hand on the hard, swollen belly. She wasn't sure what she was looking for but she knew Mrs Riley would ask. Just then another spasm came and the tight belly tightened still further. The bloodstain widened.

'Oh, God, please help me,' groaned Eliza, her hand fastening on Mary's arm again. Beads of sweat stood on her brow and ran into her dark hair. As if in reply, a man's voice was heard and in a few seconds George was by her side.

"Appen your George is getting a bit above 'is station!' Mary grinned and Eliza managed an answering smile.

'I need to fetch summat to ease the pain,' explained Mary rapidly to George. 'You stay wi' 'er and wipe 'er face and hold 'er 'and and I'll be back in no time.'

A small bottle of laudanum was ready on the table when Mary burst in. Mrs Riley had guessed that this at least would be needed if the birth were anything other than straightforward. A frown creased her brow when Mary explained the bleeding.

"Tis the afterbirth,' she explained. 'It feeds the baby till it's born. It should come out last but sometimes it grows too low and gets in the way. Then, when the baby is coming out, the head pressing on it makes it bleed. The only thing to do is get baby out as soon as possible. We'll try vervain and parsley,' she muttered half to herself, rising stiffly from her chair and inspecting the rows of labelled jars along the shelf behind her. 'They help the womb to contract better. It's risky, though. 'Appen it'll make the bleeding worse. But if we do nothing we may lose them both.'

Mary was comforted by the way in which Mrs Riley shared the responsibility for Eliza's treatment, but distraught at the possible appalling outcome.

'Stay calm, Mary. Remember, thou art doing thy very best for Eliza. Stay calm, then so will she and everything is much more likely to turn out well. Now, remember, no more than three drops of the laudanum in a glass of water. Any more than that and it will go badly with the baby. Repeat it after four hours if there's a need. The other bottle do thou start at one drop and increase by a drop every quarter of an hour.'

During Mary's absence twilight had turned to dark and the room was thrown into wavering shadows by two candles, which stood, one on a small cabinet by the bed and the other on a chest of drawers. The effect of the laudanum on Eliza's pain was rapid. She dozed between contractions and George took the opportunity to slip next door and check on Alfie. Sarah-Louise had tucked him up in bed, where, worn out with all the excitement, he was sleeping soundly. George had no desire to return to the bedroom, where he felt useless. In any case Mary had said she would call him if needed. Sitting on the bench outside his house, he pushed a large pinch of tobacco into his favourite pipe and lit it. The smoke curled peacefully upwards and its smell drifted into the bedroom above.

'Lucky for some,' murmured Eliza through a drugged haze. 'Next time…' But the third dose of vervain had begun to work. The spasms came frequently, the pain was worse. And so too was the bleeding. Each spasm brought with it a fresh spurt of blood. *How much blood was it possible for one person to lose?* Mary worried. And then, miraculously it stopped. And a minute later there was the baby's head. Mary stared in amazement and wonder.

'Mary, I can feel t' babby coming,' slurred Eliza.

'Yes, yes, it is. I can see it too. It'll soon be over.' Mary wondered what would happen next. What did happen was out of the control of both women. Eliza pushed and grunted and in less than five minutes a tiny boy lay in the bloodied mess of childbirth.

Now that there were two people instead of one to care for, Mary needed another pair of hands. They were not long in coming. George was by her side as soon as he heard the baby's cry.

'Eh, lass,' he said to Eliza, 'we've got another little lad.'

'Aye,' replied Eliza, 'and he's been that much trouble I'm going to call him George.'

George laughed. 'Suits me fine,' he said. 'Good-looking fellow 'e is too, like his dad.' He turned to Mary. 'Thanks, Mary. We're reet grateful. Tha' certainly knows what tha's doing when it comes to babbies.'

Mary continued to attend to Eliza, marvelling at the afterbirth, which for so long had given the baby its life and then at the end had nearly caused the death of both baby and mother. She felt the hardening of the womb, knew the worst danger was past. It could be months before Eliza recovered from the loss of blood that the pregnancy had inflicted on her but, if she looked after herself, recovery should be complete, if slow.

The baby seemed remarkably unaffected. After his piercing announcement that there was a new arrival in Station Cottages, there was no further noise and when Mary put him in the arms of his mother he slept immediately, drowsy with laudanum.

'I don't know how to thank thee,' whispered Eliza. 'I know this was t' first time, like. Tha' was grand.'

'If there's ever owt we can do in return, promise me that tha' will let us know,' added George. He turned back to his wife but already, like her baby, she was asleep.

CHAPTER SEVEN

A CHILL east wind caught at Mary's hair and billowed out her skirt as she made her way along the dark road. She wrapped the shawl tightly round her shoulders and quickened her step. Autumn leaves raced ahead of her down the lane, carrying with them the tension from her body and the turmoil of emotions from her brain. She was too overwrought to sleep and, guessing that everyone in Station House would have retired to bed, she had decided to go for a walk.

She felt exultant, triumphant. The panic that had flooded her body while Eliza was in labour and the horror of the pain and bleeding were forgotten in the miracle of new life that had lain between the mother's legs on the soiled bedclothes. She had done it! She had saved this woman's life, when she might otherwise have died. She laughed aloud as she thought of what George had said to her. 'Tha certainly knows what tha's doing when it comes to babbies.' She hadn't known, of course. And Eliza, no less grateful, had realised this and still appreciated the help that Mary, in her ignorance, had given her. Of course, the outcome might have been different, had it not been for Martha's advice and medicines. How she wished again that she could have continued to learn more about herbs and their uses, rather than being forced into an employment in which she felt constricted and uncomfortable.

The last building she passed as she made her way out of the village was Temple Farm. A light still burned in an upstairs room and Mary wondered if it was Nathaniel's. Maybe, like her, he was unable to sleep. Maybe he was lying in bed thinking about her, as she so often thought of him when she retired to her room in Station House. If only she knew what he really thought of her. If only he thought as much about her as she did about him. If only he loved her, she thought, her heart missing a beat. If only he loved her, he would ask her father if they could be married and, when they were, he would take her away from Station House.

At the place where the road performed several bends as it followed the contours of the river, she decided to turn and make her way back to the house. The bedroom window of Temple Farm was still lit. She walked slowly past, looking across at the otherwise darkened building. No figure loomed in the square of light to satisfy her curiosity as to the owner of the room or her hunger to see Nathaniel again.

'And just where dost tha' think tha's bin?'

Mary gasped in fright at the angry voice that intruded into the darkness.

'I've been helping out over t' road,' she faltered, her

heart pounding from the shock. She lit a candle and placed it with a shaking hand on the kitchen table, where it lit up to grotesque effect the flushed face of her employer. 'George's wife, Eliza, had her baby this evening, and I thought, seeing as it was my evening off…'

'I'm the one who employs you,' interrupted John Crowther rudely, 'and I'd thank thee to come in at a decent time and not at this late hour like a common trollop.'

The injustice of this remark hit Mary and she flushed. 'But I couldn't leave poor Eliza. There *was* no one else, tha' knows. Mrs Riley is too old now. Think how your Annie would have been with no one there to help.' She did not intend to start apologising when she had done nothing wrong. But neither did she want to fuel the argument. She could smell alcohol on the breath of her employer and knew that appealing to reason was unlikely to get her anywhere.

'If you'll excuse me, I must get to my bed,' she said, passing him as he sat slouched at the kitchen table.

In that same second he reached out and caught her hand. 'No, don't go,' he muttered thickly, refusing to release her from his hot grasp. 'Stay and talk, won't you. I didn't mean to be angry.' She hesitated, trying to think of a way of disengaging herself without annoying him afresh.

'Can I make thee a cup of tea?' she asked, smiling awkwardly, 'and, if it's all right by you, I'll have one too. It's been a long evening.'

'Such cold fingers. Such a lovely face,' he continued, as though he hadn't heard her. He reached up to stroke her dark hair, blown loose and tangled by the wind, and his flushed perspiring face and bloodshot eyes loomed close in the candlelight. She drew back in alarm, knocking against the cabinet, and an enamel basin crashed to the floor, spinning round and round before coming to rest against a chair. The sound brought him to his senses and he drew in his sprawled legs and sat up.

'Tek no notice o' me,' he slurred. 'It's yon wife o' mine has upset me wi' 'er high and mighty ways and 'er "don't like this" and "can't be doing with that". There's no pleasing 'er. Don't know what I ever saw in t' lass.'

Mary turned to the stove where a kettle stood simmering on the hotplate. She warmed the teapot, added tea and poured on the water, all the time uncomfortably aware of her employer sitting behind her. She watched out of the corner of her eye for any movement.

'Won't you join me?' John Crowther asked when the tea was poured and she had placed a cup on the table in front of him, hoping to escape upstairs with her own. He pulled out a chair and she reluctantly sat down.

'Never 'ad any trouble like this wi' Harriet,' he went on. 'She were my first wife, like. Always did as she were told. Reet obliging she were; none o' this nonsense. Lost 'er giving birth to my son. Been dead now these twenty years, she has. All that time wi'out anyone cuddly and soft in my bed. And now this…this…prim and proper cold fish of a wife. But she'll soon find out she can't carry on refusing me.' His voice had risen and he slammed his fist on to the table, making the cups jump and their contents slop on to the wooden table. 'I'll mek 'er see sense, if it's the last thing I do.'

Mary had risen from her chair and now she held a

second candle to the one that was lighting up the brutish face of the Stationmaster. She edged towards the door. 'If you'll excuse me, Mr Crowther, I'm very tired and I need to be up early in t' morning to see to t' house and babby.' Before he could detain her any longer, she opened the door into the hall and made her way quickly up the stairs and into her room, turning the key securely in the lock.

A whirlpool of emotions drained her strength and she sat down suddenly on the side of her little bed, extinguished the candle and stared out of the bare window into the night. Shivering in disgust and fear, she recalled his bloated face and tainted breath and his hot, grasping hands. How could he behave like that and he her employer? Had she acted correctly? Should she have created a scene, risked losing her job, jeopardised her friendship with Annie? The thought of Annie increased her apprehension. She had watched day by day the offhand way John Crowther treated his wife, putting her down, criticising when praise was what she needed, ignoring every attempt to please him. Mary suspected that her presence around the house prevented some of John Crowther's wilder outbursts. She had often heard his voice raised in anger when they were alone, had been unable to ignore his shouts echoing along the corridor when they went to bed. She had listened to Annie crying and wanted to go to her, although she knew she couldn't. She had even seen bruises on her arms after one of these episodes and suspected that, in his anger, he was hitting his wife. Mary was naive about the goings-on between a man and his wife in the privacy of their bedroom. Strange to think she had spent the evening helping to bring a baby into the world, she thought with a wry smile, when she knew so little about how babies were made. Her mother had always been too preoccupied with Alice to consider the needs of her other daughters to learn about the ways of the world. But it was obvious that something was sadly amiss in that secret part of their lives.

John Crowther had compared Annie unfavourably with his first wife. Mary had known nothing about an earlier wife and it was a revelation to her to find out that he had a son—a son who must now be twenty and a grown man. Why had John never mentioned him? Why did he never come to visit? Then there was this outburst she had just witnessed, this dark tide of threats that had hung in the air and to which she had given no reply but to flee the room as soon as she was able.

She heard a door slam and the uneven, heavy tread of boots on the stairs. She held her breath as the steps came closer and paused outside her door, before weaving on to the bedroom at the end. Another slammed door, a man's slurred voice raised in an indistinct comment and then silence. Mary released her breath unevenly. After a minute she went to stand by the window. The line of cottages showed black against the night sky. She stared at the one in which her family lay sleeping, wishing that she were there too, protected and safe.

Lying down again on the bed, she buried her face in the pillow and tried to blot out the image of the flushed and leering one that had confronted her in the kitchen. Eventually she turned over and stared wide-eyed into the darkness. She was still dressed and pulled the heavy eiderdown around her in an attempt to calm her shivering. She closed her eyes and tried to sleep but it seemed like only minutes before the cockerel's morning ritual interrupted her nightmarish thoughts and fingers of light were filtering through the silhouetted trees into her room.

CHAPTER EIGHT

THE pile of baby clothes in the nursery was growing rapidly, more rapidly even than Johnny Crowther. Annie had decided that she would sort through the chest of drawers and pass on to Eliza Morritt all that Johnny had outgrown.

'Just think,' began Annie, sitting back on her heels and looking at Mary. 'One day you'll meet someone who will want to marry you. Then, before you know it, *you'll* be collecting piles of baby clothes.'

'Oh, I don't think that will be for a very long time. I'm happy here looking after you and Johnny.'

Annie breathed a sigh of relief. 'I'm right glad to hear you say that. I was sure you'd be off marrying someone, especially with John keeping on about how attractive you are.'

Mary stopped her sorting and looked up. 'What do you mean, Annie?'

'Aw, you know, he likes your cooking and he thinks you keep the house looking nice and you're good with Johnny.'

'Oh, I see. That's all right then. But that's what I'm paid for, so I should think I do.'

'And then he says how you've got a comely figure and he reckons you'd be much more exciting than me in…'

'Annie! What are you talking about? He said that to you?' Mary put her hands up to her burning cheeks.

'Well, he sometimes has a bit to drink of an evening and says things he doesn't mean.'

Mary took out another pile of tiny clothes. 'How did you come to meet Mr Crowther?' she asked, breaking an uncomfortable silence.

'He was a churchwarden at Father's church for a long time. I think Father felt sorry for him, his wife having died and him having been left with a baby. You did know he had a son?'

'Aye, I did hear it somehow.'

'Edward, they called him. He didn't live with his dad. John's parents-in-law brought him up. He'll be twenty or so now. He works somewhere around York, I think, but I don't know what his job is. I've never met him. You see, they don't have any contact, John and his son. Anyway, Father and John got friendly—Father used to invite John to tea sometimes—and Father told me one day that John had asked if he could walk out with me and he had given his consent.'

'What did you think?'

'Well, we all have dreams, don't we, and it wasn't what I'd dreamed would happen. But my parents were getting old and what would I have done on my own? And it pleased Father. But then one day Father had a seizure in the street and was taken from us straight away, and two months later Mother died too. She couldn't live without him, you see. When the mourning was over John came to claim me, saying as how I'd been promised to him. We moved here soon after that, when he was given the Stationmaster's job. I was expecting Johnny by that time.'

'Don't you think you ought to keep some of these little clothes, in case you have another babby? There's more than enough here for little George.'

'Oh, I shan't have another,' Annie replied quickly, 'and, if I do, I'll buy some more.'

She rose from the floor and crossed to the window, from where she could see Johnny asleep in his perambulator.

'Mary!' she began and then paused. 'Do you know anything about what goes on in the bedroom…you know…between a husband and wife? I mean, I was never told anything about it. I tried to find out. You know, those books he gave me, I've looked right through for something on how I should behave in the bedroom but there's nothing. John always says how he's got rights. But it's horrible, what he does. I've tried to be a good wife, but it's getting worse. I know it's my fault. At least, he tells me it is, but I don't know what to do about it.' She turned from the window to look at Mary, tears pricking the back of her eyes.

'Mam never told me about the ways of the world. I suppose she was too busy with our Alice. But she and my dad seem happy together and so do George and Eliza next door.' Mary frowned. 'I suppose I could ask Mrs Riley if she knows anything that would help.'

'Oh, no, no, don't do anything like that,' Annie said

in alarm. 'I wouldn't want anyone else to know our business. Suppose it got round the village. John would be so angry that I don't like to think what he would do.' She closed her eyes as if to shut out the possibilities that rose before them. 'No, it doesn't matter. Forget I said anything. At least you know all about the best and the worst of me now.' She gave an unconvincing laugh and picked up the piles of clothes to carry them downstairs.

Annie was embarrassed now that she had told Mary this, her deepest secret. She hoped that it wouldn't damage the friendship that had grown between them. For Mary was her first real friend, her advent into Annie's life being a turning point. Before Mary, she had found it difficult to cope with life. Her sheltered childhood had left her unprepared for even the normal ups and downs of everyday life. If anything new came along she would begin to shake with fear, her mouth would go dry and her head feel as if it was filled with wool. She would be unable to sleep. Food would become tasteless and stick in her throat.

With Mary's encouragement, though, she was learning to cook, beginning to take responsibility for the household and, most importantly, coping with the nurturing of her young son. To her surprise she was even beginning to enjoy motherhood. She marvelled at Johnny's first words and watched with amazement tinged with apprehension his first drunken steps. Rather than being frightened by his utter dependence on her, she began to relish it. If it were not for what went on behind the bedroom door, she would be a happy woman.

CHAPTER NINE

STUBBLE stood ankle-deep in the fields and, although it was uncomfortable for walking, it was certainly easier than corn waist high or ground newly turned by the plough. Mary was making slow progress, the stalks snaring her skirt, even though she lifted the front of it high, showing an indecent amount of ankle. But it hardly mattered when there was no one around to see. She stopped to draw breath and sat at the edge of the field to tie the lace of her boot, which the stalks had succeeded in pulling undone. She looked along to the hedgerow end, where she knew the best hops were growing, twined in choking profusion up the bushes. She had promised Martha Riley on her last visit to the cottage that she would gather hops for her when they were ripe. Martha was planning to make a hop tea, very beneficial, she assured her, for digestive problems.

It was a week since the encounter with John Crowther and the first time she had been given any time off since that eventful night. He had not been near her since and she had taken care never to be alone with him. She hoped against hope that what had happened was fuelled by his over-indulgence in alcohol and that there would be no recurrence. But she was taking no chances. She sighed, breathing in deeply the corn-scented air. It was good to be out in the fields again after the claustrophobia of Station House.

Suddenly from behind the hedgerow came the sound of voices and, as she sat there, skirts awry and laces trailing, Nathaniel appeared from behind a hawthorn bush, his hair, the colour of the hops, wild about his head and his long waders slimed with the mud of the dyke they had been cleaning.

'Nathaniel!' she gasped, clambering to her feet. 'I was just having trouble with my lace. I didn't expect to see you here.'

'So I can see,' he replied, smiling broadly. 'Nor me you. It must be my lucky day! Where are you off to? On a mission for old Mother Riley, I'll be bound.'

'Nathaniel, you mustn't call her that. It's not right.' Mary tried, and failed, to look severe. 'Well, yes, as it happens, I am. I promised her a while since that I'd pick some hops for her. The best uns are growing at the bottom of this hedgerow.' He came across to her and followed her gaze down the field. She glanced down at his waders. 'If you don't mind me saying, Nathaniel, you don't smell too sweet.'

He burst out laughing. 'Jacob and I have been hedging and ditching. This dyke always needs a lot of work to get it clean. It's fortunate you've come today, though. We were working our way down this field. We'd have had everything cut back by tomorrow. Come on, I'll help you. The best hops are the ones you won't be able to reach.'

He set off along the field edge and she followed closely behind, struggling to keep up with his long strides.

'Your sisters were telling me how you helped your neighbour the other night. What a mercy you were there.'

'I was very frightened, I don't mind telling you,' she said to his back, thinking to herself that the greater fright had been caused by what had happened after the baby's birth. 'If it hadn't been for Mrs Riley's help, I don't know how I would have managed,' she continued.

'I know that…and I'm sorry; I wasn't really mocking Mrs Riley. It's just your sisters and their song about her…they entertain me in the cart when I give them a lift home from school and I finish up thinking of her as old Mother Riley.'

The hops hung pale gold in the autumn sunshine. Nathaniel reached for the higher convolutions where the best flowers grew and showers of petals, gossamer-thin, fluttered down on to her head. He brushed the petals gently from her hair, looking into her eyes until she turned her head away in embarrassment. He reached out his hand and gently took hold of her chin, easing her face round until once more their eyes met. 'How different he is from the Stationmaster,' she thought, recalling John Crowther's drunken face lit up by the light of the candle. She pushed the thought away, for fear it spoil the time with Nathaniel.

'And what will you be collecting for Mrs Riley on your next evening off?'

'Oh, I'm making some rosehip syrup for Johnny Crowther. Martha showed me how when I was helping her out last year. But the best bushes are in the lane at t' far side of the village.'

'Ah, you mean where I ride Jess of an evening. Well, happen you can do your gathering later in the day and I might be riding past. You'll certainly get on faster if you have someone to hold your basket while you pick.' He hesitated, holding her gaze. Then he tucked a damp tendril of hair behind her ear, smiled his wide smile and they turned to walk slowly up the field to rejoin Jacob.

'Good luck with the brewing then, Mistress Mary.' He vaulted the dyke to where Jacob was standing, missed his footing on the slippery side and disappeared into its depths. Mary hurried over, alarmed that he might have injured himself. One look at his mud-covered body struggling in the stinking quagmire was enough to reassure her that he was unhurt. It was Jacob who broke the sudden silence, his guffaws echoing down the land and joined immediately by the laughter of the two young people.

'I thought for a minute I would have to try out one of my new remedies on you,' she said when she could talk again.

'Are you both going to leave me here all day?' Nathaniel called from the bottom of the dyke. Mary stepped back, out of range of the foul-smelling mud.

'Take my hand, Master Nathaniel,' called Jacob, and Nathaniel emerged to stand next to the farm-hand, the sight reducing Mary once more to helpless laughter. 'You best get back to the farm and change. I'll carry on here meanwhile,' Jacob continued.

'Aye, I better had, or the smell of this ditch will still be with me next week. And then I doubt whether any pretty country girl out picking herbs will find me attractive.' He strode off across the field to the farmhouse, muddy rivulets running down his legs into his waders, which squelched with every step he took.

One evening two weeks later he rode his chestnut mare up the lane and tethered her to a tree while they gathered the ripe fruit. Jess, a spirited four-year-old, reared and broken in by Nathaniel, seemed happy enough to graze the sweet grass until the couple were finished. Nathaniel placed the basket in the hedgerow, mounted his horse and held out his hand for Mary to clamber up behind.

'Hold on round my middle,' Nathaniel said. She hesitated to do so and timidly held on to his waistcoat but, as soon as the horse took a step, her arms grasped Nathaniel tightly. In the gathering dusk he walked the horse up the lane to allow Mary time to get used to the insecurity of being so far above firm ground. Then he eased Jess into a trot and, with a frightened cry, Mary held on even tighter. Slowing the horse again, they made their way over the stubble fields until they were far out of the village and day was a mere streak of light on the western horizon. Horse and rider picked their way without mishap over the rough terrain, only because they had done it so many times before that they knew every indentation and impediment.

At last Nathaniel turned Jess homeward. Mary listened to the slow clip-clop of the horse's shoes and thought the animal sounded as reluctant as Mary was herself to end the evening, even though her thighs ached and her body was stiff with tiredness. At the approach to Station Yard Nathaniel swung his leg over the mare's head and jumped easily down. He clasped Mary's waist and lifted her out of the saddle to the ground, keeping his hands around her waist until she could stand steady, and not releasing her until he had placed a kiss on her forehead and made her promise to meet him on her next evening off.

The Stationmaster entered the kitchen as Mary was taking off her coat. Her cheeks were pink and her eyes sparkled. Her long hair, loosened by the jolting she had received on her ride across the fields, framed her face in dark tendrils.

'Good evening, sir,' she said with a sinking heart as she stepped into the scullery to hang up her coat.

'Where've you been?' he inquired, without returning her greeting.

'It were my evening off, sir. I've been picking rosehips to make syrup for your son.'

'Where are they, then?'

'Where are what, sir?'

'The rosehips! Where are the rosehips you've spent all evening picking?'

She looked around for the basket, realising, as she did so, that she had left it nestling in the long grass up the lane.

'I know what you've been doing, so don't try and pretend otherwise. I saw you from the window, so thick with that farmer's son.'

Mary started to redden, as much with irritation that

she had been observed as from embarrassment that her secret had been uncovered. 'He's a friend, sir, and I'm allowed to meet friends when it's my evening off.'

'And does your father know about this "friendship" or are you keeping it a secret from him too?'

Mary's silence confirmed that neither she nor Nathaniel had spoken to her father.

'May I remind you that I'm your employer? I do not want you cavorting round the countryside and bringing my good name into disrepute. Is that clear?'

'But Mr Crowther, we were only…'

'I saw what you were doing…and I won't have it on my land and in my time. And besides….' He came closer and looked her in the eye. 'What makes you think that a farmer's son is going to be interested in the likes of you?' A sneer crossed his face. 'No, my dear, you keep to your own kind and leave the farmers to themselves. We get on just fine here, all of us, don't we?' He came still closer. 'So just you forget all about him and go and brush your hair and get yourself into that little bed of yours.' He raised his hand to her hair but she slapped it away and turned to run from him. He caught her wrist and gripped it tightly, bringing his face up to hers.

'Remember what I told you. Forget the farmer's son. I'm the one who pays your wages.'

Winter, to everybody's relief, was not as bad as the last one had been. Snow came in November and the old farmers warmed themselves around the fire at the Wheatsheaf. Gazing into the flames, as if they could see within their changing patterns the weather to come, they predicted a return of the cold white months of the previous winter that had kept them off the land and under the feet of their wives. Not that they had minded the enforced break—after the exertions of harvest they were always glad of the chance to rest their aching bones. But by March the hard frost had still held the countryside in its grip and they had fretted in their inactivity, thinking of the ploughing and harrowing that remained to be done before the seed could be sown. This year, however, the snow dispersed quickly and further falls brought a temporary brightness to the dark landscape and only a brief lull in their activities.

Spring could not come soon enough for Mary. The short cold days and dark elongated evenings, confining her to the house, stretched her nerves to breaking point. She was unable to relax and enjoy her work because of the possibility that John Crowther would interrupt her. She made sure, whenever possible, that she was in the same room as his wife whenever she knew him to be around. And still the feeling persisted that he was watching her. At times he was attentive to his wife and she thought then that she had been mistaken about him. But she knew by his behaviour at Christmas that she wasn't.

There were no trains on Christmas Day. The rail men, from Stationmaster to lowly porter, could relax in the knowledge that for this one day in the year they would not have to forsake their firesides and brave the icy wind that funnelled through the station. The lamps remained unlit and workers and their families marvelled at the eerie silence pervading the yard and the stretch of line that it served. The Stationmaster had enjoyed a good joint of beef, courtesy of one of the local farmers who regularly sent his beasts to market on the cattle truck to Selby. The meat was accompanied by an excellent bottle of claret and John Crowther had partaken generously of its purple-red richness. Annie had invited Mary to join them in the living room after the meal and she had not been able to think of an excuse to go to her room.

John sat by the fire, his legs stretched out towards the flames, the crescendo of his snores causing his wife and Mary some hilarity. Mary was only half conscious of Annie saying something as she got up out of her chair and she fought against her tiredness, her eyes closing in the warmth of the room. She was thinking of Nathaniel, calculating how many weeks had passed since she had seen him and wondering if his feelings for her were the same as they had seemed to be last autumn. She relived the ride on Jess, feeling the strength of Nathaniel's body as she clung to him and savouring again the tenderness of his kiss on her forehead...the kiss that she had wished was on her lips, that in her imagination he was planting even now. Suddenly her eyes snapped open, to be confronted with the same flushed perspiring face that had so disgusted her on her return from Eliza Morritt's birthing.

'Leave me alone! Get away from me!' she cried, trying to push John Crowther away and, as she did so, the door opened and Annie, who must have left the room, was standing there, looking bewildered.

'What's the matter?' she gasped, looking from one to the other.

'It's Mary,' her husband replied without hesitation.

'She was dreaming. I had to wake her up, she seemed that upset.'

Mary sat forward and rubbed her forehead. 'Yes, I must have been dreaming. I'm sorry, Annie. Did you want me to do summat? I shouldn't be sitting here like this when there's work to be finished.'

'You've done everything that's to be done.' Annie put a hand on her shoulder to prevent her from getting up. 'Sit there, Mary. You've cooked us a beautiful meal and you deserve a rest, doesn't she, John?'

Her husband grunted and sat down heavily in his chair. 'I suppose so,' he muttered. 'Only just make sure you don't disturb me again.' He leaned back and closed his eyes. Mary looked at him and wondered, not for the first time, whether she was imagining what had surely happened.

The long days of winter brought with them no message from Nathaniel. Mary was restless. She was beginning to believe that his feelings towards her were imaginary or, at the least, fleeting, pale as the sunshine that forced its way between the gathered winter clouds. She spent the first weeks of the New Year in a well of despondency, willing Nathaniel to miraculously appear and take her away from the confusion of her present life, knowing that she must smother her own feelings because his were not what she had hoped them to be. On a clear blue afternoon that promised spring, she wheeled Johnny in his baby carriage along the track that led to Beckley. The endless liquid vibrato of a skylark made her stop to seek the tiny black spot in the cloudless sky.

Around them finches flitted between the leafless twigs and here and there an early blackthorn flower brightened the bareness. Mary felt the excitement all around her and longed to be a part of it again.

At Station Yard her mother was taking in the washing and Mary, reluctant to go indoors on such a beautiful day, walked along to pass the time of day.

'Well, look at Johnny. Hasn't he grown over the past couple of months! He must be walking now,' Susan said as Mary slowed the baby carriage.

'Almost! He can pull himself up with the help of the table leg and the chairs. Like as not he'll be walking in a week or two. How's our Alice?' Mary continued, immediately thinking of the sister whose progress was measured in hours without a fit and for whom walking would never be a possibility.

'Middlin',' Susan replied. 'Good days and bad. I'm just glad to see a bit of sunshine again. If this keeps on, it won't be long before your father can start to grow his vegetables and the girls will be out from under my feet. Look, here they come now. Getting a lift again. No peace for the wicked!'

Mary turned the baby carriage in the direction of Station House and watched Nathaniel's wagon approach, struggling to subdue the rising tide of consciousness that his appearance had induced. Her sisters milled around, talking of school, of how lucky they were to have a ride home, of how much the baby was growing. Over their heads Nathaniel caught Mary's eye and she knew by the look he gave her that nothing had changed.

* * *

'I wasn't sure I could get away,' gasped Mary, breathless from running between the fields to reach their meeting place. 'Mr Crowther and Annie 've been out shopping and needed summat to eat when they kem in. And little Johnny wanted his mam and I couldn't get him settled.' The matter-of-fact way in which she delivered these words was at odds with her inner turmoil, for she had felt certain that he would have tired of waiting for her and returned home. And then would he have wanted to see her again if he thought that she had gone back on her promise to meet him? These thoughts had been going over and over in her mind as she'd watched the hands of the clock move round ever faster as the time arranged for their meeting had come and gone. She had not dared show her anxiety or John Crowther would have wanted to know where she was going and would in all probability have changed his mind about giving her the evening off. She already knew what he thought about her friendship with the farmer's son.

'Don't worry, lass,' replied Nathaniel. 'I thought I wasn't going to make it on time myself. I took Blackie and Princess up to Bracken Haggs to sow the barley. It's a big field, that one, and the horses were fair lathered by the end of it.' He came to her side and they walked slowly towards the river, an awkwardness between them, brought about by the winter months that had kept them apart.

The water was high. It swirled and eddied beneath them and brown froth gathered in the hollows of the bank. A heron took off awkwardly into the air, squawking its disappointment that the river was devoid of fish. It flew over the chimneys of the railway cottages towards Low Ponds, where richer pickings were to be found. The couple made their way carefully along the bank, silent at first, the silence stretching into minutes.

'I've missed you, Mary,' Nathaniel blurted out at last. 'No one to tease and pick hops for. Only Jess and I exploring the fields of a night. I've missed you so much. I don't want things to go on like this. I want to tell my father about you but t' trouble is, Father's always got his own opinion about things and everything planned out the way he wants it to be.'

Mary's hopes had risen at his words but now she looked at him with a sinking heart. 'And how does he want it to be?' She guessed the plans wouldn't include her, for farming folk in general thought themselves above the likes of her and her railway family.

'Well…he's friendly with a farmer at Bankside. He seems to think his daughter…she's called Rhoda…would be a good match. Never met her myself, like.'

Mary had met her, though. She had been an occasional visitor at the big house in the same village, the house where Mary had worked as a maid. A thin, humourless girl she was too, not at all suited to Nathaniel, Mary thought. Jealousy bubbled up inside her as she turned to face him.

'Well, if that's what tha' wants, mebbe tha' should ask her.' Mary's dark eyes flashed. ''Appen she's cleverer than I would ever be and much more able to do t' books and such like. And she'd play t' piano for you and sing. But she's not one as likes to get her feet dirty, so tha' better mek sure t' yard is always clean and swept, and don't expect 'er to roll 'er sleeves up and 'elp when times is busy, like, or go walks over t' fields wi' thee. But don't tell *me* about 'er, cos I don't want to know.' Turning on her heel, she made off along the riverbank in the opposite direction. She had not gone many yards when he was by her side once more.

'Don't let's quarrel,' he said. 'My father's only thinking of what's best for the farm. After all, it's me that will take it over when he's no longer able to work.'

'Well, tha' doesn't think much o' me if tha' let's thy father tell thee what to do.'

'I've told you what I think of you. I've done nowt but think of you all through the dark days of winter,' he replied reasonably, 'and I will talk to him, I promise.'

'Before next week?'

'Promise!' said Nathaniel. 'As long as you promise to meet me next week.'

'Next week or the one after. It depends when I'm given my next evening off.'

They walked together then. Mary relaxed as he began to talk of farming business, about the struggles they were having with the new steam plough, about the crops they were planting, the number of cows that were in calf. He made her laugh with descriptions of the antics of the new farm-hands. She in turn talked of her family, of Annie and the baby and of her friend, Mrs Riley.

'I've never met anyone like her,' said Mary. 'She's very knowing and she did like to teach me, though sometimes it seemed that I were o'er slow to learn. And she were peaceful, like, always listening, never forcing her ideas on me, though she must have plenty, wi' her having lived so long.'

'A bit different from my father, then.' They laughed. 'You realise, lass, that I will have to ask your father's permission too, if we are to be seen out together. 'Appen I'll speak to mine first, though. If I come calling at your cottage, your sisters will spread it all round the village and then there'll be hell to pay at home!'

In the deepening dusk they picked their way along the edge of the field to Ings Lane. Just before they reached the road, Nathaniel took her in his arms.

'Don't fret, sweetheart. I'll talk to my father this week. And the other lass, she means nothing to me. It's you I love. There, I've said it now.' And, bending his head, he kissed her tenderly, straightened up and strode off in the direction of his father's farm.

CHAPTER TEN

WHEN John Crowther took his family to York, he was thoughtfulness itself. He handed Annie proudly into the carriage, took care of little Johnny when he became too heavy for her to carry and left them with refreshment in the Station Hotel while he went to meet his bosses, this being the main purpose of the trip. On his return they dined and then set out to see the Minster and as many of the shops as they could comfortably visit before the return train arrived to carry them home. Annie carefully carried the gifts she had bought—a small trinket box for Mary and a teddy bear for her son.

Johnny was restless after the day's excitement and it took Annie and Mary longer than usual to settle him. Mary had taken the opportunity of an empty house to do a more thorough clean than was usually possible and John told her that she could take the evening off. After she had gone, Annie sat in the nursery, listening to the rhythmic sound of Johnny's breathing. She was tired too and her feet ached with the unaccustomed walking. The gentle murmur of the wind outside made her feel sleepy and her eyes began to close as she leaned back in the comfort of the chair.

Behind her the door opened and John came quietly into the room and looked into the cot at his sleeping son.

'Has Mary gone?' he asked.

'Yes, I told her she could go as soon as Johnny went off to sleep. I think she's planning on visiting a friend. I told her she needn't be back until ten.'

'Good! Come with me, then. We've got some time to us selves for a change. Reckon you owe me a bit of consideration after all I've done for you today.'

Annie's heart sank. 'Aw, John, please, no. I'm so tired.' She cringed as he took hold of her arm and pulled her towards the open door.

'And I'm tired—tired of hearing you making excuses. You're my wife, dammit, and I've every right.'

Johnny stirred in his sleep as his father raised his voice and Annie turned back to him.

'Look, Johnny's going to wake up. I need to see to him.'

'You need to see to me and you will,' John muttered through clenched teeth. Tightening his grip on her arm, he pulled her from the nursery and along the corridor into their bedroom.

'Please let go of me—you're hurting,' she sobbed. In a surge of strength fuelled by panic, she twisted to try and free herself from his grasp. Caught off balance, he fell heavily against the wall of the corridor, letting go of her arm as he did so. Before he had a chance to find his feet, she was off, running down the stairs and out into the yard. Hesitating only a second, she turned into the station entrance and ran along the platform, her shoes clattering like the alarm call of a frightened bird. The long stretch of the platform ended in the signal box and beyond this was scrubland, fringed by tired bushes. Before she reached the grass her breath was coming in gasps and her steps, in her inadequate footwear, had slowed. Glancing over her shoulder, she saw that her husband had followed her on to the platform and was gaining on her rapidly. She tried to run again but her energy was spent and she halted, beginning to cry noisily as she realised that her reckless flight had made a bad situation even worse.

John Crowther's anger at his wife's refusal to accede to his wishes was in no way diminished by the ignominious chase down the platform, in full view of the one or two railway employees who remained on duty. As if to make it obvious to all that he would not countenance such waywardness, he marched back down the platform with his wife, his hand clamped firmly around her upper arm. Once inside the house, he slammed the door and almost dragged her up the stairs and into the bedroom.

'No, please don't. Please leave me alone!' she screamed, trying to roll off the bed and out of his grasp, but he caught hold of her and a heavy slap across her face shocked her into a momentary silence.

'You'll do as I wish, woman. Don't you deny me or you'll get what's been coming to you for a long time.'

George Morritt scratched his head and frowned. It was obvious that something was amiss. The evening being quiet, he had nothing to do but watch Annie's flight from the house and the pursuit by the Stationmaster. He followed their return to the house, noting how John Crowther never lessened his hold on her arm. It was not the first time his suspicions had been raised that things were amiss in Station House. He had no liking for the belligerent, opinionated man who was his boss, but he was reluctant to interfere in something that was clearly none of his business. He knew Annie Crowther to be an overwrought, anxious sort of a lady, quite unlike his own placid, even-tempered wife. He determined, however, to keep his eyes open for further trouble.

He was still pondering the episode as he came off duty and turned into the station yard, seeing the peaceful row of cottages, indistinct in the approaching dusk. Mary was coming towards him from the road.

'Goodnight, George,' she said, not slowing her progress to the back door of Station House.

'Mary…' He hesitated. She turned and looked at him. 'I hope you don't mind me saying, but I've seen things tonight…'

'What things? What do you mean, George?'

'I'm not happy wi' what's going on between t' Stationmaster and that wife of his. I think tha' best get inside and check she's all right.'

The oil lamp that she carried into John and Annie's bedroom allowed Mary to see the outline of a figure curled up under the counterpane.

'Annie,' she said softly, 'what's the matter? Are you ill?'

No answer came but a loud sob.

'Annie, tell me. I can't help if I don't know what's

wrong. Let me pull back the counterpane a little so I can
see you.'

'No, don't! Leave it. I don't want you to move it.' Her
voice rose in distress. 'Go and see that Johnny's all
right, will you? He's in the nursery.'

Mary lit a candle and left it burning on the bedside
cabinet while she hurriedly retraced her steps along the
corridor to the nursery, anxious that whatever had gone
on here had not affected the baby. Johnny was sleeping
soundly.

When she returned to the bedroom, Annie had pulled
down the cover and Mary gasped as the candlelight fell
on her friend. One side of her face was swollen and her
eye almost closed. Her hair was sticky with blood. She lay
curled up on one side of the bed, nursing her body tightly.

'Annie, whatever's happened to thee?' Mary whispered. 'Oh, God, let me look.'

She knelt down and tried to unwrap her taut arms
from round her body.

Annie cried out. 'I can't breathe. It hurts me when I
breathe.'

Slowly and gently, Mary unbuttoned Annie's dress
and pulled up her undergarments to reveal a purple
bruise, the size of a fist, beneath her left breast. Annie
cried out again as Mary helped her slowly to a sitting
position and removed her bodice to reveal further
bruises to her arms and neck.

'How did this happen?' asked Mary, as she examined
a gash on the back of Annie's head. 'Did John do this?'

'No, oh, no. I fell. I fell downstairs and banged my
head on the wall.'

'Then why isn't John here? Where is he? He should be looking after you?'

Annie looked away evasively. 'John and I had a bit of a tiff. It was my fault really. I can never give him what he wants and he gets angry with me.'

She was crying now. The tears fell steadily as she spoke and she made no attempt to wipe them away. Mary took her carefully in her arms and rocked her gently back and forth as she sobbed.

'I remember now. He said he was going for a walk. 'Appen I felt dizzy and must have fallen. When I came to, I was lying at t' bottom of the stairs. It's not his fault, all this, it's mine. I should never have married him. I can't make him a good wife. That's what he said to me today. He told me he regrets the day he asked my father for my hand in marriage. Said he'd be better off going to a whorehouse. At least they would give him what he wants and willingly.'

'Don't you dare talk like that!' Mary retorted angrily. 'He's no right at all to say that. He's never shown thee any consideration. I've seen the way he treats thee and it's not right.' She stopped, conscious that Annie and her husband were her employers but torn between this fact and that of being Annie's friend, possibly her only friend.

'Let's get you cleaned up and something put on t' bruises,' she said to fill the silence that had followed her accusation. 'Lie back for a few minutes and rest while I heat some water.' She eased Annie gently back on to the pillows, closed the door quietly behind her and descended to the kitchen. She set the kettle on the range

and, while it was heating, took a spade and, by the light
of the oil lamp, dug a root of comfrey from where it
clothed the sides of the lane. She grated this into a pan,
added hot water and left it simmering on the back of the
stove. She made a pot of tea and set it on the prepared
tray, together with a bowl of hot water and a roll of lint
from the cupboard. Lastly she took a small vial of laudanum and poured a little into a tumbler of water.

Annie lay as Mary had left her, in a half-doze. The
puffiness around her right eye had increased and a bruise
was gathering beneath it. Mary gave her the draught of
laudanum and a cup of hot sweet tea. Then she took a
wad of lint, soaked it and carefully cleaned Annie's face
and the swollen area around her eye. Next she concentrated on the scalp wound and washed the blood from
her hair as well as she could. Returning to the kitchen,
she removed the pan from the stove. The grated comfrey root had formed a gelatinous mass that Mary set on
one side to cool a little. She tore a clean white rag into
strips long enough to wrap round Annie's body.

A heavy footfall on the step made her turn round in
alarm. John Crowther was standing at the kitchen door.

'What's tha' doing?' he said to Mary gruffly.

'Annie says she fell downstairs.' Mary turned to him
with a challenging look. 'She's in a bad way. I'm making a poultice to ease the pain around her ribs.'

'Where is she now?' asked her husband.

'She's resting on t' bed.'

'I'll go on up to her, then.'

'I think she needs to be left alone,' Mary ventured.

'And I'd thank you to keep your thoughts to yourself.

I pay you to look after the house, not tell me what you think.' He pushed past her rudely on his way to the stairs and his and Annie's room.

Reheating the comfrey poultice, she wrapped it in the rags, climbed the stairs and stood for a minute outside the bedroom door, listening to the murmur of voices from within. She knocked and entered. Annie was half sitting, half lying as she reclined against her husband.

'I've brought this to ease the bruising on your ribs,' said Mary and Annie swung her legs slowly to the floor and eased herself to a sitting position. Mary applied the poultice to the deepening purple bruise, making Annie gasp with the heat, then cry out because it hurt to gasp.

''Appen there are some ribs broken and that's why tha's in so much pain,' Mary explained.

'I'll have to take more care in future,' said Annie. 'It was a stupid thing to do.' Her husband said nothing.

'John says that he'll arrange to take me and Johnny to Scarborough for a few days when I'm recovered. Won't that be lovely? I've never been to the seaside before.'

'That's grand,' replied Mary. 'It'll do thee a world of good. I've heard say that t' sea air is beneficial and lots o' folk go there when they're getting over illnesses.' She glanced at John, who turned away without speaking.

'Of course, I shall need you to stay here and look after t' house and see to t' chickens while I'm away,' continued Annie. 'I'm so excited. I hope we can go soon.'

'Just as soon as you're well enough and I can get someone to stand in for me,' said John. 'It won't be for a week or two yet. Any road, lass, you're tired. You better get some rest.'

'Will you have summat to eat?' asked Mary. 'There's a rice pudding been simmering in the oven for several hours. It should be good and creamy by now.'

'That would be lovely—' Annie smiled '—and will you get some supper for John?'

John Crowther came into the kitchen while Mary was putting the finishing touches to a meal of ham, pickles and thick chunks of bread. He looked uncomfortable as he turned to her. 'I'd be thankful if you would hold your tongue about this little episode today. I don't want it getting round t' village that my wife's taken to drink or owt like that. There's them as likes nowt better than to spread rumours.'

She looked at him, her suspicion about what had gone on causing a wave of disgust that tempered her fear. 'I wouldn't dream of saying owt,' she said, putting the meal on a tray.

'Good! Then we understand one another.' He had come up close behind her and she felt her flesh begin to crawl. 'It wouldn't do for a pretty lass to get above her station, now would it? She might need summat to bring her down a peg or two.'

'There's thy supper,' Mary said abruptly and placed the tray rather too hastily on the table so tea spurted from the spout of the teapot. 'I'm off to check that thy wife has all she needs.' And, without waiting for comment, she left him in the kitchen alone.

Annie slept. The laudanum had dulled her pain and made her drowsy. Mary crossed to the window and, pulling back the curtain, stood looking over the railway line towards the Varleys' farm. She imagined Nathaniel finishing off the work that her earlier unexpected visit had interrupted. She wished she could tell him what was happening but she feared precipitating him into a course of action for which he was not yet ready. How she longed to escape what was fast beginning to feel like a prison. If nothing else, the Crowthers' anticipated holiday would be a welcome release from the presence of the Stationmaster and might give her and Nathaniel an opportunity to spend some precious time in each other's company. Letting the curtain drop back into place, she crept to the door and along to the refuge that was her own bedroom.

CHAPTER ELEVEN

THE upside-down garden of greenery in Martha's parlour was enough to confuse visitors into thinking they had stepped into an Alice in Wonderland world, where nothing was as it seemed. Everywhere from the roof beams hung bunches of drying herbs, their leaves, ranging from deepest green to delicate silver, giving off a bewildering variety of fragrances. To the side of the door were huge bunches of dark green spearmint and lighter softer apple mint. In the corner hung long fronds of lovage and next to them several bulbs of garlic with their creamy peeling covering. A pungent aroma of rosemary predominated in the far corner of the room. Woundwort with its heads of flowers, white and yellow, added a splash of colour and, on a rack beneath the inverted herbs, maiden pinks were drying, their clove-scented sweetness carried through into the kitchen where Mrs Riley and Mary were working at the table. The day was warm and sunshine filled the kitchen with its brightness.

'Sometimes I wake up and, when I see all t' herbs

hanging there over my head, I think I've died and gone to heaven and I'm looking down on my garden to see how it's doing wi'out me.' Mrs Riley had recently given up the struggle to climb the stairs each night and, with the help of Tom and George, her bed had been carried downstairs into a corner of the already crowded living room. It was, she suggested, putting a brave face on it, the next best thing to sleeping in her garden.

'Tha' mustn't talk like that,' said Mary, lifting a heavy copper pan from the shelf. 'I hope it's years and years before tha dees.'

'Mebbe, but a body can't go on for ever and mine's had its three score years and ten. And it feels like it too. Some mornings I find it hard to get my weary bones out of bed.'

She sat in the sunshine and watched as Mary began to pick the leaves off a large bunch of lady's mantle and place them in the pan.

'It's good to see thee again, Mary. It's been a long time since thou hast been here.'

'Far too long,' Mary replied. 'Usually I only get an evening free every fortnight, or sometimes more often, if there's not so much to do. I suppose Mr Crowther was feeling generous.' She suspected he was trying to placate her after the rumpus of the previous week. He had been noticeably more civil, both to his wife and to herself, over the last few days. Perhaps he had at last seen the error of his ways and was trying to reform. She doubted it.

'I like to see the lady's mantle in the morning.' Martha interrupted the girl's thoughts. 'Each leaf with its little pool of dew. Of course, in times past they used to think it was this that held all the magic and healing powers. That's what its proper name means—"little magical one". They used to collect the dew and use it in all sorts of potions. Often thou wilt hear it called dew-cup. Of course we don't believe now that it's magic…but it is good for all sorts of women's problems. Never use it on someone who's expecting, not until her time leastwise, because it can cause powerful contractions,' she went on. 'That's right, pour on the boiling water and we'll just leave it to steep for half an hour or so. Then, do thou fill these bottles. The old medicine is best thrown away as it's likely lost its strength by now. It's a useful lotion to put on wounds and bites too, and it makes a soothing mouthwash, so we need a good supply. Later in t' year we'll dry some leaves and store them to use in t' winter months.'

There was plenty to do in the garden so, while the leaves were infusing, they made their way slowly outside. Mrs Riley leaned heavily on her stick as she walked to her favourite place beneath the gnarled and twisting branches of an ancient apple tree. She eased herself carefully into her garden seat, took a deep breath and sighed. The air was full of the scent of a large rosemary bush that was growing next to her chair. Its untidy branches, clothed in dark green needles and decorated with small blue flowers, swung lazily in the breeze. Mary busied herself with weeding and keeping the path free from the herbs that were trying to encroach on it. Heaviness had settled on her heart at Mrs Riley's suggestion that she might not have long to go before death.

Not that the old lady seemed to mind. She appeared to be resigned to the possibility, if not actually looking forward to it.

'Fetch me some forget-me-nots and sprigs of mint, Mary. And I need a cutting or two of myrtle and some sage and rosemary—and one pink rose and pull a few pieces of ivy off the wall.'

Mary carried on with the weeding while Mrs Riley busied herself with making a posy. She placed the rose in the centre, surrounding it bit by bit with the other herbs. Around the outside she made a rim of rosemary with ivy intertwined. Mary fetched twine and bound the stems carefully together, while Mrs Riley's arthritic fingers held the posy steady.

'There! It's for thee. It's a tussie-mussie. Tussie-mussies can be made with different herbs and flowers, depending on who they're for,' the old lady went on. 'This one has a pink rose for purity, mint and sage for virtue and ivy for fidelity. The forget-me-nots and the myrtle are to bring true love and rosemary signifies remembrance and fidelity.' She handed it to Mary. 'And how's that young man from t' farm?' she asked quite unexpectedly, making Mary start and blush.

'It's beautiful,' Mary replied. How on earth did Martha know about Nathaniel? She was sure she had never mentioned him.

As if she could read her thoughts, the old lady said, 'Only I've seen thee walking out over the fields, the two of thee.' Her bright eyes twinkled. 'It's a shame I can't get up my stairs any more. Thou would be surprised what I can see of village life from my bedroom window!'

Mary laughed, picturing the old lady gathering information about the goings on in the village from behind her bedroom curtains. After all, she thought, there was no other way that she could find out what was happening, for she no longer ventured out and the villagers were too in awe of her to come calling.

'His father had someone else in mind for him, tha' knows,' said Mary, pleased to be able to talk openly about Nathaniel. 'I've not met Mr Varley yet, but Nathaniel says his word is law in that house. But I told him that it weren't right to go on meeting without we said owt to 'is father. And 'appen someone would have seen us.'

'Like me, you mean,' Mrs Riley laughed.

'Aye, except I know you wouldn't 'ave said owt. Any road, he asked his father—well, told him, more like. He were none too pleased at first, but he's come round now, according to Nathaniel. I think his mam had something to do with that. I've met her, of course, in t' village, before there was anything between me and Nathaniel, like. She's a kind lady and right easy to talk to.'

'I suppose thy family knows?'

'Aye, Nathaniel went round to see Father the same evening. I hid in my bedroom at Annie's and watched them talking in t' garden. A bit like you spying on us from t' bedroom! But I were that worried he might forbid it.'

'So when are thou planning to wed? I trust thou will not leave it too long.'

'Oh, we haven't even talked about that. We've not been walking out that long. And, in any case,

Nathaniel's wanted on t' farm and we wouldn't have anywhere of our own to live. And Annie needs my help too much at present.'

The old lady became quiet. Mary glanced at her, thinking she had tired her with the talk of Nathaniel. Her face was still, her eyes looking wistful. Was she looking into the past or into the future? It was impossible to say.

'I was married once,' she said at last. 'Fine young man, he was. Joseph, they called him.'

Mary held her breath. It was rare for Mrs Riley to say anything at all about her past.

'We were very much in love,' she continued. 'We didn't want to wait to get married. We wanted to be together. I was only eighteen then, just a bit younger than thyself. Joseph was twenty-four. He was a fine figure of a man. His parents wanted us to wait till he'd had a chance to establish himself in the family business. So we waited. We are Quakers, thou knows, and he was the eldest son in a family long-established and well thought of in the city. Friends were always minded to care for people in need, so he'd plenty to keep him busy. We weren't wed till four years later. I were twenty-two. A lifetime to enjoy being together, or so we thought.'

She paused. 'It's a beautiful place, Mary, is York, but there are parts of it where the poor are gathered, the same as in any big city. He used to help out down around Skeldergate where there were a lot of families near destitute. In the summer, just a few months after we were married, a boatman who lodged there fell ill. He'd been ferrying people up from Hull and Selby and he brought the cholera with him. It spread like wildfire. Some of those who sickened were dead within the day. Joseph went to see what he could do. I begged him to keep away but he would help. So I told him about the baby. It was very early and I hadn't been sure, so I hadn't said anything before. He stopped when I told him, said he would stay with me, not go back to that plague-ridden spot. He didn't. Next morning he sickened. Started with awful looseness of the bowels. Then vomiting. It's a terrible thing is the cholera. There was nothing I could do. I kept trying to make him drink. I didn't care about myself or the baby. I just wanted him well again. All through that day I nursed him and into the night, but he got worse and worse. It was as though he was shrinking away. His eyes sank into his face and his skin hung loose on his body, and so cold and clammy. And in between the bouts he told me how much he loved me. He kept saying how glad he was about the baby and how wonderful it would be when we were a family of three. We never were. He died as dawn broke the next morning.' She paused. Mary looked away, her eyes full of tears.

'Four months we had together…and fifty years alone.'

'What about the baby?' asked Mary when she could trust herself to speak.

'After Joseph died, I wanted to die too. I couldn't believe he was no longer there. How one day we had everything to look forward to and the next it was all taken away. I felt bad that I hadn't shared with him earlier the excitement I felt about the baby, but I wanted to be sure, do thou see? Over the next two or three days I went over and over in my mind what he had said before he died and I began to think, well, what he kept repeating was how much he was looking forward to us being a family together. At least I still had the baby, a part of him. He wasn't lost to me altogether. So I would love and care for the baby and tell it about its father and how he tried to help those who hadn't the advantages we had. I didn't get a chance, though. Three days later I started with the sickness. I was more worried about the baby than about me. I'd seen how much water Joseph had lost, so I drank and drank as much as I could. Maybe that's what saved me. It didn't save the baby, though…'

'How was it that you came to live here?' asked Mary, when the old lady had been quiet for so long that it seemed she wasn't going to say any more.

'For a long time I wished I had gone to join Joseph. For months I could only think of how I was alive when my husband and baby were dead, and how I would rather be with them.

'I couldn't stay in the city. My family were there, of course, and Joseph's too, and they were all very good to me, but I needed to get away, to find peace of mind again. Both families were against the idea. I mean, it isn't what young ladies do, is it? But I came anyway. The cottage had belonged to an acquaintance who had recently died. It was standing empty. My husband's parents bought it for me when they saw my mind was made up.

'I knew straight away that I had made the right decision. The four walls of the cottage were like a soothing blanket wrapping me round and keeping me safe. It was a long time before I could take an interest in anything else but gradually I began to wake up to my surroundings. Of course I'd walked round the garden but what grew there was a mystery to me. In the kitchen there were books on the growing of herbs and their uses. I began to read about them and then I'd go in the garden with the books and match the herbs to the pictures. That was the start of my interest. I began to think how I'd been spared for a purpose. I knew that there was power in herbs if they were used rightly. Maybe I'd been spared to learn about the herbs and how to use them to prevent suffering and carry on the work that had been started by the person who lived here before me.

'There's comfort in growing things,' the old lady continued. 'Seeing nature waking up each year after the death of winter, getting your hands dirty, thinking about the garden and what's growing rather than what you've lost, watching things develop, seeing their beauty. It was sad at first. I used to sit here and cry and cry for the loss of my husband and child. I shed more tears than I ever thought possible. Gradually, though, I became engrossed with the herbs. I think there's many round here think me more than a little peculiar and stay away.' She smiled. 'But they come soon enough when they need my help. And they'll come to thee as well. Thou hast a rare touch when it comes to caring for people.'

She rose stiffly from her seat and made her way up the path towards the kitchen.

'The lady's mantle!' cried Mary. 'I'd forgotten all about it.' She was thankful that Mrs Riley had not expected, nor given opportunity for, a reply to her revelations, for what could she have said that would do justice to such a heartbreaking account?

'Annie will be expecting thee as well,' Mrs Riley reminded her. 'Mary, love, is anything wrong?' Mary's face had fallen at the reminder of Station House, which she had not thought about during Martha's story.

'Oh…well, there was something I wanted to ask. Are there any herbs that will stop bruising or help take it away? It's Annie…she bruises so easily. I wondered if there was anything I could give her to help.'

The old lady looked at her shrewdly. 'Thou art a real friend to her,' she said slowly, 'in more ways than one. Thou can make an ointment with elder leaves or marigold petals. They're both very soothing. But if the bruise is new, the best thing to try is a poultice of comfrey leaves. Thou had best get back to her any road. Mister will be wanting his dinner and happen he won't like to be kept waiting. Come and see me if ever thou needs. Don't forget thy tussie-mussie…and mind what I said to thee. Be on thy way now before I get accused of teaching thee witchcraft.' She closed the door and hobbled back into her kitchen.

CHAPTER TWELVE

AT THREE minutes to ten the porter shouted 'Right', the guard blew hard on his whistle and the fireman gave the answering 'Right away' to the waving flag at the far end of the platform. With a toot on the engine's whistle the Doncaster to York train eased out of Templesforth Station, enveloping the platform and its Stationmaster in a hiss of steam. As it picked up speed the exhaust took up a continuous snorting beat and the passengers settled back in their seats to enjoy the ride. The red number-plate on the side of the cabin, with its brass number glinting in the morning sun, identified the huge green engine which, until now, the little girls had only seen from their platform of boxes in front of the cottages. It pulled a row of gleaming wooden carriages, in the second class compartment of which sat Nathaniel and Mary opposite Mary's three younger sisters. Lucy and Laura were almost sick with excitement. Sarah-Louise, who, at the age of eleven, vacillated between being Mary's confidante and still retaining the freedom of childhood, was trying but failing to be grown-up, her excitement nearly as obvious as that of the little ones. Mary smiled at her and she grinned in return.

It had been Nathaniel's idea. Mary had told him that Mr Crowther had awarded her a day off. 'It's in advance really,' she'd explained, when Nathaniel had shown surprise, 'because I have to look after things while they are on holiday.'

'The Stationmaster is going on holiday! Maybe I'll be able to see you a bit more often then while they're away.' He'd looked at her mischievously.

'I really can't take you to York on your own, much as I would love to,' he'd said to her one day, shortly after suggesting the trip. 'What goes on in the countryside and what is allowed in the big city are two different things entirely. So let's take your sisters. It will be fun for them and for me too. And they can be our chaperones.'

He sat close to Mary, looking at the row of eager faces, and laughed. 'I can see I've taken on a difficult job today with four young ladies to look after,' he said, turning to Mary as the train began to pick up speed. She squeezed his hand in reply, keeping her eyes fixed on the familiar fields and houses, fascinated with the speed at which the countryside passed by as the train made its way towards Selby. Her face was serious, her excitement dulled by John Crowther's words not an hour before. She had been about to leave the house, knowing that her sisters would be waiting in excitement in the cottage…and, no doubt, driving their mother to despair. She was anxious to avoid the Stationmaster, and when she saw him standing on the platform, she had run quickly down the stairs and out of the front door, only to confront him as he came out of the entrance hall. It was almost as if he had been waiting for her to appear.

He'd stared at her in appreciation for a few seconds. 'Well! As pretty a picture as I'm likely to see in a long time,' he smirked.

'Excuse me, sir, but I have to see if my sisters are ready. We're catching the three minutes to ten train and I don't have long.'

'And is all this finery for their benefit?'

She glanced down at her dress, one which Annie had discarded for a more fashionable style and because it hung too loosely on her thin frame. Its cream colour suited Mary's complexion. She had decorated a straw hat with flowers and she knew from the five minutes she had spent looking at her reflection in the mirror that both hat and dress enhanced her not inconsiderable beauty.

'Well, I have to be properly dressed for a visit to York,' she hedged and, turning away, crossed the yard swiftly to her parents' cottage.

When the train pulled into the station John Crowther was hovering in the shadows at the back of the platform. Nathaniel helped Mary and her sisters into the carriage and, as he did so, Mary glanced round and saw the Stationmaster's lustful eyes following her every move.

She had been looking forward to this trip for days. Nathaniel was the only one of the group to have been on a train. He told Mary that he had twice travelled to York on farming business, but this was his first visit for pleasure alone. He was dressed, despite the warmth of the day, in a suit. Mary's sisters were wearing identical muslin dresses whose hems stopped short of their ankles and they wore straw boaters to protect them from the sun.

'Well, one thing's for sure. Three on 'em at least won't look this neat and tidy for long,' Mary said at last, dragging her gaze from the view and looking at Nathaniel.

'You've no room to talk, sweetheart. You didn't look too tidy yourself by the time we came back from our walk last night!'

Mary blushed. It was true. Just lately they had found it increasingly difficult to restrain their feelings for one another. They had wandered for miles, up the lane and over the fields, seeking to expend their pent-up passion in walking. It was useless. The perfumes released from the hedgerows in the evening air only served to stir their desire and in the flat landscape of the fields under the unending reach of sky they felt themselves to be the only two in the whole world. Their natures were such that their friendship developed rapidly. Nathaniel, outgoing and spontaneous, had fallen deeply in love with Mary and her generous but more reflective nature responded without hesitation to his passionate advances. The one thing that limited the extent of their lovemaking was the continued antagonism of Nathaniel's father to their relationship.

'I know you find it difficult to understand,' Nathaniel tried to explain to her, 'but he believes that proper speech and an equal social standing are most important.'

'So I'm not good enough for you. That's what you're saying.'

'I'm not saying that at all,' said Nathaniel shortly. 'It

doesn't matter one way or the other to me. But there's no changing my father. Anyway, he's not forbidden me from seeing you, only made it plain that he wishes "a more suitable match".'

'Like Rhoda Precious,' Mary snapped.

So it would not do for Mary to become pregnant just yet, and add more weight to the belief that Henry Varley's son could do better. Mary knew that in the countryside a pregnancy before marriage was nothing out of the ordinary and hardly frowned upon by the majority of country dwellers, as long as marriage followed. But she would not risk this possibility and further upset Nathaniel's father. It was up to her though to put the unwanted restraint on their activities. She did not believe that Nathaniel himself would ever have such a degree of self-control.

So they walked hand in hand between the fields of ripening corn. When they were far from the farm and its adjoining fields they stopped and kissed. At the limit of their ramblings was a darkening copse, in front of which they sat with the golden blanket of the land spread out before them, and watched the sun as it dipped below the horizon and painted with brightness the edges of the small clouds that hovered there. And then Nathaniel kissed her and told her that she was more beautiful than the sunset and the flowers that surrounded them. And he made as if to demonstrate how much he loved her, but she'd jumped up, escaping his embrace, and ran laughing across the fields to the lane.

If only he knew, she reflected as they swayed together to the bumpy rhythm of the train, just how difficult it was for her to relinquish the nearness of his body when all she wanted was to respond to it. The spectre of Rhoda from Bankside rose up before her and she felt a pang of disquiet. So long as she and Nathaniel were unwed there was always the possibility that her rival might steal him away—and his father would be more than pleased. Maybe her behaviour last evening would cause her lover to turn to other more willing arms. Not that Rhoda's arms would be very welcoming, she thought with a secret smile. In any case she was much too well guarded to be allowed strolls through the country lanes unaccompanied. Added to this, she would muddy her boots and get stains on her skirt and the grass would make her sneeze and her eyes would run and…

'Mary, you haven't heard owt we've said to you.' Sarah-Louise's voice broke into her thoughts. 'Nathaniel says we haven't far to go before we reach York. He wants to know what we'd like to do first.'

''Appen Mary's got her mind on higher things,' said Nathaniel, squeezing her hand playfully.

She looked at them and smiled, then glanced out of the window. In the distance she could see the river Ouse making its way south to where it eventually joined their own river at Airmyn. The railway and river began to converge as they approached the city.

'I think,' said Mary, 'that everyone will be hungry by the time we get there. Why don't we find the riverbank and have our picnic?' Her words were greeted with enthusiasm, not least by Nathaniel, who had made a point of telling the girls how early he had had to leave his bed, in order to get his regular morning chores done before calling for his charges.

Five minutes later they were standing under the huge curved roof of York railway station. The girls stared upwards in amazement. They had never seen anything on so grand a scale. Up till now the hay barns and granaries of the local farms had seemed huge. Around them all was bustle and noise. Passengers streamed from the carriages. Some of them, well acquainted with the journey, hurried to the exit and onwards to their business. Others, like Mary and her sisters, for whom the experience was new and exciting, stood mesmerised by the activity around them, watching the porters and the Stationmaster who milled around to offer assistance. On other platforms trains were preparing to leave or passengers stood waiting, surrounded by children and luggage. The smoky crescendo of a departing train filled all the building with the commotion.

Nathaniel led the sisters out of the station and they made their way, with Sarah-Louise walking in front, holding the hands of Lucy and Laura, towards the river. They crossed Lendal Bridge and turned left on to the esplanade. At a grassy spot in the dappled shade of a tree they stopped. Mary spread out a cloth and took from the picnic basket ham rolls, cakes, hard-boiled eggs and milk. She sat on the grass and looked at the view before her—the river sparkling in the sun and lined by a row of trees, dressed in their summer livery, her sisters chatting happily with the man she loved. Happiness welled up inside her and in its aftermath she began to doubt whether her interpretation of John Crowther's behaviour was a true one. Maybe she was mistaken. Maybe she had been misled by his arrogance and somewhat coarse language into thinking him guilty of impropriety to herself and misconduct towards his wife. She would never like him…but perhaps she was thinking of him more harshly than she should.

Nathaniel and Mary's sisters were admiring the bridge they had just crossed. Its span was decorated with colourful roses and in the centre a figurehead stared out, like those they had seen on the front of ships in the pictures at school.

'This bridge is the same age as Mary,' Nathaniel told them. 'Who do you think looks the most beautiful?'

'Mary, of course,' said Lucy. 'If we don't say that, she might not give us owt to eat!'

Nathaniel laughed. 'I'll tell you something,' he said. 'This bridge is a lot more beautiful than the one that was here before. That finished up at the bottom of the river.'

'How old was that one then?' asked Sarah-Louise. 'Was it worn out? Did it die and collapse?' Her sisters laughed as they pictured a bridge, like an old man, no longer able to stand on his wobbly legs.

'No, it wasn't old at all. In fact it wasn't even finished. They were just fixing it all together and one bit fell over on the next bit and that fell over on to the next and they all tumbled into the river. And that was the end of that.'

'Like dominoes,' said Sarah-Louise.

'Is it there now?' asked Lucy, peering into the murky water swirling downstream in front of her.

'Oh, no. They had to take the pieces out or the boats would have run into them and been holed. Do you see the little houses like tiny castles at each end of the bridge? Well, it was so expensive to build the new bridge and get it right that all the carriages that pass over it now have to pay money. Those castles are where the money's collected.'

Mary interrupted the history lesson. They sat around her on the grass, munching happily, drinking the warm milk and watching the couples and families as they made their way slowly up and down the path.

'What are we going to do now, Nathaniel?' asked Lucy, before he had time to swallow his last bite of cake.

'I think you've all got too much energy, so we're going to go for a walk.'

'Oh, no,' cried Laura, 'I don't like walking.'

'I think you'll like this walking,' said Nathaniel and, when they had helped Mary to pack the basket with the remains of the picnic, he led them back across the bridge. On its far side sat a small cylindrical tower and, beyond it, a flight of stone steps led upwards to the ancient wall of the city.

'Careful,' said Nathaniel to the smaller girls as they began to scramble up the steps. At the top they looked back and saw the city spread out before them, ancient rooftops clustered round a huge church, its towers reaching into the sky.

'That must be the Minster,' said Mary. 'It's wonderful.'

'Aye, it is,' replied Nathaniel. 'We'll go and look at it after we've stretched our legs.'

Holding the hands of the younger girls, for there was no balustrade here to prevent their falling, they made their way along the wall. Like birds in the trees they looked down on the trains entering and leaving the station to their right and heard and tasted the smoke that escaped from the great locomotives. They saw the horses pulling coaches and carriages through the narrow streets below. At Micklegate Bar they climbed down the steps, Nathaniel pausing in the darkness of the entrance to kiss Mary before they emerged into the sunshine to weave their way through those same narrow streets to the Minster. Mary sighed happily. She was glad of the presence of her sisters, for it meant that she could enjoy being with Nathaniel without worrying that she might have to rebuff any advances that he might make, when that was the last thing she wanted to do.

'It looks like t' railway station,' exclaimed Laura as they entered the coolness of the great building. Mary was spellbound. The Minster was huge. It echoed with feet, its floors danced with a multitude of colours reflected from the stained glass and over her head the roof soared in a hundred different patterns. For some inexplicable reason she found herself wondering what it must be like to be married in so grand a place. She glanced at Nathaniel and found he was looking at her.

'It's marvellous,' she said. 'What a beautiful church. Thank you for bringing us. I had no idea there was so much beauty in York.'

'There wasn't this much until I brought *you* here today,' he said simply. 'Come on, I think we'd better be making our way back to the station if we're to catch the four thirty-five. If we miss that, the next train isn't till after nine o'clock and we'll have some tired girls on our hands by then, to say nothing about anxious parents.'

The three younger girls were asleep before the train was fifteen minutes down the line. It was a further ten minutes before Nathaniel spoke.

'I can't go on like this, sweetheart. Shall we be wed?'

'One day,' replied Mary. 'But what would your father say if we decided to marry now? He wouldn't be o'er pleased. And besides we've nowhere to live. 'Appen we need to wait until…'

'Mary! Anyone would think you didn't want to marry me!'

A snatch of Mrs Riley's conversation came back to her. *'So when are thou planning to wed? I trust thou will not leave it too long.'* She turned to Nathaniel. 'How about in the autumn after harvest home? Would that suit you?'

He grinned at her, hardly able to believe what he was hearing. He and Mary wed before the year-end!

'I promise you I will make you as happy as you've made me today,' he said. 'And you needn't worry about my father. His bark's worse than his bite. We'll go and discuss things with him in the next few days, before he gets busy with barley harvest. Happen he'll agree to doing up one of the labourers' cottages for us, at least to start off with.'

Now that the decision was made, there was not enough time to discuss all the things that needed to be said. As the train pulled out of Selby Station they began to rouse the sleeping girls and gather together their scattered belongings. Nathaniel helped each sister down from the carriage at Templesforth Station, keeping his hands round the waist of the eldest for as long as decorum allowed. Mary glanced round. John Crowther was nowhere to be seen.

'I'll call for you on Wednesday evening,' he said as they parted, 'and we'll make our wedding plans then, before you have a chance to change your mind!'

CHAPTER THIRTEEN

A STRANGE yellow light crept over the flat land. The earth held its breath. Birds sang as if it were evening and fell silent. It was, Mary reflected, as she imagined the day of the crucifixion: *'Now from the sixth hour there was darkness over all the land unto the ninth hour'*.

Through the morning the palest blue sky had been covered with a creeping grey blanket, unruffled as a newly made bed. On the land beneath, the motionless air exhausted the villagers as they went about their work within and without the houses and farms dotted along the road. The sea breezes in Scarborough were hopefully proving to be more bracing, Mary trusted, for John Crowther had departed there two days previously with his wife and young son.

In the garden of Station House clusters of ripe black-currants draped the bushes. With time on her hands, Mary had decided to make jam. A bowl was already filled with the ripe fruit. The raspberries would be ready in a few days, so she was not going to be idle. Perspiration ran down her back. Her hands were stained red with the juice. She straightened up and walked to the kitchen door, placing the bowl of blackcurrants on the step. Then she clambered up the bank to the far end of the platform. Her gaze skimmed the ripe fields and rested on the horizon. It was from here that the untimely coloration of the sky seemed to be spreading. A sudden hot gust of wind rustled the leaves of the trees and made the dividing hedgerows of the fields sway to and fro. As quickly as the wind had sprung up it settled. In the distance she now saw a flash of yellow, followed swiftly by another and, a few seconds after, heard a low rumble of thunder. The menacing sky stood poised to strike but for a long time it hesitated to come closer. Mary stood fascinated by the spectacle. She thought of the line of almost dry washing and knew she should be collecting it in. As she turned, the lightning flashed directly overhead and a crack of thunder heralded several angry spots of rain and then a sudden ferocious downpour. Skidding down the bank, she ran into the garden, gathered up the already wet garments and raced into the house.

The rain was disturbing the peace of the interior. It battered the window panes and Mary stood watching the raindrops racing each other down the glass, trying to guess which would be the first to reach the bottom of the window. It was a game she had often played as a child, when the weather had held her prisoner indoors. After a minute she was aware of a movement in the cottages opposite. It was her mother waving, trying to catch her attention. Pulling her cloak around her, she left the house and ran across the station yard. Thunder cracked overhead.

'I'm reet glad to 'ave caught your eye,' said Susan as Mary stumbled through the door in her haste to escape the rain, 'only little uns will be coming out of school soon and they've nowt wi' 'em to keep them dry. It were fine when they set off this morning and I didn't give it a thought. There's Alfie too from next door. He usually walks back with the lasses.'

By the time Mary had called at Eliza's to pick up Alfie's coat, had admired the baby and asked after Eliza, now expecting a third child, she had to hurry to cover the two and a half miles to the school. The lane was awash with mud. Mary was soaked through before she was out of the village. She carried the extra clothing in a large bag but if the rain kept on, and it showed no sign of abating, this too would be wet before the school was reached. She trudged on, wishing that the road meandered less and she could be at the school the sooner. The sight of Nathaniel and his cart would be very welcome, but the road remained empty. The rain was beginning to flatten the ripe corn and bare areas pockmarked the expanse of fields. Nathaniel and his family must be worrying about the possible loss of the barley harvest.

The four children stood huddled together in the school porch waiting for the rain to stop.

'Look, it's our Mary come to fetch us. Mary! Mary! We're reet pleased to see thee. It's all right, Miss Thompson, our Mary's come for us,' Sarah-Louise called to the interior of the school. 'We'll see thee tomorrow.' The porch became full of children wrestling themselves into coats and cloaks. It was still raining hard as they set off. At least they could be thankful, thought Mary, that the thunderstorm had passed over.

It was a bedraggled group that made its way wearily into Station Yard and the cottages. Susan had put soup to warm on the stove and, after they had all greeted Alice, they sat round the table drinking the steaming broth while Alice shrieked with delight at their appearance.

'Will you stay on to see your father and have some supper wi' us?' asked Susan of her eldest daughter.

'I'll wait to see Father, but I've arranged to meet Nathaniel this evening so I won't stay. They'll be starting barley harvest any time now like, so he may be too busy after today.'

At eight o'clock Mary left the house and walked over the fields to the river. The storm had passed over, although the sky was still heavy and the air damp. Nathaniel was nowhere to be seen. The river level had risen and dead branches mingled with other debris in the swirling brown water. Swallows dipped and soared around her, taking their meal from the numerous insects that had been tempted out by the hazy evening light. She turned from the water with a shiver.

A man was making his way down between the fields. It wasn't Nathaniel. She recognised Jacob, the farm-hand.

'I've come with a message from t' young master. There's trouble with t' steam engine that were meant to be arriving for to help wi' t' 'arvest. 'E's 'ad to go off to Carborough to see about it.'

'How's he gone, Jacob? Is he in t' pony 'n trap, only t' road is o'er muddy after that storm?'

'No, Miss Mary, He's ridden Jess. Reckoned he'd get along better than risk t' wheels getting fast in t' mud.'

'I were just looking at t' river,' said Mary, turning back to watch it flowing swiftly by. 'Level's risen a fair bit since I were last here.'

'Aye, an' I don't think we've seen t' last of the wet weather, neither. Tha' best be getting home, miss, if tha' don't mind me saying. It's coming on to rain again.'

The sky had darkened and the rain came heavily without warning. Mary turned towards home with a heavy heart. She had looked forward all day to seeing Nathaniel. Now an empty house beckoned.

'Thanks, Jacob. It were good of you to let me know.'

'That's all right, Miss Mary. Nathaniel says he'll try and call round tomorrow. Oh, and if I may be so bold, I think the two on you make a grand couple. Nathaniel told me you were planning on getting wed. I hope you'll both be as happy as me an' my missus.'

'Thanks, Jacob. I hope so too. Now I better run, else I'm going to be drowned for the second time today!'

The hammering on the door grew louder. Mary knew it was Nathaniel but every time she tried to rise from the bed she found she was chained down. She rattled and pulled at the chains but they would not give. Now he was walking away down the path and, though she called and called his name, he didn't hear her and kept on walking. Suddenly a light was shone in her face and she woke with a start, her heart racing, and stared into the blackness.

The storm had returned. Wind rattled the window

latch and rain bounced on the panes and through the chink of open window on to the linoleum beneath. Mary threw back the bedcovers and hurried to close the window, slipping and almost falling on the wet floor. As she struggled against the wind, another huge flash of lightning lit up the countryside like day and she could see the distant glint of water.

Her dream had unsettled her and she was unable to sleep again. The house shook with each clap of thunder, and lightning lit up her room, revealing its sparse furnishings. Over a chair hung the dress she had been wearing yesterday evening when she'd stood by the river waiting in vain for Nathaniel. Was he awake too and, if so, was he thinking of her? Had he and Jess managed to get back from Carborough without mishap? Mary pictured him riding up the lane. With the coming of the light evenings he often took Jess out when work was done, trotting along the lane past Station House, waving to Mary as she went about her jobs. Once out of the village he would give the horse free rein and she would gallop along paths and jump ditches, returning at nightfall, ghostly riders at one with the elements. And Mary, sitting with a pile of mending, would smile at the sound of them as they passed by.

When morning came and she had fed the chickens and made the jam that she should have made yesterday, she would go and check that he was back safely. She was hesitant about calling at Temple Farm, for the old farmer still greeted her coolly and barely gave her the time of day. But she must go. She needed to know that Nathaniel was all right. While there she would commiserate with his mother over the wetness of the weather and the damage to the crops.

She must have slept again for when she next opened her eyes a reluctant grey light filtered through the flimsy curtains. She put her feet to the floor and shivered. The heat that had preceded the storm had dissipated and a chill dampness wove through the house. The clock in the kitchen showed half past six. She poured warm water into her jug, refilled the kettle and set it on the stove. Then she carried the water back to her room, filled the basin and washed. She went to the window and drew the curtains. A scene of devastation lay before her. Field after field of ripe barley lay flattened by the storm. In the distance a wide expanse of water stretched to the horizon. Crossing the landing she gazed at the railway lines, where men were moving about, small and industrious as ants.

Her mother was busy with breakfast when she walked in.

'What's happening, Mam? Why are the gang out so early?'

'Your dad's worried about t' bridge wi' the river rising so much in t' night. He called them up at first light and they're checking it now before they let any trains through. I think the children will have to miss school today. They'll not get along to West Haddley after all t' rain. I could do wi'out them under my feet all day,' she added crossly.

Mary would have offered to help but she could not neglect her work at the house. She would not rest easy, however, until she had seen for herself the state of the lane and the river. She quickly packed for her father a breakfast of bread and pork dripping, for when he had opened his curtains and seen the havoc wreaked by the storm, he had not stopped to eat.

Tom and his men had returned as far as the road bridge by the time Mary left the cottage with her father's food. He waved and took the steps down to the roadside where his daughter stood.

'There's no damage to t' bridge, thank God,' said Tom, unwrapping the sandwiches. 'T' river's running high and has burst its banks t' other side and flooded t' fields that way on. It's holding firm this side, so the village is safe. The rain has washed some of the top ballast loose in places and t' seating of the sleepers could be at risk, so we've some urgent repairs to do. But we should be able to keep t' trains running while we work.'

'Is there anything I can do to help?'

'You could tell your mam t' state of things and say that we'll work on late tonight to try and get things straight, like. Otherwise I don't think there's owt… Any road I'd best get back and start. Thanks, lass. 'Appen I'll see thee later on. Oh, and by the way, I saw young Nathaniel a bit back, on 'is 'oss. Said he'd stayed with a farmer at Bankside last night, as t' road made t' going difficult, like. You know who I mean—'im wi' a daughter called Rhoda. Think you know of her, don't you?'

Mary turned abruptly and began to walk down the lane. Why, when there were a dozen of Nathaniel's acquaintances, did he have to lodge with Rhoda Precious? Why was it that every step she took, the spectre of Rhoda seemed to cross her path? She splashed along under the bridge and turned down towards the river at Ings Lane. The rain had eased now but the hedgerows were so saturated with water that in a few minutes her skirts were soaked through and draped with goose grass and other sodden vegetation. As her father had said, the bank was holding firm on the village side of the river, but the water had reached its top and the strong wind was blowing wavelets over the edge, to collect in an enlarging lake which had until yesterday been a field of barley. On the far side of the river two waterfalls had formed, down which the water rushed in an unaccustomed torrent, eager to escape the confines of its path. The land, as far as Mary's gaze could stretch, was transformed into an inland sea.

How different everything looked today, and not just the watery scene before her eyes. The feelings of tranquillity and certainty that had accompanied her visits here with Nathaniel had been replaced by turmoil and confusion. Everything had been stirred up again by her father's words, like the muddied water swirling at her feet. Of course it had made sense for Nathaniel to stay at Bankside Farm last night when the weather had been so bad. She had worried about him, hadn't she? Had wished him kept safe, hadn't she? But why couldn't he have been kept safe with someone else?

Station House had lost its odd empty feel when Mary stepped into the kitchen in her stockinged feet, having removed her muddy boots on the doorstep. She was glad of the warmth from the range. The dampness left from the rain and the keen northerly wind had chilled her through. She set the kettle on the hot plate and it immediately started to murmur. The fire must be burning well to heat the water so quickly. Good. She was afraid she had neglected it with all the activity of the last day or so. She brewed a pot of tea and, when she had poured a cup, sat down at the kitchen table to try and concentrate her thoughts on what needed doing. First she must make blackcurrant jam or the fruit that she had picked yesterday would spoil. The poor weather would probably mean that the raspberries would not ripen as quickly, so they could be left until later in the week. She had promised Annie she would clean out the chicken hut. It was her least favourite job, but one that could not be put back any longer. Perhaps she should have done that before taking off her muddy boots. But she really needed this cup of tea. And, in any case, her skirt was wet and her petticoats clinging to her legs. She should change into dry things before starting. She frowned at the sight of the mud on the kitchen floor. She couldn't remember bringing so much mud into the house. Another job to add to the list. At this rate there would be no time to divert her thoughts on to Nathaniel. The day would be taken up with getting her work finished before he called…if he called. Glancing at the clock, she realised that it was a lot later than she had thought. Almost one o'clock and nothing to show for it. She had called at Temple Farm after leaving the river. She hadn't seen Nathaniel and his father, who had been in the fields, rescuing cows that were close to being stranded by the rising waters. Mrs Varley had given her a cup of tea and Mary had marvelled at her composure.

'It's ever been like this,' she'd said. 'You take the rough with the smooth. Trouble is, living here, the river always means we have more of the rough than we do the smooth.'

Then she had called on her mother, harassed by the energetic cluster of children, to pass on her father's message from earlier in the day. And had been delayed further by the need to lighten her of some of the extra burdens the day had put on her.

Mary went up to her room, undoing the buttons of her skirt as she did so. On the landing the door to John and Annie's room stood ajar. Mary always shut each door when she had finished the housework. The wind from her bedroom window must have blown it open. She shut it again and walked back along the corridor to her own room. Letting her wet skirt and petticoats slide over her hips into a heap on the floor, she stepped out of them, opened her underwear drawer and took from it a clean petticoat.

'Don't bother putting that on.'

Mary gasped and spun round in horror. In a chair in the corner, almost hidden by the open door, sat John Crowther. Lifting his leg he placed his muddy boot on the door and slammed it shut.

When Mary thought about it later, she wondered how she had neglected to see the footmarks that he had left on the stairs as he'd climbed them to her room. Forgetting that the day was so overcast that the staircase and landing had been in semi-darkness. When she thought about it later, she wondered whether, if her reactions had been quicker, she could have reached the door before he'd slammed it, or ran and reopened it before he'd grabbed hold of her. Forgetting that when he'd spoken those first words, her terror had frozen her to the spot. When she thought about it later she wondered why she hadn't realised he was upstairs, for hadn't she felt as though the house was not empty when she had returned from surveying the ravages of the storm? Forgetting that she would have dismissed such feelings as the meanderings of an agitated mind.

George Morritt, like the rest of the rail men, had slept badly the night of the storm. Although his shift did not start till two the following afternoon, he had risen early to lend assistance if it were needed. In John Crowther's absence Harold, another of the three signalmen who worked the shifts, had been temporarily elevated to the Stationmaster's job, assisted by Walter, the railway porter. They liked to think they did the job as well as, if not better than, the Stationmaster himself.

George knew that there would be some tricky manoeuvring needed to avoid accidents. Everyone was working flat out to make the necessary repairs to the damaged line. He had climbed into the box to start the early shift as well as his own afternoon stint, allowing the other men to concentrate on making sure all was safe. The twelve-thirty up train had pulled in on time, a miracle, given the difficulties, and he'd been surprised to see the burly figure of John Crowther alight from the train. Had he been worried by the possible effect of the storm on the station and returned to take charge? He'd watched as John had made his way quickly to the side of the platform and down the embankment, rather than passing Walter, who was standing at the barrier. John obviously wasn't here on official business, then. Weaving his way through the station yard, he had gone quickly up to the kitchen door and had disappeared inside, closing the door behind him. Perhaps there was some earlier domestic arrangement, necessitating his return. It seemed an odd thing to do, though, when he had only a week in which to relax and enjoy himself with that lovely but fragile wife of his. Strange too that he hadn't stopped to check on how the trains were running, given the state of the weather.

George's attention had been diverted by the need to see the Doncaster train safely out of the station. While he had still been musing on what he had seen, he'd watched Mary make her way from the lane up to Station House. She must have been expecting the Stationmaster back and had returned in time to cook his dinner. He'd thought no more about it until, less than two hours later, he'd seen the Stationmaster climb the embankment and cross the line to await the down train to York, which was expected any minute. George had watched him as he'd stood among the bushes that lined the back of the platform. Such behaviour could only mean that he was eager to avoid attention. He'd seen John climb quickly into the carriage and disappear from view. If either Harold or Walter had seen him, they gave no indication that they had done so, for John's furtive behaviour made it obvious that he didn't wish to talk. The whistle blew and the train had pulled out of the station, taking John with it. George had presumed he was bound for his family at the seaside. The whole episode was a mystery. In fact, after a while George had begun to wonder whether he had made the whole thing up.

Of Mary he saw nothing. The previous day she had been busy, in and out of the house, pegging washing, pulling blackcurrants, visiting her mother, collecting her sisters. Today, there was no sight of her since her return at dinnertime to satisfy the hunger of her employer.

CHAPTER FOURTEEN

GREY, overcast skies faded early into the twilight of evening. The windows of Station House remained unlit. Nothing stirred within, except with the vibrations of passing trains, which made their way at haphazard intervals up and down the lines, ignorant of the goings-on in such an insignificant station. In the late afternoon Mary heard a knock at the door, followed after a minute or so by another, and then silence. She guessed that it would be Nathaniel. She held her breath, wondering if he would come in, fearful that he might, desolate when he didn't. Tears came then, for the first time since her ordeal—hot, bitter tears that soaked the pillow and were accompanied by sobs racking her body and making her chest ache. She had lain unmoving since John Crowther's departure, curled embryo-like in the centre of her disordered bed. She couldn't think. Her mind was chaotic, disordered, like her bed-sheets. Phrases, sentences, entered her head, flitted around, settled for a moment, then took off, mingling with others, like flies on a rotting carcass. Every now and then she experienced a sickening thud that sent her reeling down and down into a bottomless black hole. Then she would open her eyes wide in horror and fasten them on the dwindling light at the window.

The sobbing diminished and its passing brought a clarity of thought worse than the chaos which had preceded it. Why couldn't she turn the clock back? Six hours. It wasn't much to ask. All would then be back to how it had been. Infinite possibilities. Now there was an infinity of nothingness. Now she could never again see Nathaniel. The realisation started her sobbing afresh. When her father had told her this morning—was it only this morning?—that Nathaniel had stayed at Bankside Farm with Rhoda's parents, she had been jealous of what might have been an understanding between them. Now Rhoda would have him. There was no longer any contest. And he, Nathaniel, would possess Rhoda in a way that Mary had never allowed, not because she hadn't wished it but because she had been frightened of the consequences for Nathaniel. For she had wished it, more than anything she had wished it, had wanted him, body as well as soul.

Now it was too late. It was all too late. And it was all her doing. She would never know how it would be with Nathaniel because she had refused it. It was all her fault. She had refused that beautiful thing that he'd wanted and that she'd wanted and now it was too late because that beautiful thing was defiled, desecrated, sordid. A fallen woman. That was what she was now.

Her mind had refused to let her dwell on the hour and a half that had changed her life. Now though her mouth twisted in disgust as she began to go over the sequence of events, from the moment when he'd first spoken and she had stood undressed in the middle of her room, rooted to the spot. Strangely enough he had said nothing after that, apart from the grunts and groans that had accompanied his subsequent violation of her. She ran her hands slowly up her arms and felt the pain of the bruises above her elbows where he had held her down and she had struggled vainly to escape. She stretched out her legs and gradually eased herself on to her back. Her whole body ached but the ache was concentrated in her thighs. She felt again the weight of him on her, the rasp of his unshaven chin on her face, the moistness of his kisses, the roughness of his probing hands and, above all, that animal invasion of her flesh, which had made her cry out in anguish of body and soul. She cried out again as she relived the encounter and raised her hands to her mouth to stop her cries. Then she smelled the smell of him on her skin and a sudden nausea made her throw back the bed covers and stand. Her legs nearly gave way and she clutched the bedside table. She must bathe. She must wash the smell and the feel and the touch of him away. Staggering from the room, she made her way stiffly downstairs and set water to heat. She had no fear that he was still in the house for, although she had kept her body turned from him, she had been conscious of him dressing and she'd heard him go downstairs and through the kitchen. He had closed the door quietly but she had heard, and had breathed more easily at the sound. She went to the door now and locked it, leaving the key in the lock so no one could get in. She

did the same with the front entrance. Then she went into
John and Annie's bedroom and dragged the tin bath out
from its usual corner and along the landing into her
own room. The water was insufficient and, while she
waited for more to heat, she stripped her bed of its soiled
sheets and fetched others. Next she laid and lit the fire
in the small hearth of her bedroom, a luxury she was seldom allowed. Finally she poured the hot water into the
bath and lowered herself in. Strange that, despite all the
folk she had encountered today, she should derive her
only comfort, not from any of them, but from the simple pleasure of the enveloping water and flickering firelight. Outside that cocoon all was darkness and danger.
The words of an ancient prayer kept flitting through her
mind. *Lighten our darkness...and defend us from all
perils and dangers of this night.* Well, God hadn't done
a very good job—He hadn't defended her from perils
and dangers, and it wasn't even night. She began vigorously to rid herself of the stains of the afternoon.

Later she sat exhausted and dry-eyed before the
glowing embers of the fire. Here, for the moment, she
felt safe. But it was a safety that could not last, that
would disappear on her employer's return. Whenever
that was. The family were due back at the weekend. It
was now Wednesday. At best that gave her two days, always assuming the Stationmaster didn't return earlier.
He had done so once; there was no saying he might not
do so again. He might not even have gone; he might
even now be waiting somewhere nearby, to return.
Hearing the closing of the kitchen door was no guarantee that he was not still in the vicinity. A key in the lock

was no guarantee against a further entry by someone possessed of such brute strength.

Mary knew in a flash that she could not stay even for the night. She had already decided against staying longer than this. But where could she go? She glanced at the window and saw a single line of brightness along the western edge of the sky. It must be ten o'clock at least. Putting her feet to the floor, she padded to the window and looked at the silent row of railway houses. Lights still flickered in two or three of them. The living room of her parents' cottage was in darkness but a light showed in their bedroom. But what was she thinking of? She couldn't go there. What explanation could she give to her parents and her sisters for her precipitate return? Her parents might not even believe her. And then there was her father to think of, who had to work alongside John Crowther. She couldn't do anything that would jeopardise his job and the future well-being of her family. No, a return to the cottage was out of the question. Panic overwhelmed her. Her previous feeling of safety was overtaken by one of being trapped in a cage, unable to escape.

Her heart leaped suddenly. A shape, darker against the darkness of the encroaching night, was moving along the path between the cottages and Station House. Mary's first thought was that John Crowther had returned. Looking again, she saw that the form was slighter than that of her attacker and, when he flicked his unruly hair back in a characteristic gesture, she knew with a pang of misery that it was Nathaniel. The house was in darkness, for she had no need of light to find her

way around, and she stood silently at the window, hope-
lessly feasting her eyes on the man she loved. He gazed
up at the house for what seemed an eternity, before turning slowly towards the lane. Even then he hesitated, as
though mystified by the apparent absence of Mary, before silently making his way back to the farm. Mary
watched his retreating figure, trying to encapsulate
every contour, every movement of his body, every man-
nerism of his that she knew and had grown to love. And
then he turned the corner and was gone. And she wished
that the earth would swallow her up and relieve her of
this agony.

How long she stood there looking at the faint outline
of the empty path, she had no idea. At last she turned
and stumbled, shivering, towards the hearth. She poked
the embers of the fire into life and threw a shovelful of
coal on to the reluctant flames. She went to the bedroom
door and unlocked it, pausing outside to listen before
tiptoeing along the corridor and down the stairs. She
checked that the keys were in both the front and the
kitchen door, knowing that they would prevent any but
the most persistent from gaining access. Her employer
would be unlikely to draw attention to himself by kicking the door down. She set the kettle to heat and, while
she waited for it to boil, attended to the kitchen range,
filling it with coal and adjusting the flue and the damper
to keep the fire in for the night. Finally she set a tray
with a slice of bread and butter, teacup and pot of tea,
shut the kitchen door behind her and carried the tray up
to her room. She placed it on the hearth, where the fire
was now throwing a comforting glow into the unlit

room. Before she sat down, she locked the bedroom door again and dragged a heavy chest of drawers in front of it. Now, feeling comparatively safe, she pulled the eiderdown from her bed to the fireside, sank into the armchair and leaned over to pour a cup of tea. Its hot sweetness coursed through her body and she began to relax. But the relief of tension enticed fresh tears and, every time she attempted to eat, the bread stuck in her throat and she couldn't swallow. Staring into the glowing coals until her eyes ached, she forced her brain to empty itself of the images of the afternoon.

Mary squinted at the brightness invading her room. The fire was dead but sunlight was spilling in through the windows on to the armchair that had become her makeshift bed. Her neck was stiff and her limbs ached. For a few seconds she could not think where she was or why she ached as she did but, with a sickening pang, the events of the previous day flooded back.

Slowly she pushed the eiderdown to the floor and eased herself from the chair. Walking as though through water, she crossed to the window and stood looking across to the path and the cottages beyond. The sun shone uncaring in a clear blue sky, mocking her hopelessness. She recalled Nathaniel's figure as he had stood looking up at the house and she, in the darkness, had watched him turn from her and disappear into the night. The recollection was abruptly banished by the appearance of her sisters from the end cottage. Each carried a parcel containing lunch and protection against the rain, should it decide to return. Sarah-Louise called out to the younger of her sisters and Laura turned her head and said something in reply. Then they skipped and ran down the path and she watched as they turned on to the road and disappeared from view under the railway bridge. Looking back at the cottages, she saw George Morritt make his way down the land to the pigsties, a large bucket swinging from his hand. Breakfast for the pig, she thought, imagining the smell. Her father would be somewhere along the track, hammering in the pegs and checking the line for subsidence, particularly after the floods of the last two days. He would have left the house an hour before, kissing her mother goodbye, as he always did, meeting up with the other platelayers, giving his instructions for the day's work in the normal friendly way that he had. Life went on as it had always done. Outside the house nothing had changed. She was looking out on yesterday's world. For her, that world no longer existed…washed away with the floods that had swept across the fields and devastated the ripening corn. Suddenly light-headed, she turned from the window, crossing to the bed to lie down, until the thought of what had happened there yesterday caused her to recoil in horror.

She must eat something. Apart from the unpalatable bread, no food had passed her lips since breakfast the previous day. Crossing the room, she dismantled the barricade erected in the darkness and made her way downstairs. The house was as she had left it. No one had forced an entry. The fire in the range was still in and she made a pot of tea and buttered a slice of bread, which she ate hungrily.

In the scullery the bowl of blackcurrants was covered in a grey mould. She tripped over the basket of clean laundry, hurriedly pulled from the line two days before and still unfolded. Perhaps she would heat the flat iron later and tackle the pile. She continued to move aimlessly through the house, noting the jobs that remained to be done and wondering whether she could be bothered to do them. It was growing warm now. In the living room dust danced in the sunbeams. She knew she should start the housework. It was already growing late. Instead she crossed once more into the kitchen and heated water. This she carried upstairs to her room, where the tin bath still stood. She pulled the bath over to where the sun was streaming through the window and, when there was sufficient water, lowered herself in and lay with her eyes closed until its surface began to cool and the sun had moved southward beyond the back of the house.

On Friday afternoon a loud knock came at the door. She had been sitting sleepily in the bedroom, for the closed windows and the doors bolted against intruders had made the house very warm. Her heart began to thump in her chest at the sound. She crept to the window and peeped round the curtain. The knock came again and after a brief pause the figure of the postman appeared in the back yard, a letter of some kind in his hand. George Morritt, digging vegetables in his garden, saw him hesitate, looking up at the windows, and walked over to him. They exchanged words, both men glancing up at the seemingly empty house. Mary retreated a step behind the curtains of her bedroom and, when she considered it safe, looked again in time to see the postman give George the letter and go on his way. Slowly she went downstairs, knowing that sooner or later George would come knocking at the door and spurred on by his anticipated appearance into a semblance of normality. Since her attack two days before she had done nothing apart from tend the hens and this she had accomplished at the dead of night so as to remain unseen. By the time George arrived, over an hour later, she had heated the flat irons and the pile of washing was slowly going down and the ironed garments were filling the clothes rack.

'A telegram's arrived for you, Mary,' said George cheerfully as she opened the door a mere eighteen inches.

'Thank you, George.'

'Are you all right, Mary? Only the postman knocked two or three times and couldn't make himself heard. He said as how he thought there were nobody in, like.'

'I must have been busy upstairs and didn't hear him.'

'You don't look well, Mary. Are you sure you're all right?'

'Too much staying in, I suppose, nothing more.'

'You'll be glad to have the Crowthers back and get into t' normal routine again. 'Appen it must seem strange without them.'

Mary looked at him without speaking and closed the door.

The telegram was from Annie:

Arrive Saturday, early afternoon. Stop. A lovely week. Stop. John and I much refreshed. Stop.

Forcing down the panic that suddenly resurfaced, Mary tried to think clearly. She must be gone when they returned, that much she knew. It was only now that their arrival was imminent that she made herself face the fact that she could not stay in the village. She could risk seeing neither John Crowther nor Nathaniel again and, in such a small community as existed in Templesforth, she would be bound to bump into one of them, if not both. She would go to York and find work. Nathaniel had told her of the big houses and the wealthy people who lived there. Surely they would be looking for housemaids, and she had years of experience to offer. Refusing to think of the bleak prospect conjured up by her decision, she looked at the clock. It was nearly half past seven. She knew that the down train from Doncaster to York stopped at the station just before ten in the morning. It was the same one as she had taken with Nathaniel a few short weeks ago—in her other life…her past life. If she took this train, there would be time on arrival in the city to look for a position. That would leave the rest of this evening free to pack her trunk and visit her parents with an excuse for her abrupt departure. She would also call on Martha Riley. She wrenched her thoughts away from the one she most wanted to see. She would wait until she was safely in a position in York and then write to him, although just at this moment she had no idea what such a letter would say. The early morning would be taken up with leaving the house ready for the family's return. She would also leave a letter for Annie.

It was the work of a few minutes to gather together her few belongings and lay them on the bed. She surveyed the bare room, recalling the day not so long ago when she had seen it for the first time and been so full of excitement at the prospect of her new job and her own room to go with it. Opening the back door, she looked carefully around to make sure no one was about. She would visit Martha first, leaving the more difficult confrontation with her parents for later.

It was a perfect evening, a slight breeze stirring the leaves on the trees and relieving the village of the earlier heat of high summer. Birds flitted to and fro in the hedgerows or perched swinging on the tall grasses that grew along the roadside. But all this Mary refused to see, keeping her emotions firmly under control, lest they overwhelm her. She scurried along the road and knocked at Martha Riley's cottage, entering the room before she heard a reply and closing the door quickly behind her, glad that the old lady, despite Mary's advice, never used the key. As she expected, Martha was already in bed, her knees supporting a large book, which she was attempting to read with the aid of a magnifying glass.

'Mary, this is a nice surprise. I did not expect to see thee tonight. Come over here and let me look at thee.'

Mary reluctantly crossed the room and kissed her friend, feeling the softness of her ageing skin against her lips. She looked at Martha but could not trust herself to speak.

'Sit down, Mary, sit down. Thou do not look well. Is something ailing thee?'

Mary sat on the wooden chair next to Martha's bed and forced a smile.

''Appen I've been indoors over much this week, that's all.' She paused and drew a deep breath. 'I've come to tell you that I've decided to go and work in York.'

Martha looked at the girl in astonishment. 'York! But why? I thought thou were happy working for the Stationmaster and his family. Naturally enough I like York. Thou dost recall how I told thee I was born and brought up there and several of my relatives still live in the city. But for thyself to decide to go…' The old lady shook her head. 'Thou was always saying how thou never wanted to go to the big city. What has made thee change thy mind?' Martha looked at her keenly. 'I trust all is well at Station House?'

'Oh, Mr and Mrs Crowther have been away in Scarborough for the week,' Mary said quickly. 'They took Johnny with them, of course. It were his first trip to the seaside. Annie sent to say they are much refreshed.'

'Then why hast thou decided to go now, Mary? There must be something wrong. Thou art such a country girl.' She hesitated and still Mary said nothing. 'Is it something to do with thy young man, Mary? Hast thou fallen out with him?'

At the mention of Nathaniel, Mary could hold back her distress no longer. Bending her head to the bed, she buried her face in its blankets, while her shoulders shook and hot tears wet the coverlet. Martha sat silent, gently caressing Mary's hair until the deluge was at an end. Eventually Mary looked up, her face twisted with anguish.

'I'm sorry, Martha. I didn't mean to get upset.' She took out a handkerchief and blew her nose. 'I'm better now. It won't happen again.' She paused and this time it was Martha's turn to be silent.

'I can't tell you any more,' Mary continued at last, conscious that Martha was expecting an explanation, 'so please don't ask me. I've come to say goodbye.'

'Goodbye? When art thou going, then?'

'In the morning. The ten o'clock train.'

'No, Mary! Why so soon? Stay a while.'

'I can't. I'm leaving Station House and there's no room to stay with my parents.' She started to cry again at the thought of her parents. How she wished she could tell them what had happened. But she would never tell anyone…never. It was too awful. She knew that everyone would think of her as a loose woman, as sordid and dirty as she felt herself to be.

'Stay with me, Mary,' the old woman said. 'Don't be hasty. Stay for a few days and consider. It's peaceful here. No one disturbs me. Thou dost know my reputation as a witch!' Mary looked at her and smiled through her tears. How comforting the offer sounded. She considered. John Crowther wouldn't know she was here, as long as she didn't leave the cottage. She would have to see her parents, of course, and let them know she had left the Stationmaster's employment. She looked round the room, attempting to stifle her sobs.

'But where will you put me? There's no room for me here.'

'There's plenty of room. I'm afraid that my own room upstairs is rather bare, now that the bed is down here, but there's a spare bed in the alcove and tomorrow it can be moved into my room. Then it will be thine for as long as thou dost want to stay. And I would love to have thy company. And, if anyone asks, do thou say that I need help because of my poor old bones…which is no more than the truth.'

Now that Martha's offer had been made, Mary felt that she could not bear to stay even one more night under the roof of Station House. As if Martha could read her thoughts, she went on, 'Why not stay tonight, if thy mind is made up?'

'Do you mean it? I would love to. I'll have to go back and see to the range and collect my things. And in the morning I must leave everything ready for their return.'

'Of course. Go now then and sort out some things and be back soon.'

The alcove containing the spare bed was little more than a cupboard leading off Martha's own bedroom. Later that evening Mary lay down on the bed and pulled the covers up to her chin. In the sloping roof over her head a small window showed a square of sky, sprinkled with stars. *How beautiful—and how out of reach,* she thought, before sleeping a sleep undisturbed by dreams.

She opened her eyes and heard Martha bustling around downstairs. Sunlight streamed through the window of the room next door on to the space normally occupied by the bed. She lay listening to the comforting sounds of activity coming from the kitchen, determined to suppress her dread of what today would bring. The aroma of herbs wafted up the stairs and she lay trying to identify their individual scents. Her head ached and her eyes felt heavy after her outburst of the previous evening. The window of the bedroom had been shut for months and, putting her feet to the floor, she crossed the room to open it. A fresh breeze billowed out the net curtain and Mary gazed over the ruined fields. The river level had dropped but the land beyond the river would be flooded for days. This then was the window through which Martha had seen Nathaniel and her walking across the fields hand in hand, with not a care in the world and all the future to look forward to. A million years ago.

'Come and have some breakfast,' called Martha. Mary came slowly down the stairs and smiled at her friend.

'How did you know I was awake?'

'It's the creaking floorboards. They make more noise than my old joints rubbing together. I thought that thou would be hungry, so there are boiled eggs and there's fresh bread that I baked yesterday. Come and sit here.'

'Martha, you've taken so much care. This is beautiful.' A fresh white cloth covered the scratched and scarred wood of the table and a bunch of herbs in a glass jar stood in the middle of the cloth, painting it with their pastel colours. She sat opposite Martha and began to eat her first proper meal in days.

'Nothing is as bad on a full stomach,' Martha said and poured Mary a second cup of tea. 'Now, tell me, what hast thou to do this morning?'

'I must go back to the house and see to t' stove and feed t' chickens. Annie's due back this afternoon and I want t' house right for her return. After that I shall come back here and you must make full use of me.'

'Oh, I intend to. Thou must stay as long as thou dost want.'

'I couldn't put on thee like that,' Mary said. 'It wouldn't be right. I need to be earning some money an' all.'

'There's nothing I would like more. Do not thou worry about money just now. I've enough put by. And, any road, it would be an opportunity for thee to learn more about the herbs and medicines. We both know that my days of mixing potions are over. And there are always going to be poorly people in need of our help.'

Her words were so reassuring that tears sprang to Mary's eyes again. If only it were that easy.

'Mary, stay a while. Don't decide yet. Stay here and rest. Do thou go and sort out what needs doing at Station House and then come back here. There's no one who would be gladder of thy company than me.'

Mary helped her friend clear away the remains of breakfast, washed and dressed and reluctantly made her way back to Station House, taking care not to be seen.

CHAPTER FIFTEEN

SATURDAY, 22nd July.
Dear Mrs Crowther,
I am sorry to say I can no longer work for you. I know that this is very short notice but it cannot be avoided. I have to go away.
I do hope you enjoyed your stay in Scarborough and feel the benefit.
Yours sincerely,
Mary Swales.

Mary read the letter twice and frowned. It explained nothing, but there was nothing that *could* be explained to Annie. Mary neither knew nor cared what Annie's husband would say when he read it. Unlike his wife, he would understand why it had been written.

She folded the note and placed it on the kitchen table. It was the last thing she had to do before closing the door on Station House for ever. Walking swiftly down the garden between the rows of raspberry bushes, now bowed over with ripened fruit ready for picking, she placed the key in its prearranged hiding place under the bowl of oyster shell in the chicken coop. Continuing on down the garden, she opened the small gate and crossed the path into her parents' garden.

Susan was standing in front of the range, knocking bread into shape before leaving it to prove. Alice lay in her bed. Mary's other sisters were nowhere to be seen.

'Hello, Mam,' Mary said quietly.

'Goodness, Mary, you startled me, coming in like that. What are you doing here at this time on a Saturday morning?'

'Where are the girls?' Mary asked, going over to Alice and kissing her on the forehead.

'They've gone along to t' shops and to call at Bessie's for some eggs. I needed to get them out from under my feet.' She brushed a strand of hair back with a floury hand and looked at Mary with a quizzical expression. 'Everything all right, lass?'

'I've called in to tell you I'm going to work in York.'

'Tha's going to what…? Why? What's wrong with the job tha's got? I thought it suited thee working there.'

'Oh, you know. I wanted to try my hand in the big city to see what it's like.'

'I can't imagine John Crowther will be o'er pleased wi' your decision. What does he say about it?'

'He doesn't mind really. Besides, it's not up to him what I decide to do,' Mary said heatedly.

'Well, he'll want you to work your notice, else tha'll not get a letter of recommendation to tek with thee. When's tha' planning on going, any road?'

'Very soon. Next week, maybe.'

'Next week?' She stopped to consider. 'What about Nathaniel? I thought thee and he were walking out.' She eyed Mary narrowly. 'He hasn't gone and got thee…'

'No, Mother, nothing like that,' Mary exploded and turned quickly to Alice so that her mother wouldn't see the beginnings of tears. She stroked her sister's hair and began to talk to her softly.

'Alice will miss you,' her mother went on. 'She loves you to visit.' Mary suppressed a sob and continued to look at Alice. She knew it had been a mistake to come. She should have gone away quietly, disappeared from her family's life without any of these questions being asked that she didn't feel able to answer.

'I must go, Mam.'

'Go where? Back to Station House?'

'No, not there. I'm staying with Martha Riley for a few days before I leave. I knew there'd be no room here and she could do with some help.'

'Aye, well. 'Appen she's not the only one.'

'Oh, Mam, I can't explain. I have to go. You must take my word for it.' She turned to leave. 'One thing. Please don't tell anyone where I'm staying. I…I don't want the old lady disturbed.'

'Tha'll say goodbye to thy sisters and thy father before tha' goes?'

'Of course I will. I'll call in later in the week.'

Early on Wednesday morning Martha hobbled to answer a knock on the door, while Mary ran upstairs to hide in the bedroom.

'Is our Mary here?' It was Sarah-Louise's voice. 'Only I've come wi' a message for her.'

'What's the matter, Sarah-Lou?' Mary peered round the bottom of the stairs at her sister. Her two younger sisters stood on the road waiting for her and all three were dressed for school.

'It's Mrs Crowther. She called at our house. She wants to see you. Mam wouldn't tell her where you were. What's going on, Mary?'

'Oh, I'm helping Mrs Riley for a few days, that's all. You get off to school then, Sarah-Lou, or you'll be late.'

She sat down on the bottom step, cursing herself for not leaving on Saturday as she had intended. She might have guessed that this would happen, that Annie would seek her out. It wasn't fair that her family should be involved in this mess. She would have to try and see Annie, though. She sat and thought. She knew that the line was always busy in the hour leading up to lunch. If she called in at about eleven o'clock John Crowther would be occupied with the day's arrivals or dispatches and she herself could arrive and depart before there was any danger of his appearance in the house.

Accordingly, Mary made her way later that morning to Station House, going by way of the garden, knowing that she could hide behind the bushes or in the hen-hut if anyone should chance to appear. She peered round the bushes and saw Johnny asleep in his pram under a tree. Checking the back yard, she could see that all was quiet. The kitchen door of the house stood open. Annie was sitting in the kitchen, her head resting on her hands, studying Mrs Beeton's *Book of Household*

Management. She looked up as Mary entered and jumped up to greet her.

'Mary, thank goodness you've come back. Please tell me you're here to stay. You must help me. I've got to prepare John's dinner and I haven't started yet. What am I going to do?'

'Annie, didn't you read my note? I'm going away.'

'But why? I don't understand. We were getting on so well. You've been happy here, haven't you? If it's that you're not getting good enough wages, I can talk to John about paying you more.'

'No!' Mary replied vehemently. 'No, don't do that!' she said more softly. 'I have to go away. I'm sorry, Annie. I can't explain. But it were good being friends and I am sorry to leave you.'

'But how am I going to manage?' Annie's voice was tearful now. 'I can't cook like you can and Johnny is so much of a handful.'

'You'll be sure to find another housemaid. We're ten a penny.'

'Perhaps your sister would consider it. She'll be leaving school soon, won't she?'

'No, she won't. What I mean is, yes, she will be leaving school soon but she can't help you. She's likely going to work in t' city.' Mary made a mental note to somehow warn her sister not to consider a job with the Crowthers. The hands of the clock showed a quarter to twelve. 'Annie, I must be going,' she said, backing towards the door.

'Will you come and visit me when you're in the village?'

'I don't know that I'll be back for a long time and, the chances are, you might have moved on by then.'

Annie went over and hugged Mary warmly. Then, glancing up, she said, 'Oh, look, John! Mary's come to say goodbye.' Mary gasped and turned quickly to come face to face with the Stationmaster, his bulky frame filling the doorway, blocking her escape.

'So I can see,' John Crowther murmured, looking Mary up and down.

'I've tried to persuade her to stay,' went on Annie, 'but she won't hear of it.'

'Is that a fact?' said her husband, taking a step forward. As he moved towards the two women, Mary, pulling away from Annie, stared into the scornful face of her attacker. Then she spun on her heel and made her escape through the living room and out of the front door, paying no heed to Annie's cries for her to wait. Across the yard she raced and out to the road, not stopping until she was safe in Martha's cottage. She ran upstairs and flopped down on the bed, covering her face with her hands, trying to blot out the hateful image of John Crowther. Gradually her pulse slowed and she grew calm. She sat up. She felt safe here but it was an illusion. She wasn't safe at all. She knew without a shadow of a doubt that she had to leave the village as soon as possible. She would go early the next morning, walk into Selby so there was no chance of encountering the Stationmaster again, and catch the first train to York.

Martha was sitting in the garden under the apple tree. 'I know,' she said, looking at Mary's unhappy face as the girl sat down next to her. 'Thou art about to tell me that I will not have thy company for any longer. I do not understand why thou must go but I must accept it and hope that thou hast made the right decision.'

'I'm sure I have. I will go in the morning.'

'Very well. I ask only one thing. Do not lose touch with thy family. I say this only because it was what I did when I first came here... Remember how I told thee about losing my husband and baby and how I decided to leave York and bury myself in the countryside. That much wasn't a mistake but breaking the ties with my family was.'

'Did you ever see them again?'

'I didn't but, after several years, my sister-in-law, Hannah, wrote to me. She was Joseph's youngest sister and we had been very close. I shall always be grateful to her for taking the step of writing. I could have so easily lost her friendship for ever.'

'Is she still alive?'

'Oh, yes. Indeed she is. She's sixty-four years old now and head of the Tuke family. She lost her dear husband two years ago. We've written regularly over the years. She had two children, both girls.' She chuckled. 'She wrote to me asking if I minded her calling the first one Martha...if I minded! It was an honour. Hannah's a grandmother now. She still lives in the big house in Marygate where they all grew up. She must rattle around in it now, though I guess they all come to see her regularly.'

'How strange to have all that family and never to see them...though I suppose there are plenty more of us...aunties and uncles and cousins, who we never visit. Of course it's been hard for my mother and father, with

Alice being ill. They haven't been able to go around as they might have. No, I won't forget them. I'll come back and visit…though not yet.'

That evening Mary sat against the brick wall of the garden, watching the sky turn dark and the stars appear and wondering whether the same sky and the same stars would give her comfort when she was no longer here. The cool evening air was drawing from the herbs and flowers a multitude of perfumes. The whole produced in Mary a mixture of both sadness and peace. In the distance she could hear the steady clip-clop of horse's hooves. She sat motionless, screened from the road by the high brick wall. The horse sounded tired. There was no gaiety to its step as it approached, no anticipation of an exciting ride up the lane and over the fields. The hoof beats slowed and stopped along the lane. After a couple of minutes they resumed and came slowly closer. Mary held her breath. They were now on the other side of the wall. Suddenly a well-loved voice caused her already tense body to contract.

'Walk on, Jess. It's no good you lingering. It looks as though it's you and me again tonight.' A big sigh came from the speaker. 'Walk on, girl.' The noise of the hooves picked up and passed along the road, fading into the distance. Mary sat on under the wall, frozen with misery.

In the middle of the night there was a knock on the door of Martha Riley's cottage. Mary sat up quickly, banging her head on the sloping roof above her. She looked up at the square of sky, unlit by stars. The bed had remained where she had found it on the night of her flight to Martha's. It was cosy there, enclosed in its tiny alcove. But she had slept badly and had heard the footsteps approaching. She heard Martha call out.

'Who is it?'

'It's me, George Morritt. I need your help.'

'I'll answer the door,' said Mary, running down the stairs. She opened the door a crack.

'Oh, Mary, it's you. I'm reet sorry to disturb you, but it's our Alfie. He's been took real bad and 'Liza asked whether Mrs Riley had owt that would help.'

'What's wrong?' asked Mary.

'Well, he's burning up and shivering and he keeps being sick, like. 'Liza's tried all night to get him cool but nothing's working. She thought as how Mrs Riley might have summat to cool him down.'

'Mary, the little lad really needs someone to look at him. I can't manage to get over there. Do thou go and check him and report back to me.'

Mary turned back to George. 'I'll come straight away, George. If you don't mind waiting there, only Mrs Riley's in her bed in t' room. Give me a minute while I put some clothes on.' She closed the door softly.

'Try and get the fever to break,' said Martha. 'Little ones can easily suffer a fit if they get too warm. Make sure he stays in bed, sponge his face with cool water and give him a little of the infusion of lemon balm—it may help the fever to break. Thou wilt find it on the shelf over there. Oh, and try to make him drink.'

George was waiting for her as Mary stepped from the cottage into the night. They hurried along the road to the silent row of railway cottages, the second of which was lit up as if to alert passers-by of trouble within. Alfie was as bad as George had said.

'He were took bad at school today,' said his mother, huge with her third baby. 'I didn't reckon much to it at first. He always did make a fuss. Anything to get out of school and round to the farm instead.'

Mary saw his burning face and felt the swellings in his neck. She guessed that his throat must be very sore. She carried out Martha's instructions, bathing Alfie's hot face with cool water and encouraging him to drink. She wrapped soothing warm flannels round the swollen neck. As the dawn was poking its pale fingers through the trees, Alfie slept, his fever a little less and his vomiting settled. Mary took advantage of his improvement to return to Martha's cottage. Martha was already up and dressed and preparing breakfast in the kitchen. Mary sat down dejectedly. She knew without being told that her plans for escape were going to be thwarted again. She could hardly leave this morning with Alfie so poorly and Martha unable to get out of the house herself to see to him.

'Eat some breakfast, Mary,' the old lady said, pushing a plate of fresh bread towards her and pouring a cup of tea. 'And tell me how the little lad is.'

Mary described his illness, adding, 'It's all right, Martha. I'll not go until he's better. It wouldn't be right, not when you can't look after him yourself. I'll stay on an extra day or two if that's what's needed.'

Alfie's condition had improved. Although still feverish, he was less hot than he had been and had not vomited. But when the curtains were opened and Eliza was removing his damp nightshirt, they could see a rash that covered her son's neck and spilled on to his chest. It seemed to spread even as the two women looked at it.

'I think it's scarlet fever,' said Mary.

The words dropped into Eliza's heart like a stone. 'God help us,' she moaned. 'It takes so many little uns. Please, not my Alfie.'

'Let me go and talk to Martha again. She'll be able to tell me if there's owt else we should be doing,' Mary said to Eliza as she rose from the bed. 'I'll be back very soon.'

Martha looked serious. 'I'm sure thou art right about it being scarlet fever. Two things worry me if it is. The first is that Alfie needs to be kept in bed and calm, even when he's feeling better. Not an easy thing to make him do when he's a lively little boy. But if he's allowed up and around too soon, he's more likely to suffer later.' For the minute she didn't elaborate on what this suffering might entail. 'The immediate problem,' she went on, 'is Eliza. If she starts with the illness, she will be very bad because she's expecting. She must be kept away from her son at all costs.'

'Then I shall have no choice but to stay,' said Mary, her voice cracking. She felt as though a cage was closing around her. 'I don't feel up to all this just now.' She climbed the stairs to pack some clothes in a bag, kissed Martha goodbye and returned to the Morritts' to explain what would have to be done.

It seemed to Mary that her friendship with Nathaniel belonged to another life. A few days after moving into

George and Eliza's cottage, she had written to him in a brief interlude of peace.

Dear Nathaniel,
I have decided that I cannot marry you. I don't love you enough. Rhoda Precious would make you a better wife than I ever could. Please forgive me.
I am very sorry that you have lost the barley. I hope the wheat harvest will be better.
Yours very sincerely,
Mary Swales.

The letter was the second she had written. In the first she had put *I don't love you*. The harsh untruth stared out at her from the page and she had ripped it in pieces. She added *'enough'*. *'I don't love you enough'*. Still a lie but a kinder one, one that was a bit nearer the truth. The truth was that she loved him more than she could ever put down in words.

The letter sealed and addressed, she placed it in the hands of her younger sister, Sarah-Louise, and asked her to deliver it to the farm, torturing herself with thoughts of what the hurtful letter would do to its recipient.

'How did Nathaniel seem?' she asked her sister the following day.

'He were pleased to see me. Said as how he hadn't seen his favourite lasses for days. But when he studied your letter, he seemed reet angry an' all. He said as how he'd be calling to see thee, then he took off over t' fields wi'out even saying goodbye. What's up, Mary? What has tha' said to 'im? Aren't the two on you friends any more?' But Mary was too sick at heart to trust herself with words and turned back into the house.

Nathaniel didn't come. Instead he wrote to her. A short, to-the-point letter that cut Mary to the quick and showed her by its tone how much she had wounded him.

Dear Mary,
Why have you led me on if this is how you feel? You promised me that we would marry at the year-end. If you are so fickle I'm glad you will not be mine. Perhaps Rhoda Precious will not be so particular.
Yours sincerely,
Nathaniel Varley.

The letter was delivered to Station House and Annie delivered it to Mary's parents. He didn't know, then, where she was. After two days she received another.

Dear Mary,
This must be my father's doing. I cannot believe you have changed your mind after all that passed between us in the summer. Has my father been try-ing to influence you against me? If this is the case, tell me. I do not believe you can be so fickle.
I await your reply,
Yours affectionately,
Nathaniel.

His anger she could submit to, but that she should be the cause of his misery she found hard to bear. What was she to do? She could not leave his questions unanswered. After two weeks she wrote again.

Dear Nathaniel,
Please believe me when I say I cannot marry you.
It is not your father's doing. I cannot explain more.
Do not press me to. I want only what will make
you happy.
I remain your affectionate,
Mary.

She sat in the rocking chair in the little back bedroom that had now become both sickroom and prison. Nathaniel's letters lay in her lap. She kept them always about her person; they were all she possessed of him—the anger and the hurt. All else—the love, the companionship, the laughter—seemed like a distant memory, flown from her as surely as the swallows who were gathering in their chattering flocks, preparing to take from her the last of summer.

She was not entirely ignorant of Nathaniel's behaviour in the weeks that followed. She received no acknowledgement of her last letter to him but, one day, when she was in the garden of Eliza and George's cottage, her father returned home from work, having called in at the Wheatsheaf with his men for their customary pint of ale.

'Mary, love, it's good to see thee again. And how's little Alfie?'

'He's improving a lot. In fact it's difficult to keep him in bed now he's so much better. I'm just enjoying a few minutes fresh air while he's asleep.' Her pale face and lacklustre appearance suggested that she was enjoying very little. Her father frowned.

'Young Nathaniel were in t' inn just now,' he said, watching her carefully. ''Appen e'd had a drop too much to drink. All over t' shop he were, when 'e got up to go. Never said a word, like. Looked right through me. Funny that, we'd been middlin' chatty t' last month or two. I suppose there's nowt wrong between the two of you?'

Mary coloured at the mention of Nathaniel. She had said nothing to her parents about the distance she had put between herself and her former sweetheart. Now she struggled to hold back tears of unhappiness for Nathaniel, for herself and for her inability to confide in her parents and be the recipient of their comfort.

'Yes, there is something wrong,' Mary admitted to her father. 'I've told Nathaniel that I don't think I love him enough to marry him, and he's reet upset by it.'

'I'm not surprised he's upset,' said Tom angrily. 'Nay, what's tha' playing at, lass? You and he were all set to wed. I didn't expect any daughter of mine to be so flighty. What's 'is parents going to make of it all? Still, if that's how you feel, mebbe it's for t' best. Though it won't make my life any easier, having to pass t' time of day wi' 'im in t' Wheatsheaf.' And, bidding her a brusque 'Goodnight', he disappeared into his cottage.

Alfie's improvement had not lasted long. After the fever had gone, the rash which followed it spread, then disappeared within the week, leaving skin that flaked off in lumps and a little boy whose exuberance Mary found it difficult to control. Martha had said to keep him in bed well after the infection had run its course. But how could Mary restrain an active five-year-old, anxious to be playing out with his friends and enjoying what remained of the summer? And then one morning, a full two weeks after the start of his illness, when Mary was thinking that the worst was past and everything would soon be back to the way it had been, Alfie woke with puffy eyes and a face swollen and pale. When Mary drew back the bedclothes, she saw that his ankles too were swollen.

'It's the dropsy,' Martha told her. 'Poor little lad. I was hoping he might have escaped any after-effects.'

'Is there something else I should have done?' cried Mary, distraught. 'I tried to keep him quiet but he would keep bouncing around, no matter how hard I tried.'

'No, there's nothing else. Thou hast cared for him as devotedly as any mother. It's something that happens. Do thou try to keep him as calm as possible, though he won't feel well for a while and I doubt he'll want to do any bouncing. We'll make up some nettle tea—that will help get rid of the fluid—though it may be difficult to persuade him to drink it. And give him plenty of milk to drink. It looks as though thou wilt be there for a while longer.' She looked at Mary perceptively. 'Do thou take care of thyself,' she said. 'I'm worried about thee. Thy country-girl bloom has all but disappeared. 'Appen it's the staying indoors that doesn't suit thee. Just remember how many of us love thee and there's more than one depending on thee to keep well.'

It took all Mary's powers to persuade Alfie to drink the nettle tea. Whether or not it helped was difficult to say, for the swelling in his small body grew worse before it eventually improved. Day after day he sat in his bed or on Mary's lap, pale and listless, while Mary, no less pale herself, tried to keep him amused with stories and little toys. Outside, trees loomed ghostly in the morning mists of early autumn. The day came at last when Alfie's illness was deemed to be at an end and Mary carried him downstairs to the mother he had not seen for two months. Her heart twisted as she handed him over to Eliza, for in the weeks she had been nursing him she had grown very close to the little boy. She stepped outside, breathing in the sharp smell of soot as a noisy goods train made its complaining progress northwards to York. The closing of the door behind her should have spelled freedom after the long weeks of incarceration, but she knew now with a certainty she would not previously acknowledge that a longer and more harrowing captivity awaited her. She was carrying John Crowther's child.

CHAPTER SIXTEEN

MARTHA was having an afternoon nap in her favourite place under the old apple tree when Mary returned. She had told Mary often that its knotted trunk and gnarled branches comforted her, being as old, if not older, than she was herself and even more rheumaticky. Mary tiptoed into the living room and lifted the heavy herbal off the shelf. She sat at the kitchen table and feverishly leafed through the pages, looking for information on herbs useful in establishing a woman's regular monthly flow. There were several herbs that a woman who was expecting was wise to avoid. Lady's mantle was one of them. She remembered Martha's words of warning when she had been helping to replace the old stock from the previous year. She had said that the concoction could cause powerful contractions. Even now the bottles sat in a row on the shelf, where she had put them.

She rubbed her forehead, racking her brain to recall what they had been talking about that afternoon. It was something important, something momentous even. That was it! Martha had been telling her about the loss of her husband and unborn child in the horrors of the cholera outbreak that had swept through York. She could see the sorrow still, locked at the back of her friend's eyes…sorrow at the loss of a husband, followed by the loss of a much longed-for baby. She shut the book with an abruptness that sent the dust flying from its well-thumbed pages. A surge of panic rose through her body at the thought of what she had been considering and she shook her head in disgust. She was startled by the sound of Martha's voice calling for assistance. She hurried inside, replacing the herbal on its shelf, and left it there.

'Mary, do thou help me to get out of this chair. Sometimes I sit for so long I do find it hard to move.' She took Mary's arm and pulled herself out of the chair. 'It *is* good to see thee again.' They began to stroll slowly along the path.

'It can't be as good as it is for me to see *thee*. Not that I didn't like caring for Alfie…and it was certainly good to leave him so much better.' Mary sighed. 'I don't want to be a mawk, but there were times when I thought I'd go out of my mind if I were cooped up in that room for much longer. There's them as likes to stay indoors but I sometimes think I would die wi'out fresh air around me.' She stopped abruptly.

'And how *is* young Alfie?' asked Martha, her query filling the lengthening silence. 'Is he bouncing around as much as ever?'

'He's still very pale and he doesn't have a lot of energy. He wants to play but he gets tired after only a few minutes. Eliza's going to tek him out in t' fresh air to try and fetch some roses back in his cheeks.'

'And thou art not the same fresh-faced country girl who first came to help me tidy my garden and tie up my bunches of herbs.' There was silence again. Mary opened her mouth to speak and shut it without anything being said. She looked round the garden. It had suffered from the neglect of the past few months. Many of the herbs had run to seed, their tall flower heads dried and yellowing, strung with the intricate weavings of busy spiders. Weeds had pushed their way between the stone paving of the path and weightless thistledown floated in the slanting sunbeams.

''Appen this country girl has been neglecting 'er job,' Mary said with a forced laugh. 'At least t' birds are happy wi' all this extra breakfast. Just look at 'em in yon corner.' She pointed to where two goldfinches flitted about on the prickly seed-cases of a clump of thistles, their red and yellow markings bright against the uniform decay of the plants. 'It's time I rolled up my sleeves and did some work.' She ran to the coalhole and pulled out a wooden box containing fork and trowel and a sharp knife. Then she set about the weeds as though her life depended on it. Martha sat down again and watched her hacking back the dying plants and running to and fro along the path to the corner of the garden, where a growing pile of decayed vegetation was evidence of her single-minded determination.

The delicate leaves of the lady's mantle, when Mary stumbled across it, were brittle, fringed with brown, no longer able to trap the dew with its supposed magical powers. She stooped down and, with a racing heart, touched the dying leaves. How could she have even thought of using it to put an end to the life that was growing inside her, even if she hated its existence? She hated herself more, nearly as much as she hated the man who had been the cause of her downfall. It was all wrong. The baby should have been Nathaniel's, his and hers, not that monster's. She couldn't bear it. She just couldn't bear it. She flung the fork and trowel across the garden and they clattered against the wall and disappeared in a patch of sage. Then she rushed into the cottage and up the stairs. At the bedroom window she paused, looking over the fields to the river beyond, as it curled its way seaward. It was all she knew, this flat land with its wide expanse of sky and unpredictable weather. She had no desire to leave it. Putting her head into her hands, she wished she had never been born.

When, at last, she roused herself and came softly downstairs, Martha was in the kitchen preparing tea. Mary walked straight past her into the garden, cleared away the tools, retrieving the fork and trowel from where she had thrown them, and came to sit down in the kitchen.

'I'm going now, Martha.'

'What, *now*? Today?'

'No, not today…but in the morning, before anything else happens to stop me.'

Martha poured a cup of tea and handed it to Mary. 'Yes, I thought it would be so. I see thy mind is made up, so I will not try to change it. Maybe it is the right thing to do.' She took Mary's hand and caressed it. 'I can't deny that I will miss thee, though. Remember that there is always a place for thee here when thou dost decide to come back.'

CHAPTER SEVENTEEN

MARY stepped from the train on to the bustling platform of York Station. She had not been able to rid her mind of the memories of the last journey on this line with her sisters and Nathaniel, and the arrival at her destination served only to reinforce them. She pictured her sisters' faces upturned towards the cathedral-like roof of the station and experienced another spasm of guilt and sadness that she had left the village without saying goodbye to her family. Once she had a position and was settled, she would write to Sarah-Louise explaining everything… well, not everything. In fact she didn't know what she would say…only that she missed them.

All Mary's possessions were contained in a large leather bag. Her decision to walk to Selby and catch the train had meant that she had to leave her small trunk in Martha's cottage but she was glad now, for she could not have wandered round looking for employment encumbered with a trunk. She stepped from the protection of the station into a light drizzle, which increased to a steady downpour while she was making her way to what she assumed was the centre of town. She had no idea where vacant positions for maids would be advertised and stopped a postman to ask for directions to a newsagent.

'It depends what tha's wanting, like. Burdekin's is the biggest…that's in Parliament Street. Tha knows where that is?' He looked at her leather bag doubtfully.

'No, I'm new to the city.'

'Well, tha's going in t' right direction. Carry on along this road till you reach the end, then turn left and you'll see Burdekin's. You can't miss it.'

'Do you happen to know whether they have advertisements for housemaids?'

'Oh, aye. Tha'll find plenty there. You can put an advertisement there yourself…"Position Wanted" like…' he looked at her bag again '…though 'appen tha's looking for summat straight away.'

'Yes I'm wanting something today, if possible.'

'Aye, well, like I say, you'll find plenty there.' He hesitated. Mary looked at his weathered face, legacy of so many years in the fresh air, and thought of her father.

'Thank you. You've been very helpful,' she replied and began to walk in the direction he had indicated. She hadn't gone more than a few steps when she heard him call.

'Excuse me, miss, for asking, but what kind of housemaid are you trained to be?'

'Well, I've been trained up to parlour maid…but I don't mind anything. I were a general servant in my last job. I just need to get settled somewhere.'

'I know of one family that's looking for a lady's maid. You could try there first, maybe.'

'Yes, I would like that. Where do I go?'

'The family are called Turton. He's a solicitor. Has a big practice in the city. You'll find them in Bootham Terrace, number five. Tell them I sent you…Henry Purvis is the name.' He pointed out the direction she must take.

'Thank you, Mr Purvis. I'll go right away,' Mary said eagerly, pleased at how easy it was proving to find employment.

It was a walk of less than fifteen minutes to her destination but, by the time she arrived, the persistent rain had soaked her cloak and skirt and was dripping off the ends of the ringlets of hair that had escaped from her hat. The servants' door was opened by a housemaid.

'Yes,' she said shortly. 'What do you want?'

'I've come about the job.'

'What job? We've got a scullery maid here.'

'No, the job of lady's maid.'

'The job of lady's maid…you?' The girl smirked and looked her up and down.

'Who is it?' a voice shouted from inside the kitchen.

'It's someone after t' job, Mrs Banks.'

'Well, don't keep them standing on t' doorstep. Ask them to come in. This damp is playing havoc with my rheumatics.'

Mary stepped into the kitchen, apologising for the pool of water that quickly formed around her feet.

'Don't worry about that. It can't be helped in this weather,' Mrs Banks said kindly. 'Maud, go and ask if the mistress is free. She may insist on you making an appointment if she's busy,' she said, addressing Mary again.

But she wasn't busy and word came down that she was prepared to see the new girl. Her face showed that she wasn't prepared, however, for the sight that Mary presented. Surveying her from her dripping hair to her muddy boots, she said archly, 'And what makes you think you would be any good as a lady's maid? You look as if you can't look after yourself, let alone anyone else.'

'I'm sorry, madam, it's because of the weather, you see. I've only arrived this morning. Mr Purvis, the postman, said you might be looking for someone. I need a job quickly.'

'And I need someone who's competent and efficient. Have you done this kind of work before?' Mrs Turton asked doubtfully.

'Yes, madam. Leastwise, not the job of a lady's maid, but I've been trained in everything else up to that.'

'Oh, yes? And where were you trained, may I ask?'

'I worked at the big house in Bankside, madam…not many miles from Selby,' she explained, when her interrogator looked perplexed.

'Oh, a country girl, then.' She looked disdainful. 'And why did you leave, may I ask?'

'Because relatives came to stay and brought their own servants with them, madam, and my help weren't wanted any more.'

'And how long ago was this?'

'Er…I left there about two years ago.'

'Two years ago. Then what have you been doing since?'

'I were general housemaid to a local family.'

'And why did you leave there?'

'Well…well…I wanted to better my position and I thought that I'd be able to do it coming to t' city.'

'Indeed! Let me see your "character" then.'

'Pardon, madam?'

'Your "character". You do have a reference, don't you?'

Mary's heart began to beat faster. 'Er, no, madam.'

'You don't have a reference? How do you think I'm going to take you on without a reference? Why didn't you obtain one from your last employer?' She eyed Mary suspiciously.

'My last employer acted in an improper fashion to me, madam, and I thought it best to leave.'

'Tch! You servants are all the same. You give inferior service, then invent a cock-and-bull story to cover your deficiencies. Well, I don't want any of that here. You can get out now. And if you see that Henry Purvis again, tell him not to bother sending anyone else. I shall go to the agency myself and pick one.'

It was the same at the second place she tried. She had written down the name and address off the board in the newsagent's shop. All was going well until she was asked for her character reference. Within two minutes she found herself on the back steps in the gathering twilight.

Now she was presented with a problem. There was only a small amount of money in her purse and she could not squander it on board and lodging, especially if tomorrow was to prove as difficult as today had been to find work. She wandered disconsolately back towards the station, thinking of the comforts of home and the peace of Martha's cottage. She found a small tea-shop and took so long over a cake and a pot of tea that the waitress began to sweep the floor and give signs that she was waiting to lock the door. Smiling apologetically, Mary got up to leave and continued on towards the station, knowing that here at least she would find warmth. In the Ladies Waiting Room she watched the last train of the evening preparing to depart southwards towards Doncaster. Every bone in her body yearned for her to gather her things, leave the warm room, board the train and return to comfort and security. But she sat on as though in a trance as it pulled out of the station in a cloud of steam.

At ten-thirty the door of the waiting room opened and a porter put his head round the door.

'Na then, miss, you can't stay here all night.'

Mary, who had been dozing by the fire, woke with a jump. 'I'm sorry. I didn't realise how late it were. I've been looking for work, you see, but got overtaken by t' dark before I managed to find a post.' She looked round the room. 'I wouldn't be a nuisance if you let me stay.'

'It's not that, miss, only I'm not meant to keep the fire in all night. We have a coal allowance each day and it has to last.'

'Oh, I don't need a fire. All I need is some shelter for the night. Please say I can stay. I'll leave first thing.'

'Well, it's not strictly allowed…but I don't see as how it'll matter too much. You're not going to give me any bother, after all.'

'Thank you. You're very kind,' Mary said with a catch in her voice.

In the middle of the night the porter returned. 'Begging your pardon, miss, but I've just brewed up and

I wondered if you'd like to get a warm at my fire and a mug of tea.' Mary blinked back tears at the porter's kindness as she followed him into the parcels office and sat down by the fire.

The following morning Mary was examining the notice boards for 'Positions vacant' before most folk were behind their counters in the grand shops that lined the streets in the centre of the city. As she perused first one and then the next, wondering which was least likely to need a reference, she heard a man's voice to her left asking what price it was for two weeks advertising. The transaction was made and the man turned to go, Mary noticing as he did so that he was wearing clerical garb. She watched the shop assistant pin the piece of paper to the board and, peering over his shoulder, read the words:

'General Maid required for clergyman and large family. No experience necessary.'

Perhaps a cleric would be less critical of her failure to produce a reference, she thought, and, turning on her heel, hurried from the shop in time to see the man weaving his way between the stalls that had been set up for Friday market.

'Excuse me, sir,' she panted, breathless from her pursuit, 'but I saw you hand in that advertisement and I'd like to apply for the job.'

'Good gracious,' the cleric said, looking at her over his spectacles. 'That must be the swiftest episode of divine intervention I have yet experienced.' The man who faced her was of medium to tall stature and inclined to be portly. He wore a bushy beard, greying in parts and connected to his hair by luxuriant sideburns. A pair of round-rimmed spectacles perched on the end of his nose, lending a severity to his face that it might not otherwise have possessed. 'You'd better follow me then and we will see what Mrs Thoroughgood says about you.' And he set off again at such a pace that Mary had difficulty keeping up with him. They passed several churches, at each one of which Mary expected their journey to end. Eventually the Reverend Thoroughgood turned into a side street and stopped at the door of an imposing house, next to which stood the church of The Holy Trinity within a peaceful graveyard, shaded with trees on the brink of discarding their worn summer finery for the richer shades of autumn.

'Here I am, my dear,' the Reverend boomed, throwing open the door and stopping in a long and cluttered hall to remove his hat and gloves, which he threw on the table, adding to the pile of assorted outerwear already gathered there.

'In here, Percival,' a tired voice replied and the man opened another door into a large untidy parlour, in the middle of which lay a woman on a chaise longue, indifferent to the chaos around her.

'We have an answer to our prayers, my dear. Come child, come and let my good lady look at you.' He turned and beckoned Mary into the room. 'This young lady has answered our advertisement while it was still hot off the press, as it were. Surely she must be who we are looking for. Come forward, girl, and let my wife see you. My good lady is a little indisposed at present and must of necessity run the household from her bed of sickness.'

To Mary's eyes the woman looked remarkably healthy. She stepped forward so that the cleric's wife could look at her without craning her neck.

'My wife needs someone to help with the general running of the household. Normally she would have to do this herself, for my wages engaged in the Lord's service do not leave enough over to employ servants. But she is expecting our twelfth child and the doctor has said she must take it easy. Naturally we cannot pay a maid a large wage but we are sure you will accept this, knowing that you too will be sharing in the Lord's work in this wonderful city. You will be expected to do the general cleaning of the house under my wife's supervision. The children have a nurse but you must cook their meals and those for my wife and myself. From time to time we will entertain such church dignitaries as is deemed necessary and you, of course, will prepare refreshment, light or more substantial, as each visit occasions. Is that understood?' The cleric smiled at her benevolently.

Mary's emotions had gone from annoyance that she should be expected to accept lower wages because her potential employer considered himself on 'the Lord's service' to exasperation at the amount of work she would be expected to do and worry about whether she would be able to combine the dual roles of cook and housemaid for such a big family in such a huge house. Beneath these feelings was the unacknowledged one that she was experiencing the very same indisposition as the cleric's wife but with much less support. It was, however, a job and she was fortunate to have obtained it. The next moment, though, she thought it had slipped from her grasp.

'Does the girl have a reference, Percival?'

'Oh, yes, of course, may we see your reference, child?'

'I don't have one, sir,' Mary muttered.

'She doesn't have one, my dear,' the cleric whispered to his wife.

'Why ever not?' his wife replied. 'No one comes for a job without a reference.'

The cleric looked expectantly at Mary, who sighed and began as before, 'My previous employer acted improperly, madam, and I had to leave.'

Mrs Thoroughgood began to fan herself rapidly. She looked at her husband. 'Percival, I really do not think we can take on a girl with such morals. Think of the risk to our children.'

Mary picked up her bag. 'I'm sorry to have disturbed you, madam. I wouldn't dream of staying to inflict harm on your children's morals.' She turned to go.

'No, wait, there's no need to be hasty,' the cleric said to his wife, before turning and giving Mary an appraising look. 'I'm sure we can show a little Christian forgiveness to the young lady. Let us see how we all get on. If you are not satisfied,' he said, smiling at his wife, 'then she shall go. But we need to consider,' he said in a low voice, 'that it is not every young lady who would be willing to do what we require of her.'

'Very well.' The woman rested her head back on the cushions as though the conversation had tired her. 'But if there is any hint of misbehaviour, you will be out. Is that understood?'

'Yes, madam.'

'I will need to leave you in the care of my husband. The doctor has told me that I must rest for several hours each day. Show the girl to her room, please, Percival. By the way, what is your name, girl?'

'It's Mary, madam…Mary Swales.'

Her attic room compensated for being small and sparsely furnished by having a magnificent view of the roofs and towers of the city, surrounding the most magnificent of them all, those of The Minster. Indeed the room was as much as she wanted, for she had brought few possessions, and the vista was more than she could have hoped for. The children's nurse slept in the nursery with the younger children, so Mary had the top of the house to herself, the other rooms on this floor being shut and locked. She had followed her new employer as he'd climbed through three floors, explaining with an increasingly breathless voice that the children slept either alone or in pairs, for he liked to give them growing space. She tried, and failed, to do quick calculations in her head to determine the number of rooms she would have to clean.

'I trust you will find this satisfactory,' the Reverend Thoroughgood said, throwing open the door of her room. 'I presume you are well acquainted with your duties, having done this job in the past. I suggest we take you on for the next month and, if you prove satisfactory, we will keep you for as long as we are happy with your work.'

* * *

A week after Mary's arrival at the vicarage, she wrote to her family. She addressed the letter to Sarah-Louise, for her parents struggled with reading, and she knew her sister would convey any necessary information to them.

The Vicarage,
Church Lane,
York.
Sunday 1st October.
Dear Sarah-Louise,
I am writing to let you know that I have found a position in York. It is with a clergyman and his large family. I am sure I will be very happy here. There is plenty to keep me busy.
Please let Father and Mother know that I am set-tled. You have the address, in case there is any need for them to contact me.
I do miss you all but I am determined to settle down and do a good job here. Please write to me and let me know how everyone is at home and in the village.
Your loving sister,
Mary.

A few days later she received a reply from her sister.

5, Station Cottages,
Templesforth,
Wednesday 4th October.
Dear Mary,
Thank you for your letter. I read it to Mother and Father. They send their love to you and say they

hope you are settling well. They ask to be remembered to the vicar and his wife. I am missing you very much and so is Alice. Please do not stay away too long.

I have called to see Mrs Riley and took her milk and eggs from the farm. She said her legs were giving her pain but apart from that she was well. I told her I would call in each day to see if she wants anything.

Father came to school this week to see Miss Thompson. They have decided that I must leave next Easter, when I shall be twelve. Already I'm the oldest girl there. Only Tom Wild is the same age and he's leaving soon to help his dad on the farm. I will most likely be a maid, like you are, but I do not know where I will go. I wish I could come to York and be with you.

Yesterday Nathaniel gave us a ride home on his cart. He told us that his father is not well. The loss of the harvest upset him a lot and he has not been right since. Nathaniel did not seem happy either, not the same as he always used to be. He does not laugh and joke with us any more. He asked how you were and I told him you had gone away to York.

Please write to me soon and tell me what you are doing. Laura and Lucy send their love.

Your affectionate sister,

Sarah-Louise.

That was that then, Mary thought. *'I told him you had gone away'*. The stark words would do more than her letters to show him that she meant what she had said. Now he would for sure forget her and turn to another. Until this point she had entertained always in the back of her mind the possibility of his waiting for her, should she ever in the future decide to return. The fragile hopes melted away in the force of her sister's words. But it was as it must be. Now she would stop looking over her shoulder and instead face the future. Mary knew that the vicar's benevolence would only extend for as long as she could keep her pregnancy hidden and she had no idea how long that would be. For now though she would try to ignore it and get on with the not inconsiderable amount of work that the house in its present state of neglect would undoubtedly bring.

CHAPTER EIGHTEEN

IT HAPPENED one Sunday in early November while she was listening to another of Reverend Thoroughgood's dreary and interminable sermons. At first it was no more than a fluttering somewhere deep inside, no different from what Mary had felt many times in the last fearful months. Why it should occur now, when she was not at all overwrought, merely bored, was a mystery. But then it came again, more persistent this time, and suddenly Mary knew, and the consciousness washed through her body and retreated, leaving her a changed woman. It was the first perceptible movements of her baby.

The first weeks in the Thoroughgood household had been spent in a whirlwind of activity which, mercifully, had left little time for dwelling on the problem that had brought her here. Mary had never been so busy. It was immediately apparent that the neglect of the rooms could not be blamed on Priscilla Thoroughgood's present state. They were suffering from the accumulation of years.

In her methodical way, Mary set about bringing order out of the chaos. Realising that it was going to be the

work of months to have the house looking as she would
like it, she decided to clean one room a week, in addition to the general cooking and cleaning and waiting on
the family. She learned from Matilda, the nurse, that
there had in fact been a succession of maids employed
to do the work that she was now doing. Each of them
had left for more lucrative and less arduous employment
after a few weeks, and the accumulation of unwashed
pots and pans, the greasy kitchen range and the army of
cockroaches that nightly invaded the sticky floor of the
neglected kitchen and scullery made these the first
rooms upon which Mary would expend her energies. So,
between cooking meals, lighting fires, dusting, sweeping and running around after the mistress of the house,
she boiled water and soaked and scrubbed the dishes
until they were heaped in gleaming piles on the draining board and Mary's hands were rough and chapped
with the effort. Then she cleaned the cupboards and
washed them, before giving her attention to the range
and finally the floor. At last she stood, exhausted but
content, at the sight of the sparkling room and revelled
in Mrs Thoroughgood's surprise and pleasure when she
made a rare appearance in the kitchen to pay the visiting butcher.

Slowly she made her way through each room, pro-
gressing from the kitchen to the living room, the dining
room, the parlour and the study. She found that if she
rose at five, she would have two peaceful hours before
the family stirred. First she cleaned and lit the fires, for
the dark cold mornings of winter had arrived. Then she
would set about the daily dusting and polishing, before

preparing breakfast for the eight children who were old enough for school and who would gather round the kitchen table, argumentative and hungry, to await the arrival of their porridge. After they had been dispatched, the vicar would arrive back after saying matins and she would have to start breakfast all over again. His wife would have hers in bed and a tray would also be needed for the nursery, where the youngest members of the family and their nurse would be having a more leisurely start to the day. It would be halfway through the morning before Mary was able to apply herself to the cleaning routine that she had set herself.

The Reverend Thoroughgood insisted that all members of the household, if they were old enough, should attend church on Sunday. Accordingly both Mary and the nurse were obliged to go, although care of the babies necessitated one of them staying behind for Morning Prayer and the other for Evening Prayer. Mary, although she hadn't exactly fallen out with God, didn't feel very well disposed to Him either. So, during the long service, her bodily presence was assured but her mind was free to wander where it wanted. Just now, it was counting up the number of rooms still to be cleaned and wondering whether there was any possibility of finishing the huge task before Christmas was upon them. Seven bedrooms, the nursery—if Matilda allowed—and the top floor were all to be done. Goodness knew what she would find behind the locked doors of the attic rooms, when she reached those eventual heights.

The sudden subtle stirrings of the baby jolted her out of her comfortable charade. Of course there had been earlier times when she had been sickeningly reminded of its existence, often as the result of a chance remark made by Mrs Thoroughgood on the progress of her own pregnancy. But, more often than not, Mary could pretend that there was no baby and could even argue away her expanding figure by saying that she was eating more than was good for her in her new surroundings. Now, though, she would no longer be able to ignore its increasing presence in her life. But it was not this that shook Mary as much as the overwhelming realisation that it was *her* baby, utterly dependent on her for its life…and this realisation banished in an instant her earlier feelings of revulsion. Despite all that had happened to her, the awful circumstances of its conception, the loss of the one she loved, the separation from her family…this baby was hers…all that remained, hers and no one else's. Somehow she would manage. She would get through the next difficult months. No one could take the baby away from her. It would be hard, she realised that. But she would cope, just as her parents had coped when Alice was sent to them, just as she herself had coped in the difficult months that had led up to where she was now.

A nudge in the ribs brought Mary back with a jolt to the church service. The sermon had, contrary to everyone's expectations, come to an end and the congregation were preparing to sing. She stood in a daze, fumbling with the book, joining in eventually with the tuneful words of the closing hymn.

'There's a home for little children
Above the bright blue sky.'

The congregation sang lustily, joyful at their imminent release, and the Reverend Thoroughgood
beamed down on his children and Mary, who stood in
the middle of them, contemplating a future home for
her own child.

'It's quite an honour, my dear,' the vicar was saying to
his wife as Mary entered the dining room. The steaming dish of mutton stew that she carried seemed at odds
with the spring sunshine streaming through the sparkling glass of the windows. 'The Dean could have asked
any one of a number of incumbents to sit on the board.
He told me that mine was the name that sprang to mind
immediately.' The Reverend Thoroughgood straightened in his chair and beamed at his wife. Mary served
her mistress with a small portion and then ladled a generous helping into the plate of the delighted cleric. 'Of
course I have made arrangements to go and see the
workhouse for myself. The Dean tells me it is exception-
ally well run. Thank you, Mary. That will be sufficient.'

'It needs to be well run and a close eye kept on the
expenditure,' Mrs Thoroughgood replied. 'It really
wouldn't do for its inmates to be better looked after than
those outside or they will never want to do for themselves. There are more than enough scroungers living
at the expense of those who do an honest day's work and
see their money disappearing into the Relief.'

'Yes, Priscilla, I know your views on these things but
you must remember they are all children of God, whatever they have done or left undone.' The vicar took a
generous mouthful of stew and dumplings.

'And, as for all those girls in difficult circumstances…well, it's immoral. They should be shown the error of their ways.'

'I believe they are, my dear. It isn't easy for them. They have to give up their children when they are born. Just imagine that.'

'Oh, come now, Percival. Are you telling me that they want it any other way? They're in all likelihood only too pleased to be able to hand over their care to others.'

'Come, come, my dear. We must try and show a little Christian charity. After all, we ourselves are so blessed with our family and I for one am looking forward to the new addition to our little brood.'

'I'm sorry, Percival. I just don't feel very charitable today. The sooner this baby is here, the better it will be for everyone.' Priscilla Thoroughgood shifted uncomfortably in her chair. 'Mary, please take this plate away. I really can't face any more food. And help me up from my seat. I'm going for a rest.'

'Yes, madam.' Mary crossed swiftly over to her mistress's side and struggled to heave her out of the chair. 'Is there anything you wish me to fetch, madam?'

'A cup of tea would be nice. I shall have it in my bedroom.'

'Very well, madam.'

'My wife is very tired.' The vicar sighed as Mary turned back to clear away the plates. 'Her time is nearly here.'

'Yes, sir. It must be hard for her. Though not as hard as for those poor girls in the workhouse.' The words were out of her mouth before she could stop them.

'Wouldn't it be better if the Union paid them a little so they could continue to look after their children?'

The vicar looked at her in surprise. 'They need to be shown the error of their ways, Mary. If life is made too easy for them, they will go and sin again. Now don't concern your pretty head about things like that.' He patted her hand and, seeming to like the feel of it, enclosed it in his. 'You be thankful that you are here with us. My wife and I are very grateful for your help, you know.'

'Thank you, sir.' Mary pulled her hand away and continued to collect the dishes.

Priscilla Thoroughgood was sitting on the edge of the bed when Mary entered with a tray of tea.

'Thank goodness you've come. Go and tell my husband to send for the midwife. The baby is about to arrive.'

Mary assumed and hoped that she would be able to continue with the normal running of the household while her mistress was in labour. Instead, the midwife requested her assistance and she was obliged to listen to her mistress's screams, which were ear-splitting, and view the progress of the baby, which was rapid and trouble-free. With every scream that Priscilla uttered, Mary's terror increased. She longed to run from the room and hide in the attic or in the cellar or in the grave-yard next door...anywhere away from the noise of childbirth. As she did what was asked of her—fetching water, passing towels, sponging Priscilla's brow—she attempted to swallow her rising panic. How was she going to manage when she herself was in a similar po-sition? She did not know when it would be but she guessed it to be very soon. Perhaps her employers would send for the midwife to help *her*. After all, they often told her how grateful they were for all she had done. Her thoughts were interrupted by the rapid appearance of the baby's head and Mary was reminded suddenly of the time she had assisted Eliza Morritt to give birth to little George in the cottage next to that of her parents.

'Here it is,' the midwife said. 'A lovely little boy. And how easy. Just remember what you were like with your first.'

'I do remember,' Priscilla said wearily. 'It's a wonder I ever had another, it was that long and painful. Left to myself, I'm sure I wouldn't. But we must accept what the good Lord gives us. Mary, go and tell my husband we have a son.'

If Mary had thought that her life would be easier once the new baby had arrived, she was sadly mistaken. In addition to her normal tasks, she was expected to be up and downstairs, seeing to her mistress's every whim. The baby had been taken to the nursery and Nurse Matilda's new charge meant that she herself needed help with the younger children.

It was a week now since the birth and in that time Mary seemed never to have stopped running. Even the daily outing to the shops had become more of a chore than a pleasure. The vicar had celebrated Easter over two weeks before, its early position in the church's calendar for that year meaning that only a few hardy blooms had defied the chill easterly winds and shown their spring colours. But now the weather was turning warmer and the daffodils, restrained for so long, had burst open in a riot of colour in gardens and parks and on the banks supporting the ancient city walls. But Mary hardly noticed.

Opening the kitchen door, she placed the heavy basket of groceries on the table, sitting for a minute to regain her breath. Her boots were uncomfortable and her feet ached and for the last two days there had been a nagging pain in the small of her back. Her corsets dug into her ribs and she longed to remove them and allow her baby to kick as it wanted. She had noticed how its movements had become less recently and hoped that she was not doing damage by lacing the corsets so tightly. She struggled wearily to her feet as the door to the kitchen opened and the vicar entered.

'Ah, Mary, my dear, I am expecting a visit from the Rural Dean later this afternoon. I would be grateful if you could provide us with tea as soon as he arrives. Are you feeling quite well, my dear?' Mary had felt her abdomen contract painfully, causing the colour to drain from her face.

'I'm fine, thank you, sir. It was just a little warm outside and the basket was heavy.' She began to unpack its contents and turned to the cupboard. The vicar stood by the table watching her.

'I would like to say, on behalf of my wife and myself,' he began, 'how much we have appreciated your help over these last days with my wife's confinement. You have, over the past months, and recently, made my life…our lives, that is…very comfortable. I am very grateful to you.'

Mary continued to fill the shelves with her purchases. 'Thank you, sir. It has been a pleasure working for you.'

'I hope you will continue to give us pleasure,' the Reverend Thoroughgood said, making her start, for the words were spoken in her ear and at the same moment she felt him behind her and his hands around her distended abdomen. She jumped away in horror and gazed at the cleric, whose face showed a horror even greater than her own. Another spasm made her wince.

'You're…you're…with child,' the vicar spluttered. 'I don't believe it. You're with child. What do you mean by this?' His face had gone very red and he towered over her.

'Please, I need your help. I told you how my last employer was unkind to me. This was the result. Please, you've got to help me.'

'Help you? Help you? I'll help you all right. You immoral hussy! How could you have deceived us like this? After all the kindness we've shown you. The humiliation of it! What would my poor wife say if she knew? It would kill her. She must not know about this. She was worried from the outset about your morals and how they would affect the children. You must go now, before the children come in from school.'

'Go? Go where? I don't have anywhere to go. I thought I could stay here with you and continue to look after you and your family just like I've done these past months. After all, sir, it weren't my fault that this has happened.'

'Not your fault! What are you talking about, girl? Of course it's your fault. Don't pretend to me that you're not to blame. You will have led this man on, whoever he was. You women are all the same.'

'We're not all the same!' Mary screamed at him. 'It weren't me, it were him.'

'Be quiet, won't you,' her employer demanded, 'or my wife will hear you.' He went up to her and she winced again, this time because she thought he was going to hit her. But he took her by the arm and pulled her towards the door.

'Where are you taking me?' she breathed. The vicar hesitated, then smiled as if a sudden thought had come to him.

'To the workhouse, of course. You will be my first customer.'

'No, I won't go. I can't go there, sir. Don't make me. They'll take my baby away. Please, sir, no!'

'Be quiet. That's what the workhouse is for, the likes of you, who need to see the error of their ways. Now, wait there while I fetch my hat and coat and we'll go together.' He spun on his heel and hurried from the room.

She had no intention of waiting anywhere, not if the result was incarceration in the workhouse and, worse, the removal of her baby without her having any say in the matter. Snatching up her cloak from the back of the chair where she had thrown it, she quickly opened the back door and stepped into the sunshine, closing the door quietly behind her. Then she hurried, as fast as she was able, away from the church and its adjoining vicarage and into the heart of the city.

CHAPTER NINETEEN

WHY she entered The Minster Mary didn't know. After all, her abrupt dismissal at the hands of the Reverend Thoroughgood, a representative of this particular branch of the church, should have been enough to send her in any direction other than this edifice to the glory of God. But perhaps this would be the least likely place that he would come looking for her. She shivered as she thought of him. Underneath all his saintly words and charitable works he was no better than John Crowther. The Stationmaster at least did not pretend to be something that he wasn't.

It was always peaceful in The Minster. She sat gazing up at its vaulted roof and towering columns, watching the light spilling through the stained glass to make shimmering patterns of colour on the stone floor at her feet. Her eyes rested on the Madonna and child. Even they, for all their hardship, were not as alone as she. The pains were coming more often now. But they were nothing new. They had troubled her for a few weeks. It was just that they were getting more frequent and more severe than they had been. She supposed this to be the nature of things. She looked at the impassive face of the Madonna, as if to derive guidance as to what she should do. It was something in the set of the Madonna's lips that reminded her of her old friend Martha. Or perhaps it was the serene expression, as she gazed down from on high.

Martha would know what to do. Mary had always been able to turn to her when she was in any kind of trouble. She wished she were with her now. It was hard being alone with her pain. Martha had warned her not to lose touch with her family. But she had done. Not that they would be over pleased to see her in this condition. She looked at the statue again and frowned in concentration. Martha had told her that she had nearly lost touch with her family in York… She waited until a stronger than usual pain coursed through her body and died away…Martha's family in York. What was it that she had said? It was her sister-in-law…and her name was Hannah. She was a widow and she had two daughters and some grandchildren. And she lived in Marygate—that she had no difficulty in remembering. Perhaps, if she could have a word with Hannah, she would help, just as Martha had always done. She got up quickly and just as suddenly sat down again as another pain lanced through her. Waiting until it had ebbed away, she pulled herself out of the pew, more slowly this time, and whispered her thanks to the enigmatic Madonna.

Outside, dusk was gathering. Walking very slowly, Mary made her way towards the river. She had an idea that she would find what she was looking for in this direction. Instead she found the picnic spot where she and Nathaniel had sat with her three sisters the previous summer. She stared at the grass, imagining the blue checked cloth and on it the ham rolls and cakes and milk, warmed by the sun. She remembered it all so well.

Suddenly she felt too weary to go any further and, easing herself down on to the grass, she sat with her back against the trunk of a tree, watching the river flow darkly away beneath the bridge. She closed her eyes and allowed herself to think of Nathaniel. How she missed him. How she wished he were with her now. No, she thought, not with her now...not when this baby was not his. He must never know, would never know because she would never go back. She would never tell him.

It was darker now. The pains were worse. She eased herself down into a lying position to try and get some relief. She looked at the stars and remembered looking at them in Martha's garden...wondering if the same stars would be shining when she reached the city. They were the same, of course, but equally as unattainable. Martha's garden! She forced herself to think clearly. She had been thinking about Martha's garden and what they had been talking about there. She was meant to be finding her relative, Hannah. With a huge effort, she rolled on to her knees and dragged herself up. As she did so she felt a rush of fluid and an unbearable spasm of pain. When it had passed she set off again along the esplanade, calling on Nathaniel or Martha or even the Madonna to help her. She turned into the first road that she reached and read its name by the light of a nearby gas lamp…Marygate. Now she knew that someone was taking care of her.

A lamplighter was making his way down the far side of the road. Endeavouring to pull herself together, she called to him, 'Do you know anyone by the name of Hannah who lives in this road?'

The lamplighter put down his pole and came over. 'Hannah? Hannah who? Don't you know her surname, like? You all right, miss? You don't look too good to me.'

'I'll be all right when I find Hannah's house. It's a big house. She lives in it on her own.'

'Well, miss, the only one in this road that I know of is Mrs Tuke…widow of William Tuke, the Quaker.'

'That's it! She's the one…Tuke…that's what Martha called her. Will you show me which one it is?' She gave a groan of pain.

'Yes, miss, it's that tall un halfway up the hill… straight on to t' road,' the man said anxiously. 'Would you like me to go and knock?'

'I would like to take hold of your arm while I climb this bit of a hill,' Mary said breathlessly. Side by side and very slowly they made their way up the road to the house that the lamplighter had pointed out. A young to middle-aged woman answered the knock. She was small and plump with a friendly face and a ready smile.

'Excuse me, madam,' the man said, 'but this young lady is looking for Hannah Tuke. Is she in…? Only the young lady doesn't look well at all.'

The woman at the door gasped and opened the door wide, catching hold of Mary as she half stepped and half fell into the hall.

* * *

All through the long night huge shadows came and went across the ceiling of the room. Through her pain Mary could hear the whispered voices of women and every now and then the deeper tones of a man. Eventually light began to creep into the room and, when she next woke, the candles had been extinguished and sunlight was flooding in through large windows, hung with heavy curtains of a rich crimson colour. She slept again and woke to the sound of screams, realising with a thumping heart that they were her own. The next time she looked it was dark again. The pain and the darkness mingled and coalesced, like some awful nightmare from which she could not rouse herself.

In the distance a woman's voice was calling her name. She fought to open her eyes. How strange that sunlight had once more chased away the shadows. What was happening to her? How long had she lain here?

'Mary! It's Hannah. Can thou hear me?'

She tried again and this time her eyes focused on an ageing face framed with grey hair and language that reminded her of her old friend in Templesforth.

'Mary, thou hast a baby daughter. Listen to her greeting the day.'

Mary turned her head and saw, sitting in a chair next to the bed, the same woman who had opened the door to her that night when she'd arrived unannounced and unexpected. Cradled in her arms was a baby with black hair and an insistent cry. Mary looked from the baby to the woman who was holding her and from her to the elderly woman leaning over the bed. She closed her eyes and shook her head slowly from side to side, tears seeping from beneath her eyelids.

'I'm sorry,' she began. 'I'm so sorry. I never meant to put you to all this trouble. What have I done? Oh, what have I done?'

'Don't worry, Mary. You've done exactly the right thing.' It was the younger woman speaking. 'Martha has told us about you.'

'Martha! How does she know I am here? How do you know that I know Martha?' She shook her head in confusion.

'You said an awful lot while you were under the influence of the laudanum,' went on the younger woman. 'I'm Esther, by the way, and this is my mother, Hannah. It was Hannah you were seeking, if you remember.'

'I thought she might help me. Martha had told me about her. But I didn't intend for this to happen. What an awful thing to turn up on your doorstep.'

The mother and daughter both laughed, identical laughs that rang out across the sunlit room.

'How long have I been here? I seem to remember a lot of night and a lot of sunshine.'

'Thou hast been here for two nights,' Hannah said. 'Thou were not in a good state when we did take thee in. Thy baby has not been in a hurry to arrive.'

'I thought I heard a man's voice. Am I right? Who was it?'

'We called the doctor. Your little girl was turned around and it was more difficult for her to make progress. That's why she was so long in coming. Do you not want to see her?' Esther put the baby on the coverlet beside Mary, who gazed down at the little girl, her own flesh and blood…and that of John Crowther.

'She has clothes! Where did they come from?'

'From my sister. She has had two children of her own and, though they are grown big, she has kept the baby things. Maybe she thought I would need them in time.'

'She's very tiny.' Mary put a finger into the baby's palm and the little girl clenched her own tiny fingers tightly round her mother's.

'She needs thee to feed her,' said Hannah.

'Oh, no, I couldn't do that.'

'Of course you could,' said Esther gently. 'She's hungry. She's been waiting for you to wake up. Come, I'll help you.' And she put the baby to Mary's breast and watched as that strongest of bonds was established between a mother and her newborn infant.

CHAPTER TWENTY

THERE was a gentle tapping on the door of Mary's room and Hannah entered. Mary turned from the window where she had been studying the people in the street far below and the river sparkling in the spring sunshine. Hannah had insisted that Mary rest after dinner and, although she'd tried to argue that in the countryside she would have been working as normal by now, in truth she was glad of the chance to be alone and to think of what she was going to do. It was a week since the birth of her baby. Hannah had been kindness itself but Mary knew that she could not stay with her indefinitely. And she could no longer ignore the fact that the baby would make it impossible to find work. There seemed no solution to the problem. For hours each day she agonised, turning over the possibilities in her mind and dismissing each one.

'Mary, do thou come and meet my eldest daughter, Martha. She arrived half an hour ago and is particularly anxious to be introduced. Is all well with the baby?' Hannah tiptoed over to the crib and peeped in.

'She's fine, thank you, Hannah. I think she's grown bigger already.'

'Will you bring her down to meet Martha?'

'No, I don't think so, not while she's asleep.'

Immediately on entering the parlour Mary was struck by the similarity of mother and daughter. Both were tall and well-built, moving with poise and serenity. Both had deep-set grey eyes and a square, firm jaw. They were dressed, in the Quaker manner, simply and without adornment. Hannah's hair was silver and lay gathered into a coil at her neck, her daughter's similar but dark brown with, here and there, the first strands of grey.

'It's good to meet thee, Mary,' Martha said, coming forward to shake her hand. 'My mother has told me of thee and thy care of my aunt Martha. Thou must sit down and tell me all about her.' *Her aunt Martha!* How strange that sounded. How odd that in all these years the two Marthas, aunt and niece, had never met. Martha introduced her children, a boy and a girl, like their mother tall and striking. Both were about to return to school after the Easter holiday. At home children of their age would have left school and be working in the fields or on the railway, Mary reminisced.

'Thy thoughts betray thee,' said Hannah, laughing. 'Thou art wondering why these two grown people are not out earning their living.'

Mary blushed. She had no idea her thoughts could be so easily interpreted.

'It's the way of Friends,' she explained. 'We believe that education is very important. And we believe that men and women are equal in God's eyes and should be given the same opportunities to learn. These schools in York, and some others too, were founded by Quakers and are run by them.'

'And I left school when I were only twelve,' Mary said. 'I would like to have stayed on to learn more but that's the way of things in t' countryside.'

'My husband helped to start a school for adults,' Hannah said. 'In 1848, it was. Boys and men from fifteen to twenty went there. Now it takes men up to twenty-five. Most of them haven't had much education and have even less money but many are employed in the city. They tried to run a similar one for lasses, but that was never so successful.'

'There's nothing to stop thee doing some learning while thou art staying here, is there, Mother?' Martha said, looking from Mary to Hannah.

'Oh, but I can't stay here,' Mary said quickly. 'I've overstayed my welcome, as it is.'

'Nonsense! We love to have thee and the baby here. And just where were thou thinking of going?'

Mary looked down at her hands. 'I hadn't decided yet.'

'Then we'll hear no more about it,' Martha said decisively. 'Would you like to do some more learning, Mary?'

'I would like it very much. It's something I've always wanted to do.'

'Mother, we could ask Esther to help Mary. She has time to spare now that the adult school for girls has finished,' Martha said, excited at the prospect.

'But she must be busy with raising her own family.'

'No, Mary,' said Martha. 'Esther has no children of her own, which is how she came to be teaching in the adult school at such a young age. It took away some of the sadness of not having her own family. Esther may be very happy to help.'

Mary had warmed to Esther immediately, when the effects of the laudanum no longer prevented her from understanding and remembering the identity of the small vivacious woman with the twinkling brown eyes who'd sat at her bedside nursing the baby girl.

The following day, when Esther visited her mother, the idea was put forward and she was as excited as her sister had been. They decided that, to start with, Mary should spend two hours each afternoon with her books. This would follow the hour's rest which Hannah insisted upon.

Esther brought a copy of *The Old Curiosity Shop* and Mary began to read about poverty and hardship in the cities, worse than ever she had seen in the countryside. Esther told her of the part the Quakers had played in reforming conditions in prison and in abolishing slavery. She explained how important she thought it was to see the good in everyone. Secretly Mary wondered if Esther would be able to see the good in John Crowther. Together they studied maps and Mary learned about places she had never heard of and ways of life she could not have imagined.

'How do you know all these things?' asked Mary in admiration. 'I'm sure I could never learn so much.'

'I'm sure you could if you had the opportunity,' Esther said. 'I was very fortunate that my parents were so much in favour of education for girls as well as boys. We both went to the school founded by the Quakers. I did well, so my parents helped me to gain a place at Cambridge University. They'd just opened a women's college a year before. It was the most exciting time. There weren't many of us and we were treated quite differently from the men. We had to get on with our work and keep quiet. We weren't allowed out alone and we had to have someone with us, even when we went to lectures. We never mixed with the men students…though, strangely enough, it was at the Meeting House there that I first set eyes on my Timothy. He was travelling round in the ministry, as they say amongst Friends, and was planning to come north. When I moved back after finishing my studies, here he was. We've been wed now for eight years. He's been a wonderful husband…it seems as though this gift of learning has come in place of children. And I've my niece and nephew to enjoy as well as the books, so life is never dull.'

Esther chose from her mother's bookshelves a selection of poetry. Mary wept over Wordsworth's descriptions of the fields and rivers and flowers because they reminded her of home. She choked over Byron's words, which spoke more eloquently than she could ever do of the feelings she had had for Nathaniel.

'I'm sorry to cry like this,' Mary explained, 'but the words put me in mind of home and someone very special I used to know.' And she told Esther about her love for Nathaniel and how it had all come to nothing.

'What of the baby, then?' asked Esther. 'Are you not telling him about it?'

'It's not his babby,' Mary replied, and she explained about that too.

It seemed to Mary that Esther was the only person to whom she could talk about her doubts. Both Hannah and her eldest daughter, Martha, were so definite. They acted as though there was no problem about Mary's future. She feared their disapproval if she spoke. Esther was different. Esther would walk up and down with the baby on her shoulder, listening in silence to Mary's worries. Mary would watch with a heart full of sorrow as her friend bathed and dressed the little girl in the clothes that had been put away for the baby that Esther and Timothy never had. Esther made light of the fact that she and Timothy had no children but Mary had seen a similar sadness in her eyes as had been present in her old friend Martha's when she'd spoken of the loss of her baby.

Every night, when the house was quiet, Mary fed her baby and laid her back to sleep. Then she paced the floor or stared out of the window at the stars or cried hot tears into her pillow, as she agonised over her future and that of her baby.

It came to her late one evening as she sat at the window of her room, looking out at a new-moon sky, speckled with stars. The baby was restless, so Mary too was unable to sleep. It was a month since the birth. Leaning her elbows on the windowsill, Mary breathed in the cool air. She felt her usual conflict of emotions…happiness at being with her friends in York, for that was what they had become…sadness that she must soon leave them…exhilaration at the book-learning she had never thought she would have the opportunity to do…and over it all her sorrow at the inevitability of the decision that must be made—should she surrender her baby and give them both a future?

'Esther,' she began a few days later, as soon as they had exchanged greetings and sat down. 'There is something I have to talk about before I lose my courage.'

'What is it, Mary? Do you not like all this booklearning? If so, I shall understand. I do sometimes get carried away in my enthusiasm.'

'Oh, no, it's not that at all. I love it. Although, I suppose in a way it is part of the problem because it's making me think about the future.' Mary got up from her seat and walked slowly to the window, where she stood looking down at the busy street below. Taking a deep breath, she continued in a level voice. 'I have come to a decision about the baby. I can't go home because my family don't know about her and, any road, I'd have nowhere to live. And, besides, them as I love most and hate most are still there. I can't do as you say and see the good in everybody. I can't see the good in that man and I still hate the thought of this babby being his. So what I'm suggesting is…that is…I wondered…whether you and Timothy would have her. I know that the idea may be strange and not what folks commonly do. But I've seen the way you care for her. And I've seen t' look in your eyes when you talk about the family you and Timothy would have liked.

'I can't keep her. I know that now.' She paused, momentarily unable to continue. 'I can't keep her. And I'd like nothing more than for you and Timothy to bring her up as your own.' She stared at Esther with a face full of anguish. 'Tell me I'm not completely mad, Esther.'

Across Esther's face had flitted conflicting emotions of delight and sadness, hope and despair, as Mary talked. Now she stood up and, crossing the room, put an arm round Mary and hugged her.

'Mary, you don't know what you're saying. You love your baby. I can see you do. You can't give her up. It's against nature. It wouldn't be right for me to take her, though I would willingly do so.'

'It's against nature to be attacked by such a beast as John Crowther is,' said Mary bitterly. 'No, I've thought about nothing else for the last few days and it would be best for all of us. But only if that is what you would like, of course.'

'To be truthful, Mary, Timothy and I have often talked about taking one of the orphans out of the work-house. There are so many whose mothers died through lack of care and we would have had our own little one to bring up. The only thing that has stopped us was the thought that one day we might have one of our own, but that seems increasingly unlikely.'

'Then please say that you will at least think about it,' said Mary. 'If it wasn't for Martha at home and your family here, I could be in the workhouse too. This would be a way of thanking you for all your care.'

CHAPTER TWENTY-ONE

Now that Mary had made her decision, she resisted her natural inclination to pour all her love and affection into caring for her daughter. She did not waver from her intention to give the little girl to Esther, if her friend was agreeable. Esther told her that she must discuss it with Timothy and the following week they both came to see Mary.

'Art thou very sure that thou wilt not regret thy decision?' Timothy looked at her over his spectacles, his pale eyes full of concern.

'Oh, I'm very sure that I will regret it…many times. But what else can I do? Hannah and Martha say I should stay here and they will find work for me, but that wouldn't be right. Besides, a child needs a father as well as a mother and I'm sure you would give her what she needs. No, I have decided.' Mary hesitated before continuing. 'There is one thing that worries me about all this. Esther has told you about the circumstances that led to me having the baby?'

'She has…but be assured that what thou hast been through will make no difference to how we feel.'

'I only meant that you might regret taking on the offspring of such a man as he is. I know we are taught to see the good in everyone but there's a deal of difference between what we are taught and putting it into practice.'

Timothy smiled and Esther interrupted before he could reply. 'Timothy and I have discussed it for many hours and we're both perfectly sure of our feelings. It's your baby and that's good enough for us. And if in the future God is good enough to give us one of our own, so much the better. Your little one will be as our first-born and no one will know otherwise.'

'Then that's final,' Mary said with an attempt at a smile.

After a further two weeks Mary began to wean the baby and insisted that Esther should come and feed her from a bottle. They found the instructions in *Cassell's Household Guide* and into a quarter of a pint of milk and the same of water mixed a teaspoonful of sugar. At first the baby struggled and objected to the new routine but slowly she settled and began to drink greedily. Mary encouraged Esther to come as often as she could and to dress and bath the little girl. During these times Mary would watch impassively, her still, quiet body concealing a turmoil of emotions. She knew that it must be a difficult time too for her friend and she imagined her trying to hide her growing excitement while fearful at the same time that Mary might change her mind.

The weather was warm now and Mary suggested that Esther should take the baby out in the perambulator. She could walk along the nearby esplanade and anywhere else that took her fancy. At first Esther was reluctant.

'Suppose I see any of my acquaintances when I am out walking, what shall I say to them? After all, nothing is settled.'

'Everything is settled,' replied Mary. 'It has only to be finalised. And it is to be expected that you and t' babby should get used to one another.'

The hardest decision in those early weeks was the one not to have the baby christened and so risk eternal damnation. Mary had always, without giving it much consideration, accepted the ceremony as part of the early weeks of a baby's life. Words of the parson's prayer echoed in her mind, that the baby should be delivered from the wrath of God and received into the ark of Christ's church. She now discovered that the Quakers believed that such ceremonies as these were unnecessary. Esther explained that the Friends preferred simplicity rather than symbols. So Mary decided that if the baby were to be raised in a Quaker family, she must abide by their beliefs. The naming of Mary's daughter, however, ceremony or not, must still be carried out. Esther felt that the choice of name belonged to Mary, but Mary insisted that it was Esther's. In the end it was decided that they ask Timothy and he called her Ann. Mary thought, but didn't say, how ironic it was that the baby, who was half John Crowther's, should be named after his wife.

As spring blossomed into summer, Mary hovered between motherhood and a future, at the same time lonely and hopeful, hesitating to look beyond the next few difficult days.

At the end of June, Esther and Timothy collected the baby for whom they had waited so long and their house was silent no more.

Mary was exhausted. She felt as if she had walked for miles. Setting out in the mid-afternoon she had gone first to the Minster. Taking advantage of its cool interior, she lingered, enjoying the ornate majesty contained in its height and space. Then she set off again, along Minster Yard into Stonegate with its many bookshops. It was here, she remembered, that Hannah had said that her husband had worked until his death. She wove her way through a cluttered maze of little streets, the ramshackle overhanging dwellings shutting out the brightness of the sun, and found herself on wide and spacious Parliament Street. Nearby, the lantern tower of All Saints' Church dominated the Pavement. Another beautiful church graced the skyline at the end of Ousegate and a third as she made her way to Lendal. At the bridge she descended to the Esplanade, stopping to listen to the distant sound of a train as it groaned its way out of the station and began to pick up speed. It was a sound that always brought a pang of homesickness. She walked where she and Nathaniel and her three sisters had walked on that sunny day just a year ago. Was it only a year ago? She felt as though she had grown ten years older, not one. She had regained the slender figure of her country days but not the healthy glow to her skin that had always made her so attractive. Like a plant too long indoors, her face was pale and her normally exuberant hair lustreless and neglected. She looked up at the bridge. What was it that Nathaniel had said to her sisters? 'This bridge is the same age as Mary. Who do you think looks the most beautiful?' Looking now at the impressive figurehead staring out from the curving span of the bridge, she suspected that the answer would not be the same now as then.

Now that her baby was gone, Mary was eager to do the same. Much as she longed to see Ann again, she knew this was not only unwise, but also unfair to Esther and Timothy. Understandably Esther would want to visit her mother and show her the miracle of the everyday things that her baby was doing. She would feel awkward doing this while Mary was still at the house. But it wasn't just this. There was a restlessness inside her, a feeling that she could make a fresh beginning only by moving to a new place entirely, hard though that would be for the second time in a year.

'Hannah,' she began, two days after Esther's departure, 'I don't feel as I can stay any longer. Please don't think me ungrateful. But it would not be fair on Esther for me to stay and it would be hard for me too when she comes to visit.'

'Don't think that I haven't noticed,' replied Hannah. 'Do thou feel like returning to thy home, only I know Martha would be overjoyed to see thee again?'

'Oh, Hannah, I can't, not at the moment. Not while them as did me harm are still there. Of course I would love to see my family again. I miss them very much, especially Sarah-Louise. She's just started working, you know. Helping out at Temple Farm, of all things. Nathaniel's parents are elderly and last year's bad harvest brought them a lot of worry. So she's working there a bit—general housemaid, like. And she looks after Martha the rest of the time. Of course, what she has always wanted to do is move out of the village to somewhere bigger, but just at the moment it seems she's needed there. 'Appen she'll be able to do that later. I'm not like Sarah-Louise. I never wanted to leave the village and move to a big city. Although, to be fair, you wouldn't think we were in t' middle of a big city now.'

She had sought out Hannah in her favourite place, a large, enclosed and peaceful garden at the back of the house. A high surrounding brick wall kept out all but the most insistent of the city sounds and had grown its own covering of mosses and ferns to soften its bareness. Around the borders ostentatious peonies wept their red petals over the lawn, interspersed with irises, keeping quiet sentinel, and coreopsis, echoing the colours of the sun. The scent of roses was heavy in the June air.

'Well, I can't deny I'll be more than sorry to see thee go, but it is no more than I had expected. Hast thou thought what thou would like to do?'

'Well, I've had several years' work now as a general maid. I shall look for another post, though it will need to be somewhere away from York. But there are always places looking for a maid.' She stood up and walked slowly over to a large rose bush. Drops of dew still lingered within the velvet pinkish-yellow petals of the blooms. Mary bent to smell the fragrance.

'Nonsense!' exclaimed Hannah. 'Thou could do so much more than that. Why, I know from Martha that thou art well versed in the herbs and using them to treat illness. Thou has nursed sick people and, from what Martha says, thou hast a rare touch with them. And, since being with us, thou has shown thyself a willing pupil under Esther.'

'I suppose you're right,' said Mary, surprised. 'I hadn't thought of all that. But I still don't know what kind of a job that would suit me for.'

'Well, as I said, it doesn't surprise me that thou has asked to leave. So I've been giving it some thought. How about seeking work in one of our boarding schools? Not in York, of course, but there are others not so far distant. There is all kind of help needed there, not just teaching but caring for the children day by day and when they're ill. They've no parents there to look after them, remember, so the members of staff have to be mother and father to them. And, of course, there's all the cooking and sewing and cleaning for hundreds of children. Never a dull moment, to be sure.'

'But they wouldn't have me. I'm not a Quaker.'

'Not so. They do have members of staff working there who are not members. Consider it, Mary. It might be just the new start that I think thou art seeking.'

CHAPTER TWENTY-TWO

BY THE time the carriage was making its way up the steep hill to the start of the village, the horse was beginning to tire. The journey had taken most of the day, for both horse and driver were elderly. They had stopped at Tadcaster for refreshment and again in Pontefract. A warm wind was blowing from the south and clouds of dust rose from the dry mud of the road, giving a nebulous look to the travellers as they neared the brow of the hill. Used as they were to the flat countryside of York, it was hard work negotiating any inclines, let alone such a hill as this one.

The way through the village was lined with huge trees, whose branches linked arms across the road to form a cool green canopy, through which the sun scintillated and sparkled. Houses lurked behind the trees, only the roof tiles and an occasional window being visible to passers-by. On the triangular village green an ancient elm presided over a weatherworn stone cross, and at the highest point of the green a lych gate marked the entry to an equally weatherworn church, whose tower could be seen above the tall trees of the churchyard. On the opposite side of the road stood two or three shops and a long, low row of almshouses. The female occupants of these houses were seated in the sunshine outside, exchanging the latest gossip about the village and its inhabitants. They looked up in interest as the driver slowed to ask a passing farmer directions to the Quaker school. He pointed in the direction they were taking and, half a mile further on, the imposing buildings of the school were visible among the trees.

Mary had enjoyed the journey and the sense of adventure that came with it. Hannah had insisted that Robert drive her in the coach, although Mary had argued that she could easily have travelled the distance by train, there being a direct line southwards from York. It was her first time in countryside other than the low-lying flat plains that drained the Aire and Ouse rivers and she gazed at the undulating fields in wonder. There, the huge expanse of the sky had influenced every mood of the countryside and the people beneath it. Here, the sky was subservient to the rippling hills and luxuriant trees that covered so much of them.

She had been pleased when she'd learned that the school was in a village. She'd imagined a school such as the one of her childhood in a village like the one she had left behind. But this was altogether different. The brief glimpse of the houses they had passed had shown them to be on a much grander scale than anything back home. These resembled the big house in the neighbouring village, in which she had learned to be a housemaid. The dwellings were strung along the road but, here and there, others could be seen in terraces, rising steeply up side streets or edging the horizon of the hill. At home it was the work of a few minutes to walk from one end to the other of the village. Here, she imagined it to be the work of an afternoon.

Robert slowed the carriage and turned into a narrow opening that ended in a cobbled yard with a row of stables, all of them empty at present but several showing signs of recent occupation. Mary climbed down from her seat and stretched.

'You see to the horse, Robert, while I go and see if anyone is expecting me.' She walked through a stone archway and found herself facing the imposing frontage of a large and beautiful Georgian building. Its walls formed three sides of a square, the fourth side of which was bounded by a black iron railing that separated it from the road. At both ends of the railing large gates opened on to a semicircular driveway, enclosing a garden. A young man was so intent on turning the soil that he did not notice Mary approaching and started at her voice.

'I'm sorry to disturb you,' she said, 'but I've come to work here and was wondering if you could tell me where to go.' The young man straightened up, smiling. He was slim and tall, with a mass of dark brown hair that he brushed back from his eyes as he turned to look at her. Her heart missed a beat. It was not because he was good-looking, though he was, or because he looked at her in a more friendly and open way than she had been accustomed to in the city. It was the feeling, not entirely pleasant, that she had seen him before. She knew this was impossible. It was the first time she had been in the vicinity and, if he had been to Templesforth, she would have recognised him.

'I'm pleased to meet thee,' said the young man. 'I'm Ted, one of the gardeners, and thou must be Mary. Jane Moxon asked me to keep an eye open for thy arrival, but I was so carried away by my digging, I entirely forgot. Did thou have any trouble finding the school?' he asked, taking out a handkerchief and mopping his brow. He wore cord breeches and an old leather waistcoat over a white shirt, the sleeves of which were rolled up to reveal tanned, muscular arms.

'What? Oh…no, it was quite straightforward really. I'm sorry. I'm a bit tired after the journey. It's so warm today and the road was very dusty.'

'Aye, it is that,' Ted said, laughing. 'It'll be worse still if we don't get some rain soon. If you'd care to follow me, then, we'll go and find Jane. She's bound to find thee summat to eat and drink.'

He led the way to a large double door that stood open and she stepped inside and found herself at one end of a long, cool and very gloomy corridor. Their footsteps echoed on the stone flags. Mary turned to him.

'Where are all the children?' she asked. 'It were never this quiet in school at home.'

Ted smiled at her. 'It's not this quiet usually. The lads and lasses have all gone to their homes for the summer holiday. School finished a week ago and there was plenty of noise and chaos then, while we got everyone packed and off. They need it though, poor little bodies. They've had no break since Christmas. And of course it gives us five weeks to thoroughly clean the place and do the repairs that we haven't had time to do all year.'

At the end of the corridor Mary could see, to one side, an expanse of grass with gardens and trees beyond. Skirting this, a second corridor led to a wide flight of stairs, splitting to right and left above. They were just about to climb them when a door on the right opened and a woman's shape filled the doorway.

'Ted, you've found her, then. I was beginning to wonder when she would arrive. Welcome, my dear. Come on up.'

'Mary, this is Jane. I'll leave thee in her capable hands and go and get on with my work.' Ted turned and began to retrace his steps. Mary watched his familiar stride as he walked back along the corridor, shook her head in perplexity, smiled up at Jane's welcoming face and climbed the stairs to where she stood.

Hannah had been right. It *was* the new start that Mary needed. Her first few weeks at the school brought with them the peace she craved. Though situated in the centre of the village, the school was not dependent on it. Indeed, there was very little need to venture beyond the walls and fences that enclosed it and contact with the world outside was minimal. It had its own farm and its own laundry. House linen was sewn and clothes repaired on the premises. Many of the teachers had themselves been educated in the school and had little experience of life beyond its rarefied atmosphere.

Peaceful she may have been; idle she was not. As Ted had said to Mary on her arrival, the five weeks' long summer holiday was the only opportunity to clean the building and undertake the many repairs and alterations that were not possible in the presence of nearly three hundred energetic scholars. Corners that only rarely saw the light of day were exposed and swept, sending spiders racing for cover and mice scurrying back into their holes. Curtains were taken down and washed in the huge stone basins of the laundry room and hung out to dry in the hot sun. All the bed linen was examined for holes and signs of wear were made good. The kitchens, scene of so much industry in term time, were thoroughly cleaned and the stone floor scrubbed till it shone. Mary rolled up her sleeves and enthusiastically set to work. She had warmed immediately to Jane Moxon, whose job as housekeeper meant that she directed the staff in this flurry of activity. Jane had been at the school for more years than she cared to remember. She had joined the staff as a young teenager, employed as housemaid, and had worked her way up to her present position.

'There's nothing that I haven't lent my hands to,' she would say, 'apart from the job of cook. And that's just as well, 'cos I can't be doing with any more weight, what with all the sampling of meals that I would be called upon to do.' And, as she chuckled, her plump body shook beneath its voluminous starched apron and her eyes disappeared into the folds of her face like currants in a teacake.

At the end of a day's work Mary would wander into the gardens in the warm sunshine. The buildings forming the main part of the school appeared similar to those at the front entrance. They were ranged around three sides of a huge square of lawn, down the centre of which ran a path of flagstones. This path was known as 'The Flags' and Mary was told that this was the only place where boys and girls were allowed to talk to one another and, even then, only if they were related.

'Even brothers and sisters aren't allowed to talk to each other at any other time?' asked Mary, whose rudimentary schooling had not allowed for such conventions.

'Aye,' replied Ted, who had been showing her the gardens where he spent a good part of each day, 'although I've heard that many call themselves cousins so they can get to walk together on t' Flags.'

Beyond the grass lay the gardens. Mary had discovered them early. They reminded her of Hannah's walled and secret garden in York, for they grew a similar riot of flowers and the scent from them was just as sweet.

'Why is it,' she asked Ted, 'that the gardens lower down are divided into squares? Are you experimenting with different kinds of flowers?' She had noticed how one plot contained a confusion of marigolds, another was more delicately patterned with pink and purple edging plants, and a third contained three or four herbs that she immediately recognised.

Ted laughed. 'These are the garden plots belonging to the boys. I help them—when they want help. Advise them what things are best to grow and how to grow them. It's a long tradition of the school that those as want can have a little plot of their own. I think it helps them to have summat to care for, when they're away from home for so long.' He paused, then went on. 'Thou must miss home, Mary. Do thou have family nearby?'

'Oh, I've been working in York for some time now,' she replied evasively. 'I'm not expecting to go back home yet, though I have to admit I do miss them all very much, especially my sisters—and my old friend Martha who was very good to me.'

'York! I was brought up there and learned my trade in and around the city. I've no family there now, so I don't think I'll be going back. Besides, here it's like being in a family. You'll find that out for yourself in time.'

She felt it already. She had been accepted as one of them by the household staff and by as many of the teachers who had remained during the holiday. How it would feel when the children returned for the new term, she had no idea.

It was true what she had said earlier to Ted. She did miss her family and her friend Martha…and another whom she had not mentioned and would never mention. To talk of Nathaniel would be to stir up feelings that threatened to overwhelm her. So she refused to let her mind dwell on her past love, pushing the recollection of him and anything to do with him into the hidden depths of her mind and heart. The problem was that this isolated tranquil spot, so far away from the hustle and bustle of activity in the school, encouraged those very feelings she was trying to suppress. Here, nature around and enveloping her, drew from her those emotions which both gladdened her heart and made it weep. Here, she had the greatest difficulty in denying the exhaustion heaped on her body and her spirit by the months of pain and anguish that had preceded her journey to this place of opportunity.

But deny it she did. And, pushing the lid firmly back on the Pandora's box of emotions, she would make her way slowly back through the fertile summer vegetation to the school gardens where, like as not, she would see Ted at work in one of the greenhouses. And she would wave to him and go on her way. It was good to have someone of her own age to talk to, especially someone with as open and friendly a nature as Ted's. But he was still a relative stranger and she would not and could not unburden herself to someone she had known for so short a time.

Mary assumed that the start of the school term would mean an end to the peace she had come to enjoy. But she soon discovered that the children brought with them a peace of their own. Like all children—and she thought again of her sisters—they had boundless energy. But when they rose from their beds, they dressed in silence. And in the dining room they ate in silence. She was amazed at the way they could sit quietly each morning in the Meeting House, without so much as a fidget between them.

The return of the children brought a dilemma. Mary had been accepted on the recommendation of Hannah. There remained, however, an ambiguity as to what her role would be. Would she be a housemaid—a job she had been doing very willingly over the past month? Or would she be asked to put to good use the other skills that Hannah's family were so certain she possessed? Charlotte supplied the answer.

Charlotte had just turned eight. She had endured the

long journey from her home in Devon in increasing dis-
comfort. Her bones ached and her throat was sore and,
every time she nodded off to sleep, grotesque images of
snakes and monsters caused her to wake with a pounding heart and feverish skin. In London she and her
brother had boarded a second coach in the charge of an
elderly Friend, who had agreed to escort them, together
with two other children bound for the school. By the
time they arrived at the school gates, the little girl was
in a sorry state. At the top of the stairs she encountered
Jane Moxon who, with Mary, was seeing the last of the
girls into the dormitories.

'Why, Charlotte, what in the world is the matter
with thee?'

Mary knew immediately. The sight of Charlotte's
blotchy face and the strange pallor round her mouth reminded her of the weeks she had spent nursing Alfie in
the railway cottage next to her own home.

'I think it may be scarlet fever,' Mary whispered to
Jane. Jane looked at her in consternation.

'Oh, my goodness! That would be a dreadful start to
the term. Let's hope you're wrong.'

'I hope so too. But she looks awful like a neighbour's little boy I looked after with the illness. And
there's her brother who were travelling with her—and
the two other children—they are all at danger of starting with the illness.'

'Oh, my goodness,' repeated Jane, clapping her
hands to her cheeks and more and more flustered with
every word that Mary spoke.

Charlotte was accompanied to the small room kept

for such emergencies and a brief inspection of the rash spreading rapidly over her hot body confirmed Mary's suspicions. Sarah Pumphrey, the school nurse, was fetched and she, in turn, sent for the kindly and ageing Dr Wood, who lived in the village and looked in on the children on the few occasions they needed it. Mary breathed a sigh of relief that she was not to be revisited with the worry and responsibility she had previously had to bear. She was not, however, to escape so lightly. The doctor wanted to know who had identified the illness and been alert enough to isolate Charlotte's travelling companions. Jane was quick to speak up for Mary.

'It were Mary, our newest member of staff, sir. She were able to say what the illness was, just by looking at t' little lass's face. I were right impressed. She's only been here a month, but she's worth her weight in gold.'

Dr Wood turned to the nurse. 'If you take my advice, I would suggest that you ask whether Mary can assist you in caring for the boys and girls. She has either had plenty of experience in dealing with illness or she possesses a rare talent.'

So Mary found herself once again in the sickroom, caring for a feverish child. How much older and wiser she felt herself to be now than when she had been doing the same thing only a year before. She nursed Charlotte back to health and, when her brother succumbed to the infection, she nursed him too. Miraculously neither of the two children who had accompanied them in the coach from London caught the fever. To Mary it was a miracle too that both brother and sister recovered without any of the problems that Alfie had endured.

After being confined to the sickroom for the first weeks of the school term, it was good to be in the fresh air again. Her surroundings had a strange, unreal quality to them, as if she was seeing them in a dream or through a distorted looking-glass. The leaves were beginning to show the rich tints of autumn and Mary took a deep breath of the sharp tangy air and shivered. She looked across the gardens to where her favourite spot lay beyond the trees and the cricket field. It suddenly seemed a long way to walk but she had been given the rest of the day off before resuming her normal job, whatever that was to be, so she could take her time…all day if she wanted. She set off across the grass, still wet following a heavy dew that morning. Sunbeams glinted intermittently between the thinning trees and she shielded her eyes from them, aware of a nagging pain across her forehead. Her hands gave a welcome coolness to the skin of her face. She dragged her feet slowly through the woods, amazed at how the enforced inactivity of the sickroom had drained her energy. Eventually she reached her favourite spot overlooking the stream and the fields beyond and sat down on the stile. There was no sound of children to mar the peace, for school was in progress and all heads, including those of the children she had nursed, would be bent more or less over their books.

Over the curve of the hill two carthorses, led by the farmer, were dragging a heavy plough. The land stretched into the distance, covered with stubble, spiky as a man's unshaven chin. She shivered at the memory that sprang to mind. Then, pushing the thought away, she drew from her pocket a letter that had arrived not half an hour before. Screwing up her eyes, she tried to focus on the writing. It was in a hand she did not recognise. She tore open the envelope and the address hit her with a jolt, not least because of what she had that moment been thinking about. It was from Annie Crowther. She had heard nothing from Annie since leaving Templesforth. As she read, the past flooded back.

Station House,
Templesforth.
Friday 5th October, 1883.
Dear Mary,
Sarah-Louise gave me your address. I do hope you do not mind my writing to you. I was surprised to learn that you are working in a school. Sarah-Louise says that you are happy there.
I miss our friendship very much. It is lonely here and there is nobody to talk to. Little Johnny is growing into a fine young man. You would hardly recognise him. I am coping well with everything there is to do. John does not think so. He says I am not a patch on his first wife and he wishes she had not died. I try to be a good wife to him but I cannot behave how he wants.
I know it is wrong for a woman to talk about her husband behind his back. I would not do so normally but I am very worried about him. He is drinking heavily every night after he has finished work and sometimes earlier in the day as well. I fear that he might lose his job or that he might

have an accident. I try to talk to him about his
drinking but you know how he gets.

I am sorry to burden you with my troubles. I know
you cannot help but it helps me to tell you. Please
write back if you can.

Your affectionate friend,

Annie Crowther.

By the time she came to the end of the letter, Mary
was shivering violently and a cold perspiration stood out
on her brow and trickled down her back. It was the
mention of that man, she knew, that had caused such a
reaction. She must pull herself together, for she realised
that the letter was a cry for help. She pulled out a handkerchief and mopped her brow. Then she began to read
the words again. But now she could not understand
what was written at all. Why was Annie lonely? She was
married, wasn't she, and had little Johnny to look after.
She couldn't be lonely with a husband, surely. Her husband! Her husband! What was he called? She glanced
at the page again. Ah, yes! John. John Crowther. John
Crowther, with his alcohol-laden breath and his coarse
unshaven chin. John Crowther with his rough hands
and brutish insistent body. His face leered in front of her
as she stared at the dancing black specks on the page.
Then she fell forward on to her knees and retched and
retched into the long grass. At last she sat back, leaning
for support against the rough wood of the stile, closing
her eyes against the sun's glare. Tears leaked from beneath her eyelids but she was too exhausted to lift her
hand and brush them away.

She sat there for several minutes, feeling the dampness of the long grass seeping through her skirts. Eventually she opened her eyes and folded the letter, replacing it in its envelope and pushing it into her pocket. She would reply later, when its contents ceased to upset her so. Now she must get up before she was soaked through and make her way back up to the school and attend to all the things that she had neglected while she had been looking after Charlotte and her brother. She put her hand on to the fence to steady herself and was overcome by a second bout of nausea which caused her to bend her head once more to the ground. Afterwards she lay there, grateful for the cool comfort of the grass on her hot face. She must have fallen asleep, for when she looked again the sun had moved out of the shade of the trees and was making its way towards the horizon of hills behind her. She sat up suddenly, her head spinning, and clasped her arms tight around her body in an attempt to ease her violent shivering. She lay down again and closed her eyes. She would wait for her energy to return and then she would set off up the path to the school.

Strange yellow suns whirled and spun around her, licking at her shut eyes and hammering at her brain. Suddenly a black oval appeared in the seething yellow mass and a deadly creature made its way towards her through the blackness, bloodshot eyes matching its forked tongue, its face glistening and bloated, rough claws clutching at her throat, choking her. She tried to scream but the words would not come. Then the creature spoke her name, the voice one that she recalled with horror. She tried to push it away, arms flailing uselessly in the air.

'Mary, Mary! It's all right. You're safe now.'

She tried to say that she was not safe, that she had been captured and was being taken far away. And then she was falling, falling and there was nothing to hold on to, no one to stop her descent into the blackness beneath her. The blackness surrounded her—comforting, soft. And she remembered no more.

It was on days like this that Ted relished his job the most. To go out into the garden after breakfast and be greeted by the colours and the mists of October and know that the day would be spent in tidying and pruning the decaying and discoloured borders was as much as he had ever desired. He could never decide whether it was this or the exciting new growth and delicate freshness of spring that he loved most. It mattered little for one would follow the other within a few months and he had no wish to change what he was doing.

He had been in the greenhouses, coaxing the last of the tomatoes to turn red before the first frosts rendered their turning impossible, when Mary crossed the lawn. He had waved at her and she returned his salute, not interrupting her slow progress towards the cricket field. His heart continued to beat at the faster pace it had adopted on first seeing her as his eyes followed her across the lawn. It was good to see her enjoying the sunshine again. She had been shut indoors for so long, only venturing out for short intervals when someone else was free to watch over the sick brother and sister, that he was afraid she would lose the improvement brought by her first months in the school.

Mary had told him about her favourite walk and he respected her privacy, although more than once he would have liked to walk by her side. If he were honest, which he liked to be, he knew that the garden, spring or autumn, was no longer as much as he desired. Mary's presence in the school had awoken in him for the first time yearnings for a woman's company and hers in particular. The work had certainly tired her, he thought, watching her figure grow slowly smaller. He had been attracted from the first by her energy and enthusiasm. Now, though, she seemed listless and slow, when he had imagined she would be skipping with the joy of being in the fresh air. He turned his hands back to the tomato plants but his thoughts remained with the young woman who had now disappeared among the trees.

At six o'clock in the evening there was a knock on the door of his room and an anxious Jane Moxon popped her head into the room in answer to his invitation.

'What's the matter, Jane?' He was surprised at her presence at this late hour in the men's quarters.

'Begging thy pardon, Ted, but we wondered if thou did have any idea of Mary's whereabouts.'

'Maybe she's walked into the village, making the most of the time before she gets back to her ordinary work. How long has she been missing?'

'She didn't have any tea…and she wouldn't be out walking now. It's nearly dark.'

Ted glanced towards the window. He had nodded off

on his return from work and hadn't realised how late it was getting. 'I suppose thou hast been to her room?'

'Yes, of course. Her cloak is missing, so she must still be out somewhere.'

Ted got up and took his jacket from the back of the chair. The strong smell of tomato plants that clung to the fabric reminded him of when he had last seen her. He remembered too the less than energetic progress he had witnessed that morning. Surely she would not still be in her favourite place at this late hour. But where else would they start looking?

A storm lantern hung in the work shed. He lit this and set out along the path that led towards Mary's haunt. He had no idea where she liked to sit, so he swung the lantern back and forth slowly to light up the cricket field and the woods beyond. It was an almost impossible job, he thought, to successfully cover such a wide area with such a small light. Keeping more or less to the path that led to the periphery of the grounds, he came at last to the stile. His heart sank as the lantern lit up the beginning of the broad sweep of field. How could he hope to find her now? He made to climb the stile when his boot caught fast in something at the side of the step. Projecting the lantern towards the impediment, he saw that his foot was snagging the hem of a skirt. Mary was unconscious at his feet, her head half buried in the long grass. He placed the lamp carefully on the ground and put his hand to her cheek. The skin was burning. She groaned and turned her head, staring at him with unfocused eyes.

'Mary! Mary! It's all right. You're safe now.'

He picked up the lamp and rested it on the stile before bending to Mary. She flung her arms out, mumbling that he must leave her alone, but he picked her up and the next second her head rested unmoving against his chest. Taking up the lamp, he proceeded very slowly up the path. Were it not for anxiety about her condition, he would have revelled in the proximity of her body to his own. In the event, he could hardly wait to reach the open back door of the kitchens, from which light was streaming to assist his path.

CHAPTER TWENTY-THREE

NATHANIEL stretched out his long legs beneath the table that held his beer, cupped his hands behind his head and closed his eyes. The evening sunlight slanted across the river and set fire to the distinctive mass of fair curls. It was over a year since he had last set eyes on Mary but he could still hear her laugh and see her dark curls as though it were yesterday and his body ached for her now as much as it had done on that last Sunday evening before the storm of the following week. He knew that every day that passed took with it the possibility that he would ever see her again.

He had ceased trying to make sense of it all. He had cursed himself for not going to see her, as he had told Sarah-Louise he would do, when she had brought him that first letter of Mary's. Instead he had written back, concealing his perplexity and hurt with angry words. After his anger had subsided, he preferred to believe that something had occurred to force Mary to change her mind. What it could be, he had no idea, when only that Sunday evening they had sat together in the field making plans for their wedding in the autumn. She had assured him that it was not his father's doing and this was, in any case, not likely when his father had already agreed, though reluctantly, to let them rent a farm cottage that was standing empty. Mary and his mother had wasted no time in attacking the cottage with scrubbing brushes and tape measures.

That Mary had simply fallen out of love with him or had met someone better, his pride refused to acknowledge. After all, it was a step up the social ladder for her and the reason his father was so against the match.

'What did I tell you?' his father rounded on him, when Nathaniel could no longer put off telling his parents that Mary and he were not going to be married. 'The hussy! I said no good would come of this. She's 'appen gone off with some common lad not worth the time of day. I told you that you should have chosen someone from your own class, not such an illiterate as she is.'

His mother said little. She and Mary had got on well from the start and she had made no secret of the fact that she regarded Mary as a replacement for her own daughters who had long since married and whom she seldom saw. They had Mary's sister, Sarah-Louise, working for them now. Of course his father had objected to that too. He wasn't having any relative of 'that wanton' working in his house. But his wife needed help and there was little other help to be had in the village. So Sarah-Louise came four days a week and was proving a godsend.

It was Sarah-Louise who first told him that Mary had gone. He had known that she was still in the village for some weeks after they last met. Where was she that evening when he had come looking for her and Station House was in darkness? Why hadn't he knocked? After all, he'd known that the Crowthers were away. There had been nothing to stop him. He had wanted only to prevent Mary's embarrassment if she had been in her night attire and, if he were honest, he was unsure what his own reaction would have been if she had greeted him scantily dressed.

He knew Sarah-Louise was trying to help, had sensed that she hated being the bearer of bad tidings in the form of those letters. He felt sure that she was as baffled as he by the sudden reversal of the wedding plans. 'I'm sure she still loves you,' she said when she handed over the second letter. He kept his distance, however, for the tone of that letter made it clear that she did not wish to see him. In late October he gave Mary's younger sisters a lift home on his cart. He always enjoyed doing this, for the Swales girls were fun to be with. But the main reason for his generosity, if he were honest, had always been the possibility of a glimpse of Mary when he arrived at the cottages. He turned to Sarah-Louise, who was occupying her usual place by his side, and asked how Mary was.

'She's gone away.'

'Gone away? Where?'

'She's gone to be housemaid to a family in York. I've had a letter from her. She likes it there. But I miss her. I wish she didn't have to go.'

It wasn't often that he agreed with his father but he had to acknowledge that there was something to be said for choosing someone of a similar standing to himself and not a woman so lacking in conventional good manners, who was so prepared to trifle with his affections.

Opening his eyes, Nathaniel took a sip of his beer and gazed across the bend in the river to the road beyond as it wound its way on to Bankside. The harvest had been gathered and this year it had been a good one. The fields stretching into the distance stood shorn of corn and lay relaxing in the rays of the setting sun. Tomorrow he and his father would begin ploughing. So the seasons continued to turn, regardless of the ups and downs of the people who made their living from the soil. At least there had been no repetition of the disastrous weather of the previous year. The family had come close to losing everything and the worry had made his father ill.

Nathaniel sighed. His father was growing old and had not regained his former strength since last year's difficulties. More and more he was relying on Nathaniel. For all their disagreements, Nathaniel acknowledged how hard his father had always worked on the farm. It was only natural that he should be concerned about his son's future. Recently he was again dropping hints that Nathaniel could do worse than pursue a friendship with Rhoda Precious. Henry Varley had gone so far as to invite Arthur Precious and his daughter to the Harvest Supper, and had arranged things so that Nathaniel had found himself seated next to Rhoda. She was a nice enough girl. She always dressed well, although her ample skirts looked as if they concealed far too scrawny a frame. Not really the build of a farmer's wife. He would not mind if she could be a little more cheerful.

But she sat at his side and surveyed the proceedings with an air of condescension, as if she was above the feasting and merriment that the end of harvest and a drop of good ale had induced. He tried and failed to engage her in conversation and eventually gave up and drank more of the good ale than was prudent. Nevertheless, he would persevere. She was probably shy and found such social gatherings difficult. Arthur Precious had mentioned to his father that he would like the family to join them for the Christmas Day festivities. A further opportunity would present itself for better acquaintance then.

A shadow fell across him and he looked up to see the large frame of George Morritt.

'Na' then, Master Nathaniel, do you mind if I join thee?' He sat down at the table without waiting for a reply and looked across at Nathaniel. 'I was on t' early shift today and just fancied a half or two while t' weather holds. To tell you t' truth it's good to come along here for a bit of peace.'

'Aye, it must be noisy, having the trains up and down every hour of the day and night. It's not as if you get a break from the railway when you're at home.'

'You're right. There's always summat going on in t' station yard or on t' lines. But you get used to that after a while. It becomes second nature, like. No, it's Station House that's causing a breach of the peace, if you know what I mean. Just between you and me, t' Stationmaster's getting very partial to his drink and he could end up in a spot of bother, to my mind. Trouble is, he's not waiting till he's finished work before he's having a drop. Don't get me wrong, I've no complaints about his work—he's a good boss to work for. But I am worried t' passengers will be put at risk if it goes on. What do you think I should do, lad? You've always been keen on relations between workers and their bosses.'

'Aye, that's right, I have. Mind you, it's an uphill struggle. I try to encourage our men to join the Agricultural Labourers Union. That way they have a voice and they're less likely to be exploited by the bosses. And there's more chance of them getting a fair wage and being able to better themselves. They're reluctant to get involved though; they think they're more likely to suffer intimidation if they join—and they're sometimes right, they do. I've often been at loggerheads with my father over it all, but it's something I feel very strongly about… But that isn't helping your problem.' He was silent for a while, thinking.

'If it gets to be where his drinking is affecting his work and may put lives in danger—and it's the safety of the passengers you have to consider—and the staff that work with him—and his own safety too, then you have no choice but to report it to the railway bosses in York. But it might be best to try and talk to him first, man to man. How do you think he would take that?'

'Not at all well, I suspect. He's got a reet temper on him when he's roused. And he's not a man as makes friends easily. But I were thinking along t' same lines. I'm not one for grassing on a colleague. I'll try and raise the subject with him.' George frowned and went on. 'It's not just work I'm troubled about, though. There's summat up between him and his missus, I'm sure of it. Ever since they moved here with that babby they've had their ups and downs. We all do, like, but them more than most. It's Annie I'm worried about. She never goes out of that house, and I hear him ranting at her summat awful. What goes on between a man and his wife is their business, I've always thought, but I can't stand by and do nowt if he could be hurting her. Once or twice last year I did suspect that he might be knocking her about. I said as much to your Mary one evening. Didn't hear owt else about it, like. But then I wouldn't expect to…your Mary was never one for spreading gossip. Oh, I'm sorry, Nathaniel, talking about Mary, when I've heard how things stand between the two of you. It's helpful to talk about the problem, though. I'll try and act on your advice. Can I get you another drink for your trouble?'

'Thanks, George, that would be very welcome.'

George rose from his chair and made his way into the murky interior of the Wheatsheaf. Nathaniel mulled over what the signalman had been saying. The mention of Mary had made it difficult for him to concentrate on what George was telling him. It was true, though—Mary never passed on gossip. She *was* always loyal to her friends. She had spoken not a word to him about any trouble at Station House. A disturbing thought took seed in his brain. Could it be that Mary's departure was in any way connected with troubles in the Crowther household? Had she been given the sack for seeing or hearing more than was good for her? Had she perhaps challenged John Crowther's behaviour in order to protect Annie? His skin ran cold. Was it possible that John

Crowther had threatened her—or worse—had actually attacked her?

He thoughtfully sipped the beer that George set down on the table in front of him. The sun had dipped below the horizon now and the undersides of the clouds and slow-moving water of the river reflected the pink of its passing. Trees and fields were losing distinctness in the encroaching twilight.

'You must be able to sit and watch the world go by from your elevated position in the signal-box,' Nathaniel said with an attempt at light-heartedness.

'Well, I'm pretty busy with the trains mostly. But, yes, there are quiet spells when I can sit and study my surroundings. You can learn a right lot about animals and birds and their habits through the seasons from up there. Sarah-Louise always came for her nature lesson after school. I miss her company, now she's working for your parents at the farm. She used to sit on t' top of the steps and tell me what she had learned in class that day. And then she would want to know the latest about the pheasant family or the swallow babbies in t' eaves of Station House.'

He hesitated. 'The truth is, I've seen some rum goings on over the months. 'Appen folks forget I'm up above when they're going about their business down there on t' ground. Take last year, for example. T' Stationmaster and his wife and babby went for a week to t' seaside. Left Mary to look after the house. Any road, middle of t' week John Crowther comes back. Didn't tell no one he was coming, like, but that were not so surprising as t' weather had been bad and there was middlin' of flooding. I guessed he had come to take charge. But no! He gets off the train and runs down t' bank and into the house. Not long after I see Mary making her way to the house. Skirts all wet and covered in mud. She must have been seeing for herself how far the river had over-flowed its banks. She goes into t' house and then there's nothing, not a glimpse of anyone for hours. I were on extra duties that day—all hands to the plough, as it were—because of the weather, so I were still in t' sig-nal-box later in t' afternoon when I see the kitchen door open and t' Stationmaster appears. He creeps back to the line and hides in t' bushes, waiting for the train. And then he's gone, as mysteriously as he came. And I'm left wondering whether I've imagined it all.' He shook his head slowly and peered into his mug.

'What about Mary?' prompted Nathaniel when a minute had passed and George seemed disinclined to say more.

'That's the strange thing. I didn't see her at all. Normally she was in and out all day—pegging out wash-ing, collecting eggs, picking fruit—that kind of thing. The evening drew on and the house stayed in darkness. 'Appen she had popped out to her mother's or to Martha Riley's and I missed her. I saw her on the Friday, though. T' post-man had come wi' a telegram and he couldn't make her hear, though he knocked several times. I told him I'd take it round later on. She were there then, when I went round, but she didn't look good at all…like she hadn't been out of the house for days, though the weather were good by then. And she said nowt…couldn't wait to get back in-doors. Not at all like the Mary we all know and love. The day after that the family were back, but not Mary. She never came no more.'

'Where did she go…back to her parents?'

'Nay, lad. They'd no room for her there. She were planning to stay wi' Martha Riley but then our Alfie were took ill and she came and looked after him. Our 'Liza were expecting, like, and Martha Riley said it were dangerous for her to mix wi' t' scarlet fever. She must have been wi' us…oh…best part of two months. Then she left and I never saw her no more. Sarah-Louise told us that she'd gone to York, like. I thought it were strange. She never seemed one as fancied the big city. Always seemed contented with her lot here.' He glanced sideways at Nathaniel, drained his tankard and set it down on the table. 'Any road, I'd best be off. T' missus will be expecting me and it doesn't do to keep a good lady waiting. Thanks for your company, lad.'

'Thank *you*,' replied Nathaniel, his head spinning with the story he had heard. Was it possible that John Crowther had attacked Mary and she was too frightened to continue working for him? It certainly made some sense of the mystery of her departure. But why had she not come to him? Why had she written to him that she no longer loved him enough? Surely she did not have that much loyalty to the Crowther family that she would protect them at such expense to herself. He replayed the picture that George had described—John Crowther's unexpected and secretive arrival at the house, Mary's return soon afterwards and then several hours spent in each other's company before John departed as furtively as he had arrived. His stomach lurched. Of course, there was another possible explanation. Mary and John Crowther had an understanding. They had arranged this liaison, knowing that Annie was out of the way and the house would be theirs for the afternoon. Although the realisation sickened him to the heart, it was the only explanation that made sense. Mary would know that she couldn't stay in the Crowthers' employ, neither would she be able to stay in the village. She had gone off as soon as she could get away to arrange employment at a decent distance. There could be no other reason for her suddenly breaking off their engagement and her subsequent refusal to see him.

He stood up abruptly and nodded his goodbye to the landlord. Behind him a harvest moon hung yellow above the eastern horizon, not yet high enough in the sky to give any light to the road ahead. Martha Riley's cottage, when he passed it, was in darkness. It came to Nathaniel then that she was the only one who could confirm or deny his suspicions and clear up the mystery of Mary's behaviour. He did not know Martha but she must surely know of him from Mary. Should he go and ask her to explain? Would she be willing to tell him what had been going on or would her loyalty to Mary prevent her from talking to him? Did he really want his suspicions confirmed? As things stood now, he could still believe in her innocence. Was there any point in troubling the old lady, when Mary had gone and would not be coming back? He would decide over the next week or two whether to call on Martha.

Passing the end of the track that led to Station Cottages, he thought of George. Poor George. He sensed that the older man had been seeking to help. Instead he had, without realising, made things much worse.

He breathed deeply. The weather was set fair for the start of ploughing. Quickening his step, he passed under the railway bridge and up the lane. Blackie and Princess, the shire-horses, had been stabled in order to be fully rested for the hard work ahead of them tomorrow. He gave each of them a handful of sweet-smelling hay and watched their breath steaming around him in the cold air as Princess nuzzled his pockets, looking for further titbits. Moved by this simple act of friendship, he buried his face in her soft mane and caressed her neck. Then he turned and walked over to the farmhouse and, opening the kitchen door, went inside to join his parents.

CHAPTER TWENTY-FOUR

MARY could remember nothing but a sea of faces that swam in and out of her field of vision as the time passed. How *much* time had passed she had no idea. She knew only that her throat, which had been too inflamed even to allow her to swallow water, was now settling and she could attempt a few spoonfuls of the thin broth that Sarah arranged to be sent up from the kitchens. When she looked at her thin arms she saw that the rash covering them had now faded but that the skin of her palms was dry and flaking. Worst of all now were the pains that flitted from her back to her hips and then to her knees or her elbows, flaring without warning and then moving on just as quickly to other joints…this, and the tiredness that made her feel as though she had cleaned the whole school single-handedly in a day. When she attempted to do anything, even sit up in bed to ease her back, her heart would thump in her chest and she would become too breathless to talk.

'You must have complete rest,' Dr Wood said. He had been a frequent visitor to her bedside, his kind and caring face looming out of the blackness into which she had been plunged. She recalled words spoken in a whisper to Sarah Pumphrey during the darkest days of her illness.

'I blame myself for putting her in charge of those two young people. Her resistance was so low, of course, after all that she had been through. If I had known sooner, I would not have risked it.'

She remembered wondering then how he could have known what she had been through, for she had said nothing about her previous life to anyone at the school. She asked Sarah one day when the nurse had been vigorously rubbing her back and helping her to turn on to her side to avoid the bedsores threatened by her immobility.

'Well, at the beginning of thy illness, the fever did loose thy tongue and we did unwittingly learn a lot about thy past life.'

Mary's pale face flushed in alarm at the thought that she may have talked about her baby or, even worse, the attack by John Crowther.

'Don't worry. Thy secret is safe with me,' the nurse said enigmatically, plumping the pillows up behind Mary.

'How long have I been here, Sarah?' asked Mary, looking out of the window to the bare branches and grey sky beyond.

'It's November now. Thou were very poorly at first. We all thought thou weren't going to pull through, thou were that ill. It were Ted that found thee, though I doubt thou can recall that. Thou were down by the field end, slumped in t' grass. If thou'd been there the night, I doubt whether thou would have lived. Leastwise that's what Dr Wood says. He's been reet good, coming every day, like, to check on thy progress. He's taken to thee, right enough.'

'You have all been very good to me. I don't deserve it,' Mary said in a small voice and began to cry and, in her weakness, couldn't stop. She cried for the baby she had given away and for the man she had lost and for the ending of the life that would never return.

'Come now,' Sarah said brusquely. 'That's enough of that. Thou must put on a brave face, else thou't never going to get better.'

The doctor's orders had been that Mary was to stay in bed at least a month. Every day he continued to come, listening intently to her chest, while she looked optimistically at his professional face that gave nothing away.

'Is my heart affected?' she asked him one day. He looked at her sharply. 'I do know a bit about scarlet fever,' she told him. 'When I lived at home, I were taught by a wise woman what the after-effects could be. I know that it can cause trouble with the heart or with the kidneys.'

'You certainly know something about it. It's true that your heart was affected but I can no longer detect signs of weakness. You should make a full recovery.'

'When can I start work again? Only I've been here at the school since July and I've been in bed for weeks. Look at the state of my arms and legs. I need to be doing some work again.' She held out her wasted arms in front of her face and examined them.

'You are not ready to start work again just yet. But you can begin to get up for a short time each day.' He turned to Sarah Pumphrey. 'Next week she can start going for a daily walk to regain her strength. But make sure she doesn't go anywhere in a hurry!'

The other visitor who came every day was Ted. He never arrived empty-handed. He might bring a bowl of shiny horse chestnuts, salvaged from under the fallen blanket of golden leaves…or a late rose, sheltered by a protecting wall from the chill autumn winds. Sometimes he would pick an apple or a pear from the cellar, where he was storing this year's crop of fruit. Sarah told him what the doctor had said and Ted asked Mary if he could accompany her on her walks to make sure she came to no harm. He was not anxious, he told her, to be obliged to come looking for her when she had gone on one of her nocturnal meanderings. The following week, therefore, he waited for Mary by the kitchen door and they set off slowly, doing a circuit of the garden, she leaning heavily on his arm for support. As her strength returned, so did her independence. The doctor, however, was not prepared to let her return to her full duties for a few weeks yet.

Sarah Pumphrey, the school nurse, seemed intrigued with Mary's knowledge about herbs and their uses. When Mary was well enough, she helped Sarah in the restocking of the medicine cupboard. Sarah's own arrival at the school ten years before had been a lifesaver, she confided to Mary, the dirt and smoke of Leeds having played havoc with the delicate state of her lungs.

'Thou has to see it to believe it,' she explained to Mary one day, as they checked on their supplies of chlorodyne, camphorated oil and oil of cloves, before the expected rush of winter coughs and colds. 'Such a crush of houses, side by side, back to back—rows of them, running up hillsides, huddled under huge factories, and the smoke billows out from the chimneys and falls straight down into the back yards, over the washing. On a bad day the women have to take the clothes in and wash them again. The lads and lasses run around in rags and barefoot, even at this time of the year, and they breathe in all the smoke and fumes and their chests get bad as a result—the grown-ups too. The powers-that-be are beginning to clean up the streets now and put in proper drains, so there's less cholera and typhoid and such like. But folk are so poor and their children so hungry that they pick up every disease that comes their way.' She was interrupted by a vicious spasm of coughing, which left her struggling for breath.

'It would have been the death of me if I'd stayed any longer,' Sarah went on. 'Mother said I always suffered from a weak chest, right from being a tiny baby. I suppose working in the Infirmary, in the middle of all that smoke, was not really sensible. I couldn't believe my eyes when I arrived here and there was all this space and the air so fresh and clean.'

'It's like this at home,' said Mary. 'Fresh air and fields stretching for ever. Except, of course, for the trains. My father works on the railway, see. He's a plate-layer.' Sarah looked at her blankly. 'That means he looks after the track,' Mary explained. 'He makes sure it's in good condition and he and his men repair the line. He's the ganger—he's in charge. It's dangerous work but he's very good at his job,' she added proudly. 'Any road, our house is right next to the railway so every time a train goes past there's such a noise and rattling and the garden's full of smoke and soot. Mother goes on alarming about her washing—odd times she's had to wash hers again too! But somehow it's different—it's still the countryside. There's still room to breathe.' She paused as a sudden rush of homesickness swept over her.

'Why do thou not return home, if thou dost miss it so much? Dost thou not want to admit to thy parents what thou did with thy baby?'

Mary stared at her. 'What do you mean?' she stammered. 'What do you know about the baby?'

'We all knew about it, when thou were ill. Thou did talk about nothing else. There's some of us think that thy illness were God's punishment for the sin of giving thy baby away,' Sarah said slyly.

'Who thinks that? It were summat as couldn't be helped. Whoever thinks that doesn't know owt about it.'

'Well, all I know is, if I had a young man, I would make him marry me, especially if I was carrying his child.'

'I don't have a young man!' Mary protested.

'Oh, so where did thy baby come from, Mary? It's the Virgin Mary now, is it? I always thought a baby needed a man. Maybe it's for the best that thou hast got rid of it, in that case.'

Sarah's harsh words haunted Mary over the next weeks. Was her illness really the result of what she had done? Was God angry with her? Was her baby safe or had she condemned her to everlasting damnation because of her decision not to go ahead with a christening?

Mary felt Sarah's ambivalence towards her keenly. At

times she seemed genuinely interested in Mary's knowledge of herbs. At other times her spiteful words would wound Mary deeply. She remembered the words of the doctor after she had identified Charlotte's scarlet fever. He had suggested to the nurse that Mary's talent should be put to good effect. Perhaps Sarah was jealous...although she had no reason to be, Mary thought, because the nurse's knowledge far outweighed her own.

'Don't let her bother thee,' Jane Moxon commented, when Mary mentioned her worry. 'Sarah has always had a bit of a chip on her shoulder, especially when there is someone around who is younger and prettier than herself. I've heard tell,' she whispered, 'that she had a young man in Leeds, who left her for someone else, and she's never got over it. So it's not surprising, I suppose, that she's a bit envious of thee.'

Mary shook her head. 'Well, she's no need to be envious of me. I'd give anything for the last year not to have happened.'

'Where did thou learn to use the fruits of the hedgerow to such good effect?' Sarah asked Mary a couple of days later. Twice on her recuperative walks she had taken groups of the older children to gather rosehips, and the bottles of thick pinkish-red syrup now filled one shelf of the store cupboard.

'I had a dear friend who used to grow herbs in her garden,' Mary replied. 'In her younger days she used to walk miles, gathering them from t' fields. She showed me where I could find all the best ones. Then, little by little, she taught me how to make the medicines and what they're used for. I shall never know as much as she did.

She keeps a huge book on the shelf in her room. It contains all there is to know about the uses of herbs and such like. Mind you, that hasn't stopped Martha adding to it over the years, so every time you try to look summat up, bits of paper flutter out everywhere like a snowstorm.'

'Does she not make medicines now?'

'Not for a long time. She taught me so that I could carry on her work in t' village and around. But it didn't work out that way. She's old now. She used to say when I were with her that she wasn't long for this world. I should dearly love to see her again before she goes.'

'Hast thou decided not to return home then, Mary?' Sarah questioned, as though she could not resist goading Mary.

'It's all right, Sarah,' Mary replied. 'I shan't get under your feet…and I've no intention of staying here for ever.' In uttering the words, however, she realised how sorry she would be to leave the people who had taken her in and made her feel so welcome.

If Mary had been disposed to return to her home village, there was little chance of her being able to do so for some time. As her strength returned, the housekeeper was determined that Mary's training as a housemaid should not be neglected. Along with several other women, she cleaned and polished and laid fires, for the cold days of winter had arrived. The schoolrooms were heated, not very efficiently, with a series of steam pipes. In the Meeting House, where the children gathered every morning before the start of lessons, under-floor heating with hot air flues helped to delay the onset of chilblains but in the library and the headmaster's room, as well as the staff quarters and the rooms where the children spent their evenings, there were more fires to be laid and lit and tended than Mary cared to count. She tired easily, so Jane Moxon suggested that at the end of the school day groups of girls join Mary in the sewing room and help with the endless stack of mending. This way Mary could continue to work, tackling the endless job of sewing and mending, while, at the same time being able to sit and rest. As well as the making and re-pair of the pupils' clothes and the bedding and furnish-ings of the school, orders were frequently taken from the village and beyond, and the manufacture of baby clothes and the sewing of quilts was much preferred to the darning of socks and the turning of hems in a pile that never grew smaller.

Mary loved this quiet hour in the day. She sat among the girls and helped to lessen their homesickness by lis-tening to their talk of homes and parents and much missed brothers and sisters. *Such little lasses to be traipsing around the country,* she thought. As the days shortened and winter's icy fingers began to poke their way into every unheated corner of the school, the girls began to talk of Christmas.

'When I first came to the school,' explained one of the oldest pupils, 'there was no holiday in the winter. The only time we went home to see our families was in the summer. That's better than it used to be, though. We were told in lessons last week that there used to be no holiday at all. Imagine coming here as a tiny lass and not seeing thy parents again till thou was grown-up.'

'I would like to see my mother during term time, like

some of the boys and girls do,' said Charlotte wistfully, having endured her bout of scarlet fever without the presence of either parent.

'It's easier for some to visit when they live so near,' said the first, 'but thou hast hundreds of miles to travel from thy home.'

'My parents couldn't afford to come and see me,' added Charlotte's best friend. 'Father has a bad leg and can scarcely walk now and hasn't been able to work for years. In mother's last letter she wrote that we would have to "make do" at Christmas. I think that's her way of saying there won't be any money over for little presents.' The girl was busy rectifying this situation by sewing gifts for her parents and many brothers and sisters—a lavender bag for her mother, a linen handkerchief for her father, small rag dolls for her youngest sisters, bookmarks of differing designs for her brothers. Her three brothers were also pupils at the school and Mary knew from what Jane had told her that such families were only there because the Quakers paid for the children of Friends 'not in affluence'. Indeed the school had been founded to give an education to these children. Still, she thought, it was a rum do when children were cut off from contact with their parents for so much of their young lives. She smiled, thinking of her younger sister, Sarah-Louise. She would probably have jumped at the chance of being here. Sarah-Louise always did have a yearning to be free of the restrictions of family life and away in the big city. She might not like it so much though if she came up against the conditions in Leeds that Sarah Pumphrey had described. Indeed she might not like it so much if she came up against the sharp tongue of Sarah Pumphrey herself.

For all Sarah's harsh words, however, Mary was grateful for the way the school let her put her knowledge to good use. Some might be cautious about accepting Martha's mixture of folklore and herbal remedies. But here there was no such hesitation. In addition, she was allowed to help the younger girls with their reading, although the time she had spent herself with the books had been so limited.

'I often feel as though I should be one of the pupils myself,' she said laughingly to Ted one day. She was helping him to carry baskets of apples to the cool dark cellars beneath the classrooms. There they carefully examined the fruit for any blemishes, before laying it in rows on the wooden racks, arranging each apple so it was close to, but not touching, the next.

'I'm really grateful for the way the staff encouraged me to carry on with the things I'm most interested in, and even put them to use in t' school. After all, they ran a bit of a risk taking me on.' She stopped, conscious of the fact that she was approaching the dangerous ground of her baby's illegitimate birth. 'My parents would be made up if they could see me now in such a grand place,' she said to divert the conversation on to more commonplace concerns. 'They've had plenty of scratting and saving to do all their lives.'

'Aye, I know what thou means. My grandparents brought me up and I know they found it hard to make ends meet. After all, it's not what they expected to have to do at their time of life. My mother died giving birth to me,' Ted added by way of explanation. He lifted another rack on to the shelf and settled the remaining few apples into its grooves. ' I was her first—luckily, I suppose, or there would have been even more for my grandparents to do. They never complained, mind. I always remember being happy and I never felt as though I went without.' He paused, deep in thought. Then, frowning, he looked at Mary. 'I'd like bairns of my own—and I'd make sure I could support them. How about thee, Mary? Is there someone back home that thou dost have a special regard for?' He stepped closer and held her gaze.

'No, not at all,' said Mary quickly. Then, realising that she had given Ted the perfect opportunity, should he wish it, to make advances, added, 'Well, at least, there was someone who was interested…' Her voice trailed off.

'Then he's daft not to come after thee now… but I'm glad he hasn't.' Ted hesitated and then went on, 'I…I wanted to say what a high regard I have for thee. Such a lovely face,' he murmured, reaching out his hand to touch her hair. Mary recoiled in horror, her heart racing.

'Don't touch me,' she cried, retreating into the darkness of the cellar.

'I'm sorry,' said Ted in a shocked voice. 'I only wanted to say that I do think a lot about thee and if thou would ever consider walking out with me…' He stopped, lost for words at the ferocity of her response.

Mary was immediately contrite. 'I only meant that I think of you like a brother to me and I don't want to lose the only brother I ever had.'

'Aye, well, if that's the way things stand, 'appen you're like a sister to me too. That's how it better stay, then.' He turned to climb the stairs that led from the cold cellar to the warmth of the kitchen above. Mary reluctantly followed.

'Any road, that's a good evening's work we've done, sister. Thanks for helping me.' Mary was so shocked by the extravagance of her response to his advances that she did not answer him.

Mary found her comfort in the small room she had been given when she'd first arrived at the school. It was one of a rabbit warren of rooms situated in the basement of the school beneath the classrooms. It did have one small round window high up on the wall. When she looked out, her eyes were on a level with the grass. A true rabbit's eye view, she thought.

Now it was winter and darkness had already fallen when she arrived back at the end of a day's work. She drew the curtains across this lookout on the world and lit the fire. Pulling her easy chair close to its warmth, she sat and wrote to her family or read one of the many books that she had chosen from the library. Sooner or later, depending on the endeavours of the day, her eyes began to close and her head to nod.

The reply to Annie's letter had remained unwritten. For weeks it had lain forgotten in the pocket of Mary's skirt and, when she did find it again, she didn't know what to write. She wanted to help her one-time friend but it was too painful having to be reminded about the person she was most trying to forget. Eventually she could put it off no longer and, several weeks after receiving the letter, she wrote back to Annie.

Ashworth School,
Saturday 2nd December, 1883.
Dear Annie,
I was pleased to hear from you and I am sorry I
have taken a long time to write back but I have
been ill. Johnny sounds to be growing into a fine
young man. You must be a good mother to him,
despite what some would think.

I am enjoying work at the school. There is a lot to
do from morning till night and I am often tired. I
like having the children around. They are not so
different from my own sisters.

I do not know how to advise you about your husband. I think you are a good wife to him. I am
sorry he does not realise it. Have you tried asking
one of the railwaymen to talk to him? My father
might do so, but it would be better to ask George
Morritt. My father was never one for stirring up
trouble. Mr Morritt knows your husband better,
with them working together, and might be able to
say something.

It seems so long ago that I was in Templesforth. I
do miss our friendship. If you should ever wish to
visit, you would be most welcome.

My very best wishes to you and your family.
From your friend,
Mary.

The letter sat on the table in Mary's room for a further three days before she found the courage to walk
down the lane and post it. She did not want to send her

best wishes to John Crowther but it seemed churlish not to add them at the end of the letter. Besides, it would have seemed odd to Annie, as she read what Mary had written.

By the middle of December the children were so excited about the Christmas break that it was proving difficult to maintain the peace and decorum that marked the school day. In less than a week they would depart by wagon to the local station and thence by train to their homes. There were few places now that were not within easy reach of the great spider's web of railway lines that had spread to cover the country. The school was to be closed for three weeks, although staff remained if they had no alternative arrangements. Mary assumed that she would pass the festive season where she was. She knew of several of the household staff that would be there and Ted had told her diffidently that he had nowhere else to go. It would not be so bad, she thought. Infinitely better than the miserable time she had spent last year with the Thoroughgoods, pretending to the family that all was well and knowing that the secret of her pregnancy would soon be a secret no more.

How she longed for home. She missed her family dreadfully, especially when all the talk was of seeing loved ones again. Sarah-Louise would be almost a young lady and the two little ones grown tall. Alice had not been well during the year and her parents struggled more, as they grew older and she more demanding. But she would not visit yet, not while *he* lived opposite.

CHAPTER TWENTY-FIVE

DISASTERS, such as the one at Abbot's Ripton eight years before, were not easily forgotten, George Morritt thought. He warmed his hands at the stove and inspected the line in front of him and the station along to his left. Patches of white frost still lingered where the sun had failed to reach. There would be no further thaw today. The sun was already dipping towards the horizon, although he had only just started the afternoon shift.

It had not been the most recent rail disaster. That was the collapse of the Tay Bridge, a mere four years ago. The engine and all its coaches had plunged into the icy waters below, with the loss of everyone on board. Her Majesty had crossed it herself only three months before that, he recalled. What a rumpus that had caused and rightly so, for the design of the bridge had left much to be desired and the workmanship had been shoddy. Even in the awful storm of that night, the accident need not have happened.

But it was the earlier crash that was imprinted on his mind because it was a failure of the signalling that was the cause. At that time he had only been a signalman himself for five years—since the opening of the station in 1871, in fact. He remembered the crash as if it were yesterday and the memory made his blood run cold. Even now it was unclear who had been to blame but if it had not been for a spell of extreme cold causing the signals to freeze, the accident would probably not have happened. It had been much like the weather they were having now, which was the reason he had thought of it. At least he didn't have snow to contend with today, as the poor blighters had then. It had been a routine procedure. The coal train had been on the up line, delayed by the weather. Behind it the Flying Scotsman had been closing on it fast. The coal train should have been stopped and shunted on to a sideline but the distant signal had been frozen at clear. At Abbot's Ripton, where the signals were also frozen, the goods train was stopped by the hand signals but, before there was time to shunt it off the main line, it had been hit from behind. To make matters worse, the Leeds express from King's Cross had been fast approaching on the down line and had ploughed into the wreckage of the first collision.

He shuddered, remembering how he had heard the news so quickly on the telegraph, sitting here in his box. He had felt sick at heart. He tried to imagine how the signalmen must have felt in that small station, not so different from his own. The following morning the newspapers had been full of the crash.

Frosty weather was always a worry if you worked on the railway, especially for himself and the other signalmen, and for the platelayer gangs. The frozen signals and points meant that, more often than not, they had to resort to using the hand signals, at least until the approach of the midday sun brought a temporary thaw. And then, by evening, the freeze would have set in again. It was a constant worry for George and he was finding it difficult to relax, even when he was off duty. Tom and his men had it bad too, he thought, for they were at the mercy of the weather all day. At least he could get a warm at his stove when he wasn't busy. The gangs were helping to keep the points free and the signals working, as well as attending to their routine work. Then there was the additional hazard of ice on the lines. The fast express trains didn't stop to pick up water but collected it from the water troughs as they passed, splashing it in all directions and for yards along the line. In the low temperatures it turned immediately to ice, so the men had to set to with picks and shovels, before the build-up of ice caused a derailment. It was cold work and very dangerous.

There was no denying that today had been a beautiful day. The sun shone in a clear blue sky. The rooks were cawing to one another in a nearby copse and a noisy flock of fieldfares were feasting on the berries alongside the line. Last night, as he lay in bed, unable to sleep, he had heard the scream of a vixen.

It was not only the weather that was keeping him awake at night. It was the worry over John Crowther. As Nathaniel had suggested, George had tried to approach him over the problem of his drinking. It had started off amicably enough. John had been standing on the platform, watching a herd of young bullocks being unloaded from the sidings into the station yard. One had been acting up and causing Nathaniel and his father no end of trouble, as they struggled to bring some order to their adolescent charges.

'Sooner them than me,' said George, who had just finished his morning shift and was looking forward to an hour or two 'putting the garden to bed for winter', as he liked to call it. Then he would spend a bit of time contemplating the progress of the pig. Finally he anticipated a half hour in the company of a jug of ale along the lane at the Wheatsheaf.

'Aye,' said John Crowther, 'there's worse jobs than on t' railway. We might have a bit o' dust but at least we avoid all that mud and muck year in, year out. And the trains are a bit better behaved than that lot over there. Any road, what are your plans for the rest of the day?'

George told him. Then, because he could think of no other way to introduce the subject, said, ''Appen you'd care to join me for a drop of ale when you finish work this evening?'

'Thanks, but I prefer to have a drink at home. I was never one for frequenting the local hostelries. Besides, there's my wife and bairn to see to.'

'I reckon it's best to 'ave a drink wi' me mates, rather than by missen at home. That way I do more chatting and less drinking.'

'What are you implying?' John Crowther rounded on him, the colour rising up his neck and into his face. 'Are you suggesting I'm o'er fond of my drink? I would suggest you watch what you're saying. You've got a job and a family to keep, just remember that.'

Having gone this far, George saw no point in retreating now. He went on bravely. 'We all like a pint; there's no denying that. It's just that I've noticed how them as likes to start supping early in t' day often get themselves into trouble, like. And I don't wish to see people put at risk as a result…or families hurt…'

'How dare you suggest I can't do my job or look after my own?' John Crowther's face was purple now, his fists clenched. 'I'd 'ave you mind your own business. You'll be hearing more about this, mark my words.' He turned on his heel and made his way, not altogether steadily, into his house.

After this George had waited in trepidation, fearing for his job, knowing that the loss of it would also mean the loss of a roof over the heads of his family. But he'd heard nothing and, in time, had assumed that John had seen sense enough to realise that giving him the sack would be likely to draw unwanted attention to himself and his drinking.

He heard John Crowther's voice again, raised in anger, and realised that, though he had been daydreaming, the voice he was hearing was no dream. He looked along the platform towards Station House, where Annie and her son were making their way through the garden to the kitchen door. How much like his father the boy was, George thought, looking at his sturdy frame and dark hair as he zigzagged his way through the bushes. Annie followed. She appeared thinner than ever. It was a thousand pities that Mary had left. Annie had begun to bloom under the influence of Mary's friendship. That bloom had faded again, although, from the little that George saw of Annie and her husband together, he sensed in her a steely resolve that had not been present in the early months. He endeavoured to see her face, but she was warmly wrapped against the cold and at some distance from his lookout in the signal-box. He had taken to checking, whenever possible, for any telltale signs that John Crowther had been over-zealous in the handling of his wife.

'Where have you been, woman? I've been waiting here for my tea this half hour. And what do you mean by having my son out in this weather? He'll catch his death.' He looked at Johnny, who was pretending to be a horse, galloping and neighing in and out of the black-currant bushes. His coat and shoes were muddy and his hair dishevelled. 'Look at t' state of him. You'll have the whole village thinking my son's a street urchin. Get along in, the two of you.' He grabbed Annie's arm to pull her inside and the little boy ducked away from his father and ran into the house ahead of them.

It was as George had thought. By nightfall the frost was setting in. His barometer had signalled a change, though. The pressure was falling and, with any luck, there would soon be an end to this cold snap. He checked the signals. Right now they were in working order. The Stationmaster came out on to the platform for the five twenty-seven from York. George wondered whether he had been drinking again. John Crowther was very good at disguising it, even if he had. He stood, outlined by the indifferent light of the oil lamps, as a couple and a lone man alighted from the train. When it had departed, he stood chatting to the man, whom George recognised as a farmer from the next village.

It was clear that tonight there would be no peace in the Crowther household. George looked at his watch. Six-twenty. What was the Stationmaster shouting about now? He strained to hear but could make no sense of the words. The shouting continued and then he heard a woman's voice raised in protest. The voice carried along the line in the frosty night. Silence fell again. From his position in the signal-box he could see only the darkness of the side of the house. An opening door threw a brief light over the garden and the next minute George could see Annie's slim figure on the platform. Looking to right and left, she let herself down on to the rails and quickly crossed to the down line. He sighed and shook his head. *Poor lass,* he thought. *It wasn't right for anyone to be so ordered about as she was.*

By nine o'clock there were just a couple of goods trains and the nine fifty-seven from York to see through the station. The bell sounded from the down box and George replied, accepting the next train. He heaved the levers into position to change both distant and home signals to off, indicating to the driver of the coal train, when it appeared, that his block of line was clear. The signals were moving freely, he thought with relief. The barometer must have been right. A scarcely human shout made him look up. He could see his boss thrashing around on the platform. The porter was trying in vain to restrain him. Snatching up the lantern from the side of the door, he hurried down the steps, almost losing his footing on their icy surface. As he cautiously made his way along the stretch of platform, he could see Tom emerge from his cottage door and run through the station yard. It was immediately obvious to the men that John Crowther had been drinking heavily and was completely out of control.

'If you know anything about this,' he was screaming at the porter, 'you best tell me now. Did you see owt? I'll not have any of you helping that minx.' He turned to Tom. 'She's gone and left me. Taken t' little un with her. No word. Nothing. Just upt and left. I'll bray 'er when I lay hands on 'er, making a laughing stock out o' me.'

'Hold on,' said Tom reasonably. 'How do you know she's gone? Have you looked all over t' house? Could she be with t' babby? 'Appen she's been out visiting or owt like that. Are you sure nowt's happened to her?'

'What do you take me for—a fool?' John Crowther roared. 'She were there at teatime—got me my tea—late as usual, like. Then she put t' little un to bed. Of course I've looked everywhere. She's nowhere to be seen. She's gone and left me, like I said.' He turned drunkenly, his arms outstretched to demonstrate that he had looked everywhere. George was hurrying along the platform towards the group.

'And it'd pay thee to keep thy nose out of my business,' he said, pointing an accusing finger in the signalman's direction. 'Tha's done enough of meddlin' in my affairs. Wouldn't surprise me if you had summat to do wi' her going.' And, staggering towards George, he aimed a swing at him with his fist. George stepped to one side and John Crowther lurched towards the edge of the platform. Tom and George grabbed to stop him falling but he shrugged them off, the alcohol fuelling his powerful body.

'Look,' said George reasonably. 'It were nowt to do wi' me. Why don't you come inside out of t' cold and let's make us all a cup o' tay while we think what to do?'

'I want none o' your fuss…fuss…fussing. Get out of t' road, all of you. I'm off to look for her. She can't take my bairn and get away wi' it.' He turned to make his way towards the exit from the platform, walked into a pillar and staggered backwards on to the ground. The bell sounded to notify them of the imminent arrival of a goods train on the up line.

'This is dangerous,' said George. 'I'm going up to my box to stop that train.' He grabbed the lamp and made his way back along the platform. The whistle of a train carried through the frosty night air. Climbing the steps, he flung himself on to the lever to manoeuvre the distant signal into the 'on' position. It was frozen fast. He signalled six bells to the down signal-box to warn of danger and tried to move the home signal to 'stop'. Like the distant signal, it refused to move. He turned to the hand lamp signal, struggling to light it, clumsy in his haste. Setting it in the window, he lit the fog lamps and made his way with them to the door of his box. As he ran down the steps he glanced up at the platform, saw Tom and the porter wrestling with the drunken man, and slipped on the last three steps. The lamps flew out of his hands and fell clattering to the ground, their lights extinguished. George raised himself stiffly, rubbed his elbow and groped for the lamps. It was too late. The red light in the signal-box had alerted the driver but, try as he might, he was much too close to the station for the brakes to make any difference to his progress. George shouted to his colleagues but his voice was lost amid the engine's turmoil and the clamour of its haul of wagons. Limping back along the platform, he saw the Stationmaster wrench himself free once more from Tom's grasp with a momentum that sent him over the platform's edge into the arms of the oncoming train. The three railway workers stood frozen with horror and disbelief as the huge locomotive thundered on down the line, its firebox glowing red, like the mouth of hell, carrying with it the remains of John Crowther's body.

CHAPTER TWENTY-SIX

A LETTER arrived from Hannah, inviting Mary to stay with them in York for the Christmas period. She was overjoyed, having resigned herself to staying at the school for Christmas. The misunderstanding with Ted had strained their relationship and she was not looking forward to spending more than the usual amount of time in his company when it was obvious that he wanted more than she was able to give.

The first weeks of December had been marked by crisp frosts and clear blue skies. Frost lingered in the shadows, white-patterning the ground with trees and fences and roofs and chimneys. Water froze in pipes and Ted and the other men worked hard to clear them and keep the school supplied with fresh water. Mary loved the clarity of the sky and the sparkle of the frost and she spent a little time each day in the gardens or, occasionally, walking into the village. But on the day that she received Hannah's invitation the temperature had risen suddenly overnight, the frost scattered by a strong blustery wind from the north-east. Mary drew her cloak tightly round her shoulders as the wind whipped her hair across her face and tore at her skirts. By the time she reached the girls' quarters her clothes were soaked with the rain that the wind hurled at her like needles. The wind caught the door and slammed it back against the wall as Mary entered. She glanced up at the heavy, doom-laden sky.

By half past three the oil lamps had already been trimmed and lit. Smoke billowed out from fireplaces and draughts blew under doors and along corridors. Leaves and small twigs were flung against the downstairs windows and the buildings shuddered with the force of the storm. The children were at first excited and then frightened as its intensity increased.

'There's going to be no settling them down to sleep tonight,' shouted Jane to Mary, as the two of them made their way to the washrooms to inspect the progress of the girls. ''Appen we'll be reading them bedtime stories for a few hours or until this storm passes over.'

It was as Jane had said. The girls were much too disturbed by the maelstrom outside to give any thought to sleep. Fires were lit in the dormitories and the usual rules ignored. Girls, big and small, brought blankets and pillows and made themselves comfortable around the hearth.

'I do feel like a mother hen and thee are all my little chicks,' laughed Jane, as two or three of the youngest girls huddled close to her.

The two women let the girls chatter on with tales of home and family. Mary was glad of the diversion. She felt strangely agitated and knew she would settle to nothing alone in her tiny room. A stronger shudder than before was followed by the tearing of branches as a tree was toppled by the wind, its naked twigs rasping down the dormitory windows as it fell.

'What an awful night,' said Mary, as they all turned towards the noisy darkness. 'Thank the Lord we are all tucked up safe and sound inside.'

The York to Sheffield mail train was running late. In the half-covered cabin there was little protection from the gale, and the jackets and trousers of both driver and firemen clung to their soaking backs, while their fronts basked in the heat of the firebox. They had encountered no debris on the line but the chances of doing so had made them slow their progress. Eventually they drew alongside the tiny platform of Ashworth Station. A solitary passenger alighted, arms encircling a large bundle.

'Not a night to be out and about,' commented the driver, as he watched the figure cross the yard and disappear into the darkness. 'Can't wait to be home wi' me missus. 'Appen she's summat tasty waiting for me.'

'Aye,' replied his mate, 'and, if you're luck's in, 'appen it'll be more than apple pie and custard.'

The driver chuckled and eased the train slowly out of the station into the wildness of the night.

When her visitor was catapulted into the room Mary was certain she was dreaming. It must have been the freak conditions of the storm that had disorientated her mind. But no, Annie didn't disappear, even when Mary shook her head and blinked her sleep-heavy eyes. At least, she thought it was Annie, but it was a very different person from the neat and tidy Annie Crowther who had been her one-time friend and employer. Her crumpled hat clung to the back of her head, offering no protection to her hair, which had worked loose and trapped small twigs and leaves within its length, giving it the consistency of a bird's nest. Her coat and dress were heavy with rain and rivulets of water coalesced into puddles on the floor. Her boots were covered in mud and her eyes reflected the wildness of the storm outside. A plaintive voice came from the unwieldy bundle that Annie clutched to her, a voice that would never have been conjured up by an overactive imagination.

'Mummy, down. Me hungry. Want down.' A dishevelled toddler peered from the bundle, a head of unruly dark hair flopping over eyes so uncannily like those of his father that Mary gasped.

'Annie, what on earth are you doing here?' she began. 'What's the time? How did you get here?' Her questions came thick and fast now, her brain struggling to make sense of her friend's sudden appearance in what seemed like the middle of the night.

Annie sat down suddenly on the bed and Johnny wrestled with the blanket in which he was wrapped and which was now sodden and cold. She began to shiver violently.

'It was fortunate I heard her knocking,' said Jane Moxon, who had entered the room behind the two unexpected visitors. 'I only went down the corridor to make sure all was well with the headmaster and his family, the storm being so violent, like. And I heard this banging on t' door and thought, now who's this out in weather such as we've got?'

'Stand up, Annie,' Mary ordered. 'Let's get these wet things off you. Jane, can you take Johnny's coat off? And then would you mind lighting the fire? I didn't bother when I got back from the dormitory; I went straight to bed.' She wrestled to get Annie's wet coat off her shoulders. Annie started to whimper.

'I was so afraid,' she started. 'I had to get to you. You said I might.'

'I'm not surprised!' Jane broke in, as she struggled with Johnny, who was running round her in circles. 'Anyone would be afraid, out on a night like this, let alone a little scrap like thyself.'

'How did you get here?' asked Mary, who suspected that Annie's fear was not caused by the weather.

'We came on the train. Last night we stayed in the Station Hotel in York. Then, today, I didn't know what was for the best, not wishing to impose, so we wandered round York all day. But the weather was getting bad and the light started to go. I decided then that I couldn't go back.' She glanced at Jane, then continued in a low voice. 'Things have been very difficult lately. I had to get away. For Johnny's sake.'

'What's this, young man? Hast thou been tumbling?' Jane was removing Johnny's jacket to expose a dark bruise mottled with yellow on the upper part of his arm. As he pulled free a second bruise could be seen in a similar position on the other arm. Mary looked at Annie in alarm.

'Now you see why we had to get away,' Annie replied to Mary's unspoken question.

Jane bustled around, piling the wet clothes into a heap and lighting the fire. Soon it blazed brightly and warmth began to reach the shivering occupants of the room. 'I'll fetch some hot water,' she said to Mary. ''Appen thy friends would like to wash off some of the effects of the storm.' She left the room, closing the door quietly behind her.

'Oh, Mary. You've no idea how awful it's been,' said Annie. She buried her face in her hands and began to cry noisily. Mary put an arm round her damp shoulders and listened as her friend went on. 'I could cope with John hitting me. After all, I knew I wasn't a good wife to him. And life wasn't so bad…some of the time.' She looked at Johnny and smiled, her smile fading as she went on. 'But then he started on Johnny. It was almost as if he was trying to hurt the only thing that gave me pleasure. I tried to reason with him. When he was sober he was always really upset that he had hurt his son. He does really love him, you know. But then he would start drinking again and Johnny, as well as me, would be his punch-bag. You see those bruises on his arms? That's where he took hold of him and shook him. *I* could put up with it, but Johnny shouldn't have to. After all, he's only little and he could get badly hurt. Any road, it's not right, is it?'

'Of course it isn't,' Mary agreed. 'But how did you leave? Did you tell him you were going?'

'No, of course not. He'd never let us. It was the night before last. He started again. He'd been drinking, of course. Complained because I'd taken Johnny out in the cold…and we were a bit late back for his tea. It's always

284 THE RAILWAYMAN'S DAUGHTER

little things, never anything important that he gets upset
about. Any road, after tea I gave Johnny his bath and sat
reading him his bedtime story when John comes in. He
seems upset, seeing us together, getting on so well. I try
to get him to join in looking after his son but he won't
do it. So he snatches the book from my hands and
throws it across the room and takes Johnny from me. He
puts him on the bed but Johnny hadn't heard the end of
his story so he gets up again. And then John hit him
hard. Look.' She pulled the top of his trousers down to
reveal a purple bruise developing at the top of his leg.
'That's when I decided to go,' she continued. 'There and
then. I wasn't going to risk staying another night. He
was on duty till late. Not that it stopped him drinking.
He sat in the parlour with the bottle. I got on with the
chores, the same as I always do before I sit down. But
I was putting together a few essentials in a bag. I
couldn't take much because I had Johnny to carry. When
I looked in again, John was asleep. I knew the last train
to York was due in half an hour, so I dressed Johnny and
we put our coats and hats on ready. It was difficult keeping him quiet, although John had drunk so much by that
time it would have taken a train through the house to
wake him. The only thing I didn't have was money of
my own. I knew where John kept it, though, so I went
and took a bit. I hope he doesn't mind. Then I left by
the back door, so as not to disturb him, and we crossed
the line for the York train.'

'Did no one see you, then?' asked Mary.

'There was no one about. I stayed in the shadows
until the train arrived. There was only Walter on duty

in the office. He came out to see the train on its way but I made sure I got on while he was busy and he didn't see me.

'We were in York within the hour and I booked in at the Station Hotel for the night. For the first time in ages I felt safe. But this morning I started thinking he might work out where we'd gone and come after us. After all, it was the obvious thing to do, to catch the train. How else could I have got away? And he would have guessed that I would go to York. After all, he took me there once before and we had dinner in the hotel.

'So then I started to get anxious. I paid the bill and we left. I couldn't think what to do, so we walked around a bit. Next thing I knew we were at the steps of the Minster and that was when I thought of you…remember how you used to say how beautiful it was? Even then I wasn't sure what to do. I mean, I didn't know whether I'd be able to stay, not with Johnny as well. In the end, like I said, the weather started getting bad and it was dark again and Johnny was cold and tired. So I had to take the chance. Please say that we can stay. Otherwise I don't know what else I can do.'

Jane had come into the room with a jug of hot water and some towels, while Annie was speaking.

'Of course thou can stay,' Jane said, setting the jug on the washstand and putting the towels by the fire to warm. 'I think the best thing is if we make up some beds on the floor tonight.' She turned to Mary. 'It's warm in here now and far more cosy than cold beds in the spare room. In the morning, we'll see what we can do to make thy friends more comfortable.'

'Are you sure that will be all right?' asked Mary anxiously.

'Of course it's all right. What else are we going to do? Throw poor Annie and t' little un back out into the teeth of the gale?' They all laughed. 'Any road, the poor girl looks as though she could do with a bit of the milk of human kindness. Sounds as though she's had little enough recently.'

Mary smiled. Nothing much escaped Jane's eagle eyes.

Mary and Jane dragged a mattress along to the small room and they made up a bed in front of the fire. Johnny, exhausted by the day's tramping around the streets of York, was already asleep on Mary's bed, so they drew the covers snugly around him and left him there. In the firelight Mary and Annie sat, sipping the hot cocoa that Jane had brought them and discussing the future. Mary had noticed, without comment, the numerous bruises on Annie's body and marvelled how she could have stayed all this time with a man who had so damaged her. He certainly had a lot to answer for. And more than Annie was aware of.

'I hope he'll be all right without us,' Annie said, gazing into the embers of the fire. 'He's not very good at looking after himself.'

'Why should you care, after what he's done to you?' replied Mary hotly. 'He deserves all that's coming to him.'

Annie had never heard her speak so sharply before.

'But it's the drink that's to blame. If it weren't for that he would be a fine husband and father. And it's probably me that has driven him to it.'

'Don't be ridiculous. Of course it's not you. He's

never shown you any consideration in all the time I've known you. All he thinks of is himself—what he wants, what he needs. Satisfying himself. Lusting after the flesh…that's what it says in the Good Book.' Mary clambered to her feet and started to pace up and down the room. 'That's what he does. And he doesn't care how many lives he ruins. He doesn't care who he tramples under his feet. Well, *I* don't care what happens to *him*. However bad it is, it's too good for him. I hope he rots in hell for ever—with weeping and gnashing of teeth.' She burst into tears and sat back on the floor, burying her face in the cushion of her fireside chair.

Annie stared at her friend in amazement.

'Mary, don't get so upset. I'll be fine. Don't worry. I've no intention of going back to him. I knew last night that when I left, it would be for good. But you *know* what I'm like. I've got to think of how I'm going to live in the future. I've never been out earning my keep like you have. And there's Johnny to think of. You're lucky. You've worked in so many different places, and had the chance of going to York. It must have been grand working in a big house in the city. I can't think what made you want to leave. I'm sure, if it was me, I'd have stayed there.'

Mary's indignation at these unwittingly hurtful words burned within her. She longed to correct the misapprehension, but knew she couldn't. It was not Annie's fault that John Crowther had misused her as he had misused Annie. To say more would only have added to the hurt that her friend was suffering. She calmed herself and gave a small twisted smile.

'Well, there we are, then. What's done is done. And I'm happy here, any road. Happier than I've been in a long time.'

It was true. She was busily engrossed in all that went on in the school and, were it not for Sarah Pumphrey's hostility, she would indeed be happy, only to be bettered by the blissful months with Nathaniel. Still, she thought, every word of what she had said about John Crowther was true. She did hope that, when the time came, he would rot in hell…and the sooner the better.

It seemed to Mary that the school was fast becoming a home for waifs and strays. The next day the three made their way along the draughty corridors to the girls' quarters, where Jane was waiting for them. Annie stared at the scenes of devastation visible from the windows. Branches of trees lay about, littering the gardens. A beech tree lay in its entirety close to the side of the building. In the distance she could see greenhouses flattened by the storm.

'I had no idea the storm had done so much damage,' she said to Mary.

'That tree came down while we were sitting with the girls in the evening. It was very frightening. Little did I know then that you were on your way here in t' middle of the storm. You were fortunate not to have been hit by anything yourselves.'

The sight of Annie in the subdued and unadorned dress of a Quaker matron loosened the restraint caused by the events of the night. For all his supposed shortcomings, John Crowther had always insisted that his wife was dressed in fashions as up-to-date as it was possible to purchase from the nearby market town. Where Mary had always worn plain or polka-dot skirts, loose or hitched over two petticoats, Annie's had frills and flounces, pleats and buttons, as fashion had dictated several years ago in London and more recently in the provinces. To see her now in the plain brown dress with white lace collar reduced both women to laughter, especially when Johnny wanted to know, 'What has Mummy done with her pretty dress?' Once Mary had become accustomed to the transformation, she had to admit that the style and colour showed off Annie's features to perfection.

Her son proved more of a problem. The boys started school at nine and, although they were often small and Johnny was big, they could find nothing in the linen cupboard to fit.

'Well, little man,' said Jane, entering the room just as Johnny tripped and fell headlong, 'thou does look like a two pence-halfpenny rabbit in those clothes.' Johnny struggled to stand upright amid a flurry of trouser legs and more hilarity from the three women. Jane turned to Mary. 'Why do thou not take thy friends down to the farm and ask Judith for help? She has a little lad Johnny's age and 'appen she can lend thee something that fits until such time as Annie can make some or can get to the draper's.'

Her suggestion gained Johnny a set of clothes and a new friend. Judith's first boy was the same age as Johnny. Together they chased chickens, inspected sheep and fed hay to the horses, watched over by Annie, Judith and the new baby.

Mary was about to make her excuses and return to the school, for the day was slipping by and she had done very little of her work, when Judith said unexpectedly, 'Why don't Annie and the lad stay here with us? The farmhouse is plenty big enough for us all. And it will be easier for thee, Annie, than having to keep Johnny quiet when school's in progress. And it would give our little lad a friend to play with and keep him from under my feet!'

'But I've no clothes and neither has Johnny,' Annie said apologetically.

'All the more reason for thee to stay here with us. Thou art a similar size to me and the lads are much the same. I reckon we can fit you up with something until we can get something made.'

So it was settled and Mary made her way back to the school, leaving Annie in the company of the farmer's wife. Everywhere the workmen were struggling to repair the damage of the night before. Several slates had been dislodged from the roof of the girls' house. Some lay smashed on the ground and others perched precariously on the roof, against which the men had erected ladders and were attempting to make safe.

'We've got off lightly,' one of them said to Mary as she stopped to speak. 'The church has been badly damaged. Parts of the tower were blown down and went clean through t' roof. There's other houses in t' village too suffered a worse fate than this.'

'It's a mercy this didn't happen next week when the children are to go to their homes,' Mary replied. 'We would have had a lot of disappointed boys and girls on our hands.'

'Aye, not to mention the grown-ups.'

She continued on her way. His words brought with them the sudden realisation that she was now presented with a dilemma. With Annie's arrival, what would Mary do about her invitation to York? If circumstances had been different, she was sure that Hannah would not have minded two extra guests. But she could not risk Annie finding out about the baby and to take her there would be as good as telling her. As it was, Mary was finding it difficult to face the likely possibility that she would see her baby again. She had tried unsuccessfully to blot from her mind the image of the little girl. While the busy days kept her fully occupied, body and thoughts, in the night she had no power to control her dreams. She remained haunted by what she had done and Sarah Pumphrey's words came back to her time and again...'the sin of giving thy baby away'. What if the baby looked like John Crowther, as was quite possible? Could she stay with Hannah then, if she saw in Ann's face the image of her attacker? Suppose she felt again the feelings that had made it so difficult to give up her baby? What would she do then? She could not escape the stubborn feeling that she had let go the only thing that was exclusively hers. For John Crowther had no claim to the baby, not even knowing of its existence. His connection with the baby grew more tenuous, in her mind, with each passing day. But it might not be so if the baby looked like him.

Dragging her thoughts back to the week ahead, she considered the immediate problem of how she could protect Annie from John Crowther's possible attempts to track her down. That was just as important as the need to keep from her friend the knowledge of her husband's unfaithfulness and the resulting baby.

The austere offices of Crombie and Ashington, Solicitors, stood nearly a mile distant from the railway station but, as Edward Appleby made his way through the narrow alleyways of York, he was oblivious to the street vendors selling sweets and toys for the Christmas tree and kissing boughs and garlands to decorate the houses of the rich who had no need or inclination to dirty their own hands.

'Do come in and sit down.' Josiah Crombie indicated a chair on the other side of a huge mahogany desk that formed the centrepiece of the dark wood-panelled room. Its windows looked down on to the bustling scene that his visitor had just left. The young man sat down wearily.

'It's no good,' he said. 'I've been everywhere that I can think of. I've followed up every suggestion that's been made to me. I seem to have travelled halfway round Yorkshire in the last few days. It's a waste of time.'

'We're more than grateful for your help,' said the older man, 'and, rest assured, the police will continue to search. There will have to be an inquiry into the circumstances of the incident, of course. As far as the money is concerned, that will come to you when all investigations have been completed. The eventual outcome of the search will make no difference to that. The will makes no other provision. Of course, there's the little matter of services rendered, but the bill for those will be sent on to you in due course.'

'It all seems so unfair,' continued Edward Appleby, as though he had not heard the solicitor's intervening words. 'After all, I don't even know the man. What is the amount of money involved?'

'It's impossible to say for certain at the moment, but it could amount to several thousand pounds. It seems the Appleby family made some sound business investments. This part of the money was entailed on the daughter and, by marriage, to her husband. It has been sitting in the vaults accruing interest. Unfortunately other investments made by the family fell in value and they lost a lot of money. I understand they struggled to make ends meet towards the end of their lives.'

'Several thousand pounds! The old miser. The unfeeling, uncaring good-for-nothing bastard…I'm sorry. Do forgive me. I've no right to talk like this.'

'It's understandable, given the circumstances.' The solicitor got up from his chair and walked to the window, gazing down on the festive tableau below. 'What do you intend to do now?'

'Oh, I shall go back to my job for the next few days. Nothing more can be done until next week. I shall travel over then.'

'You realise what a difference this could make to your life? You could set up in business yourself. Do something altogether more profitable.'

'Maybe. There's a lot to think about. And, anyway, I wouldn't want to do anything while the police are still carrying out inquiries.'

'Indeed. Rest assured that we will be in touch with you as soon as we have further information.' The two men walked to the door and shook hands. 'And, on behalf of the firm, may I wish you and yours our sincere Christmas greetings.'

CHAPTER TWENTY-SEVEN

ALTHOUGH Mary had been working in the Quaker school for nearly six months, she had forgotten how eerily quiet it was without the children. They had all dispersed without mishap the previous day, most travelling on the school wagon to the local railway station and from there to the four quarters of the country. The teachers breathed a collective sigh of relief that the weather had been neither too cold nor too stormy for the long journeys home.

The household staff cleaned and mended, taking the opportunity to work without three hundred pairs of feet impeding their every move. It was while Mary was polishing the windows of the girls' dormitory that she saw Ted and two of the other men trying to make sense of the jumble of glass that had been the greenhouses. Clearing up the wreckage of the storm had kept the men fully occupied and Mary had not seen Ted to tell him about her invitation to Hannah's, let alone introduce him to Annie…that was if she could persuade her and Johnny back from the farm, of course.

Just before midday Mary put on her cloak and walked out into the gardens. Ted and the other men had piled up the shattered glass and had started to repair the frames. Ted was rescuing the cuttings he had so painstakingly made in the autumn, before joining his colleagues for dinner. He smiled at Mary as she approached. He looked tired and there were dark rings beneath his eyes.

'Mary, it's good to see thee again. What a mess everywhere is! We don't really know where to start, there's such a lot of clearing up to do. I had no idea it was this bad. How are things with thee?' He shot a glance at her and looked away again. 'I've missed our walks.'

'Me too,' said Mary, awkwardly, uncertain how to continue. 'I hope we can still be friends, Ted.'

'I hope so too,' replied Ted, his eyes fixed on the far reaches of the garden. 'Who's that over on t' green?' he asked suddenly. 'I had no idea we were taking them that young!'

'It's Johnny, my friend's little lad. They've come to stay.' She waved to Annie, who was following Johnny across the grass. Annie waved back and started to walk slowly in Mary's direction. Johnny raced ahead, his energy still not exhausted despite the morning's activities, and threw his arms around Mary's skirts, laughing up at her. Mary looked from Johnny to Ted and back again, conscious of the rapid beating of her heart.

'Mary! Dost thou feel unwell?' Ted took her elbow. 'What is it? Can I do owt to help?'

'No, it's nothing.' She cradled her forehead in her

hands and struggled to regain her composure. Shrugging him off, she said, 'I'm tired, that's all. 'Appen it's the extra cleaning. And it's a long time since breakfast…I must be hungry.' She stared at him for several seconds before suddenly remembering her friend approaching across the green. She turned to Annie to introduce her to Ted. But Annie had halted and, as Mary watched, the colour drained from her friend's face and she crumpled in a heap to the ground. Both Mary and Ted were on the ground beside her in a second.

''Appen the last few days has all been too much for her,' Mary said unevenly, feeling Annie's forehead. Johnny ran up to his mother and began whimpering.

'Ted, I think this is just a faint. Will you carry her to the house and I'll bring Johnny. Come, Johnny, Your mam's not feeling well. Let's get her indoors. You come with me.' Ted put his arms beneath Annie's body, scooped her up and began to half walk, half run towards the school, while Mary followed, hand in hand with Johnny. Her head was spinning. She was right, then. It wasn't her imagination. Annie had noticed it too…and that was the reason for her body's unforeseen response.

'How's Annie?' said Ted. The encroaching darkness had limited his activities and he had sought Mary out as she went about her jobs in the school. She was in the library when he came across her. A cheerful fire was blazing in the grate and the brass candlesticks she was polishing twinkled and glowed in the light of the flames.

'She's asleep in my room,' said Mary, looking at him

quizzically. 'Johnny too. He's worn out after a day playing in the farmyard.'

Ted set down the wicker basket of logs at the side of
the hearth and sat down suddenly, holding his head in
his hands.

'What's wrong, Ted?' Mary asked anxiously from the
other side of the room. 'Are you not feeling well? You
don't look right good.'

'I've been away for a few days. Maybe thou did not
know.'

'I had no idea. I thought you were busy with clearing
up after the storm and that's why you looked so tired.'

'My father died,' Ted said without preamble. 'Yes, I
know I told thee I had no family. It was true what I said.
My father left when I was born, so I never considered I
had a father.' He shook his head slowly and looked up
at Mary. 'I told thee how my mother died, giving birth
to me. Well, he wanted nothing more to do with me after
that. Remember me saying that I was brought up by my
grandparents? They were my mother's parents. Of
course I knew nothing of this at the time. When I was
older they told me. I don't think they liked him much,
right from the start. They lost trace of him. He just disappeared and they never saw him again. It must have
been hard work for them, bringing up a baby at their age.
Thou would not have guessed, though. What they lacked
in money they made up for in love and care. They had
very little, you see. He gave them nothing.' Ted walked
to the window and stared into the blackness.

'How did you know he had died then, if you had lost
touch with him?'

Ted turned to face her. 'I was contacted by my grandparents' solicitors. My father still had dealings with them, though he kept it a secret where he was. Didn't want to part with any of his brass, I wouldn't be surprised. Anyhow, it turns out there's money in the bank that's coming my way. Not yet, of course. The solicitors have things to sort out first.' He paused, seemed about to say more, but turned back to look out of the window.

'So when was he laid to rest?'

'The funeral won't take place until next week. Circumstances have forced a delay.'

The door opened quietly. Annie entered, then hesitated when she saw Ted.

'I'm sorry. I didn't mean to interrupt, only Johnny is asleep and I came to find Mary. I'm sorry about earlier. Only when I saw you, you reminded me so much of someone I knew…' She looked at him and shook her head disbelievingly.

'Please, come and sit down,' said Ted. 'I was just telling Mary that I have been away for a few days on family business. Do thou sit here by the fire and warm thyself. How long hast thou been here? When did thou arrive?'

'Johnny and I arrived last Friday.'

'Hopefully before the bad weather struck?'

'Well, no. Actually we arrived in the middle of…' She stopped, knowing that, if she went on this way, she would have to explain what she had been doing out in the middle of the storm. She looked to Mary for assistance. Mary put down her polishing cloths and went to where Annie was sitting, putting an arm round her shoulder.

'Annie needed to get away from home for a bit, so she sought me out. It was quite a surprise, her arriving unannounced.' The two women smiled at the recollection of Annie's bedraggled appearance.

'Did thou have far to come…from York, perhaps?'

'No, from the same village as Mary. My husband is the Stationmaster there.'

'Ah! So thou wilt be returning soon to spend Christmas with him?'

'Well, no. That is…I don't think we'll be returning.' She glanced at Mary and back to Ted. 'You see…I ran away. He was ill-treating me and then he started on Johnny. It was the drink, you see. It wouldn't have happened otherwise. I'm sorry, I shouldn't be telling you this. I can see by your face that you think I've done wrong to leave him. 'Appen there's a lot of people think like you. I made my vows…"for better or worse"…I wonder myself if I should have…'

'No, no, it's not that at all,' Ted said hurriedly. He was staring at her fixedly and his face had drained of colour. 'I can't believe it,' he muttered to himself. 'It's too much of a coincidence.' He sat down opposite the two women and continued to stare at Annie. 'Would thou mind if I asked what village thou do come from?'

'Why do you want to know?' asked Mary, unwilling for any possible link to be made between her and John Crowther.

'Is it Templesforth, near the town of Selby?' he went on, ignoring Mary's question.

'How do you know that?' Annie looked at him in astonishment.

'Then thy name must be Annie Crowther, married to John Crowther, Stationmaster at Templesforth.'

'That's right. But how do you know all this?'

Ted turned to look into the fire, ran his hand down his face and turned back to face Annie. He drew a deep breath. 'I'm very sorry, Annie. I hate to be the bearer of bad news.' He flashed a look of warning at Mary and continued. 'I have to tell thee…I have to tell thee…that is…there has been an accident. John Crowther…thy husband…has been killed.'

Annie looked at him calmly and shook her head. 'No, he can't have been. I don't believe you. It can't be true. I only left a few days ago.'

'It was last Thursday evening. It seems that he was…'

'Last Thursday evening?' Annie echoed. 'That's when I left. Last Thursday evening.' Her breath came in short gasps. 'Then it's all my fault. I knew I shouldn't have done it. I should never have left him. What have I done? It's all my fault.'

'What happened?' Mary's voice was a whisper.

'It was a frosty night. He was on the platform. It seems he slipped and fell. The train was coming. He didn't stand a chance…' He stopped, anxious to spare the two women the horrific details. There was silence as the women filled in the details themselves.

'How could he fall?' cried Annie. 'He knew the station and the platform well. I don't understand.'

'It seems he'd had a bit to drink. There was a fight. The men tried to restrain him but he pulled away. That's when it happened.'

Annie burst into tears. 'I should have been there, then this would never have happened. It's all my fault. I should have been there.' She looked at Mary with wild eyes. Mary sat by her, unable to speak, cradling her until she was quieter.

Yes, it would have happened, she thought. *Sooner or later, this would have happened. And meanwhile he would have continued to use you and your son as a punch-bag.* She turned to Annie. 'The drink had become his master. There was nothing you could have done that would have made any difference. Sooner or later, something like this would have happened.'

'No, I could have stopped him. I should have been there. What are we going to do now, me and Johnny? Poor Johnny! He'll have to grow up without a father. What are we going to do?'

It was several hours before Mary was able to seek out Ted again. She had made Annie a soothing chamomile tea and stayed with her friend until she slept, exhausted. She would return later to see if there was anything she needed. Ted was in the library, where they had left him.

'I knew that there would be some questions to answer,' he said, after asking how Annie was. 'So I came back here to wait for thy return.'

'What I don't understand is how *you* know about John Crowther's accident. After all, you're nothing to do with the railway and you've never been to our village.'

'Thou art wrong there, Mary. I have been to thy village. I had been charged with looking for Annie and her child. I searched high and low, never, for one minute, thinking that they would be here waiting for me on my return.'

'Forgive me if I appear stupid, but why should *you* be looking for Annie and her child?'

'Because, Mary, Johnny and I are half-brothers. John Crowther was my father too.'

Apart from the crackle of logs on the fire, there was silence as Mary struggled to assimilate this information. 'You mean, all that talk earlier about your father abandoning you as a baby and leaving you to be brought up by your grandparents…that was him…John Crowther?'

'That's right.'

'And the money that's coming to you…that's John Crowther's money?'

'Just so. It was money of my mother's that came to my father on their marriage. She was Harriet Appleby, his first wife. When my father walked out after her death, the money was left untouched, gathering interest. I don't mind admitting I was furious when I learned how it had sat in the bank all those years, while Grandfather and Grandmother Appleby were struggling to make ends meet. And then, to add insult to injury, the solicitor told me of the existence of a second wife and child, for whom no provision had been made in the will.'

'To think that you never knew you had a brother…well, half-brother. If this hadn't happened, you might never have met.'

'Who can say? It was only when I went to York following an urgent telegram from the solicitors that I found out that his wife and child not only existed but had also gone missing. The police were out looking for them. At first there was some suggestion that his wife might have had something to do with his death. The evidence of the railway workers soon disproved that. Then they carried on looking because they were worried as to their whereabouts, the weather being so awful and all. I joined in the search. I've been up to the police house this evening while thou were busy settling Annie down. I've asked for a message to be sent to call off the search.

'It sickened me, the thought of what his actions had done to his nearest and dearest. I spoke to the men at the station in thy village. They'd all been worried about Annie, tha' knows. They knew John Crowther drank too much and one of them, at least, had his suspicions that he was beating her. I'm sure they didn't suspect that he had started on his son as well.

'I can't believe that his wife and child have turned up here, of all places. Thou can have no idea what it feels like to have no kith and kin in the world. To suddenly find two on my doorstep is strange…and marvellous. I know the circumstances are dreadful now for Annie and her son…my brother, but they need have no fear for their future. John Crowther may have made no provision for them, but I intend to remedy that.'

Mary sat, looking at him, fitting together the pieces of the jigsaw. She recalled the first time she and Ted had met and her confused impression that she had seen him before. And that time in the cellar when he'd touched her hair and she'd reacted so violently that she'd surprised even herself. What was it he had said? *'Such a lovely face'.* Of course! That was what John Crowther—his father—had said to her that night when she had arrived back late from Eliza's birthing. He had been sitting in the kitchen, in the dark. She had smelt alcohol on his breath. He'd caught her hand as she'd gone to pass him. He'd reached up to touch her hair. *'Such a lovely face'.* Those had been his exact words. His bloated face and bloodshot eyes had loomed close in the candlelight. …And that had only been the beginning of it.

She shut her eyes, swallowing the nausea that rose in her throat. *He's gone,* she told herself. *He can't ever bother you again.* Those angry words on the night of the storm flashed into her mind. *'I hope he rots in hell'.* By her calculation, he already was before the words had passed her lips.

Mary opened her eyes and smiled at Ted. Poor Ted. She had done him a disservice. He may look like his father…and there was no denying that he did…she had seen it earlier in the likeness between him and Johnny…but his behaviour could not be more different. And yet she had unwittingly pushed him away.

'Do you not feel sad never to have known your father?' she asked him.

He thought for a moment. 'We are encouraged to see the good in everyone…'

'Oh, yes,' Mary interrupted. 'A good friend of mine was always saying that. But it can be very hard.'

Ted continued. 'From everything I've heard, it sounds as though he was a nasty piece of work. But he must have really loved my mother, to be so upset by her passing that he left home…and me. I can't help thinking that if he had stayed I could have made him happy. Now I'll never know. But, of course, thou must have known him. He lived in the same village as thyself. Did thou know him well?'

'I worked for him and Annie as housekeeper,' she replied, seeing no reason to hide the fact, which would be sure to emerge soon in any case. 'Of course, I was mostly with Annie and Johnny. Johnny was just a baby then. Annie had a bad time after he was born and needed help. I was only with them for a year or so and then I moved to York. Your father was busy with the railway most of the time I was there.'

'So thou did not have much to do with him during thy stay?'

'Not a lot, no.'

Ted got up out of the chair and poked the embers of the fire. Mary extinguished the lamps and they walked to the door.

'So what dost thou feel, having known him? Canst thou see the good in him?'

Mary stopped and looked at him. 'To be honest with you, and I think that's what you want…honesty, I never saw him do one kind act. He was cruel to Annie. She was young and inexperienced in the ways of the world. He expected her to be…as your mother must have been, I suppose. And she wasn't. I can't forgive him that. He was selfish. He was selfish in the beginning…to leave you, when you were his responsibility. And he was selfish when I knew him. He took what he fancied, regardless of the consequences. No, I can't see the good in him. I don't wish to upset you in any way, but I think we are well rid of him.' And, taking up her lamp, she made her way along the shadowy corridor and down the stairs to where Annie and her son lay asleep.

CHAPTER TWENTY-EIGHT

MARY did not attend John Crowther's funeral. The reason she gave for declining the invitation was that Ted would be able to take care of Annie now. They were, in any case, intending to stay in Templesforth for a few days, to sort out Annie's belongings in Station House and any outstanding business connected with her late husband. Besides, Mary had received a letter from Hannah, who wrote that they particularly needed her to be in York and, as it had not been possible for her to be with them at Christmas, could she not visit the following week? The real reason for her staying behind was that she could not mourn the passing of someone she was heartily glad to be rid of, and she was not prepared to pretend otherwise.

The rhythm of the carriage on the rails beneath brought a strand of poetry into her mind:

'The best laid schemes o' mice an' men gang aft a-gley'.

She smiled as she recalled the struggle she and Esther had had with the strange Scottish dialect of Robbie Burns. Without doubt he had a way with words, once you could understand what he was saying…and what he had said was undoubtedly true. Her plans for the Christmas holiday had certainly been thrown into confusion. There had been no question but that her proposed trip to York should be cancelled. Annie had been far too distressed by the news of her husband's death for Mary to suggest that she and Johnny accompany her, even if the circumstances had been different. And then, of course, there was Ted. It would not have been right to separate him from his newfound family. And really, she considered, he was the head of that family now and any decisions that needed to be made should be his.

What was it that Hannah particularly wanted to see her about? Would Esther be there? And, if so, would she have the baby, *her* baby, with her?

The flat bare fields of the Vale of York replaced the slag heaps of Pontefract and Mary was reminded of home. Her decision to stay away from the funeral meant that she had also turned her back on the opportunity to see her family. She and Sarah-Louise wrote often and she knew that her sister longed to see her again. She would be quite grown-up now; nine months out of school, and her time filled with looking after Martha and housekeeping at Temple Farm.

She thought of Ted and Annie. They had set off for Templesforth the previous day, taking Johnny with them. Today they would arrange the funeral and it would take place within the next day or two. A relief Stationmaster was staying in the village until a permanent replacement was found for John Crowther and the house cleared of the acquisitions of Annie's three-and-a-half year marriage. She imagined the grim job of packing John Crowther's possessions and was relieved that Ted would take the responsibility for this, as he was doing for the funeral.

Shortly after two-thirty Mary alighted from the train. The day was dry and cold, the sky heavy with clouds that held the possibility of snow. She drew her cloak tight beneath her chin and, skirting the city wall, crossed Lendal Bridge and took the steps down to the esplanade. The waters of the Ouse, grey as the sky above, flowed rapidly past as she walked the well-remembered route to Marygate Lane.

Her heart was beating fast as she knocked on the door of Fothergill House and stood back to greet Deborah. A long pause followed—Deborah must be having more trouble with her old legs than before. There was the brief flutter of a curtain to her left and a few seconds later the door flew open to reveal…Sarah-Louise. Mary stared at her in happy disbelief. Her sister had grown tall and slim in the year since she had last seen her. Her dark hair was looped round her ears and drawn into a low bun behind. She wore an ankle-length blue dress, protected with a white apron.

'Sarah-Lou, how did you get here?' Mary gasped, hugging her sister tightly. 'How grown-up you are. No wonder Hannah wanted me to come. I had no idea that you would be here. Let me have a better look at you.' She took her hand and they stepped into the street.

Sarah-Louise's eyes had lost none of their sparkle as she replied. 'I thought you'd be surprised to see me. And it's grand being in t' big city at last. But there's some-

one else here that I think you'll be even more surprised
to see.' Keeping hold of each other's hands, they entered
the hallway with its arching ceiling. Sarah-Louise took
Mary's cloak from her shoulders and led her through a
door to the right into a room rarely used for entertaining. A fire blazed in the hearth. Hannah, who was seated
in a low chair to one side of the fire, rose to greet her.
A second armchair completely hid its occupant. Making
her way into the room, Mary turned to see a diminutive
woman, silver wisps of hair escaping from her lace cap,
eyes even more sunken than they'd been the last time
they'd met.

'Martha, how good it is to see thee!' She knelt down
in front of the old lady and hugged her warmly.

'Mary, lass, not as good as it is for me to see thee.
How I've missed thee around the place; not but that thy
sister has been doing a very good job of keeping me in
order.'

'When did you arrive?' said Mary, looking from one
to the other of the two visitors.

'Hannah sent t' carriage for us,' said Sarah-Louise. 'I
felt real grand, travelling like that. We arrived the week
before Christmas. We were going to surprise you, like.'

'Well, you certainly did that! It's wonderful to see
you both.'

'What an awful thing to happen to Mr Crowther,
though,' went on Sarah-Louise, 'but why was Mrs
Crowther staying with you?'

'It's a long story. I'll tell you some time. Annie is
back in the village now, arranging the funeral, which
will no doubt be tomorrow. It's been very hard for her,

but she has some help now.' She turned to Martha. 'Now, tell me honestly, Martha, how you are. Look at your hands,' she said taking one of Martha's hands in her own and gently caressing the bent fingers. 'How did you manage the journey?'

'It was tiring, but since arriving I have done nothing but rest. Everyone is so kind. I've a lot to be thankful for.' She gazed at Hannah fondly. 'And to think that all these years I've kept myself distant from my family in York. There's a lot to be said for families.' She paused and looked at Mary. 'But thou dost look very thin, Mary. Does the school life not suit thee?'

'It suits me fine. I'm very happy there, happier than for a long time. But I've been ill with the scarlet fever. I were looking after two of the pupils and then I started with it. And to think…all that looking after Alfie, when I lived at home and I never caught it.' She smiled at her sister. 'I do miss my family, though, and would love to go back home. Perhaps I shall soon.'

Sarah-Louise insisted that Mary share her room. It was the one that had been Mary's for the three months of her stay and Hannah was secretly worried that Mary would be reminded of the time spent there with her baby.

'You don't need to worry, Hannah,' Mary assured her. 'It's different now, with Martha and my sister here. As if the separate parts of my life are beginning to come together.'

They lay awake that night, the two sisters.

'What I don't understand,' said Sarah-Louise into the darkness, 'is why you had to go away from us. You always said that you didn't like the city…that you were

happy living in t' countryside. I were the one who talked
of going away all t' time. I were reet lonely without you.
And Mam and Father weren't too pleased neither and
they were always cross wi' me.'

'I know how it must have been. And I'm sorry. It
were John Crowther. He were the reason for my going.
He were cruel to Annie, tha' knows. That's why she left
him and turned up unexpected at t' school. He'd started
on little Johnny as well by then. She couldn't stand it
when that happened. That's when she left.'

'But why did *you* go, Mary? Didn't Annie need you
there? After all, tha' were always so much stronger than
her. Tha' could maybes have helped.'

'I know that and I felt bad about leaving her.' Mary's
voice dropped. 'But he attacked me, you see…John
Crowther. I couldn't say owt to Annie, for fear of causing trouble. And I didn't like to mention it to Father, in
case he spoke to John Crowther and lost his job as a result. Think how I would have felt if that had happened.
So I thought it best to leave and look for other employment. I didn't want to stay in the village and risk coming across him again.'

'You didn't tell us much about what your job was like
when you came to York.'

'Oh, it were just a job, like any other. I were working
for a family wi' a lot of children, so I were kept busy like.'

'Then why did you leave?'

The questions were getting more and more difficult
to answer truthfully and Mary did not want to lie to her
sister.

'Martha had mentioned that she had relatives living

in Marygate and one day I decided to visit them,' she said with supreme understatement. 'Hannah persuaded me to stay for a while. But I couldn't stay for ever. I needed work. And she put me in touch with the school.'

About the baby Mary said nothing, even though it made explanations awkward and incomplete. She longed to confide in her sister but she didn't know how Sarah-Louise would take the news and she was reluctant to risk further suggestions that she had done the wrong thing. In any case it could cause embarrassment over the next few days if Esther came to visit.

Sarah-Louise returned to the original subject. 'What I don't understand is why you didn't tell Nathaniel that Mr Crowther had attacked you. He would have done summat. He didn't know why you had gone. He were right put out with your leaving. Father said he were drinking more than he should. He's better now, like. Just as well, really. I heard him and his dad talking and it seems t' farm isn't doing so well. His ma's been poorly too. She can't do so much as she'd like. Why didn't you talk to him, Mary?'

'I couldn't, that's all. Don't ask me to explain any more. Any road, I'm glad he's got over me,' Mary added, her voice sounding unconvincing. 'Does he have…er…is he walking out wi' anyone now?' she ventured to ask.

'Well, I've seen him and that Rhoda Precious going out riding together sometimes. Folk say that he's courting her but I don't know for sure. 'Appen it's just talk.'

Mary considered. She knew that, unless she had the courage to go back and face the possibility of seeing them together, she was never going to see her family again.

* * *

'Mary,' Hannah said to her the following day, as they prepared vegetables in the kitchen, 'Martha knows all about the baby.'

The knife that Mary was using clattered to the floor as she stared at the older woman. 'How does she know? She can't know. I didn't say anything to her before I left Templesforth and no one else at home knows about it.'

'I told her. How else could I explain thy sudden arrival in Marygate last year…and Esther's baby, when Martha was only too well aware that Esther was childless?'

Mary thought about it and realised that Hannah was right. How else indeed would she have explained all that had happened without telling the truth?

'She wants to talk to you, Mary. Do thou go and see her. Don't look so worried. When hast thou ever seen Martha angry?' She laughed. 'Go and talk to her, child, now, while the house is quiet.'

When Mary approached her old friend in her chair by the fire, Martha indicated that she sit on the stool at her feet.

'There,' she said. 'We're just as we were when we had tea in my garden after a day of tending those herbs.' She patted Mary on the shoulder.

'That seems a very long time ago,' Mary replied, staring into the fire.

'Why did thou not tell me?' Martha continued.

'I thought you would be angry…I thought you would try and persuade me to keep the baby.'

'I would never have tried to persuade thee to do anything that thou did not feel was right.'

'But you lost your baby. I remember now how sad you were when you told me about your husband and your baby dying. How could I tell you that I didn't want mine? And then, later, when she was born and I decided to give her away, how would you have understood that?'

'It's not for me to understand or not understand. I grieve only that thou did not feel able to tell me about all that thou did have to go through at Station House. It might have been easier, had thou been able to talk about what happened to thee.'

'I'm sorry, Martha. I wanted to. But I just couldn't. He made me feel so awful. I didn't want to go on living…and I certainly didn't want his baby.'

There was silence for a while before Martha asked, 'Did thou tell Nathaniel about John Crowther's attack?'

'No. I didn't see him again. It wouldn't have been fair. It wouldn't have been right to see someone he loved so defiled.'

'Shouldn't he have been the best judge of that?'

Mary looked at her in disbelief. 'No, oh, no, I could never have told him what happened. He was the main reason I went away. I couldn't bear him to be so near and for me never to see him or speak to him. I wanted it to be Nathaniel that loved me first, not that monster.'

'So he knows nothing about the baby?'

'Nothing. He must never know. It was all wrong. It should have been Nathaniel's baby. His and mine. It should have been part of Nathaniel inside me. I shall never ever tell him.'

'Well, Mary, whatever has happened over the past year, one thing is certain. Thou hast made Esther and

Timothy very happy with thy decision. And I do hope that thou will be able to see for thyself how happy they are before thou dost leave us to return to Ashworth.'

The plan was for Mary to stay for the New Year and travel back to Ashworth the day after, to complete the necessary cleaning and repairs before the return of the children. She and her sister had willingly taken over Hannah's household chores. Deborah was now so arthritic that she could do little to help and spent much of her time chatting to Martha, the aching joints of the two elderly ladies eased by the warmth of the fire that was kept in day and night. Hannah too was feeling her age and sat at the kitchen table directing operations, rather than taking part. Each day after dinner Mary and her sister dressed in their warm outdoor clothes and explored the city. Snow had fallen but not too much that they could not get about. Sarah-Louise loved all that she saw and Mary wanted to show her all the places she had discovered during her time living in York.

On New Year's Eve they returned with faces glowing to find Esther and her baby in Martha's room. It was what Mary had been anticipating with dread and curiosity. And yet the baby seemed so much a part of Esther, and Esther so happy with her, that Mary could not imagine it otherwise. She looked closely for signs of John Crowther in her daughter's appearance but she could see none. Apart from her dark hair, which she could equally have inherited from her mother, she showed likeness to neither parent. Sarah-Louise picked up the baby and went off to the kitchen to feed her, thereby showing a tolerance for children that no one, least of all Sarah-Louise, realised she possessed. Mary sat with Esther and her Aunt Martha in the small room that had now become Martha's own.

'I am glad you took her,' said Mary. 'She's growing up so bonny. If I had kept her, I would always have been reminded of what John Crowther did to me. Now, with him gone, I feel I can really make a fresh start.'

'It's what I hoped to see,' said Martha. 'Thee happy and looking to the future again. Thou were always such a cheerful and starry-eyed girl when I did first know thee.' She stared into the fire in a way that reminded Mary of their days in the herb-filled living room of Martha's cottage. 'I must say this, while Sarah-Louise is attending to t' babby. I am not long for this world. I shan't be going back to Templesforth. I shall die here among my family. I want to thank thee for all thy help. Do thou thank thy sister after I am gone. I don't wish to upset her by talking of these things, she being so young.'

'Don't talk like this, Martha,' said Esther, who had sat silent until now. 'You've not been here long and how can you be so certain?'

Mary said nothing. She knew Martha spoke the truth. The old lady had a lifetime of watching and listening to the workings of her own and others' bodies. She knew when her end was near.

Martha smiled at Esther's question and went on, 'What I want is this, Mary. I want thee to have my herbal. Tha' knows where it is kept. After I am gone, thou must go to the cottage and take it. Wilt thou promise me that?'

'Of course I will. I'll take care of it. I'll use it. It's

time I got back to studying about all t' herbs and plants. I fear it's been sadly neglected recently, with all t' other things to take up my time.'

Sarah-Louise entered with the baby. 'She likes her food, just like her mother,' she said, handing her back to Esther. Mary looked at the two of them, Esther and Ann. It was true. No one would have doubted that Ann was Esther's daughter. Her sturdy little frame bouncing on the equally sturdy frame of her mother put a smile on Martha's lips and an answering one on Mary's.

'Martha will be staying here,' Hannah said to Sarah-Louise on the evening before Mary's departure. 'She's not well enough to travel. In any case, now we have her here we don't want to lose her again.'

Sarah-Louise glanced uncertainly at Mary. She had confided in her just the night before that she was not looking forward to going back to the village. Now she would lose half her wage as well.

'So what I am suggesting,' went on Hannah, 'is that thou dost stay here and look after Martha and keep house for me as well. I have discussed it with Deborah and she admits that she isn't up to the work now. She will stay with us as a guest. After all, we've more than enough rooms.'

The last three sentences were lost in Sarah-Louise's ecstatic cry. She hugged Hannah and then her sister. 'It's what I always wanted, to live in t' big city.' She paused and frowned, looking at Mary. 'I shall have to make sure that Father agrees. And there's my other job, working for Mr and Mrs Varley. Will I have to go back home to talk to them, do you think?'

Mary considered for a minute. 'You could write to Mr and Mrs Varley,' she said, 'but Mam and Father would find it difficult to read a letter. Why don't I write to Annie and Ted? They're staying in Templesforth until the end of the week at least. Ted would go and talk to our parents. And, if I mention that you have written to the Varleys, I'm sure he would go and see them too, just to explain things.'

It was settled. The letters were sent. Mary said good-bye to her friends, promising to return at the first op-portunity to see Martha. Sarah-Louise walked with her to the station to see her off.

'I wish I didn't have to leave you quite so soon,' Mary said, hugging her sister and stepping into the carriage.

'Come and see us on your next day off, Mary. Martha will be anxious to see you again…and so will I!'

'I should be able to visit regularly, thanks to Hannah's generosity,' Mary replied but her voice was lost in the hiss of steam. The sisters smiled at each other and waved as the train rounded the curve in the rails and Sarah-Louise and York were left behind.

CHAPTER TWENTY-NINE

THE expected rush of winter coughs and colds didn't materialise. A few children arrived back and succumbed a few days later to mild fevers that their families had been nursing. Sarah Pumphrey dosed them with Mary's rosehip syrup and nothing more serious developed.

Mary began to put on much-needed weight and lose the pallor that had hung around her since her illness. She resumed her work as a housemaid but was allowed a certain amount of time to hear the smaller girls read and to supervise the older ones in the sewing room. She avoided Sarah Pumphrey's sharp tongue whenever possible and made sure that she was not alone in Ted's company, for fear of a repeat of his earlier declaration. Ted, however, spent much of his spare time getting to know his young half-brother and Mary saw them often about the grounds, as Ted attempted to teach Johnny the rudiments of gardening. Annie had recovered from the disaster of her husband's death more quickly than Mary could have thought possible and was helping Judith on the farm with all kinds of activities, agricultural and culinary, that she would previously have resisted.

Once a month Mary was given a day off and she caught the train to York to visit her friends and Martha in particular. On Easter Day Martha did not wake up. Mary had arrived at Fothergill House the previous day, the children of Ashworth School having departed to their homes for the Easter break. She was taking a breakfast tray into the little room that was now considered as Martha's own. It had become a regular feature of her visits, this tray of breakfast. When Martha had accused her of fussing, Mary had said that it was reward for the breakfasts she had received at her hands in the cottage.

Mary drew the curtains and sunlight flooded the room. She could hear the bells of the Minster ringing out their Easter message. Martha lay curled peacefully, the sunken pallor of her face making it immediately obvious that she was dead. On the bedside table was a letter addressed to Mary:

My dear friend,
I shall not see thee again this side of the grave. Do not grieve for me. After so many years I am at last going to see my dear Joseph.
Remember to go to my cottage for the herbal. It is thine to use as a token of my thanks and for the good of those around thee. Thou art a brave lass, Mary, braver than I ever was.
There was a holy woman hundreds of years ago, who wrote this: 'All shall be well, and all shall be

well, and all manner of things shall be well.' We may
have to wait a long time, but I do agree with her.
I know that this day is the first anniversary of thy
baby's birth. I have not forgotten. Neither shall I
forget thee.
Martha.

Four days after the resumption of school the first pupil
went down with a fever and sore throat, which turned,
within days, into a cold and cough. Several more followed. The nurse opened the sick bay in an attempt to
isolate the infection. Within a further three days most
of the class and several other pupils had all succumbed.
Unlike the first sufferers, who were now well on the way
to recovery, those who had lately acquired the infection
began to complain of colicky pains and several began
to vomit and suffer diarrhoea.

'I can't understand what's happening,' complained
Sarah irritably. 'The first children are recovering without any problem. Why are these later ones getting colic
and sickness? It must be your medicine, Mary. I never
did have any faith in all these herbal remedies.'

Mary was upset by the accusation. 'It can hardly be
my medicine, otherwise all the children would be suffering. They've all had some.' Nevertheless, the hint was
enough to worry Mary and that night she didn't sleep.

The headmaster called the following morning and
Sarah Pumphrey lost no time in telling him her fears. It
was while she was talking that Annie put her head round
the door of the sick bay. Mary was sweeping the floor

between the beds and listening miserably, as Sarah continued to suggest to the headmaster that they should be relying on what the chemist dispensed. What did some girl fresh from the countryside know about medicines, taught as she had been by an old woman who sounded nothing short of a witch?

'It's Johnny,' Annie whispered. 'He's started with the sickness too. He's not well at all.'

'I'll tell Sarah when she's finished talking to the headmaster. You'd be best keeping him on the farm, Annie, unless he gets really bad. Sarah will come and see him there.' As Annie turned to go, Mary realised with relief that Johnny had not been near the school recently, let alone had any of the medicines.

The headmaster suggested that the doctor be called. By the time he arrived a further five children were complaining of colic. A lad who had gone down with the illness the day before was complaining of headache and becoming delirious. Dr. Wood examined each of the children carefully before announcing that he thought there might be something in the water that was causing the problem and that the house staff should be summoned to check that all water supplies were satisfactory.

It was Johnny who provided the clue. Mary called to see him later in the day, at Sarah's suggestion. Ted was sitting on the end of the bed, it being his dinnertime break.

'He's very thirsty,' said Ted, passing him a cup of water, 'and he keeps complaining of his mouth tasting funny. Have any of the other children been the same?'

'They're all thirsty,' Mary replied thoughtfully, 'but

I don't know about t'other. The doctor thinks it's summat in t' water.'

'I know. I've been helping to check the pipes all
morning. Johnny doesn't go up to the school much,
though. He plays around the farm most of the time with
Judith's little lad…and there's nothing wrong with him.'

When Mary started asking the other young patients,
she discovered that they were all noticing a peculiar
taste in their mouths. She mentioned it to the doctor on
his afternoon visit.

'Aah,' he said. 'Well, Nurse Pumphrey, thanks to
your assistant here, we might well have the diagnosis.'
Sarah Pumphrey shot Mary a vindictive glance, before
smiling at the doctor. 'I think the children may very well
be suffering from acute lead poisoning,' he continued.

'Is that serious?' Mary asked in alarm.

'Well, yes, it is if we don't catch it early and the children continue to drink the affected water. The important
thing is to trace the source of the contamination. And
we can try a dose of syrup of ipecacuanha for them all,
in case there is any lead left in their stomachs.'

'What does that do?' asked Mary and received a
nudge in the ribs from Sarah.

'I'll tell thee all about it later. Don't bother the doctor now. He's got better things to do.'

'It's all right, Nurse. It makes them sick, Mary. But
it does mean that there is nothing left in the stomach to
enter the bloodstream and cause more damage.'

The search continued to find where the contamination of the water source was occurring.

'It's obvious,' Ted said suddenly, after an afternoon's

examination of the school waterworks. 'If Johnny has the same as the rest and he's been nowhere near the school, then there must be contamination around the farm.' He and two of the other men started to examine the farm and its outbuildings. Behind the farmhouse was a large barn, once used for lambing. Along one wall a tap, infrequently used, fed an old stone sink. It seemed an unlikely source of the problem until Ted questioned Johnny, still feeling queasy after his dose of deceptively sweet medicine.

'Oh, aye. I gave them all a drink. They were thirsty from playing cricket and they asked me for a drink and I gave them one.'

'And you too?' asked his mother.

'Oh, aye. I had one too!'

Mary slept more easily that night than she had since the outbreak began. The next day a further three children went down with the feverish chill. Under Sarah's instruction Mary dosed them with medicines from the cupboard and within twenty-four hours each had begun to vomit.

'I said so,' the nurse began. 'I said it was thy quack remedies all along. Trying to worm thy way out of it with thy superior knowledge.' She tossed her head. 'Well, talk thy way out of this one.'

Mary stared at the bottles of rosehip syrup in disbelief. It couldn't be them, she thought. She had dosed all the early sufferers with it and they hadn't started to be sick. She began to question the children, most of whom were back to normal after their ordeal. Several of them had not been playing cricket and neither had they been near the lambing shed. Again she began to fret that it might be her fault. She walked down to the farm to check on Johnny. He was in the shed, watching in rapt attention as Ted dismantled the lead piping that ran along the wall and fed the stone sink.

'Imagine this place full of bleating lambs.' He laughed. 'Thou wouldn't be able to think straight. I don't suppose thou hast seen all these farm buildings before, Mary.'

'Yes, I were here last backend. It were when I were recovering from my illness. We went picking rosehips, the older girls and I. And we came in here to wash them in t'…' She gasped in horror as she realised what she was saying. 'It *were* me, then. It were my fault that some of them were ill. I washed the fruit in the sink in the water from that tap. Oh, no! I could have killed them. What would I have done then?' She hid her face in her hands.

'Mary, thou must stop this,' said Ted sharply, coming over to her. 'Thou art not to blame. This could have happened anywhere in the school at any time. It is only that the water has been in this pipe for months, just because it is not used often. It's soaked up more lead than would normally be the case. It wasn't thy fault.' He put his arm round her shoulders and she buried her face in his neck.

'I'm sorry,' she mumbled into his shirt. 'You're quite right. Now I come to think of it, the first lot I made were fine. We gathered that from the lanes the other way on and took them to the kitchen straight away. The next batch, though, we brought here because the girls were muddy from the track and we didn't want to trail mud into t' kitchens.'

'So all thou does need to do is go up to the sick bay and throw out all of that second batch and there will be no more danger.'

'You make it sound so straightforward,' she said, smiling up at him.

'Well, it is straightforward.' He smiled back and then his smile faded as he continued to hold her gaze. 'I wish the rest of life was as straightforward.' He kissed her forehead and let her go and they walked, the three of them, Johnny holding hands between them, up to the school.

CHAPTER THIRTY

THE tenant farmers at Temple Farm received the news of Sarah-Louise's departure with dismay. She had been, in Henry Varley's words, 'a grand little worker'. For Nathaniel it was a further worry to add to the growing list, for which there seemed to be no solution.

It was an inescapable fact that his parents could no longer cope with the day-to-day running of the farm. They were elderly now and the cold weather was playing havoc with his father's rheumatics. Never a man with the sunniest of dispositions, the combination of weather and stiff joints was making him positively cantankerous. Already this year disagreements with his labourers had twice needed to be resolved in Selby County Court. What particularly upset Nathaniel about this was the fact that he himself had always been on the side of the workers, encouraging them to join their Union, which he saw as the fairest way to ensure them a decent wage for a decent day's work. But, at every turn, his father unwittingly, or otherwise, undermined his work on their behalf.

There was another problem, though. The last harvest may have been a better one than the disastrous result of the year before, but overall they were not making ends meet. There had been a run of summer storms, just at the time the corn was almost ready for harvesting, and they had lost money for several years in a row. British corn did not sell so well either. When the government had repealed the Corn Laws in the earlier years of Queen Victoria's reign, there had been an influx of wheat from Canada, America and Russia. For a while, despite fears to the contrary, English farmers had continued to hold their own against the imports but now people seemed to prefer the hard, firm wheat of Canada for their bread making. Despite the downturn in their fortunes, Nathaniel's father had gone ahead and invested in two pieces of modern machinery, a reaping machine four years before and, more recently, a threshing machine. Money was still owed on these and of course the labourers had complained because the machines did much of the work that they were previously employed to do. The trouble was that the farm, while covering three hundred acres or so, was just not big enough to warrant the new machinery that Henry Varley had bought.

At least the cattle were still bringing in money, Nathaniel thought. The advantage of a mixed farm was that even if one part did badly, there was still the chance of the other part doing better. But even this side of the farm had its worries, for his mother had not recovered her strength since the illness that had laid her low in the summer. She badly needed someone to help in the dairy, but they just couldn't afford it. Perhaps if and when Rhoda married him and came to live at the farm, she would take over from his mother. But he had his doubts.

Thank goodness they had accepted the invitation to spend Christmas Day with the Precious family. It had been a pretty lacklustre affair but infinitely preferable to his father's original idea of Rhoda and her father visiting them. Their servants had served up a good joint of beef, followed by Christmas pudding, all accompanied by wine enough to make them forget the troubles of farming for one day in the year.

He had been invited to join them for Sunday dinner on two occasions since then. Awkward, ceremonious affairs they had been. The best silver cutlery twinkling in the light from the candles set in elaborate silver candelabra. Matching plates and tureens and cups and saucers on an immaculate tablecloth. Everything as formal and starchy as the collars he wore with his best suit when he visited them. After dinner he would sit in the parlour opposite her father while Rhoda played from her extensive repertoire at the piano. Finally her father would leave the room for fifteen minutes, to allow the two young people time to themselves. There they faced each other, trying to think of things to talk about until Nathaniel made his excuses and stepped into the freedom of the fresh air and a welcome walk home.

It had been on one of these occasions that he'd decided to call on Martha Riley. After George Morritt's revelations concerning the strange goings-on at Station House, Nathaniel had at first been determined to go and see the old lady, so that she could verify or deny his suspicions.

But the weeks had gone by and other things had filled his time. Eventually he'd come to believe that if he could prove Mary's guilt he would pursue his friendship with Rhoda with greater enthusiasm. He knew, in any case, that any chance of a future with Mary was long gone. She was probably now in the arms of another—maybe that young man who had materialised at the time of John Crowther's funeral to confirm that Sarah-Louise had defected to York. But, even so, he hated mysteries and this one had dragged on for far too long. On a Sunday in late January, returning from dinner with Arthur Precious and his daughter, he had made up his mind.

He knocked on the door. No one came. There was no sound from within. It was hardly surprising. The old lady was probably having a nap after her dinner. Besides, her arthritis had made her slow—Mary had said as much. Opening the wooden side-gate, he found himself in a neat and tidy garden, plants cut back, soil turned, ivy trimmed to the wall. Someone must be in, then. He knocked at the kitchen door. Silence. Turning the handle, he stepped inside and called Martha's name. Silence again. He walked through into the living room. Bunches of herbs hung from the ceiling, dried now and a little dusty. The fire was dead in the grate. A small bed in the corner was neatly made. A damp chill hung about the place. It felt as though it had been empty for weeks.

Nathaniel sat down in one of the fireside chairs. Where had the old woman gone? He felt cheated. Having at last decided on visiting her, he couldn't believe that she was not here to answer his questions. He looked around the room. This was where Mary had spent so much of her time before she was working for the Crowthers. He had heard that she had even stayed there a few nights before her mysterious disappearance from the village. He got up and walked slowly round, letting his hand trail over the backs of the chairs, along a bookshelf, over a huge tome, worn and dog-eared, that rested on the shelf. He climbed the stairs to the room above, looked from the window across the fields—his father's fields—had turned to a bed that nestled in an alcove, a bed with a tiny window slanting over it in the roof. He lay down on the bed, had imagined night and a view of the stars such as she would have seen, lying here after she had told him that she didn't want him. He left then, clattering down the winding stairs and out of the door as though the devil were after him.

He had gone back though, one more time, although he had found out by now that Martha was staying in York. The same emptiness had greeted him, the chill more intense, the silence more profound. He had lain on her bed again. And it was then that he had decided that she was dead to him. What she had done, she had meant to do. Rhoda was free and there was every chance that she would have him. He went downstairs, shut the door behind him and left the cottage.

In May Nathaniel attended the annual area meeting of the Agricultural Labourers' Union. It was twelve years since their formation and he had been attending for the last five, ever since he had reached the age of majority, in fact. It was his one act of defiance against his overbearing father.

It seemed the farm labourers were much less inter-

ested in the Union than he was. Even now there were
only fifteen thousand members nationwide. Nathaniel
knew that, compared with workers in other parts of the
country, those in the north were fairly well off. Their
weekly wage was now over sixteen shillings. No matter how hard he tried, however, he could not rid them of
their complacency. He told them the story of how the
predecessors of the Union had demanded a 'living
wage', and how they were now benefiting from the re-
sults. He warned them that the increasing use of machinery meant that their jobs would be under threat. He
reminded them that loss of a job also meant loss of a
roof over their heads, for many of them lived with their
families in tied cottages. They retaliated by reminding
him that the farmers threatened them with loss of their
cottages, even if they did belong to the Union.

What made it more difficult for Nathaniel was that the
men were suspicious of him and his motives. To them
he was one of the bosses. They could not conceive of a
boss on the side of the workers. It was, and would always
be, 'them and us'. It was understandable perhaps when
the machinery on the family farm was doing just what
he warned them about—threatening their livelihood.

He sat by the window in the Station Hotel restaurant,
absent-mindedly stirring a cup of tea. The heavy damask
curtain to his side and the dark oppressive furniture
around him contrasted with the bright sunshine outside.
He knew that his position as boss's son and workers' ad-
vocate was an incongruous one. The only way of secur-
ing the future of the farm and that of his family and the
farm workers was to sell the unnecessary machinery.

His idea would unleash a torrent of anger from his father, not least because he would be seen to lose face amongst the surrounding farming community. But it was his and Rhoda's futures that were at stake here. She would not be eager to become mistress of an ailing homestead and he couldn't blame her. Yes, that is what he would do. He would make enquiries at the next market and set his plans in motion.

The burden eased, he looked up from his cup and studied the cheerful faces of the inhabitants of York as they made their way along the pathway. They sauntered in pairs, couples out for the day, enjoying the spell of good weather. Or they looked purposeful, intent on carrying out whatever business they were engaged in, so that they too might enjoy what remained of the day when their duties were done. He had invited Rhoda to join him on his visit to the city but her father objected to her being left alone while he was talking to those men. He suspected that the real reason was that her father objected to his dabbling in Union business and did not want his daughter similarly tainted.

A slim young woman, more purposeful than most, walked briskly past the window at which he was seated. He watched her familiar figure as it grew smaller and realised with a start that it was Sarah-Louise. Hastily calling the waiter, he paid the bill for his untouched refreshment and ran down the hotel steps into the sunshine. He could no longer see her but he hurried along in the direction she had gone. In the middle of Lendal Bridge he paused for breath. She was nowhere to be seen. She always was a quick walker, legacy of all those years in the countryside. He turned to look down at the river and, as he did so, saw her emerge from the shadow of the bridge to make her way along the esplanade.

'Mr Varley, what a surprise! You're the last person I expected to see. What are you doing here?' Sarah-Louise began, as she turned at Nathaniel's shout and stopped to wait for him.

'Trying to catch you up, for a start!' he gasped. 'You're a fast walker and no mistake. And please, call me Nathaniel. Do you have time to stop and talk for a few minutes?'

'Of course. I've been delivering messages for Hannah. She's not expecting me back just yet. I were going to walk along t' river bank for a bit and enjoy t' weather.'

'Then I'll join you, if you don't mind. My train doesn't leave for over an hour. I've been here on business,' he added, by way of explanation. They proceeded, at a more sedate pace, along the path, as he tried to explain to her a little of what he had been doing that morning. 'So, how are you getting on in your new job? Is it everything you wanted?'

'It's grand. I always wanted to work in t' city, right from being little.'

'And what about Mrs Riley? How is she?' Even now he had some vague notion that he may be able to speak to her.

'She passed away last month. Easter Day, it were. It turns out she knew she were dying, like. She wrote a letter to Mary the night before she went.'

'Was Mary with her?'

'Aye, she had come to visit that weekend. She'd been coming regularly, with Martha being so ill and not likely to last.'

'Mary's not living here, then?'

'Oh, no, she's been gone for nearly a year now.' She did not say where and Nathaniel did not like to ask.

'I called on her,' Nathaniel went on.

'Mary?' asked Sarah-Louise, shocked.

'No, Martha Riley. Earlier in the year. I didn't realise she wasn't coming back. I wanted to speak to her. The cottage was empty.'

'What did you want to say?' asked Sarah-Louise. 'I didn't know that you knew her.'

'I didn't. I thought she might be able to clear up a puzzle.' He looked at Mary's sister and, on impulse, said to her, 'Perhaps you can clear it up for me.'

'Perhaps…' she replied uncertainly.

'Is it true that Mary and John Crowther had an understanding?'

'Had an understanding? Of course not! Why on earth should you think that? Nothing could be further from t' truth.'

'What is the truth, then? It seems that no one knows or, leastways, no one will tell me. Don't I have a right to know?'

'Aye, I think you do. John Crowther attacked her against her will. He…he forced himself on her, like. That's why she went away.'

Nathaniel stood rooted to the spot. Of course! He had not for one minute thought of this as the possible explanation for Mary's conduct. A wave of anger passed through his body, to be followed by another when he realised that John Crowther's death made any attempt at revenge impossible. Struggling to keep his voice calm and focusing his eyes on the dissipating smoke that rose from the direction of the station, he said, 'She could have come to me. She could have told me. It would not have made any difference. I would still have loved her.'

'That's not all,' went on Sarah-Louise in a low voice. 'She had a baby. She ended up staying with Martha's family. I didn't understand either, why she had left. She never told me…probably thought I were too young to understand. Martha told me, just before she died. That's why Mary couldn't stay in the village.'

Nathaniel's brain felt fit to burst with this new and unpalatable information. The whistle of an engine brought him to his senses. He glanced at his pocketwatch, noticing that there were only fifteen minutes remaining until his train left. He would have to sprint back across the bridge if he was not going to miss it. He took a step in the direction they had come from, then turned to face Sarah-Louise.

'Where are Mary and the baby now?'

'Mary doesn't have the baby any more. She gave it away. She gave it to Martha's niece. Esther and Timothy don't have any family of their own, you see.'

'And Mary? Where is she?'

'She left here last summer. She's working in a school now. Pontefract or that way on. She seems right settled. I've been studying t' job and I don't think she'll be coming back.'

CHAPTER THIRTY-ONE

ON THE platform of Ashworth railway station a small group were saying their goodbyes. The porter, who didn't know any different, no doubt assumed that it was a young family seeing off a friend who had been to stay. And in a way it was, though not in the way that the porter had assumed. It was, of course, Ted and Annie, and Annie's young son, Johnny…and it was Mary who was leaving.

'Do come and visit us soon,' said Annie. 'We're not short of space and, even if we were, there would always be room for you.'

'Aye, and plenty of work an' all,' said Ted and they laughed.

'I still can't believe how you've taken to those hens,' said Mary. 'When I think of your struggles with them in Templesforth. Remember that cockerel? He got the better of both of us.' They were silent, each remembering those early months of Annie's marriage. 'It's no good inviting you to stay with me; I shouldn't think you would want to return. And, to be honest, I don't rightly know where my parents are going to put *me*. The coal shed, I wouldn't be surprised!'

They saw the smoke from the engine before the train emerged from the bend and, slowing, approached the station. Annie threw her arms round her friend.

'Thank you so much for everything. I don't know where I would have been without you.' Her voice was too full of tears to continue. Ted passed Johnny to his mother and carried the trunk to the goods van at the rear of the train. He held out his hand to Mary.

'I shall miss thee,' he said. 'We shall all miss thee. Come and see us soon.'

'Thank you for being so understanding.' Mary faced him, overcoming the embarrassment she felt at having to raise such a delicate topic. Her sense of fair play would not let her go without saying something. 'I know you wished for more than I was prepared to give. But you have been a true friend to me and I'm very grateful for that.' She stood on tiptoe and kissed his cheek.

'Aye, well, I can't deny that my hopes ran on beyond just friendship.' His dark eyes held her gaze. 'Some lucky man's going to benefit from thy return to Templesforth. And, to be honest, there were times when I could see that thou were like a caged bird, straining to be free. I thought that this would happen in the end. I wish thee well, Mary. We both do.'

She stood at the window to wave as the engine enveloped the little group in a cloud of smoke. By the time it had cleared, the train had rounded the bend and the family were out of sight.

Mary's sadness at leaving her friends and the school

was soon eclipsed in the anticipation of seeing her family and village again. She had taken time before coming to this decision. There was nothing now to keep her away. Her time in York and then at the school had been a necessary interval and much of it enjoyable—more so than she would ever have thought possible in those last dark days in Martha's cottage. But the countryside was where she belonged. Only there did she feel really free. Ted was right. Even the school, always accepting and helpful, restricted her spontaneity. She wanted to sing when music came to her, run when she wanted to run, be quiet when she felt the need to be so and not when she was told she must.

Annie now appeared to be fully returned to health. It was as though she had emerged from under a huge grey cloud into the sunshine. There had been no excuse for her husband's behaviour but it wasn't just this that had made it all go wrong. Annie had been so young, so innocent of the ways of the world, so protected by her ageing parents. If she had married a younger man, someone who loved her for her inexperience and helped her to develop, like an unfolding plant…someone like Ted, in fact…her life could have been very different, could still be very different. It was clear to see that Ted had played a large part in Annie's speedy recovery. The two had become good friends. Both were overjoyed to discover relatives they didn't know they had. Mary smiled as she thought of Ted and Johnny's antics. She could see that the little boy looked to Ted as a father figure.

It was taking a long time for Crombie and Ashington, the solicitors, to sort out John Crowther's will. Ted had told Annie that her husband had made a will and that, in the course of time, a substantial amount of money would be coming her way. He'd neglected to say that John had in fact made no provision for her and her son. As he'd told Mary later, there was no need for Annie to be further upset by knowledge of this betrayal. He had, as yet, no firm idea of what he would do with his share of the money. For now, he continued to live simply in his room at the school, taking meals with the staff and tending the gardens, as he had done since the day of his arrival.

Mary could see Annie blossoming as she discovered in herself skills that she didn't know she possessed. She'd learned how to sew and was soon spending time in the linen room with the girls, where she did her share of repairing and darning, as well as making clothes for herself and Johnny. Her friendship with the farmer's wife and family had blossomed. She'd become proficient at milking cows, feeding horses and collecting eggs from the fluffy undersides of broody hens, while avoiding their angry beaks.

Yes, Mary thought, as the train carried her homeward, *this is the right decision. Annie is settled now and doesn't need me there any more. And I want to be where I belong.*

At Selby she learned that she would have more than two hours to wait for her connection to Templesforth and, as she was impatient to be home, she decided to go on foot. In any case she preferred to gather her thoughts at her own speed, rather than be disgorged straight from the train into her parents' house without time so much as to draw breath. Accordingly she made arrangements for her trunk to be put on the next train and set down again at Templesforth Station, and started to walk.

Her way took her along the canal. In its heyday it had been busy with traffic but, with the opening of the much more convenient Goole and Knottingley canal, its use had declined. It was the railways though that had delivered the death knell to the whole canal system. Now it was just the occasional coal barge or a supply of animal feed to an out-of-the-way farm that disturbed the peace of its water. The only hindrance to Mary's progress was the hogweed that, in full flower, was attempting to spread across the canal path and entangle her feet. A startled heron took off awkwardly from the bank with a loud 'crawk' and flew on languid wings in the direction she was going, as if to announce her imminent arrival. She left the canal and set off across country, making towards the railway line, skirting the edge of well-remembered fields as she made her steady progress homeward. She trailed her hand over the soft brush of ripening corn. In a week or two they would be harvesting again. She turned into the lane and walked past the farm. She was nearly home now.

A group of children stood under the railway bridge arguing. One of them, a fair-haired girl in a pinafore that had been white but now bore the signs of a long day at school, left the group to their debating and came on along the lane. Suddenly she stopped and stared ahead.

'Look, Lucy, it's our Mary come back. Mary! Mary!' The taller of the two girls, who had been sorting out the minor dispute between the remaining schoolchildren, looked up. Together Mary's two younger sisters sped up the road and into her waiting embrace.

The cottage seemed very small and Mary's sisters very big. Lucy was now the age that Sarah-Louise had been when Mary had left, and Laura, the baby of the family, was eight. Alice looked much the same. The fact that she was as obviously excited as the younger girls by Mary's unexpected arrival supported Mary's belief that her sister understood a lot more than she was able to convey. Mary sat at the side of the cot, stroking Alice's hair and chatting to her mother, who was preparing the meal. Susan too seemed pleased to see her daughter.

'How long are you stopping for, love, only you don't seem to have brought much with you?'

Mary jumped up in alarm. In the excitement of her return she had forgotten to retrieve her trunk from the train. She need not have worried. A tall young man, dressed in the uniform of Stationmaster, greeted her and took her to the parcels office, where her trunk was waiting. George Morritt, who had been chatting to the Stationmaster, introduced her before swinging her trunk on to his shoulder and accompanying her back to the cottage.

'Eh, lass, tha's looking grand,' he said, a grin stretching from ear to ear. 'I hope you're here to stay this time.'

Her father had arrived home when she'd returned. She'd heard his voice as she'd approached the open door and stood for a minute anxiously, listening for signs of displeasure, before stepping over the threshold. Would his manner be as cool as in the months before she'd left, when he'd blamed her for Nathaniel's distress?

But he greeted her warmly. 'Na' then, Mary lass. It's reet good to see thee again. Are you stopping?'

'Aye. I hope that's all right with you. I'll look for work, so you don't need to worry on that score.'

'I know you will, lass. And of course you can stay, though I don't rightly know how we're going to put you up, like.'

'I'll be fine down here with Alice. It'll give Mam a break and allow her to stretch out in a proper bed for a change.'

'Aye, that's a good idea, isn't it, Susan?' Tom said with a twinkle in his eye. 'That would suit us very well.'

It was several days before Mary felt able to leave the cottage. Plainly her mother was worn out with looking after Alice. Her steps were leaden, her face more lined and her hair had turned quite white.

'Why do you not go next door to pass t' time of day wi' Mrs Morritt?' Mary suggested. 'I can look after Alice. It would give you a break and Alice and I would be able to have a chat.' Her mother was reluctant. Having spent so much time confined to the house, she had lost the art of being sociable. Mary persisted and eventually Susan was persuaded to pay a call on Eliza Morritt and, later in the week, to have a cup of tea at the farm with Bessie Simpson.

One hot afternoon her mother had stoked up the fire in the range in order to bake bread and the atmosphere in the room was unbearable. Grabbing her straw bonnet from the peg, Mary flung open the door and stepped into the sunshine. A warm breeze caressed her skin and set the leaves of the trees overhead dancing, so that they made an ever-changing pattern of light and shade on the ground beneath. She breathed deeply to rid herself of the restrictions of the cottage and resolved to renew acquaintance with her previous haunts. On the way back she would call in at Martha's cottage and pick up the herbal, as she had promised Martha she would. It was time she set herself some serious studying. She was in danger of forgetting much of the knowledge that the old lady had imparted to her, although she had to admit that the chances were that much of it was not written down anyway.

Martha's cottage was hot and airless. Mary had no idea what arrangements had been made for its future but clearly no one had yet come to claim it. She left the front door open and walked through into the kitchen to open the door to the garden. The wood had swollen and Mary had to put her shoulder to it and push with all her strength, whereupon it suddenly gave way and catapulted her into a garden rampant with herbs and flowers. Roses clung around the door and showered her with petals as she burst through. In the middle of the garden, under the apple tree, Martha's chair still waited for its occupier who would no longer come.

Mice had left telltale signs that they now considered the kitchen to be their territory. In the room the bunched herbs were skeletal or crumbled to dust as Mary reached to touch them. The hearth contained the cold ashes of winter. She ran her finger through the thick layer of dust that coated the herbal.

For all its neglect the cottage still spoke of Martha.

Mary could not be sad. Her friend had lived her last days surrounded by the love of her family. If she had died here alone, that would indeed have been a reason for sadness.

Still, Mary thought, she was not going to leave the cottage in this mess. Until such time as it was reclaimed, she would come whenever she was free and restore it to its previous state. Once that was done, and only then, she would set to work on studying the herbal. It was too late to start cleaning today. She had promised her mother she would be back to see to Alice, so that Susan could walk along the lane and meet her daughters coming home from school. Her eldest daughter's encouragement was taking effect. Susan was beginning to enjoy life outside the four walls of the cottage.

There was no reason, other than the lack of a conveyance, why Alice should not accompany her on these expeditions to Martha's cottage. It would give their mother a chance to have some time to herself and Alice a change of scenery. The cottage was a mere stone's throw along the lane but Alice could not get there without help. Their father and George Morritt put their heads together and, with the help of several planks of wood and a set of wheels from an old railway trolley, they made a rudimentary cart. Mary lined it with an eiderdown and put a pillow at one end. It was a chariot fit for a queen, the younger sisters exclaimed, as they pushed Alice up and down the path.

The days that followed were happy ones for Mary as she swept and polished the cottage back to its usual state of tidiness. Alice lay in her chariot under the apple tree. She seemed to be listening to the birds that twittered and sang in the branches over her head. Mary popped in and out, checking that she was all right. After a while she would join her in the garden and talk to her, as she weeded the flowerbeds and attempted to restore some sort of order to the tangle of herbs. When they were hungry, she prepared a meal in the tiny kitchen. She was sure Martha would not mind. She sat under the apple tree on Martha's seat, feeding her sister before eating her own meal.

It was good to be away from her parents' cottage. Mary could see that there was really no room for her there and she had to admit to herself that she was finding the constant presence of the family a little wearing. She was not sure where else she could go but eventually she would have to find work and maybe a live-in job. Though she didn't think her mother would relish the idea, when the last couple of weeks had given her a first taste of freedom in years. For now there was the harvesting. She felt sure of work in the fields over the coming weeks. Not all the farmers had invested in reaping machines and even the ones that had took on extra labour at harvest time.

In the two weeks since her return she had seen nothing of Nathaniel. Her father had mentioned talk he'd overheard at the Wheatsheaf. It was said that the farm was not doing so well and that old Henry Varley had made some unwise investments. Young Nathaniel had been in for a drink a time or two, he'd told her, but of course all gossip stopped if he arrived, and he said nothing himself about the state of things.

The cottage and the garden were as Martha would

have liked them. There were no excuses for Mary to stay. After they had eaten and Alice had dozed off to sleep, Mary heaved the herbal from the shelf and carried it into the garden. She sat down next to Martha's rosemary bush. 'Remembrance and fidelity' her old friend had told her; that was what the herb signified. If that were the case, she was being faithful to Martha in carrying out her wishes. She opened the book, whereupon the loose collection of recipes and other useful information slipped from its pages and fluttered to the ground. The breeze caught one or two of the lighter pieces and carried them into the far corner of the garden. Putting the book down on the table, she jumped up to collect them before the wind could spirit them away over the wall and across the fields. She sat down and, trapping the loose papers under the book, opened the first page. In it Martha had written:

To my dear friend and companion, Mary Swales, I bequeath this book and all that is to be found in it, in the hope that its treasures will bring her enjoyment, and others the help that she is best able to give.
From her affectionate and ever grateful friend, Martha Riley.

She placed the book on the table and began to leaf through the pile of papers in her lap. There was a recipe for beef broth from a neighbouring farm and one for castor oil pomade. Hannah had sent 'a good treatment for tapeworm' in a letter dated 1851, the recipe consisting of:

Oil of male fern…1/2 to 1 drachm.
Mucilage of acacia…1 ounce.
Peppermint water…1 ounce.

The dog-eared state of the letter suggested that the recipe had been concocted frequently.

On another piece of paper she read:

For weakness of the stomach:
Infusion of chamomile…1 ounce
Peppermint water…1/2 ounce
To be taken three times a day.

Again the formula appeared to have been well used. Martha probably had a queue outside her door after the Harvest Supper, Mary guessed.

Next she picked up an envelope not yet opened. Martha must have received it when her interest or abilities had been on the wane. Mary turned it over and saw that it was addressed to herself. Not a recipe, then. But how had it come to be in the herbal?

She read:

My dear Mary,
Good, thou art exploring my book. I would have hated it to be neglected and all its vast knowledge to be lost.
I did say that there are treasures to be found inside its pages. Apart from the obvious ones that it will take thee a lifetime to study and learn, the other is my cottage. I wish for thee to have it. I

know it will be a sanctuary for thee, just as it was
for me in the dark days and I know that thou wilt
care for it and for the garden, just as before.

In case there are people who do not believe this
letter and who may want to cause difficulty, I have
written to a firm of solicitors in York. My dear husband's family engaged them in connection with
their business interests. They are Moxon, Bayliss
and Son at Monks Bar. They will be expecting to
hear from thee. May the cottage always protect
thee and may it be as happy a place for thee as it
always was for me.

From thy loving friend, Martha.

CHAPTER THIRTY-TWO

IT WAS a blustery overcast morning that heralded the annual Harvest Supper. The women glanced anxiously at the speeding clouds as they went about their preparations. The village being such a small one, it had been the custom for as long as any of them could remember for the farms to combine in celebrating the Harvest Home. There were three farms in the village and the farmers had, until recently, taken it in turns to host the festivities. The middle farm, however, was still vacant and Edwin Simpson, who continued to work the land as well as looking after his own sizable acres, had been host the previous year. Nathaniel was relieved when Edwin called to say that the landlord of the Wheatsheaf had suggested holding the supper on the field outside his hostelry, neutral territory that would involve no loss of face on the part of Nathaniel's father. The old man believed that no one knew of his troubles and was eager to keep it that way. The villagers, all of whom were well aware that Temple Farm was not flourishing, were sorry for the family. Old Henry had always been aloof and irascible but his wife was friendly enough and the eldest son a 'reet good lad who would do owt for anyone'.

Geoffrey Marriner was standing at the edge of the field as Nathaniel approached leading Princess, harnessed to the farm cart and its load of trestle tables.

'Na' then, Nathaniel, up good and early today, for a change,' Geoffrey said jokingly.

'Aye, not like some I could mention, carousing till all hours of the night and then not able to get up in t' morning,' Nathaniel replied. 'Mindst you, I'm surprised you could sleep at all, with t' thought of all the extra money you'll be making today, especially if the rain comes and we all have to take shelter inside. No wonder you're rubbing your hands together.'

The landlord chuckled and crossed over to the cart to help Nathaniel unload the tables, which they erected in three long rows, joined at one end by the top table, the resulting configuration resembling the head of a giant pitchfork. At the top table the farmers and their families would sit. It had long been recognised that the railway workers and shopkeepers, along with the farm workers, all played their part in the prosperity of the farms and the village, so everyone was invited to the celebrations.

By the time Nathaniel had completed his second journey and arrived with the remaining tables and a supply of benches, Geoffrey Marriner had armed his youngest son with a shovel and bucket and set him to clearing the field of the liberal heaps of manure deposited by the horses while they waited for shoeing. Joints of beef and ham, cooked the previous day and left to go cold were brought up from their place of safety in the cellar of the inn, along with pastries and pies. The landlord's wife and daughters were preparing large quantities of vegetables and the landlord was occupied with checking the casks of beer that he had kept aside for the occasion. Nathaniel returned to fetch his parents, together with the dishes specially prepared that morning, leaving Bessie Simpson, overweight and comfortable, to bustle around, organising her tribe of little ones into setting the tables. The two farming families put any differences behind them and prepared to make this an occasion that the villagers would not forget.

In Station Cottages there was great excitement as Mary's sisters dressed for the feast. With Mary's help Susan had made each of the little girls identical dresses, blue with short sleeves and a hem to mid-calf, allowing their not-so-new but highly polished boots to show. The outfit was finished off with a straw boater each and Lucy looked doubtfully out of the window at the lowering sky as she secured hers on her head. Susan appeared as excited as her daughters. It was the first time in many years that she had been along to the feast. She had rescued her best frock from the back of the cupboard.

'It's not very fashionable,' she complained to Mary, shaking out the creases of a dozen years.

Mary was heating up flat irons on the range. 'It'll look fine once we get it straightened out. Just look at all the petticoats. You'll feel like a grand enough lady, once you have all these on. Certainly as good as all t'other women there.' Tom, who had gone regularly to the harvest feast, was also wearing his best and together they looked a family to be proud of, according to Mary.

Mary had chosen to stay at home, arguing that someone would have to look after Alice and, since her mother had done it every year, it was only fair that she herself should stay behind. Her mother had protested but Mary knew that her remonstrations were half-hearted and that Susan was overjoyed at the chance to kick up her heels. In truth, Mary was worried about leaving Alice, for her fits were lasting much longer now and made her drowsy and unresponsive for hours after. And there was another thing. She had no appetite to encounter Nathaniel again in the middle of a crowd of villagers, eager for the latest gossip. When she did meet him, it would be in her own time, if at all. Probably not at all, for her sisters had informed her that he was courting, and she had no desire to meet Rhoda Precious.

Rhoda Precious pirouetted in front of the mirror causing her pale blue silk dress to swish and sigh as it caught up with her spinning figure. Her light brown hair was piled high at the back of her head, lending her neck an even more elongated look than was usually the case. Her eyes were bright and at the top of each cheek there was a spot of colour, although whether natural or artificial it was impossible to say. On the bed lay a bonnet, its large bow matching the colour of her dress. She picked it up and secured it to her hair with her favourite hatpin, the one topped with glistening mother-of-pearl.

Now she was ready. Rhoda took one last look in the mirror before closing the door of her boudoir and walking sedately downstairs to meet her father. She may be going to spend the afternoon with the villagers but she had her standards and she was not going to lower them for any old riff-raff she might come across. She thought back to last year's feast. She hadn't known Nathaniel for long then but he had done her the discourtesy of having a little too much to drink. She would keep a very careful eye on him to make sure that didn't happen this year. If she were going to be mistress of Temple Farm, things would operate as she wanted them and not in the slovenly way she suspected they had previously been run.

The arrival of Arthur Precious and his daughter in their carriage coincided with Nathaniel's on the farm cart drawn by Princess. His mother had requested that he return to the farm to retrieve a batch of apple pies, which she had put on one side to cool and then forgotten to load on to the wagon on its last journey along the lane. Arriving back at the farm, he'd found that a visitor had arrived in his absence. It was an acquaintance from a neighbouring village, a farmer with whom he had discussed the sale of the costly and uncalled-for farm machinery.

Nathaniel had changed earlier into his better clothes but now, a couple of journeys later, he had discarded his jacket and sat on the cart in his waistcoat, shirt sleeves rolled up, fair hair dishevelled and boots exhibiting the mud and aroma of the farmyard. He was in high spirits, having successfully concluded the transaction with the local farmer. Explanations to his father could wait until later. As he alighted, two little girls ran up and hugged him.

'Come on, Nathaniel.' Laura pulled at his sleeve.

'Where've you been? We've been waiting for you for ages. We're starving. When are we going to start?'

'Our mam only gave us a teeny weeny breakfast so as we'd have room for all t' food here,' Lucy explained.

'Can I sit next to you?' Laura began again, before Nathaniel could reply to the first question. 'I'll be very good—and I've got summat very special to tell you.'

'I would like nothing better—' Nathaniel laughed '—but I'm afraid that place is reserved for Miss Precious. She's my special guest today.'

'Oh,' said Laura, looking crestfallen but brightening up again in an instant. 'Well, you've got two sides. Can I sit next to your other side?'

Before he had time to reply Arthur Precious was interrupting. 'Aren't you neglecting your duty, sir? My daughter is waiting for you to see her down from the carriage.'

'I'm sorry,' Nathaniel said, turning to him and then to the carriage. 'Let me take your hand, Rhoda.' She alighted and, looking him up and down disapprovingly, gave him a brief peck on the cheek.

'Really, Nathaniel, you look as if you've just come from milking the cows.'

Nathaniel laughed. 'Well, my dear, you know the saying…"Where there's muck, there's brass".' He turned to the two little girls, who were still standing behind him. 'Rhoda, meet my special friends, Lucy and Laura.'

'We're pleased to meet you.' Lucy spoke for them both.

'I like your dress,' said Laura, stroking a sweaty palm down its silky skirt. Rhoda stepped back so abruptly that she nearly tripped.

'I think…' said Nathaniel, coughing to suppress a giggle. 'I think, girls, that I will escort Miss Precious to her seat and you must go and find your parents. I wouldn't like to see you starve.' He cupped Rhoda's elbow in his hand and led her towards the top table, where her father was already hovering, waiting to take his place. A sudden gust of wind lifted the hat from her head and sent it skimming across the field and over the riverbank. The village children who were not yet seated tore after it and returned empty-handed to report that the water had carried it far out of their grasp.

'Well, really!' exclaimed Rhoda petulantly. Nathaniel gave her a wide smile.

'You look much better without it,' he said and squeezed her hand.

The feast was as good as everyone had hoped and expected. Nathaniel, together with his mother and Edwin and Bessie Simpson, did their share of serving. Geoffrey Marriner took charge of the ale and his wife made tea for the more abstemious among them. As the meal finished and they were clearing the tables to make room for dancing, the sun made a brief appearance as it slanted towards the horizon and bathed the revellers and the surrounding fields in a golden brilliance.

Rhoda stayed at her seat while the women of the village removed the dirty dishes and remains of food from the table in front of her.

'It's a reet good do, wouldn't tha' say,' an elderly villager commented, removing the tablecloth and sending a cascade of crumbs into Rhoda's lap. 'What a pity that the Varleys can't afford to act as hosts as they used to, like.'

'Oh, it's not that,' Rhoda said quickly. 'Nathaniel told me that the landlord offered to have it here because it was more convenient for the villagers.' She frowned. She couldn't remember whether Nathaniel had actually said that or whether she was imagining it.

'Aye, well, 'appen you're right. It's not what I've heard, though.' The old woman went on along the table, clearing and scattering food as she went.

'Nathaniel…' Rhoda turned to face him when he eventually returned to her side. 'You haven't said anything to me recently about the farm. Has it been a good harvest?'

Nathaniel looked at her in surprise. 'I didn't think you'd be interested in business matters. Aye, the harvest has been quite a good one, as it happens. But we don't want to talk about that now. Today is the day for forgetting about work and enjoying ourselves. Will you dance with me?'

She opened her mouth to say more but he took her hand and led her quickly into the middle of the cleared space. A small band had struck up and a group of village children were already skipping in a circle in one corner. Other grown-ups now followed Nathaniel's lead and soon the whole company were dancing more or less vigorously, making allowances for their age and standing in society.

Mary could hear the sounds of merrymaking as she sat reading. In the last few weeks she had been awash with alternating feelings of contentment and excitement. Upon reading Martha's letter she had decided there and then to move into the cottage and, from the beginning, enjoyed the comfort and security that Martha herself had known. Now, at last, she was able to continue her study of the plants and herbs that grew in the garden and beyond. She had begun by examining Martha's stock of remedies, many of which she had to tip away because their usefulness had declined with age. She had washed the bottles and stood them in gleaming rows along the windowsill to dry, anticipating the day when she could fill them with fresh herbal extracts. These she would have learned how to prepare during the winter months when the ground was barren. Accordingly she sat down in the evenings, when the day's work was done, and by the light of a candle studied the herbal and planned what she would do in the New Year, when the garden sprang into life again. Of course she had helped with the harvest because she had as yet no other means of supporting herself but, by next year, if all went according to plan, she would be making the same medicines that Martha had done for so many years. She would sell them to those who had money but she would never withhold their benefits from those who could not afford to pay.

It had grown dark early, for the clouds that had briefly dispersed in the early evening had returned. She placed the herbal on the floor and stood to light the oil lamp before sitting down again to one side of the range, so she could keep an eye on Alice in her cot against the opposite wall. It had not been a good day as far as Alice was concerned. She had eaten nothing and Mary was having difficulty persuading her to drink. After a while she put down her book and went to the table. Her father had brought a plateful of food from the Harvest Supper and amused her with a description of the antics of the assembled villagers. Before returning for the rare pleasure of a dance with his wife, he'd crossed to Alice's side and stroked her hair.

'How's my little lass, then?' he whispered and kissed her tenderly on the cheek. 'Sleep well,' he murmured. 'Sweet dreams.'

There was enough food on the plate for three meals at least, Mary thought—several slices of ham and beef, a whole pork pie and jacket potatoes. She reached up for another plate and placed a small amount of the food on to it. Before returning to her studying, she went over to Alice and tried to persuade her to drink a little. But it was no good. The liquid dribbled down the side of her mouth and formed a wet patch on the pillow. Mary laid her sister's head back, noting an increased resistance in the muscles of her neck. Her skin was dry and her eyes unfocused. Mary sighed. She had long since ceased to consider the unfairness of it all. There was no point in doing so. Alice was theirs to care for, for as long as she lived. That was all there was to it.

The music had stopped. She glanced at the clock. The band were no doubt using their arms to lift a pint or two of ale while the villagers would be giving their corns a much-needed rest. It would not be long before the music struck up again and the dancing resumed. She closed her eyes and imagined herself whirling round the field in the strong arms of a handsome man.

She woke with a start. She could hear the music of the band again. From Alice's corner was coming the grunting that always accompanied one of her fits. The cot began to shake as Mary flew to her side. Alice had bitten her tongue and the drool of saliva was tinged pink. Mary held her hand and stroked her hair as she had done so many times before, waiting for the convulsions to stop and the breathing to quieten. Only this time it didn't happen. The rhythmical shaking continued for minutes, which lengthened into half an hour, an hour. Mary filled a bowl with cold water and sponged Alice's face in an effort to allay the fitting. She talked to her but there was no response. Still the fitting continued. Still the music went on. She prayed for it to stop and ran to the door to see if there was any sign of her parents' approach. She couldn't bear to leave Alice alone while she fetched them. But she knew that each passing minute weakened Alice's already diminished constitution. At last she could wait no longer. Leaving the door wide, so as not to sever the connection with her unconscious sister, she sped up the path and along the lane towards the wavering lights and intensifying noise of the Harvest Supper.

Nathaniel had done everything that was expected of him. He had taken his share of waiting at tables and had chatted with the elderly villagers, many of whom had at one time been in his father's employ. He had danced with the more agile of the matrons and taken care to avoid the advances of the younger women, for fear of upsetting Rhoda. He had even entertained the children by joining in with them in their animated corner of the field. Mostly, though, he had danced attention on Rhoda and throughout the evening had done nothing that could bring from her even a hint of a rebuke. He had been careful to drink only enough ale to loosen his joints but not his tongue and they danced until she grew weary and asked to rest.

This was the moment he had been waiting for. He was determined to put it off no longer. He sat down on the chair next to her and mopped his brow.

'Rhoda,' he began, 'you know how much I admire you and have done for many months. I was wondering…if you would do me the honour of becoming my wife. I have, of course, asked your father and he has given his consent.… It would make me the happiest of men if you would agree.'

'Thank you, Nathaniel. I accept.' She beamed and bent her head to his. 'I think the spring would be the best time for the wedding, don't you?'

'Well, I was thinking more of the winter, when there's less to do on the farm, but, of course…'

'But it's so much nicer to marry when the daffodils are in bloom and the sun is shining. And, in any case, I shall need time to prepare my trousseau. And you will have to decorate the farmhouse and make the necessary repairs before I move in. Of course I shall have to come and look it over to advise what changes need to be made.'

'Well, I was hoping that it might suit you as it is.' Nathaniel thought of the hard won money from his recent transaction disappearing in a flurry of wallpaper and paint. 'But, whatever you wish, my dear.' He leaned over to plant the required kiss on her cheek and, as he did so, glanced across the field. It was dark now and lanterns had been strung around its periphery, casting intermittent patches of light on the evening revellers. Around the furthest lantern, villagers were gathering and dispersing at speed, like ants receiving orders and hastening to carry them out. It was obvious that something was amiss. Had one of the children gone astray? If so, there was indeed cause for concern, for the river was a mere fifty yards away.

'Nathaniel, that's a very half-hearted display of affection, I must say,' said Rhoda, but Nathaniel was not listening. His attention had been caught by the distraught figure in the centre of the group of people. The woman's dishevelled appearance could not hide the supple beauty of her body nor could her tears disguise the face that he had known and loved so well, until forced by events to push it to the back of his mind. Now cruel circumstance had resurrected it at just the moment when he had promised himself to another.

As he watched, he saw Mary's parents precipitated into the well of light and Mary and her father setting off at a run along the road. Her mother followed them as fast as she was able, accompanied by two or three other women. Nathaniel stood up abruptly, staring along the road after the retreating figures. Ignoring Rhoda's angry protestations, he made his way across the field. Laura intercepted him.

'Nathaniel, you promised that you would have a dance with me. Can we dance now? I've got summat to tell you, remember.'

'Laura, has your Mary come home to stay?'

'Aw, Nathaniel, that was *my* surprise. *I* wanted to tell you that.'

'Didn't she want to come and dance?' he asked bitterly.

'She said she would look after our Alice so Mam and Father could come to t' supper.'

Of course, there was Alice, her sister. Mary had talked of her often enough but she was spoken of so infrequently now that it was easy to forget she existed. Concern tempered his bitterness. If she had been looking after her sister then something was seriously amiss to have caused the disturbance he had just witnessed. He stood uncertainly in the centre of the field. Around him villagers began to say their farewells and disperse into the blackness.

Alice lay as Mary had left her, her head to one side, the pillow soaked with saliva and covered with froth. Her body was unmoving, her exhausted muscles relaxed and peaceful in death, as they had never been in her short life. She had not waited to say goodbye and now, however hard Mary tried, she would never be able to reach her sister again.

CHAPTER THIRTY-THREE

THE doctor, when he had been sent for, told them there was nothing they could have done. He had not seen Alice for years because there was little he could suggest that had not already been tried. He offered his condolences and departed, handing Tom a certificate and his bill. Tom seemed at a loss what to do and stood by the door, looking blankly at the doctor's signature in the corner of the form. Mary went up to him and took it from his hand, telling him that she would catch the first train into Selby on the Monday morning.

It was Mary's first encounter with death at such close quarters. She could recall only two of her grandparents and, although they had not reached the hoped-for three score years and ten, she only remembered them as old…and such deaths were to be expected. Her sister's, though, like her life, was unfair, unnatural.

A chill wind funnelled down the mean street of buildings, as Mary made her way to the Registry office after a weekend of hushed inactivity. The ageing and meticulous registrar rose to shake her hand as she entered his office.

'Won't you sit down, Mrs Swales?'

'Miss,' she said, correcting him. 'Mary Swales.' She handed him the Medical Certificate of the Cause of Death. 'I've come to register the death of my sister.' Her voice trembled. 'My parents didn't feel up to it; that's why I'm here.'

'I see,' he said, his voice softening. 'I'm very sorry to hear it.' He shuffled some papers on his desk and drew out a form. 'I'm sorry, my dear, but I'm afraid I must ask a few questions, just to make sure I have the correct information. I need to know the date and place of death and the full name of your sister.' Mary supplied the details in a steady voice. 'And what was her age?'

'She was eighteen December last.'

'And her occupation?'

'She didn't work—only at staying alive. She was ill, right from t' day she was born.'

'It's a blessing, then?'

'There's some as might see it like that. But she were my sister and I loved her and I think she…well, is that all? Do I need any more forms?' She rose abruptly from her seat.

'You need this form for the undertaker,' he said, filling in the required details on a further certificate. 'They will make all necessary arrangements. Do you know where to find them?' She shook her head and he wrote down the names and addresses of two firms of undertakers in the town. 'There you are, my dear. Make your way to one of these and I'm sure they will deal with things to your satisfaction.'

'Thank you,' said Mary. 'Thank you for your help…
You've been most kind,' she added, conscious that she
had brushed aside his attempt at sympathy. She stumbled from the room and out into the street, his words
echoing in her head. 'It's a blessing then?' *'For whom?'*
she thought, as she attempted to follow the registrar's
directions. Was it a blessing for Alice? Who could say
whether Alice would rather be here or wherever she
was now? A blessing for her parents? Yes, she had no
doubt that it would be so for them, after a lifetime of
being tied to their daughter. A blessing for herself,
who had caused her death? No, she would never forgive herself for leaving Alice alone in those last few
minutes. If she had stayed with her sister, the two of
them would be together now. She pressed her lips in
a firm line, as if to stop them speaking her thoughts,
and stepped into the offices of Chas. Dearlove,
Undertakers.

Her mother was well versed in the rituals of mourning, having lost Tom's parents and her own, as well as
a sister many years earlier. When they'd returned from
the Harvest Supper and discovered Alice, Mary had
watched Susan open the windows and door wide to
allow her daughter's soul to depart, while she herself
crouched, numb and disbelieving, holding Alice's thin
hands in her own. Her father had picked up his daughter as though she weighed no more than a baby and, carrying her upstairs, laid her on his own bed.

There was a woman in the village, who, for a small
sum, would come and lay out the body after death.
Mary, summoning every ounce of determination she

possessed, had helped her to wash Alice's wasted body. Stony-faced, she ran the cloth reverently down each arm and leg and gently dried her with the towel. They'd dressed her and Mary had gathered the last of the sweet peas from the garden and laid them in a bunch at her waist.

They could make no immediate funeral arrangements, Alice having died on the Saturday night, so the following morning Tom had walked to the carpenter's house in the next village. That evening a plain wood coffin had been delivered and Alice made as comfortable as Mary and her mother could manage. Word spread of their loss and those who had been reluctant to offer help during Alice's life had made haste to come and see her body after death. Invitations to the funeral were posted to relatives far and near. Susan dragged out the heavy trunk containing her mourning clothes—ugly, old-fashioned and smelling strongly of mothballs. Then she made a list of what she would need for the funeral tea—beef, ham, cheese, bread, tea, sugar, gingerbread—and visited the butcher the next morning to order the meat.

Mary knew that Sarah-Louise must be sent for and decided it should be she that undertook this task. Although Sarah-Louise had often resented the attention that was given to Alice when they were growing up, she would be no less upset than her other sisters at Alice's death. So, after visiting the undertaker, she went immediately to the Post Office and sent a telegram:

Alice passed away. Stop. Come immediately. Stop. All love, Mary. Stop.

It was good to see Sarah-Louise again, so good that Mary's recent reserve nearly gave way. Hannah had insisted she leave straight away and she arrived home on the evening train. She brought with her an envelope from Hannah. It contained a letter of condolence and a not insubstantial amount of money, which she explained away by saying that it was money set aside for the relief of Friends at such times, and she had no better friends than Mary and Sarah-Louise. The cottage was in turmoil when Sarah-Louise arrived, preparations for the funeral tea being in full swing. The following day the two daughters and their mother busied themselves with baking bread and cakes and preparing suitable mourning dress. On Wednesday Mary watched dry-eyed as Alice was lowered into the cold darkness. Sarah-Louise returned to York and Mary stood alone on the platform waving as her train disappeared into the distance. Then she turned away from the station, walked the short distance to her cottage and shut the door.

George Morritt was in a quandary. He needed a new supply of strengthening medicine for Alfie, who had been taking it ever since his illness over two years before. He had mentioned it to Mary the day before the Harvest Supper and she had promised to mix something suitable. It was now three weeks since the funeral and he had seen no sign of her. He knew that etiquette dictated he should not call too soon after a death but it was this reminder of the transitory nature of life, even amongst those who had spent only a short time on the earth, that made him decide to visit. It was not as though the rest of the family had kept themselves apart. Susan seemed to have accepted Alice's death with equanimity. She appeared soon after the funeral, dressed in black, talking to her neighbours and shedding tears as they spoke of her daughter. But her step seemed altogether lighter and her face more alive than during the later years of Alice's disability. He had seen the little girls returning to school, skipping in and out of the cottage as they had always done. Tom had taken it the hardest, it seemed to George, this loss of a daughter to whom he had been particularly attached. He had been back at work in charge of the gang the day after the funeral, his black armband an unnecessary reminder of the death. George and the other railwaymen had expressed their sympathy and he'd thanked them and got on with his work. But his friendly, outgoing manner was absent and they didn't know how to respond to this change in their colleague.

'Step inside, won't you?' Tom opened the door wide and George entered the room. He noted that Alice's cot had been removed from its usual place along the far wall and thought how much bigger the room looked without it. The two younger sisters were sitting at the side of the range in the dwindling light, examining a piece of cloth spread out on Lucy's lap.

Laura jumped up as he entered. 'Look, Mr Morritt, look what Lucy's made. She brought it home today.'

George crossed over to where Lucy was sitting. 'Why, Lucy, that's beautiful!' he said as she held up the sampler for him to examine.

'I made it at school. It was going to be for Alice, but

I didn't get it finished in time. Father says he will make a picture frame and we can hang it on t' wall over where Alice slept. That way, we'll never forget her.'

'See,' interrupted Laura, 'that's Alice's name in t' middle. Then, all round the outside there's flowers and rabbits and bees cos them's are all the things that Alice likes.'

'Alice *liked*,' said Tom, correcting her. 'What can I do for you, George?'

'I were wanting a word with Mary, if that's all right. Only she promised me a bottle of medicine for our Alfie a few weeks back. I didn't want to disturb you before now, like.'

'Thanks for your consideration, George, but life must go on,' said Tom with a sigh.

'How *is* Alfie?' Susan asked. 'I haven't seen him playing out recently.'

'He's been through another bad patch. He's not very strong, you know, and any little cold or cough seems to take a hold, when other children can throw it off in a day or two. 'Liza has a job looking after him when he's bad, what with the two little uns under her feet. Mindst you, it's thanks to your Mary that he's here at all, if you ask me. If it weren't for her help the other year, we would have lost him. Where is Mary, any road?' he asked, glancing round the room and seeing no trace of Mary's presence. 'I haven't seen her at all the last week or two. Is she all right?'

'Oh, aye,' replied Tom, 'but she's living in Martha Riley's old cottage now, tha' knows. She's 'appen making things to her liking, now she's moved in.' He opened the door of the range and threw in half a hod full of coal, the noise creating a temporary pause in the conversation.

'Well, thanks, Tom. I'll get along and call on her there, then.'

It was dark when George knocked on the door of Martha's cottage. By rights he should call it Mary's cottage now, he thought, but old habits died hard. He could never understand why Mary had decided to go and live in the city, her being such a country girl, but he was glad she was back now. It was surprising, though, that he had seen nothing of her since her sister's funeral.

A candle burned in the window of the cottage. Mary must be at home, then. There was no sound from within. He knocked again, slightly louder this time.

'Who is it?' The voice sounded strangled, distant.

'It's George—George Morritt. You said as how you would make…' His sentence trailed off as Mary opened the door and he looked at her. The extreme pallor of her face contrasted with the hair that tumbled around her shoulders and her eyes shone unnaturally.

'Why, lass, I'm sorry to have disturbed you. I wouldn't have come if I'd…'

'You're not disturbing me,' she said abruptly, fixing her eyes on him. 'As a matter o' fact, I've just come in. I've been talking to our Alice. It's lonely for her out there, tha' knows.' Her gaze slid over his shoulder and fastened on the distance.

'It's o'er late to be visiting the grave, isn't it?' he said, trying not to let the worry show in his voice.

'It's now that she needs me there. She gets cold at this time of the evening. Any road, I needed to say how sorry I was that I couldn't give her the grand funeral she deserved. I've seen them, you know. When I were living in York, I saw them. Fine carriages, coffins draped in black, men in black walking alongside, black horses leading t' way, ostrich feathers fluttering in t' breeze. My Alice should have had that. It weren't right, her going like she did.'

'You all did what you could,' George replied. He had stepped into the room now. There was no fire in the grate and it felt chill. 'Funerals like that cost more money than you or I have ever had. You gave her a reet good send-off.'

'She had no right to leave me,' Mary went on, as though she hadn't heard George speak. 'We were getting on so well. I wanted her to come and live with me here, you know.'

''Appen she'd have found it brassy tonight.' George tried to joke her back to reality. 'Have I to light t' fire and give thee a bit o' warmth?' He went over to the hearth and held a match to the paper and sticks already there.

'There, lass, that'll soon burn up. Why don't you sit down here and warm your hands and I'll make thee a cup of tea.'

'They all do it, don't they?' she went on.

'They all do what, Mary?'

'They all leave me, that's what they do—first Nathaniel, then t' babby, then Martha and now Alice. They all go.'

'Nay, lass! You've lots of folk here love you and won't leave you.'

'Is that right? I don't think so. You wait. They'll go.

Any road,' she said suddenly, looking scared, *'you* must go. It's not proper, you being here at this time of night. I'll see you out.' She rose from the chair.

'I'll call in again and see how you are,' George said, as she propelled him towards the door.

'There's no need. I'm all right. And, in any case, I might be out. I have to go and take care of our Alice. No one can look after her like me, you know.'

He stepped unwillingly over the threshold and, before he could say goodnight, she had shut the door in his face. He stood for a few seconds, staring at the peeling paint of the old wooden door. Then he turned and made his way thoughtfully back to the cottages. He knew that death could affect people in different ways but he had never seen anyone behave like Mary had just done. It was so unlike her usual self. Clearly her parents didn't realise how upset she was. Should he say something to them? Or was there, perhaps, someone else who might be better able to help?

CHAPTER THIRTY-FOUR

'How dare you go behind my back?' Henry Varley exploded, when Nathaniel told him about the proposed sale of the farm machinery that had been his father's pride and joy.

'But Father, there's no other way. You know as well as I that the farm is losing money. We can't pay off what we owe on those machines and they'll fetch a good price at the moment. If we leave it any longer they'll go rusty and no one will want them. I've worked out that with the money we'll raise from their sale, we'll be able to pay off any debts we owe and break even at the end of this year. I know it's not what you wanted…me, neither. But what other solution is there?'

'You've no right. This is my farm and I'll run it how I want. I know what's behind this. It's your jumped-up ideas about looking after the farm workers and their families. Well, I'm telling you, my lad, we need to look after us-selves, never mind t' rest of them.'

'It'll be my farm soon.' Nathaniel turned on his father, no longer able to contain his frustration at the old man's intransigence. 'And look at it this way. Rhoda's going to think twice about leaving the comfort of her father's home and coming here if all I can offer her is a farm that's losing money.'

He stormed out of the kitchen and slammed the door, crossing the courtyard in angry strides. He took hold of the fork and began vigorously mucking out Jess's stable, a job that would be done by the hired hands at Rhoda's father's farm, he had no doubt. A hand on his shoulder brought him to an abrupt stop.

'I'm sorry, son. I know you're talking sense. It's just that it's hard to give up my plans after so many years of being in charge. I realise we don't always see eye to eye but I know you're doing your best for the farm and for your mother and I.'

'Look, Father.' Nathaniel put down the fork and turned to face his father, the look on the old man's face making him regret his angry words. 'We have to come to terms with the fact that your rheumatics make it unlikely you'll be able to take an active part in the running of the farm much longer, more's the pity. I want the farm to be running at a profit, for all our sakes, and so you and Mother can have a bit of rest in your later years.'

'Hmph,' was his father's reply. 'I suppose you're right. It's hard, though, to sit back and see you taking over the reins. 'Appen what we need to do is to sit down together and work things out, man to man.'

Nathaniel clicked his tongue to persuade the mare to lower her head and quickly slipped on the head collar before leading her out into the yard, where her breath condensed into clouds in the cold air. He unbuckled her blanket and slipped it from her back, then began to brush her brown coat vigorously, beginning at her neck and mane and working down to her long black straw-entangled tail. Then the mare obediently lifted each hoof in turn so Nathaniel could rid them of the impacted mess of the stable. She put her head down and nuzzled his pocket, looking for something to eat.

'Now then, madam, you'll get your breakfast soon enough.' He finished the grooming and untied the lead rein. 'Walk on,' he commanded and she responded with alacrity, knowing that a net of hay hung waiting just inside the entrance to the field. He walked back towards the stables and repeated the process with the second horse, a young grey gelding which Rhoda's father had asked him to bring on for Rhoda to ride. He was ready now and Rhoda would be arriving later, as she often did on a Saturday, to try out the gelding. If her father had offered to contribute towards his feed, Nathaniel would have been better pleased but no offer had been forthcoming and Nathaniel certainly wasn't going to ask and risk Arthur Precious finding out how ill they could afford the extra money. He led the second horse into the field and left them both tearing at the hay while he returned to the yard to muck out the stables.

His father's financial dealings still left the farm balanced on a knife-edge between ruin and success. The sale had gone ahead, his father having eventually agreed that it was the only solution. The farm was beginning to break even, he thought, even if it had plunged them back into the Dark Ages, in the words of his father.

Nathaniel had not spoken of all this to Rhoda. His parents were keen for the match to go ahead, seeing it as a way to bring greater stability to the farm, and it would not do to rock the boat. They might not be so keen, he thought, if they realised how little she was willing to get involved in its everyday running. If they expected a rosy-cheeked milkmaid, they would have to think again.

A month had passed since the night of the Harvest Supper. Try as he might, he could not erase from his mind that picture of Mary, appearing ghostlike at the conclusion of the festivities, when he had only two minutes before asked for the hand of Rhoda in marriage. There were two reasons why she haunted him. The first was that she was the same beautiful Mary he had known and loved and who had left him more than two years before. But he was haunted too by the anguish in her face when he'd caught sight of her there in the middle of the field. He'd heard later that her sister had died. He remembered how attached Mary was to Alice and how she used to talk to him about her. If he could find out how she was, he would rest easy.

He swept the yard and filled the water trough. The horses were at the fence again, wanting more food.

'Get along, the two of you. There's no more now; we're riding out soon. I'll feed you again later.' He delivered a slap to the hindquarters of the grey and the two of them trotted off into the middle of the field.

By the time Arthur Precious drove his carriage into the stable yard, Nathaniel had finished the mucking out and had changed into his riding breeches and coat. He invited his future father-in-law to stay for tea when he returned for his daughter and then he helped Rhoda on to the grey. The two of them set off along the lane through the village. Nathaniel had done a good job of breaking in Rhoda's mount and he behaved well with a different rider's weight on his back. He passed under the low railway bridge without hesitation and when, a few seconds later, a train crossed the bridge with a deafening roar, the horse continued along the road without a murmur. Only when they drew alongside Martha's cottage did he stop and seem reluctant to continue.

'Walk on,' Rhoda commanded. 'What's wrong, you silly creature? Walk on when I tell you. Why is he stopping here, Nathaniel?'

Nathaniel knew only too well why the horse was stopping. It was no more than he had done a score or more times before when Nathaniel had been exercising him and had stopped to look over the wall into the herb garden. A certain amount of staking and tidying had been carried out but the garden lacked the firm hand that the season required. Nathaniel assumed that Mary must have been visiting the garden since her return to the village and she must have done the tidying. There was no sign of her now. She must be in the cottage comforting her mother. They urged on the reluctant horses and in a short while set off along a bridle path between the ploughed fields.

By the time they walked the horses into the farmyard the afternoon sun was low on the horizon. Rhoda's father had returned. His horse had been disengaged from the gig and was tethered loosely, munching with relish on a generous helping of hay.

'You've worn me out,' Rhoda said. 'Ask your man to see to the horse. I'm going indoors to join my father.' Nathaniel opened the door for her, then turned back into the yard to free the two horses of saddles and bridles and brush them down before they had their feed. He was so engrossed that he didn't see the man approach and started when he heard his name.

'Sorry if I startled you, Master Nathaniel,' said George Morritt. 'I've just finished work and I thought I might have a word with you before I went home.'

'Certainly, George, how can I help?' It was a long time since he had spoken to the railwayman and he was a little mystified as to what had brought him to the farm.

'Well, I hope you don't mind me coming to you, like. It's a bit of a delicate situation. I've tried talking to her parents but they don't seem to think there's anything wrong.'

'What is it, George?' said Nathaniel, his head buried in the flank of his horse as he manoeuvred the hoof-pick. 'Don't tell me you're setting yourself up dispensing moral advice to the young!'

'Nothing like that,' said George, smiling. 'I've come to you because you knew her better than anyone.' Nathaniel straightened up slowly and looked George in the eye. 'I hope I'm not speaking out of turn,' George went on, 'but I couldn't think what else to do.'

'What, George? Who are you talking about and what's wrong?'

'It's Mary.'

Nathaniel let his breath out very slowly.

George frowned and shook his head. 'She's not right

at all. 'Appen she's grieving over the loss of Alice, but I've never seen anyone behaving how she is.'

'How is she behaving? Is she upset? Is she crying?'

'No, nothing like that. 'Appen she'd be better if she were. No, most of the day she spends down at t' graveside, talking to her sister.'

'Talking to her sister?'

'Aye, she seems as though she don't want her to leave. I think she'd be there all night if I didn't go down and fetch her back. And, when she is back, she sits staring into space. I don't think she's sleeping much, nor eating neither, not by what I've seen. She's living in Martha's old cottage now, if you can call it living. There's no one there to see she's all right. It's a rum do.'

'And you say you've spoken to her parents?'

'Aye, but they seem o'er anxious with their own concerns. Seem to think she's coping—just because she always has in t' past.' He paused, then went on. 'She said as how everyone left her—her sister, yourself...the babby. That's what made me come to you Master Nathaniel. You see, me and my family, we keep ourselves to ourselves, like. I never knew you and she had a babby.'

'Oh, no, George, that's where you're wrong. The baby didn't belong...' He hesitated. If he told George who was the rightful father, Mary's reputation would be dragged through the mud even more than was likely at present.

'Nathaniel, what are you *doing* here? The tea's gone cold and we're all waiting for you.' Nathaniel turned abruptly at Rhoda's voice. How long had she been standing there?

'I'm almost finished. Go inside and make some more tea,' he said curtly.

'Well, really. I'd thank you not to speak to me like that,' Rhoda said, colouring. She looked George up and down and said to Nathaniel, 'I'll tell them you'll be in immediately.' She turned abruptly and flounced into the farmhouse.

'Look, George,' Nathaniel said in a low voice, 'you were right to come to me. Like you say, I knew her as well as anyone. I'll go and see her tonight, as soon as I can get away.' He glanced at Rhoda's retreating form.

'I'm sorry, Nathaniel. I hope I haven't made things difficult for you.' George too looked towards the house as Rhoda slammed the door.

'Don't worry about me. I'll be quite all right.' He had already made up his mind what he would do. And wild horses wouldn't stop him.

The iron gate of the graveyard creaked as he swung it open. The moon was nearly full and the shadow of each gravestone fell black on the grass behind. Nothing moved. He guessed that the new graves had been dug behind the church, a part that was not visible from the lane. The oldest ones, he knew, occupied the spaces on either side of the path to the church porch. He had seen them on the occasions, admittedly less recently, that he had attended the Sunday service. Ancient lichen-covered headstones, leaning drunkenly, with lettering that was weathered and, in some cases, indecipherable. He walked quietly along the grassy path, through the shadow of the church's bulk and into the molten whiteness of the moon. She was sitting on the grass, hugging her knees, the tip of her chin resting on them, like an angel at rest. He would not have known it was she, had he not expected to find her here. He had been first to the cottage but it was in darkness. He had taken the precaution of knocking and even peeped in to see if she was sitting in the dark. But she wasn't there. She was so still now that he wondered whether she had fallen asleep. As he came close, however, he could hear her talking. Her voice was low, monotonous.

'Mary,' he said gently, 'I've come to take you home.' She paused, lifted her head from her knees as if considering who it could be talking to her, then her voice began again, like an incantation. 'Mary, sweetheart, you're cold. Come on, it's time to take you home. Say goodbye to Alice now and come along with me. You can talk to her again tomorrow. She needs to rest now.'

Mary stopped to consider. 'Yes, you're right. She needs to rest now. I'll come again tomorrow.' She rose stiffly to her feet. Nathaniel went over to her. She was shivering and her hands were icy cold.

'Can you walk back? We've quite a way to go.' He put his arm round her and led her to the gate. 'Put your arm through mine now. You'll get along better that way.' She did as she was told and they made their way slowly along the road.

'Did you come to talk to Alice too?' asked Mary, when they were halfway back.

'Yes, I did, but I came to talk to you as well. Alice wouldn't like it if you made yourself ill. You need to look after yourself. We're all worried about you.'

'What are you doing here, Nathaniel?' Mary stopped in the lane and looked at him in surprise. 'My father told me you are getting married to someone else. Not me. You shouldn't be here. You should be with her. Everyone leaves me, remember.'

'I think you need me more than she does at the moment,' he said, turning to her.

It was a further twenty minutes before he pushed open the door of the cottage and ushered Mary inside. By the light of the moon he could see a candlestick, half burned down, and he lit this and stood it on the mantelpiece while he put a match to the fire. He sat next to Mary on the low settee and put his arm round her. Together they watched the flames take hold and listened to the cracking of the sticks. Nathaniel, uncertain what to say, said nothing. It was Mary who broke the silence.

'She will be all right, won't she?'

'Who do you mean, sweetheart?'

'Alice. She won't come to any harm?'

'Of course not. She's in the safest place. She would want you to rest and get well again.'

Mary smiled, a sad reflection of the unrestrained smiles of their early days together. They sat until Mary's cold hands were warm again and her eyes began to close. Nathaniel roused himself.

'Come on, Mary, let me see you to bed. You need to sleep.' He helped her from the couch and they crossed to the foot of the stairs. She hesitated and looked at him doubtfully.

'Don't worry, Mary. You're perfectly safe with me.

I just want to be sure you're resting properly and then I'll go. But I'll call in tomorrow and see how you are.'

They climbed the stairs together, his arm around her waist to support her. She lay down on the bed beneath the window and he pulled the covers gently over her.

'Don't leave me, Nathaniel,' she murmured sleepily.

He sat on a low chair by the bed and watched her eyes close and her lips open slightly as she relaxed. The familiar curl of hair had fallen over her eyes and he leaned forward to tuck it behind her ear, feeling its softness between his fingers.

'Don't worry, Mary. You're perfectly safe with me,' he had said downstairs. His words were at odds with the desire that was stirring within him but he knew that to take advantage of her vulnerability would be to make him no better than the man who had so violated her in the past. Besides, it would jeopardise his forthcoming marriage if Rhoda ever found out. Still he sat, the minutes stretching into an hour, two hours, his eyes never moving from her sleeping form. Eventually he leaned over until he could feel her even breath on his face. His lips touched her own slightly parted ones and he jerked back as though they had stung him. Turning from the bed, he made his way quickly down the stairs and let himself out of the cottage, closing the door silently behind him.

CHAPTER THIRTY-FIVE

'Why did you say nothing to me about the state of the farm? Didn't you consider that I have a right to know what I am marrying into?'

'But, my sweet, it's me you are marrying, not the farm.'

'Don't be so naïve, Nathaniel. Do you honestly think I would have considered marrying you if I'd known before how little you had to offer me?'

'Well, my father and I *were* having difficulties at the time we became engaged but it was nothing to worry you about. Farms are like that…they have their ups and downs, as your father will no doubt know.'

'*My* father considers you have been very unwise in your investments. He thinks you should have put your foot down and stopped your father buying equipment he could ill afford.'

Nathaniel's normally even temper snapped. 'Look, I know we have problems but I'm trying as hard as I can to put them right. I'll agree the size of the farm just hasn't warranted the machinery we bought and we lost money. But I've sold off the machines now and made a decent profit. We should break even this year. It would be more help to me if you could offer a little support, rather than lecture me about the farm's shortcomings. You were eager enough to agree to marrying me when you thought all was going well.'

It was the previous day that had been his undoing. Their late return from riding had meant that his parents had been entertaining Rhoda's father for nearly an hour before they had been joined by the young couple. Whether it was his father who had lacked discretion or Arthur Precious who had wheedled the information out of him, he was unsure. The result was the same, either way—a torrent of indignation from his betrothed.

They were walking back from church to his house, the same path that he had taken the previous evening with Mary. As they left church he had glanced surreptitiously at the graveyard but it was thankfully empty. She would have woken by now and was no doubt thinking that he would not come.

'Who was that man you were talking to yesterday?'

'What man? I don't know who you mean,' Nathaniel said, dragging his thoughts back to the present.

'The man who accosted you in the stable yard yesterday and kept us waiting for our tea.'

'Oh, him. That was George Morritt, one of the railwaymen.'

'Whatever did he want with you? You're nothing to do with the railway.'

'No, but the railway runs over our land and sometimes they need to check with us so they don't go trampling over crops and such like when they're doing their repairs. Any road, we're back now. Mother will have dinner ready. Let's not keep her waiting.'

Mary woke and gazed at the bright blue square of sky outlined by the window over her head. She lay still, her head filled with wool, trying to remember what had happened the previous night. Someone had been with her here in the bedroom, she was sure of that, someone who'd promised to return today. Nathaniel! The last thing she remembered before closing her eyes was his untidy mass of curly hair.

She staggered from the bed. Her limbs felt heavy and her brain refused to focus. Downstairs at last, she glanced at the clock on the mantelpiece. It was one in the afternoon. What was she thinking of? She should be down at the graveyard. Alice would be missing her. She dragged herself into the kitchen. She was light-headed now and, when she stopped to consider it, realised that not a crumb had passed her lips yesterday. A jug of water stood on the table and she filled a cup and drank thirstily. The larder was empty, except for half a loaf of her mother's bread, as hard as stone and blue with mould. She sat down suddenly on the kitchen chair and began to cry. She didn't have the energy to go to Alice. Nathaniel had not come back, as he had promised. In fact she wasn't sure now whether she had invented him and he hadn't been there at all.

It was here, sitting in the kitchen in her nightdress, that Nathaniel found her half an hour later.

The fire was blazing up the chimney, chasing the damp back into the far corners of the cottage, from where it had crept to taint the cosiness that Mary had always so loved about Martha's home. They had eaten the fresh bread and cheese and the slices of beef that Nathaniel had taken from the kitchen at Temple Farm, telling his mother that he was calling in to see a sick friend. This, although not the whole story, was at least true. A glass or two of the beer that he had brought with him had loosened Mary's tongue and, now she had started, it seemed that she would never stop pouring out her heart.

The autumn afternoon was at an end and darkness had fallen. They sat, side by side, the firelight flickering on their faces. Mary was quiet now. She had described to Nathaniel her time at the school and something of her life in York, how Martha had been brought there to die and how much she missed her old friend.

'Why did you leave here, Mary?'

'I…I…Mr Crowther was being over-familiar and…I didn't like it. I had to get away from him.'

'You could have told me.'

'No, I couldn't. You might have made a fuss, then Father would have lost his job and Annie would have been upset.'

'We would have managed, somehow. You know what I thought about you, Mary. How do you think I felt when you wrote me those letters and then went away without even saying goodbye?'

Mary was silent. Then she said, 'I do know how you felt. I felt the same when I read your letters. No…no, that's not fair. It *was* worse for you because you didn't know the real reason why I left. I told you I didn't love you enough.' She gave a small laugh. 'That was never the truth. I'll tell you the truth…I owe you that. And you belong to another, so I lose nothing by telling you.' Silence again, apart from the crackling of the logs on the fire.

'I had a baby. John Crowther forced himself on me and I had a baby. That's why I left and went to York. I got a job…housemaid to a clergyman and his very large family. Then he found out I were expecting a baby…and he wanted to put me in the workhouse, but I ran away. Martha had told me she had family in York. I found them and they took me in. And it were there I had my baby. They let me stay there. They wanted me to stay longer. Wasn't that kind of them? Not like that vicar and his family. I worked really hard in his house and then he just wanted to be rid of me.' She looked pathetically at Nathaniel. 'You see I couldn't stay here and shame my family and…let you think t' worst of me.'

'I should never do that, Mary,' said Nathaniel, taking her hands and caressing them as she went on.

'You will when I tell you what I did. I gave her away—that's what I did. I had a little girl and I gave her away. I was her mother and I loved her. I didn't think I would. I hated it when I found out I were expecting his child. Everything to do with him was disgusting. But, once she was there, it was different. She was so small and she depended on me for everything. I forced myself not to become attached to her. And, when she was old enough, I gave her away.' She began to cry.

Nathaniel put his arm round her. 'But you gave her

to someone who would love her as much as you did, am I not right?'

'Oh, yes. Hannah's youngest daughter, Esther, she has her. She had no babbies of her own, so she was over-joyed when I gave her mine. I can't ever let her see how much I miss little Ann. It's my punishment for being so wicked.'

'Nonsense, Mary, you did the best thing for the baby.' But Mary didn't hear him, convulsed as she was by sob-bing. He realised there was nothing he could say that would take away her sorrow, so he sat by her side until her sobbing grew less and she became quiet.

'I'm sorry, Nathaniel. I'm sorry I didn't tell you. I re-alise now I was being selfish. I couldn't face you not lov-ing me any more. It would have been best if I'd explained in t' first place. 'Appen it would have saved a lot of heartbreak. It's all finished up t' same way, any road.

'My mam and father don't know anything about t' babby, so I would ask you not to mention it to them—or anyone—and especially not to Rhoda Precious. Father tells me you and she are to be married. She's a reet fine lady,' Mary added without malice. 'I hope you'll both be very happy.'

Nathaniel rose and threw another log on to the fire. He scowled as he made safe the log with his boot. At last he spoke. 'Aye, well, what's done is done. As you say, I'm promised to Rhoda and we're to wed in the spring. I'm maybe speaking out of turn, but I wish… Nay, never mind….I'm grateful for your good wishes.'

Mary took his hand and pulled him down beside her on the sofa. 'I know,' she said. 'I know what you wish.

But, as you say, what's done is done. And I'm maybe acting out of turn but I'm going to anyway.' She took his face in her hands and kissed him longingly. Then she let go abruptly and turned away. 'I think you better leave me,' she murmured, 'before there is even more to add to the things that must be hidden from your wife-to-be.'

CHAPTER THIRTY-SIX

THE fruity aroma from a generous glass of brandy and the warmth of a roaring fire were combining to make Nathaniel feel very sleepy. In the corner of the room the candles on the towering Christmas tree turned to indistinct wavering spots of light as he struggled to keep his eyes open. He had eaten far too well and lost count of how many times his wineglass had been filled. If only he didn't have to get back to see to the animals. Arthur Precious was still talking. Something about banking and investments. Couldn't he give it a rest on this day of all days? Thankfully he didn't seem to expect a reply, so Nathaniel didn't attempt one.

The door opened and a blast of cold air preceded Rhoda into the room. Nathaniel got to his feet unsteadily.

'Come and sit next to me by the fire, my sweet.' He patted the sofa invitingly and Rhoda sat down, her full skirt rippling around her like an incoming tide. He glanced at her, hoping that some of the Christmas spirit might have softened the sharp edges of her tongue. Over the past few days, whenever he had seen her, she seemed

to be ready with some cutting remark or other. He was
at a loss to understand what was wrong.

'Well, the two of you, I hope you will excuse me for
an hour or two. I promised to ride over to Carborough
to pay my respects to the squire and his family. If I
don't leave soon, it'll be dark before I'm back. Help
yourself to brandy when you want, Nathaniel.'

'Thank you, sir,' said Nathaniel, staggering to his
feet once again as Rhoda's father left the room. He sank
back into the cushions and turned to his fiancée, taking
her hand in his. 'This is an unexpected pleasure. A
whole hour to ourselves.' She snatched her hand away
and began to toy with the ribbons on her dress. The action jerked Nathaniel into wakefulness and he frowned
at her.

'Now what's wrong? I hope this isn't a foretaste of
what you're going to be like when we're married.'

'*If* we're married, more likely,' said Rhoda archly,
moving to the end of the sofa, as far away from
Nathaniel as she could get.

'Whatever do you mean? What on earth is the matter?' Nathaniel was getting a little weary of Rhoda's
endless complaining.

'It's you that's the matter…you and your behaviour.'

Nathaniel paused, trying to think what he had done
over the last few days to cause offence. From recent experience, he knew it didn't have to be anything remark-
able to provoke her. Perhaps she took exception to the
second glass of brandy that her father had suggested he
might like.

'Look, if I can't have a little bit extra to drink on

Christmas Day, it's a poor do.' He got up deliberately and crossed to the drinks tray to refill his glass.

'It's the little bit extra you've helped yourself to already that concerns me.' Nathaniel looked at his fiancée in bewilderment.

'I saw that railway fellow last Wednesday…the one who came to chat to you several weeks back when we returned from exercising the horses. A very interesting conversation we had. It seems you've a lot of explaining to do.'

'What kind of explaining?'

'It seems that not so long ago you were running round the countryside with an uneducated hussy from the railway. It turns out that everyone in the village knew about it. What do you have to say for yourself?'

'Mary wasn't a hussy and she wasn't uneducated. She knew a lot about things that you and I have no idea of. And I wasn't running round the countryside, as you put it. There was nothing improper about it. I'm sorry, my sweet, that I didn't mention it but it was so long ago that I didn't think you would be bothered.' He tried to take her hand but again she snatched it away and got up, pacing backwards and forwards until Nathaniel began to feel dizzy.

'You didn't think I'd be bothered? How dare you? You've made a laughing stock of me. I can't begin to suppose what the villagers have been saying behind my back. And, in any case, if it was so long ago, why was George Morritt talking to you about her?' She sat down so abruptly that her skirts puffed up in a cloud of pink and purple.

Nathaniel rose from the sofa and went to stand with his back to the fire, looking down at her.

'She had been ill and George was worried about her. Her parents didn't seem too bothered, so he approached me, seeing as she and I had been friendly in the past.'

'More than friendly, I would say. He told me you were to be wed. Is that true?'

'Well, yes, it is. But…but in the end we decided against it. She went after a job in York and that was an end to it.'

'Was it now? Was it now? That was an end to it? You didn't tell me about the baby. I would never have agreed to marry you if I had known.'

'Good God! Did he tell you that?'

'Is it true, Nathaniel?' Her voice dropped. 'I've a right to know.'

'Yes, my dear, of course you have. Yes, there was a baby.' His next words remained unspoken as Rhoda launched herself at him and rained blows on his chest with her fists. He tried to restrain her and eventually caught hold of her arms and held her firmly until she was silent. For a few moments nothing was said and they stood locked in acrimony. He glanced at her and looked away again.

'The truth is…the truth is this. She decided she didn't want to marry me. She wanted to go to York, as I told you. There was nothing I could do to stop her. I'm sorry, Rhoda. I realise how upsetting this must be for you. It all happened a long time ago. It…it makes no difference to my feelings for you.'

'Maybe! But it makes a lot of difference to my feelings for you. And just think what my father will say if he finds out.'

'He'll only find out if you tell him. He'll not find out from George and there's no one else knows about the baby.'

'I want you to go now, Nathaniel, before my father comes back. I shall have to decide whether I say anything to him.'

'And will I see you for our usual ride tomorrow, if the weather holds?'

'I don't know. Don't bother me any more now.' She turned away and walked to the window, gazing out at the gloom. Nathaniel followed her and put his arm round her shoulder but she shrugged him off.

'Just go, will you? Go!'

The second glass of brandy was beginning to take effect as Nathaniel put his foot in the stirrup and swung himself into the saddle. Thank goodness Jess knew her way home without much prompting. As he walked her into the lane and set off westwards the first huge flakes of snow began to fall from a leaden sky. He held his face up to let them cool his burning cheeks. By the time Jess turned into their courtyard, the snow was muffling the echo of her hooves and turning the darkness into day.

CHAPTER THIRTY-SEVEN

KILLING the pig produced a range of emotions amongst the villagers generally and those of Station Cottages in particular. For the menfolk it brought satisfaction, the feeling of a job well done. They swelled almost visibly with pride as their friends and neighbours gathered to admire the hapless animal snuffling in its pen, waiting unwittingly for the local butcher to finish his day's work and arrive with his range of knives and choppers. The women were glad of the chance to repay what they owed their acquaintance, for they had been the recipients of joints of pork at the last killing and it was taken for granted that these debts in kind were paid before the rest of the animal was dealt with. It also gave them the opportunity to give a little kindness to those around who had been kind to them or who were in need of help themselves. It was often the only time in the year when there was enough and some to spare. But mostly the women knew that pig-killing heralded hard work. As soon as the killing had taken place and the beast had been rolled in the burning straw to remove the hair, there would be a frenzy of activity as joints were salted and hung, the fries distributed and the pig feast prepared.

The occasion induced in the children the excitement of a holiday. They raced around, gathering straw from the field boundaries and heaping it on to the already substantial pile, which stood ready to be fired at the appropriate moment. They leaned precariously over the walls of the sties to compare the sizes of the remaining pigs and to warn them of the fate that was in store for them in the coming months, all the time watching impatiently for the butcher to make his appearance at the end of the day. It was the children who each evening made their way along the well-worn paths to the pig-pens, clasping the heavy buckets of food. The food, an unappetising brownish-grey sludge, was in fact as nutritious as any the children received. When there was money to spare, it was barley mash mixed with the liquid in which the family meal had been cooked. When times were hard, boiled pig potatoes were used in place of barley. Then the peelings, stalks and any other parts discarded from the vegetables in preparation were added to the mixture. Nothing was wasted. To supplement this diet the children collected dandelions and long grass on their way home from school, the pig being the first to be greeted on their return.

It was George Morritt's animal that was about to be sacrificed. George had conferred with Tom, who had a pig of his own, and they all agreed that it had reached a good size and the time was right to end its life. This would also mean that he could buy a weaner and bring it on through the summer months, enough to withstand the harsher weather of winter.

The February day was bright and cold. The pig had been starved overnight. By the time the butcher shut up shop and arrived with his basket containing an assortment of instruments of dispatch, the sun had already set and across the darkening sky a handful of stars were scattered. The families from all five cottages had assembled and a few other villagers had been invited to join in the ceremony. The children were kept at a distance while the gruesome task of killing and bleeding the pig was carried out. George stood ready to give assistance to the butcher when it was needed. He smiled as he listened to his eldest son relating the life history of the doomed animal to the other children gathered round him. Alfie, though only seven, had developed an interest in pig-breeding and nurturing and was now a daily visitor at the Simpsons' farm along the lane. There he watched the progress of each litter, gauged the sow's mothering ability and developed a healthy respect for the bad-tempered boar. After each visit he arrived home to fill the house with a porcine aroma as he reported on the latest events.

'He were born year before last, back-end, this un,' he told his waiting audience. 'There were thirteen on 'em and this un were unlucky. The sow—that's the mother pig, tha' knows—has twelve dugs and t' babbies choose one each and that's their own special dug. So there were none left over for our little pig. Mrs Simpson had to feed him wi' her baby's bottle. And he did reet well and grew bigger than all his brothers and sisters. So me and Dad chose him and I called him Lucky, cos he started off unlucky and finished up lucky.'

'He's not so lucky now,' Laura said solemnly as a high-pitched squealing announced the sticking of the pig and its approaching death. They all turned to look as Lucky was strung up on the branch of a nearby tree, his lifeblood dripping out into the bowl beneath. The straw was lit and a shower of sparks shot upwards into the dark sky, as if in an attempt to join the stars multiplying overhead. Everyone gathered round to watch as George and the butcher quickly rolled the pig in the burning straw. The children stared, poised between the excitement of the kill and sadness for the loss of the pig, which they had fed and talked to over the last eighteen months.

Eliza had prepared bowls and saucepans to receive the joints of meat as soon as the butcher's job was done. An ample supply of salt stood ready in jars. Her two younger children had been under her feet all day, determined to trip her up at every turn, but they were outside now, leaving her free to concentrate on the salting. George staggered into the cottage with the first joints of meat and she set to work. Turning, he almost bumped into Susan, who had come quietly through the open door.

'I thought as how you might need a hand,' she said to Eliza, rolling up her sleeves to join in the work.

'Have you brought your Mary with you?' George asked.

'Aye, she's stood outside, talking to t' little ones.'

George smiled to himself and went on his way.

The butcher's first job before dismembering the animal was to remove its more unsavoury parts, most of which were cooked in the fire and distributed amongst the onlookers. They were the titbits that everyone most looked forward to, as long as they didn't consider too closely their origins. The burning straw was fed with branches blown down in the winter gales and folk gathered round, their eager faces lit by the firelight. Soon a wonderful aroma wafted through the evening air. Mouths watered and stomachs rumbled. George passed round the fries, offering the plate first to those whom he considered most deserving, and forgetting neither the station staff, who could not leave their posts, nor those elderly people in the village who were too old or infirm to venture out on such a cold evening. Standing to one side of the fire, he ran his eyes over the group of villagers, looking to see if any were missing of those he had invited. He loved gatherings like these, although he had worried all day that his arrangements for the evening might go wrong. A great deal was invested in occasions like this and more in this one than most.

Mary had regarded the evening with a mixture of anticipation and apprehension. It was the first time since her illness that she had joined with others beyond her own family. In fact, when she thought about it, she realised that it was the first time since her return from the school in Ashworth that she had met any but the occasional villager. All that was a lifetime ago. Such a lot had happened since, most of it wretched. Her recovery, initiated with Nathaniel's help and continued with the help of her parents when Nathaniel had made them aware of her condition, was slow and fitful. She knew that her parents too were grieving over the loss of their daughter—more than Mary had at first realised—but as soon as they'd realised that Mary was ill, their care was unstinting.

'Eh, lass, why not move back in wi' us, where we can tek proper care on you?' her father had urged, but she would not hear of it, preferring to stay where she felt safest. By Christmas she had been able to join them to eat their dinner of beef—supplied by an anonymous well-wisher—and plum pudding. After that, she visited her mother often or her mother came to Martha's cottage, commenting on the tiny rooms and admiring the tidy design of the dormant garden. By the time Mary felt strong again, any distance between her parents and herself, caused by her rejection of Nathaniel and her subsequent departure, had been bridged.

About Nathaniel too she felt happier, now that she had explained her behaviour to him. He had understood. He had not reprimanded her for her actions. If it were not for his concern, she didn't know what would have become of her. And yet they had done nothing during that brief time together in her cottage that would jeopardise his forthcoming marriage with Rhoda Precious. If she were to meet him in the lane now, she would do so with equanimity, knowing that he understood and forgave.

She must hurry. Through the window she could see the glow of the bonfire and she knew the pig-killing must be well underway. She dressed herself in her warmest coat, wrapped a scarf round her neck and picked up her gloves from where they lay, beside the herbal. She glanced briefly round the room, checking that the fireguard was in place, and left the cottage to join the merrymaking.

'Mary, love, I'm glad you're here. I were just off to Eliza's to help with t' meat. You go on down and talk to your sisters,' Susan said, closing the door of her cottage.

'If you're sure I can't help.' Mary was alarmed suddenly at the sight of so many people. She wandered down to the land beyond the last cottage, where the pigsties were to be found. One or two of the folk made way for her and she found her two young sisters chatting happily with Alfie. He had improved despite the recent cold weather and Mary's failure to provide the bottle of tonic that George had requested. She looked at the lad now and recalled the weeks spent nursing him. It had all been so mixed up with the horror of finding herself with John Crowther's child and with her need to break her engagement to Nathaniel, that she hadn't stopped to consider how big a part she had played in Alfie's recovery. A surge of enthusiasm passed through her. As new life returned to Martha's garden with the coming of spring, she would be all set to continue the work that Martha's age and infirmity had prevented her from doing. She smiled, seeing herself as she had so often seen Martha, sitting on her seat in the shade of the apple tree, stripping soft greyish-green sage leaves from their woody stems into a basin on her lap or weaving the lavender into scented plaits to hang among the dresses in the wardrobe. Her sisters would come and visit and she would teach them the crafts that she had learned from Martha. And much later her nieces and nephews would picnic with her under the apple tree.

How long she stood there in a reverie she did not know but when she looked up the children were gone, summoned to their beds at last, and the crowd of villagers around the fire had thinned. The flames were dying down, leaving in their place a glowing mound of wood. Mary was conscious of someone standing to one side of her in the shadows. She glanced round. It was Nathaniel. She had no idea how long he had been there.

'I didn't like to disturb you,' he said, walking over. 'You were so lost in your thoughts. How are you, Mary? You look…quite back to your normal self.'

'I'm very well now, thanks to you and to my parents.' She smiled at him. 'When did you arrive? There was such a crush of people at first, I didn't see you.'

'Oh, I was delayed by the cattle. My mother's not so well again and they needed someone to milk them. Jack of all trades, that's me!' He laughed, looking into her eyes for so long that she became embarrassed and turned her head away.

''Appen Rhoda will be able to help you with some of the chores after you are wed. Has she not come with you tonight?' Mary scanned the remaining folk for a glimpse of Nathaniel's betrothed, aware suddenly that it would not do for the villagers to see the two of them alone in animated conversation.

'She's not with me,' said Nathaniel.

'She must be looking forward to your wedding next month. What day is it you're getting married?'

'She's not with me,' he repeated evenly. 'I mean there's to be no wedding.'

Mary gave a gasp of astonishment. 'Why? What's happened? I don't understand.'

'She's changed her mind. We're not going to be wed.'

He paused, watching Mary's face, as she struggled to take in what he had said.

'But…but…what can have happened to make her change her mind?'

'I…I don't think she realised at first what her life was going to be like, being the kind of wife that I need. Her father is a gentleman farmer—he employs others to do his work. Rhoda's used to using her fingers to make pretty tunes on the piano, not wrap them round the teats of a bad-tempered cow. She began to see that life with me would mean just that. The only time she's willing to get the littlest bit muddy is when she's out riding. And even then someone else has to get the horse ready for her and clean it up when she gets back.

'And, to be honest, things have been difficult financially, and my parents being elderly and not so well hasn't helped. I do feel sorry for her in that respect. It wasn't like that when we first started walking out together. She's a right to expect the same type of life she's been used to. I suppose, as time went on, she began to see she wasn't going to get it. I think that's the real reason. She can use the other as her excuse.'

'The other? I don't understand. What do you mean?'

Nathaniel held her gaze so long before he spoke that her pulse began to quicken, despite all her attempts to quieten it.

'Well…' he said, fixing his eyes on the fire. 'It was like this. George came to tell me you were ill. Apparently he had called for some medicine and found you, you know, not yourself. He came to tell me, seeing as you and me had been so close.' He glanced at her, then looked away quickly. 'While he was talking to me, we didn't notice that Rhoda was standing there. We had been riding and she came to say tea was ready. Any road, she overheard some of what he said…enough to know we were talking about a woman. Later on she found out who George was and went to see him and learned that it was you we were talking about. She knew we were once sweethearts…I don't know how…I had never told her.'

'Poor Rhoda. That must have been horrible.'

'She challenged me about it. I told her that George had asked me for help. He had said as much to her. Then she suddenly blurted out that I hadn't told her about the baby and, if she had known, she would never have agreed to marry me.'

A knot of fright began to unravel deep within Mary's body. 'I don't understand. You didn't *know* about the baby. And how can she have thought it was yours?'

'It was you let slip to George that you'd had a baby, the first time he saw you ill. He assumed it must have been mine and he mentioned as much when he first came to see me. And Rhoda overheard.'

Mary was horrified. 'How dreadful for her. She must have been very upset. You soon put her right, though?'

'She was angrier than I've ever seen her, I'll grant you that. For fifteen minutes I couldn't get a word in. And in the time she was haranguing me I made up my mind not to tell her.'

'Why ever not? Apart from being unfair on her, it was a big stain on your own character.'

'I knew she was regretting her decision to marry me.

It gave her an excuse to break off our engagement. But that wasn't the main reason.'

'What was the main reason?' asked Mary, bewildered with this twist in the story.

'She asked me whether I still had feelings for you. I told her the truth. I wasn't going to lie and I'd had enough of failing to act when I should have acted. I told her that I had always loved you and that nothing or no one would stop me doing so. No, I didn't tell her the baby was not mine. I wished it were. I wished it had been me that had loved you first and not that man. I shall always regret that.' His words were echoing the very same thoughts she had voiced to Martha in York, when she had finally acknowledged the truth about her ordeal. Tears sprang suddenly to her eyes.

'No, my love,' she said softly, putting her hand up to his cheek. 'What he did to me was not love. He never loved me. You must try to forget that, just as I have tried to forget. The only feelings I ever had towards him were fear and revulsion. You must remember that. You are the only man I have ever loved. But I think you have done Rhoda a lot of harm by allowing her to believe this lie.'

'No, I don't think so. It's only her pride that is hurt. I fully believe that it has given her a way out of an engagement that she no longer wanted. And remember how *you* led me to believe something that you didn't feel when you wrote me those letters. I have never stopped loving you, Mary. To marry Rhoda would be to do her a disservice.'

Mary was silent. He spoke no more than the truth. She had no argument against what he had said; neither did she want one.

'Do you think you could love me again, Mary?' Nathaniel stepped closer to her.

'No, I don't think that's possible,' she replied.

Nathaniel looked at her in alarm. 'Why? Don't tell me that someone else has claimed your affections while I've been coming to my senses?'

'Of course not,' she said seriously. 'I only mean that I can't love you *again* when I've never stopped loving you.'

The villagers drifted away until at last Mary and Nathaniel were the only two left. Then he drew her into the shadows and kissed her. And they held each other close for protection against any unseen forces that might try to part them again.

George and Tom made their way along the path. George began to rake the embers of the fire, causing a further shower of sparks to fly upwards.

'It's been a grand evening, George. All of us enjoyed it.'

'Aye, it were a good turnout too. Lots of village folk here, apart from us railway families.'

'If I'm not mistaken, I thought I saw young Nathaniel a bit back. He's not been around here for a long time. I'll never be able to understand why him and our Mary broke off their engagement. Still, it wouldn't do to go meddlin' o'er much in t' lives of our children.'

George smiled into the shadows. 'You're right there, Tom. You'll not catch me meddling. Any road, let's go indoors. We've made everything as safe as we can do here.'

The two men turned and strolled back to the row of cottages in companionable silence. Candlelight flickered briefly in the windows. A crescent moon sank to touch the horizon, making a deeper darkness. Across the railway line a vixen's scream was answered with three short barks and a minute later any who still lingered in the darkness could hear, close by, the whickering greeting of the dog fox and his mate.

A young woman disappears.
A husband is suspected of murder.
Stirring times for all the neighbourhood in

THE STEEPWOOD

Scandals

A young woman disappears.
A husband is suspected of murder.
Stirring times for all the neighbourhood in

THE STEEPWOOD

Scandals

Volume 5 – March 2007
Counterfeit Earl by Anne Herries
The Captain's Return by Elizabeth Bailey

Volume 6 – April 2007
The Guardian's Dilemma by Gail Whitiker
Lord Exmouth's Intentions by Anne Ashley

Volume 7 – May 2007
Mr Rushford's Honour by Meg Alexander
An Unlikely Suitor by Nicola Cornick

Volume 8 – June 2007
An Inescapable Match by Sylvia Andrew
The Missing Marchioness by Paula Marshall

Enjoy the dazzling glamour of Vienna on the eve of the First World War...

Rebellious Alex Faversham dreams of escaping her stifling upper-class Victorian background. She yearns to be like her long-lost Aunt Alicia, the beautiful black sheep of the family who lives a glamorous life abroad.

Inspired, Alex is soon drawn to the city her aunt calls home – Vienna. Its heady glitter and seemingly everlasting round of balls and parties in the years before WW1 is as alluring as she had imagined, and Alex finds romance at last with Karl von Winkler, a hussar in the Emperor's guard. But, like the Hapsburg Empire, her fledgling love affair cannot last. Away from home and on the brink of war, will Alex ever see England or her family again?

M&B

Set in 1940s London during the Blitz, this is a moving tale about family, love and courage

Queenie McLaren and her daughter Laura have long had to protect each other from Jock Mclaren's violent temper. In 1940, the evacuation of women and children from their homeland in Gibraltar is the perfect chance to escape, and Queenie and Laura eventually find themselves in London during the height of the Blitz.

During the darkest of war years, mother and daughter find courage in friendships formed in hardship, and the joy of new romances. But neither of them has yet heard that Jock is in England – and he won't rest until he's found them…

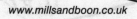

www.millsandboon.co.uk

**A vivid
recreation
of 1850s
Yorkshire,
packed with**

Abandoned as a baby and brought up by the cruel
farmer who found her, Joanna dreams of a rich
family and a better life. As a potential marriage
and a forbidden attraction develop, the truth
about her real family lurks just around the corner
—and is getting ready to reveal itself on the
most important day of her life…

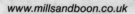